Praise for Mark Sc

Red Diamond, Private Eye

"It's easily the best mystery book of the year"
-*The Washington Times*
"A tour de force. Schorr has the tough guy lingo down pat."
-*The New York Times*
"Enormously entertaining"-*Newsday*

Ace of Diamonds

"Breezy, fast-moving...vivid and evocative...refreshingly
different." -*The Los Angeles Herald Examiner*
"Marvelously engaging" -*Newsday*
"...swift, raunchy, very funny adventure" -*Publisher's Weekly*

Diamond Rock

"This Diamond is a gem in his own right...One of the most
gifted detective fiction writers to come along in a long
while." -*The Washington Post*

An Eye for an Aye

"...beautifully plotted and has the kind of accelerating pace
that will have you hanging on for dear life during the last 50
pages of the book." -*The Los Angeles Daily News*
"...intense, vivid...a meticulously crafted tale..."
-*The Orange County Register*

Overkill

"Schorr's sentences, his paragraphs, his choice of words are
superior to Robert Ludlum and Clive Cussler. He can write
rings around them, and does." -*L.A. Daily News*

Borderline

"Impressive..Schorr hits on a wonderful occupation
for an investigator." -*Booklist*
"Schorr's new series launch is a winner. His sense of place is
reminiscent of William Bayer's, and his perfectly drawn
characters recall those of Peter Abrahams." -*Library Journal*
"A fast-paced thriller that keeps you
on the edge of your seat. I loved it!"
-Steve Hodel, author of the bestselling *Black Dahlia Avenger*
"Schorr crafts an ingenious plot,
full of clever twists and surprises." -*Kirkus Reviews*
"Gripping. Hanson is a complex, compelling amateur
sleuth." -*Publisher's Weekly*

Fixation

"Excellent…has suspense, action, surprises and edge of the
seat thrills"-Phil Margolin, bestselling author of legal thrillers.
"*Fixation* offers gripping characters with a rich sense of
place, and the kind of psychological insights that only a
counseling professional could bring to a thriller. It is a
stunning novel from a multitalented crime star."
-*Fantastic Fiction*
"Will continue to haunt long after reading-moving, affecting
and powerful. Hanson is a unique hero, and Schorr a unique
talent." -Greg Rucka, author of *The Old Guard* and the
Atticus Kodiak series
"This gripping west coast thriller, a la Robert Crais,
is one of those rare crime novels where very little
suspension of disbelief is required…"
-*Booklist*

The
Master Mind

By
Mark Schorr

www.AMInkPublishing.com

www.AMInkPublishing.com

For Emily and Ben
and all they have brought to my life

"Something could be a miracle and a trick at the same time"
- Teller (the quiet sidekick magician in Penn and Teller)

The Master Mind

The bartender nicknamed Tats told Diana Wynne she was five minutes too late.

Tats had called, alerting Diana that her sister was drunk again and being hustled by a couple of predatory guys. The bartender, in between pouring drinks in the noisy bar, described them as "big, bushy-bearded creeps." She hadn't seen them before but knew their type. Tats, who had sleeve tattoos on both arms and a floral pattern across her chest, had been too busy to play Mother Hen. Diana figured Tats was also fed up with keeping Diana's sister out of harm's way. Diana was near that point, and they were blood kin.

Diana thanked Tats and hurried outside. The bartender thought the two guys were leading Diana's sister toward the Willamette River, the more deserted part of Portland's Pearl District.

Diana scanned the streets. In the distance, toward the river, she saw a scuffle. Two men who fit the bartender's description fighting with a third. She ran toward them.

With more than a couple dozen hours a week in the gym, she closed the distance without breathing hard.

She saw her sister now, lying on the floor, looking befuddled. Where Diana was a close-cropped brunette, her sister was a flashy bleached blonde. Diana presumed the man getting attacked was some sort of Good Samaritan.

Diana hesitated, sizing up the scene. The three men hadn't noticed her, absorbed in their own battle. The Good Samaritan was almost holding his own. He was a lot less bulky than the creeps, a little taller than average. He seemed to be able to block the predators' punches the moment they were launched. She could tell that the bullies had been drinking, their moves a bit sluggish. The Good Samaritan's defense was great but his offense miserable. He was living proof that the best defense was a good offense, since the creeps were landing every fourth or fifth punch.

She raced toward them, grabbed the red bearded bully by the balls and yanked down hard. All three men froze as the man yowled. She took the pause to fire off a knife hand strike to Black Beard's throat. As he gasped for air, she clapped her hands on his ears. She hit him three times, fast and hard, the full force of her muscular body in each blow. Red Beard staggered toward her growling, and she kicked his kneecap hard enough to make an audible pop.

"Stay away from her," she growled, kicking him in the gut. He vomited.

The Good Samaritan was leaning against a fence, breathing hard and holding his side.

"Wait here," Wynne said to him as she helped her sister up.

"I'm sorry, I'm so sorry, sis." Diana was already tapping her cell phone, scheduling an urgent Lyft pickup. Not the first time, probably not the last. The ride came quickly.

The creeps had hustled away. The Good Samaritan was still leaning against the fence.

Wynne scanned him, appraising, intense. Her hands gently prodded his torso. He flinched a couple times. She ran her hand across his jaw. Not romantic, a clinical assessment.

"You can get it checked out, but I don't think there's anything serious," she said. "You might have a broken rib, not much they can do for that. You might be pissing blood tomorrow. If it continues for more than a day or two, best get it checked out."

"Are you a doctor?"

She smiled. "At least you didn't ask me if I was a nurse. But the answer is no to both. I've been around a lot of fights."

There was a long silence. He was trying to breathe deeper, but it hurt.

"Thanks for stepping in like that," she said.

"Did I hear you or her say, 'sis?'" he asked.

"Yep. Now I've got a question for you—where'd you learn to fight like that?"

"Just something I picked up."

"Where?" She had stayed close in, her intense brown eyes holding contact.

"It's a long story," he said.

She extended her hand. "I'm Diana."

He shook her hand. "Tom."

"Let me buy you a drink. As thanks for saving my sister."

"Or should I buy you one for saving me from my good intentions? How'd you find us?"

"My sister tends to go to the same couple of bars. Enough that some of the staff keep an eye out for her as she's not good at taking care of herself. One of the bartenders saw what was going on."

"Sounds like you're used to taking care of her?"

She nodded. "Since we were teens. She's five years younger, and 20 years less mature."

Then they were in the Urbana bar, a re-purposed warehouse. Exposed brick and brightly painted ducts, with pipes like a fat python winding above the dark, high-ceilinged room. Large stainless steel fragments of machinery had been left around, lit by small spotlights and sparkling in the blackness. The techno EDM music – loud, thumping bass, repetitive, primal – was at the verge of too loud. They had to lean in to hear each other.

The waitress brought IPAs. Tom downed his quickly and ordered a second. The shaking in his hands stopped.

They sized each other up. He was good-looking in a non-threatening way. He'd never be the leading man, but maybe the leading man's loyal best friend. She had the kind of looks that grew on you, with a nose that had been broken and a heart-shaped face.

"So, Tom, I've got to ask, what style of fighting were you doing?"

"No style. Just lucky." He rubbed a reddened ear. "Maybe not even so lucky."

"I call bullshit on that. Your defense was amazing. Your blocks were there almost before their strikes. Your offense was miserable, like you didn't want to hurt them."

"It's kind of weird. You probably won't believe it." He breathed in and out slowly. "Anyway, you were the one who was amazing. It was like watching a Bruce Lee movie."

"Thanks," she said. "But I'm curious..."

"Where he takes out a room full of bad guys. Have you seen *Enter the Dragon*?"

"Many times."

"How about *Way of the Dragon*? The Chuck Norris-Bruce Lee fight? Pretty incredible. But that was all choreographed. You just did it. For real."

"Yeah. I've seen all his films. And I've spent hours and hours and hours practicing since I was a little kid. Now what about your moves? It was more than just rope-a-dope. Your evasion was amazing."

He hesitated, then said, "Ever heard of mindfulness?"

"Sure. Focused attention, in the moment. I've been doing martial arts since I was eight. Some schools had meditation time, stressed the mindfulness part."

"I've been doing *tai chi* for years."

"Keeps you safe if some 80-year-old gets testy," she said. "You do *tui shou?*"

"Push hands? Whenever I find a good partner. You know your martial arts. Where did you learn to fight?"

"All over."

"You've got a black belt?"

"A few."

"You make a living with that?"

"I see what you're doing. Like the fight. Deflecting and blocking my questions. Very nice. I'll answer but you will too."

He was hesitant but nodded.

"I was a tomboy," she said. "Which was good, since my father wanted a son and got three daughters. He taught me to hunt, to do carpentry, to fight. I went to my first karate class when I was eight. Had to put up with a lot of crap because I was a girl. It made me stronger."

"I can see that. Did you wind up going into that as a career? The way you assessed me after the fight was very professional."

"Thanks. Another block and deflection. It's kind of refreshing. Most guys when you first meet it's hard to get a word in edgewise with all the wonderfulness they throw out. How much money they make, how impressive a car they have, how many triathlons they've run. All in the first five minutes of a first date."

"Is this a first date?"

"It'll be the last if you don't stop that question deflection jive."

The beer steins were empty, and the waitress offered a re-fill. They ordered nachos and he asked, "Okay, what do you want to know?"

"What's your secret? And if you block and parry again, I'm going to assume you've got some dark secret and walk away."

He hesitated, then said, "I was a bit of a troubled teen."

"Who wasn't?" she responded, looking annoyed.

"I was sent to a counselor. She helped me get on track. Part of the trouble was I used to get into fights. I wasn't very good. But this therapist taught me mindfulness and a bell went off. That's a mindfulness bell, not a bell to signal a round starting."

He liked her smile.

"That awareness helped me avoid fights in terms of reading people's intent. If I did wind up in a scuffle, I would notice a shoulder drop signaling a swing before it happened. Or a slight step back to position for a kick. It was early on in mindfulness. The mid 80s. Still pretty woo woo. There hadn't been all the fMRI and PET research."

"Validating what they'd been doing in martial arts for a couple thousand years." She glanced at her watch. "Damn, I teach a class in six hours. Better get home and get some sleep." She reached for her purse.

"Let me. You'll get it next time."

"I'd like there to be a next time too. I better run. If I don't get my beauty sleep I'm a cranky bitch. And I can be a cranky bitch even when I do."

"I doubt that."

"You obviously don't know me very well."

"I hope to change that."

Chapter Two

"I wish I coulda seen you go all Buffy on those assholes," Lisa Moreau said.

"They were drunk, and I had the element of surprise." Diana grinned. "But it was pretty cool. I was pissed."

"Way cool," Lisa said.

Wynne had already told the story, but Moreau seemed to have an insatiable appetite, like a child wanting to hear *Goodnight Moon* for the 50th time.

The women bantered, their typical pattern. They both could be short-tempered, and several times had to take a vacation from each other. But Lisa had noted that their friendship had lasted longer than any male-female relationship she had ever had, including two marriages.

She was strikingly pretty with almond-shaped eyes, prominent cheekbones and glowing golden skin. Coupled with a chip on her shoulder that let her strut the walkways with the perfect sneer. Tall and slender, she had worked as a model until aging out in her mid-20s. She had lots of wild memories, but little cash left by the time her party days were done. She was now the billing manager in a large medical practice.

The two had met in Wynne's cardio-kickboxing class, where Lisa had questioned Diana on every move. Diana was at the point of asking her to not attend the class when she realized that Lisa really was driven and wanted to do the moves perfectly. It was something she could relate to. They met for a peace talk after one class, got together socially, double-dated a few times, and had become BFFs. With lots of affectionate sniping.

The two women were at a weight bench in the gym, with Diana spotting for Lisa. Mirrors lined the walls to allow for perfect form as well as admiring one's shape. Rubber mats covered the floors to muffle the thunk of cast iron plates. They were the only women in the section, which was dominated by over-muscled young men. The women's curves under spandex outfits had not gone unnoticed. The women tuned out the looks, focused on their workout.

"Five more reps," Diana ordered.

Moreau growled and lowered the 120-pound weight bar to her chest. Her fourth rep was a struggle. On her fifth, Diana gently had her hand on the bar, giving minimal support until Lisa clunked it down.

"I didn't think I could do it," Lisa said.

"I knew you could." Diana no longer charged Lisa for lessons and Lisa was constantly trying to do her favors. She didn't like owing anyone anything. Lisa had paid for extravagant meals, fixed Diana up with guys who she thought were prime dates, helped her on job leads.

"When you next gonna see your boyfriend?" Lisa asked.

"He's not my boyfriend!"

"I could tell when you were talking about him he makes you wet." Lisa put on a googly-eyed girly expression and Diana slapped her arm.

"We've gone out four times. He's been a perfect gentleman."

"Must be gay if he's resisting your charms."

"We kissed, okay. It was very nice. Slow and sexy. And a little bit of touchy feely."

Lisa put on her googly-eyed face again.

"Knock it off," Diana said as they moved to the lat pull down machine.

"So what do you lovebirds talk about?"

"He's kind of vague on a lot. Good at answering questions with a question. We've talked about spirituality. Not so much religion but just questions about the universe."

"Like Neil de Grasse Tyson? I could go for that."

"Sort of like that. Last time he was telling me about spooky action at a distance. A quote from Einstein. Then into quantum pseudo-telepathy and non-local events. He saw my eyes glazing over. He got shy about talking too much and started with the questions again. I can see how smart he is. And sensitive."

"I told you he's gay."

"Don't be stereotyping."

"Ooooh, you're protective of him."

"He's a self-confessed nerd. Said he loved magic when he was a kid. He had a poster of Houdini on his wall when other kids had Pete Rose or Steve McQueen. He showed me how he can pick a lock with a bobby pin. How to get out of duct tape by lifting your arms overhead and snapping down. How to get out of a…"

"You're turned on by this guy? I could've fixed you up on a date with this cute jock who's so hot…"

"I don't like jocks. They get pissed off when I can hold a plank longer than they can."

"You're holding the wrong plank."

"I knew I shouldn't give you an opening like that. Tom is cute. He listens. He shows off in goofy ways. Like doing sleight of hand tricks with coins and a deck of cards."

"So when you gonna be playing strip poker with him?"

"I swear you're worse than a teenage boy."

"Usually we talk about the news, or the latest trouble your sister got into, or morons I deal with at work, or where we should go for a run."

"We've talked about that."

"Yeah, but you light up when you talk about Tommy-boy."

They worked out for a few minutes without talking. Then Wynne said, "He talks a lot about magic. Asked me what I believe in."

"I knew you'd crack and go back to talking about him," Moreau said with an "I told you so" grin. "Okay, maybe he's religious, so that's why he ain't trying to give you what you been wanting for a long time."

"Doesn't seem to be. Didn't ask whether I believe in God. More about ESP."

"Witches and voodoo boy?"

"No. He said two-thirds of people have had some sort of psychic experience. How the EEG was invented in part to test for ESP and how it's worked. Uri Geller bending spoons and fooling Israeli intelligence. He wanted to watch videos with me of some guy named Derren Brown. A mentalist."

"Sounds mental to me."

They worked out a couple more minutes and Diana said, "He can be a bit paranoid. Wears a ball cap and sunglasses any time we're out. He said people don't realize how many security cameras there are."

Moreau just shook her head.

"He was telling me about getting a VPN. Virtual Private Network. I didn't understand it."

"That's a way you can make your phone or computer bounce off a server in another city, or country," Lisa explained. "So no one can pinpoint you. He could be batshit crazy or maybe in the witness protection program." She hummed the theme from *The Godfather*.

"Stop it! A lot of our time was spent meditating. He's a good teacher. It felt almost spiritual even though he wasn't stressing that. We're going to do Push Hands in the park tonight."

"What's Push Hands?" Moreau asked.

"It's a sensing and off balancing exercise they use in most of the internal Chinese martial arts."

"Well, that don't tell me nothing."

"You gently put hands on the other person, try and sense where they are strong or weak, then get them off balance. You yield, you root, you release energy."

"That sounds like good sex to me."

"Everything sounds like good sex to you. Five more reps."

When Lisa finished, she pursed her lips, and she took a serious tone. "I know you told me to not dig into him, but I've always been your wing gal. You know love can be blind. And stupid."

"I'm not in love."

"Not yet. Anyway, I did a quick check, no mug shots online or that kind of obvious warning. But you probably did that yourself."

Wynne nodded.

"He's really into privacy. I didn't find much of anything. A skimpy Linked In profile with a picture that barely looked like him. Nothing on other social media." Moreau was no hacker but knew more about apps and existing databases than most. "So of course I had to dig a little deeper."

As she sat down at the machine, Lisa said, "Your guru ain't what he seems. Nothing on LexisNexis or anything funky at credit agencies. He's got one credit card that's barely used. His credit history goes back about five years." Through her office, Lisa had access to various public and private databases. "Funny thing though, I took his profile picture on Linked In and ran it through Google Face Search and Picwiser."

She took her phone out and pulled up Tom's LinkedIn picture. Diana looked carefully at the image. When she really studied it, she saw Tom's LinkedIn image had a shorter nose, a longer jaw.

"Photo turned out to be from a stock photo website," Lisa said triumphantly. "The picture your boy put up ain't him. A prettier version. He isn't the first to do it, but usually that's on dating sites."

Wynne nodded. "I've seen that."

"He's got a skimpy presence out there."

"He told me he moved a lot."

She shook her head. "I did a national search. He don't add up."

Diana sighed. "I'll let you meet Tom soon if you promise not to give him the third degree."

"Scouts honor," Lisa said, crossing herself. "You're not fallin' for your mystery Romeo, are you?"

"I'm not giving you a fair picture. Just the things that bother me. Not all the good stuff. But there's definitely something unusual there. I saw his cell phone. It's a burner like a drug dealer would have."

"Maybe that's the kind of sales he's doing now."

"I don't think so. He's not flashy."

"Not all dealers are. You turn me loose and I'll give you the full Lisa Moreau deluxe background package."

"Let me see how it goes. If he invites me to a remote cabin in Idaho and is bringing along a butcher saw and a tarp, I'll take you up on it."

"Don't wait until it's too late," Lisa said, pulling down hard on the bar.

"We're going to be at First Thursday tomorrow. How about you run into us accidentally at the Bechdel Galley at around 7:30?"

"Now you're talking."

They moved to the treadmills where they ran side by side, an unstated competition as to who could last longer. Moreau's long legs versus Wynne's athletic stamina. Wynne usually won but Moreau never backed down.

Lisa beamed at Diana. "I got your back, girl."

After a few minutes, both were breathing hard.

"Unless he's real cute," Lisa said, grinning. "Then it's every gal for herself."

When the workout was over, they went to the locker room and showered. Where Lisa was tall and thin, Diana was short and with more feminine curves. Where Lisa's skin had a golden sheen, Diana's looked untouched by the sun.

As they got out of the hot, hard spray and dried off, Lisa said, "I'm glad for you. It's been too long. I understand after what happened to Chuck. But you can't be like one of those Sicilian grandmommas mourning and dressing in black for 50 years."

Chuck had been Diana's husband for one month. They had met when she was 24, he was 27. A bit of a bad boy who had mellowed in their relationship. He was 31 when they got married, after starting to talk about having a kid. A month after their wedding, a week after they got back from their honeymoon in Belize, he was riding his motorcycle and was hit and killed by a driver who was texting.

Diana had thrown herself further into various low-paying jobs that kept her busy. She had also begun volunteering, working to support domestic violence victims by escorting them to court, even sleeping at their homes if they couldn't get into a shelter.

"I'm over it," she said.

"You know I've had big losses too," Lisa said gently. "You never get over it 100 percent. But you've thrown away most of your thirties without hardly any effort to get out there." Lisa knew her words had gotten through. "You're mean and ugly and smell funny, but some guy would be lucky to have you."

Diana was drying her hair and she blasted Lisa with hot air. "You sure know how to brighten a girl's day."

They finished dressing and Diana went to the brightly lit mirror, where she put on a barely noticeable pale pink lipstick and a bit of blush. Diana saw Lisa watching and said, "What?"

"You never put makeup on for me?"

"Can you back off?"

"Of course. It's cute. I've never seen you fired up for a guy like this."

"He's weird but there's something special. He's a nerd, right? But he was willing to take on those goons to protect my sister. I asked him and he said he knew he'd feel worse turning away and letting bad things happen than getting hurt but knowing he did the right thing."

"Deep but not too sappy." Lisa nodded approval.

"And he didn't seem threatened by my kicking ass. He said I was like the Black Widow.'"

"I'm happy for you. Even if he ain't Mr. Right, I'm glad to see you back in the game."

Chapter Three

Mt. Tabor Park is one of three in the United States built atop an extinct volcano cone. It's about 400 feet high and has been dormant for 300,000 years, going back to the Pilo-Pleistocene era. He told her all that as they rode east on I-84 in her grey Honda CRV. He told her he also got nerdier as he got nervous.

"It's interesting," she said. "I've lived here for years and never been here. Or thought about it." She took her right hand off the wheel momentarily and patted his thigh. "So I make you nervous?

"Uh, I'm, I'll spew fascinating facts you don't want to hear."

"I like it. I like you. Don't worry about it."

They walked around the top, looking down on the reservoirs and admiring the Douglas firs, hemlocks, cedars and maples. She recognized and identified the sounds of robins, wrens and chickadees. The obvious crows and jays. And squirrels. "Someday I'd like to move out of the city again." She told him about growing up on multiple Army bases, often in rural areas, and the difficult transition to city life.

Then they found a grassy, flat area on the west side, not big enough to be called a field, but with a view of the reservoir in the foreground and the city in the distance. In the far distance, the sun was beginning to dip toward the West Hills.

"What a gorgeous view!" she said. "I bet you just got me up here to distract me so you can knock me over."

"Ahh, you read my mind."

"We'll see." Then she rested her right hand on his left elbow and her left hand on his shoulder. He did the same to her. They began the gentle pushing back and forth, feeling out each other's balance points, how far could they extend, or retreat.

The rolling back and forth got more intense. She was strong, low to the ground. He took advantage of a longer reach and a soft-style inclination. As the movements got more intense, their connection increased.

"Lots of *yin*, not much *yang*," she said. The park was relatively quiet, with bird sounds, a few children yelling in the distant playground and traffic noise rising up faintly from the city below.

She pushed and he evaded, letting her stumble forward. After a few times, she caught on and had a more controlled assault. The third time, she pushed, then swept out his leg, and he was on his backside on the grass.

She reached out her hand and pulled him to his feet, saying, "That almost felt like you took a dive."

"No, you're good."

They spent close to an hour pushing. A martial dance. It was dark in the park as they headed to a Thai place he liked on SE Belmont St.

"This is the most fun I've had in ages, I hate to admit," she said after they'd ordered.

"Me too."

"Really?"

"Really."

"Now's the time to ask me back to your place to continue it," she said.

"Ahh, my place is a bit of a dive. And too messy."

"I've seen bachelor pads before. You're not really married and living with a wife and three kids?"

"Only one kid."

She looked startled.

"Sorry, bad joke. I'm single. Never been married."

"Why?" she asked.

"It just never happened. I had one long term relationship that lasted six years. In Hawaii. It ended badly."

"Whose fault?"

"Neither of us." He had begun tugging at his index finger and middle finger on his left hand. They looked slightly deformed, almost arthritic.

"Since we're having a deep talk, do you mind my asking about your hand?"

"It's a long story. An accident. Around the same time."

"You ever going to tell me?"

"Maybe. You ready to eat?"

She let him verbally block and evade and they had a great meal. Then she invited him back to her place.

She had a small house on the slope of Marquam Hill, aka Pill Hill, where Oregon Health Sciences University, the VA and Doernbecher Children's Hospital dominated the landscape. The quiet of the neighborhood marred only by ambulances making an occasional drop off. Wynne lived modestly, the functional furniture was from Ikea, no clutter, not much décor. A couple of movie posters from Kurosawa samurai films, some family pictures in dark wood frames.

They sat on the terrace and enjoyed the cool night air, the occasional sound of city noise drifting up, the whir of the OHSU tram in the distance. She poured them both a glass of *Pinot Gris*.

Then they moved to her sofa and polished off the wine, talking and laughing and snuggling. Then they wound up in the bedroom. It was quite a while before they were blissed out and resting in each other's arms.

* * *

Diana and Lisa slipped into the bathroom at the Bechdel Gallery, leaving Tom staring at a picture entitled, 'The Way the Martians Danced! Part Trois.' It was a mix of oil, acrylic and watercolors, with finger paint. Smudges of color and medium. The gallery, a double storefront on SW First Avenue, was crowded with people sipping cheap wine in plastic glasses, grabbing canapes off trays carried by black-clad catering staff who alternated between looking stressed or bored.

"So, what do you think?" Diana asked, embarrassed to be so eager for her friend's opinion. The trio had spent 20 minutes chatting. The two women stood just inside the small women's bathroom, out of sight of anyone outside.

"I like him," Lisa said, nodding her approval. "Was he good in bed?"

"How do you know we've had sex?"

"You got a happy look you haven't had in a while. And the way you stand next to each other, very comfortable in each other's space."

"Is it that obvious?"

"Only to someone who knows you." She squeezed Lisa's arm. "What's his place like?'

"We did it at mine."

"He didn't want to go to his?"

Diana shook her head.

"That ain't good. Most boys want that home court advantage. Show off their things."

"I don't know."

"Don't trust him. He's either living in his momma's basement or got a wife."

"Everything else was good."

"I don't want you getting hurt. You're a tough little bitch but you're more vulnerable than you think. I'm gonna dig into him."

"Let me think about it."

"Don't think too long. You're only going to get in deeper."

They walked out together and reconnected with him. Tom sensed something was amiss but they chatted amiably. Then Lisa said she had to go, gave them both hugs and walked off.

* * *

Two hours later Lloyd Cutler knocked and walked into Dr. Edward Kroll's office. They were in Kroll's three-bedroom condo, overlooking the Hudson in Hoboken, New Jersey. It also overlooked Sinatra Drive and waterfront park, tributes, along with the main post office, to the Mile Square city's most famous citizen. Kroll had moved there decades ago, after leaving the Georgetown University School of Medicine. It was the early days of Hoboken's gentrification and he'd gotten a bargain. He had shifted to a tenure track position at NYU.

Kroll was a millionaire, but the sort who would take home sugar packets from restaurants. His pay as a professor was less than $200,000 but he also received revenue from psychological instruments he had developed, including the Kroll Pathological Personality Inventory, the Kroll Subjective Pain Experience Scale, and the Kroll Intelligence Measurement Index, nicknamed the KIMI.

No one knew about his hidden source of income.

The one area where he spent generously was in the pursuit of the man who went by Jeremy Sherman/Tom Lord and multiple other names. Sherman/Lord was his Moby Dick and Cutler presumed the relentless pursuit would not end well for one of them. He hoped it would be Sherman/Lord who was harpooned. Cutler enjoyed the intellectual challenge of the pursuit as much as the money.

Two of the bedrooms were used as offices, one for Kroll and one for Cutler. Cutler had brought in boxes of electronic gear, setting up a personal web server powerful enough to support a university with backup generator and elaborate surge protection. Along with a world-class firewall. Cutler had his own office across the river in Manhattan but spent much of his time at Kroll's. The psychologist was cheap in most ways but never hesitated when it came to his hunting.

Though close to midnight, Kroll was at his desk, working on a journal article on the brain's default mode network and how it processed adverse events.

"Yes?" Kroll asked without looking up from his computer.

"We have a hit. Portland, Oregon. A woman submitted a cell phone picture to the FRIED system."

FRIED was the Facial Recognition Information Enhancement Database, which was used by law enforcement, credit bureaus, investigators, and anyone willing to pay the considerable access fee to track down fugitives, deadbeats, identity thieves and other con artists. Cutler, once the number two man in the NSA's technical division, had hacked it so Kroll had back door access.

Cutler was able to access virtually any database. With some, it was social engineering or bribery. The National Crime Information Clearinghouse (NCIC) and Interstate Identification Index (usually known as Triple I) were hard to hack, but most police officers could access through the computer in their patrol car. And there were plenty of cops across the country eager for under-the- table cash. With other databases, the former NSA official took pride in hopping over the firewall.

Kroll saved his material and slowly turned to face Cutler. Kroll had always had an imperious, chilling presence but a stroke a few years earlier, just after his 65th birthday, had made him more imperious. The right side of his face had a slight droop, particularly when he smiled. He rarely smiled. He was slender, with thinning gray hair and brown eyes so dark they appeared black. His eyeglasses magnified them slightly, adding to the power of his piercing stare. "How sure are you?"

"The system says it's a 92 percent match."

"It's been five years of wasting money on false alarms."

"The best we've had before this was 40 percent."

Cutler felt like a butterfly pinned to a board by his boss's gaze, a look of intense interest but with no humanity.

"Have Gunther put together a rendition team," Kroll said.

Chapter Four

Dr. Edward Kroll was consistently impressed with Gunther Klimke's knowledge of strongarm thugs, ex-mercenaries, burglars, and skilled criminals in virtually every large city, and many smaller ones, on most continents. Whether ex-*Spetsnaz* in Leningrad, or former *Sayeret Matkal* in Jerusalem, or retired GIGN in Paris, Klimke knew operators who could get things done. Klimke had been under contract to Kroll for several years. Cutler was the brain, Klimke was the brawn.

The nearest crew of rendition experts was based in Los Angeles. Klimke told him that they had only done a half dozen jobs in the United States, kidnapping dissidents and delivering them in the middle of the night to the Russian, Chinese, or Saudi Arabian embassies or consulates. The dissidents were sedated, packed and shipped in a cargo crate carried by their country's airline, back to their homeland. Where the real nightmare began.

The team had operated numerous times on foreign soil, throughout Europe, working for North Korean interests in South Korea, in Indonesia, Malaysia, a half dozen countries in Africa, and the Philippines. They had worked in Cartagena, Bogota, Miami, Houston, Phoenix and Los Angeles. The kidnappings had most often been for ransom, a few times when a Colombian drug lord wanted to show Mexican drug kingpins that they still had *huevos*.

Vinnie was the son of a Tennessee NASCAR driver, the grandson of a bootlegger, who had inherited the family love of driving but not the reflexes to manage 200 mph cars. He could barely hold a conversation unless it involved Hooker headers, Hemi V6 or the merits of a 2001 C5-R Corvette versus a 1969 Mustang Mach 1.

"Linc" got his nickname from his more than passing resemblance to the 16th president. Clean shaven but hairy, with a gaunt face, and a 6"4" 190-pound frame, he had freakishly long arms. He had been an Army Ranger in Afghanistan and been honorably discharged after four years. He did odd jobs, moving and delivery work where he could waltz a refrigerator up a flight of stairs and through a narrow doorway the way most would handle a toaster oven. He made a lot more money, all cash, doing renditions.

Amanda still looked like the cheerleader she had once been. The queen of the mean girls in her Dallas high school, she'd grown up with three bullying older brothers and was as tough physically as she was verbally. She'd become a Houston suburb cop but was forced to resign after several excessive force complaints. And this was in a department where "tuning up" a suspect was the norm.

Bobby Ramirez had met her in a Texas bar. They'd gone out for several months. He was movie star handsome to her relentless perky. The King and Queen of Prom. He was then putting together the rendition team and had recruited her, as well as Linc. Ramirez, an ex-Special Forces sergeant, had worked briefly for the Defense Intelligence Agency and then contracted out to Blackwater. Like many special ops veterans, civilian life was just too boring.

As the leader, he recognized Amanda could be a loose cannon. She was damn good at what she did, either as bait, technician, or even wrestling men twice her weight into submission. He was aware that her being amazing in bed colored his judgment.

He was indifferent to politics and believed everyone they kidnapped was bad. Drug dealers, organized crime rivals, suspected terrorists. The most innocent had been the wife of an overly ambitious dealer. She had more than $500,000 in jewelry on her when they picked her up. The wages of sin. He prided himself on the fact that the team had not even tried to take a bangle away from her.

Their 2015 Ford Econoline van had eye bolts screwed into the floor and clips for the disposable plastic tarp. Targets had lost bowel or bladder control when they realized what happened. Blood had been spilled, though the team did not specialize in wet work. Injuries that occurred were generally accidental. Under the hood the van had a 6.2 L Boss V8 engine with turbocharger that Vinnie had personally installed. The suspension had been hardened, the steering and brakes customized for maximum sensitivity. The tires were puncture resistant Bridgestones.

The ceiling of the van had a GoPro with secure video uplink mounted to it, so customers could see the cargo as soon as it was on board. There were three seats in the back, as well as space for the two suitcase-sized black Pelican cases that held necessary gear.

It had been five days since Lisa's inquiry hit the tripwire Cutler had installed.

* * *

Lisa Moreau was thinking about her friend as she left the three-story building in Beaverton that housed the Meadows practice. The building was as uninspired as the land around it. The city was named after the animal that had been killed off and its pelts helped the region develop. Like all the surrounding cookie cutter developments that had names of what had been destroyed. Forest View, Shady Pines, Quiet Creek.

Was Diana's new boyfriend a nut case or Mr. Right? Lisa was protective, curious and though she wouldn't admit it, envious of her friend and the budding relationship. She wondered if Lord had been in a psych hospital. But she wasn't even sure she had his real name let alone his birth date, the two essential pieces of information for medical records. If he had ever had any treatment paid for by insurance, she knew ways to work around HIPAA and get basic details by knowing the ICD10 billing codes. Did he have F20.0, paranoid schizophrenia or was it more F60.2 antisocial personality disorder? She could determine a lot just by knowing length of stay and what hospital ward he had been held in.

She was, as was often the case, one of the last ones to leave the building. The parking lot had a few cars in it. There was no reason for her to notice the big white van parked by the curb as she walked to her red Mazda Miata.

Linc and Ramirez jumped out, slipping a black cloth bag over her head in a fraction of a second. By the time she tried to swing her arms, Linc had her in a bear hug and off the ground. Ramirez grabbed her legs and swung them into the van. Amanda slid the door shut. The bag had been soaked in a Ketamine derivative and Moreau felt woozy and weak. They pushed her to the floor of the van and bound her hands with plastic quick ties. Her arms were pulled over her head, her legs pulled apart and tied down. The position was designed to make her feel especially vulnerable.

"Less than four seconds," she heard a male voice say.

"Not bad, not too bad," said another.

Though they hadn't been pleased they weren't allowed a couple of days of recon, they were getting a bonus for fast turnaround. Her working late had been a fortuitous surprise.

A hand pinched the inside of her thigh and she yelped. She struggled against the ties.

"The sedative in the bag over your head is short-acting," said a distorted male voice coming through some sort of speaker above her. "You can scream if you want. The van is soundproofed and all it will do is annoy us." Her thigh was pinched again.

She screamed.

"Very good. Nice lungs," said a voice with a Texas accent. After so many hours of phone work she had a good ear for accents and sounds. Hands roughly grabbed her breasts and she heard laughing. It sounded higher pitched. A woman?

A hand traveled up her thigh and brushed across her crotch.

"What the fuck is going on?" Moreau demanded.

Silence except for the rumble of the wheels on the road.

Moreau got quiet. She sniffed the air, trying to gather as much information as she could. Nothing made it through the fruity, chemically scented bag over her head. She violently shook her head from side to side, but the bag was cinched in place at her neck.

"The bag over your head is for your benefit as much as ours," Distorted Voice continued. "If you were to see faces, your chance of survival would significantly decrease. Do you understand?"

When she didn't respond she was pinched again. "I get it." She stopped thrashing and strained against the ties holding her down. They cut into her wrists and legs. Moving was harder and her brain felt cloudy. She'd done enough drugs voluntarily to recognize her mental state. She felt disconnected, oddly indifferent. Cooperating didn't seem like a bad idea.

"I hope to make this as brief as possible, for our sake as well as yours. All we want to know about is Thomas Lord. Who is Diana Wynne?"

"None of your business," she said, a slight slur but struggling to keep control.

"My associates here would be happy to question you after having their time with you. In various unpleasant ways." She heard chuckling.

Kroll sat at his desk in New Jersey, watching the scene through the GoPro. Vinnie was out of view, driving, Linc and Amanda watched from the side. Ramirez was the one pinching and groping her. His face showed only concentration, no sign of arousal. Kroll was pleased with his professionalism.

The threat of sexual assault was effective, though even more so with men. Women also often had a higher pain tolerance. So much for the weaker sex. Kroll had studied the work of several effective overseas interrogators who made no secret of what was done in back rooms and prisons. Of course, there were cultural factors to consider but not much good work was being published on the subject. Before Nazi Germany, so much had just been anecdotal. The North Koreans and Chinese in the Korean War had advanced the field. Russians in their "psychiatric hospitals" and gulags had also provided solid data. The CIA had dabbled, but in general were too squeamish to admit what needed to be done sometimes. The various nations' armed forces, where there was the most opportunity to gather data, had proven to be ineffective at truly advancing the science. The Geneva Conventions made documenting torture a liability. But there were sites on the Dark Web where techniques, failures and successes could all be discussed. Helpful data could be exchanged, even images, though Kroll found photos to be unnecessary, and frequently distasteful.

Kroll let the van grow quiet, musing on options as the driver took them west of the city to a logging road in the foothills of the coastal range. Hopefully the woman's imagination was creating the darkest possibilities. Only she would know beforehand what she really feared most. And the Ketamine derivative that the bag had been saturated with would make her more compliant. He was impressed at how strong her will was to resist this long. Though it had been a low dose since they didn't want analgesic effects. "My associates' methods could take a while and I'm in a bit of a rush," Kroll said casually.

Hands grabbed her left arm and held it even more immobile. "We're going to put a drop of acid on your arm. About where your medial brachial cutaneous nerve should be. Feel free to scream."

She felt a drop on the inside of her arm, about an inch from her elbow, cool for a fraction of a second, then hotter and hotter. A white-hot spot of pain seeming to burn right to the bone. She fought making a noise, grinding her teeth together until a scream escaped her lips. The wound continued to burn.

"I hope you'll make good choices moving forward," Kroll said. "If not, there is a lot more acid. Do you understand?"

"Yes," Lisa said through gritted teeth.

"Or you can answer questions without hesitation and this unpleasant few moments in your life will be over soon. Does Thomas Lord use any other name?"

"Not that I know."

"Provide a detailed physical description, starting from the hair on his head and down to his estimated shoe size."

She felt no loyalty to the man in her friend's life and described Lord as best she could.

The voice continued to ask questions and she answered them. She figured that they had access to her computer and knew it all anyway.

It wasn't much and Distorted Voice said so. "Now tell us about Diana."

"I've been her friend for years. We met when..."

The hand at her crotch squeezed hard.

"Enough," Distorted Voice said. "We have no interest in slumber parties you've had or other trite details. Has she ever been in legal trouble?"

"No."

She heard a sigh. "We know that's not true, Ms. Moreau."

"I made a mistake. I made a mistake."

"That you did. The question is whether it was deliberate. I'm going to be kind to you because I understand your desire to protect your friend. There does have to be consequences, however." The voice let time pass. Lisa wanted to scream, to cry, to beg. She understood he was in complete control of her life and nothing she did other than obey would matter.

"The nerves in your left arm are probably traumatized with overloaded pain signals, a little less sensitive at this point."

Hands grabbed her uninjured right arm and a droplet of acid was again put on the brachial nerve. Her scream turned into a sob.

"Good, good, let it out," Distorted Voice said. "Now, let's confirm her home address and describe the house in detail, as if you were walking through it."

Lisa did, rationalizing they could get room layout from blueprints somewhere. Under questioning, she gave vague but accurate accounts of where furniture was, answering every question Distorted Voice had. The drug weakened her ability to not answer. She told them how the couple had met, that Diana didn't know where he lived, that he had told her very little of his history. She admitted that Diana hadn't requested the online image search and didn't know about it. She told him what she knew of Diana's schedule, how she planned to get together with Lord, how Wynne was strongly attracted to him.

"I imagine you'll want to report this to the authorities," Distorted Voice said. "Not a very believable story. You don't have solid information. The drug you have been inhaling is a Ketamine derivative. I'm sure you're heard of Vitamin K as an abusable. If you go to police with this far-fetched story, no doubt they'll run a drug test and find it in your system. And by the way, when your employer inventories their pharmacy after they get an anonymous tip, they'll find Ketamine missing. As well as several bottles of Oxycontin. Which will be found in your home when police execute the search warrant. They'll also find out you were quite the party girl a while back. Are you understanding me?"

"Yes."

"There's additional motivation for your being quiet." She heard the sound of paper rustling. "Let's see now, and you've got a large family. Very cute nieces and nephews. There's Justin at Central Catholic, Kaitlin at Wilson High School, little Susie at Blue Frogs Jump preschool. And Amber at West Hills Montessori is quite a handful. Their futures are in your hands." He paused. "Do I make myself clear?"

"Yes."

The van drove for a few minutes, and she heard the side door slide open. Her legs and arms were untied. She was shoved out as the bag was pulled off her head. She landed hard on the graveled road. Even though it was dark due to the dense canopy of trees, she blinked from the sudden light filtering through tall evergreens. She wobbled upright on the potholed logging road. The white van disappeared around a curve before she could glimpse a license plate.

She reached for her cell phone but it was gone. She looked at her arms. Both had little bloody spots, not much bigger than a pencil eraser. Her right oozed blood. Her arms had a peculiar numbness with a painful tingle.

A light rain muddied the road. Her hair was pasted flat against her head. At least it made her tears less visible.

She staggered down the road. In 15 minutes, she had reached Highway 26. She stood in the roadway waving but cars just swerved around the bedraggled woman. Finally, a stout bleached blonde in a big pickup slowed and asked, "What's wrong with you, honey?"

"I need your cell phone. It's an emergency."

"No coverage here, we need to go about 10 more minutes closer into town. Hop in, I'll take you."

Chapter Five

Driving on Highway 26, Vinnie was careful to not go more than five miles over the speed limit. Ramirez made sure the lid was tight on the bottle of hydrochloric acid. Amanda monitored the electronics. Linc gently stretched his arms and shoulders in the confined space.

"I had forgotten how satisfying field work could be," Kroll said remotely, his face visible on the laptop. "Is Lloyd's equipment in place?"

"Of course," Amanda responded. "This isn't our first rodeo." She pointed to a laptop in the corner of the van. She had attached Lisa's phone via USB cable to the laptop.

"Good. Gunther is on his way to pick up the package. Assuming you have it ready at the airport, $250,000 will be wired to the account number you gave me."

"Lord will be there. Boxed up nice and tight with a ribbon on top," Ramirez said.

* * *

As soon as they were in range, the pickup driver loaned Lisa her phone. Fortunately, Wynne and Moreau had agreed one evening to memorize each other's numbers in the event of a lost cell phone. Moreau called Wynne but it went right to voice mail.

"Don't go home. I don't have my own phone right now but I'll call soon with details. Things ain't safe," Lisa said with urgency. She called both gyms where Diana might be working but she wasn't at either one. She told the staffers to warn

Diana immediately if she came in. They agreed to pass on the message.

Lisa called her friend's cell phone again. "Listen, I don't know what your boyfriend is involved in but some motherfuckers picked me up and threatened me. Asked a lot of questions about him. And you. They burned me, were talking about doing a lot worse." She sighed. "I know I shouldn'ta done it, but I took a picture of Lord and ran it through a high tech facial-recog database. They got to me through him. Some of that crazy shit he's been saying is probably true. Just go someplace safe. We'll figure this all out. You can let your boyfriend know or not. Just take care of yourself. These bastards are scary."

The pickup driver stared at Lisa. She spent hours working through her church to help the less fortunate. But the woman she'd picked up seemed on the edge of crazy. They rode in silence, the driver quietly watching her clearly disturbed passenger.

Moreau didn't consider calling police. She knew she'd be dismissed as a junkie nutjob who had burned her arm with a cigarette. But she couldn't let her friend go through the horror she just had.

* * *

"She called us scary bastards," Amanda said, smirking. "And motherfuckers."

"And confirmed Lord has disclosed something to the woman," Ramirez said.

Starting with the International Mobile Subscriber Identity catcher, devices with names like Triggerfish and Stingray can mimic a cell phone tower, overwhelm its signal, and do a "man-in-the-middle" hack.

Hacking Moreau's cell phone for all the numbers she had called in the past, they were able to set up intercepts. The call to the gyms had been routed to Cutler's office in New Jersey where he had a contract worker--an aspiring actress who specialized in impersonation--pretend to be gym employees and accept the message. Cutler had earlier recorded Diana's outgoing voice mail message. It was replayed when Lisa's call was rerouted to the Stingray set-up in the van.

"At least the bitch wasn't holding anything back," Amanda said. "I still think we should teach her a lesson for breaking her word."

"I got respect for her," Linc said. "She didn't really crack and first thing she does is try and protect her friend. Even though the doc threatens the kids she cares about."

"Whatever," Amanda said. "I just want to get it done and get paid."

Ramirez got an encrypted call from Cutler. The ex-spook's proprietary software was better than the usual PGP, not only scrambling the words, but inserting random innocuous words and then muddying the message with static. He knew the NSA scanned and would pay more attention to an obviously encrypted communication. Unless his former employer took it to the third level of analysis any communication between his phones just sounded like a garbled message.

"We've done a little research on Diana Wynne and I'm going to Vaporstream it to you." Whenever possible, Cutler believed in ephemeral messaging. Amanda had joked to the team, off-line, that he probably used disappearing grocery lists.

"What about this Tom Lord guy?" Ramirez asked.

"Dr. Kroll is very guarded about him. Details are above your pay grade."

"We're the ones taking the risk."

"And getting well paid for it. I can tell you he's not ex-military. Never worked in any field capacity for an intelligence agency. Both he and she are not believed to have any firearms. If he does it is doubtful he's proficient or capable of lethality."

"Doubtful sounds like you're hedging your bets," Ramirez said. "Just like saying he never worked in any field capacity. He some sort of spook desk jockey?"

"As you were told early on, he needs to be delivered intact. He has valuable information in his head. If you use violence, be judicious. Any damage to the package would result in lower or no payment."

Ramirez muttered an inaudible "fuck you." "And the girl?"

"Whatever force is necessary. If you do have to terminate with extreme prejudice, just be sure you clean up your mess."

"We always do," Ramirez said and hung up. "I hate these HQ types. 'Terminate with extreme prejudice,'" he mimicked. He looked at the picture of Diana. "Not bad looking."

"You get hard with your hands on the one we had?" Amanda asked.

"Maybe."

"It got me going," Amanda said, nibbling her lip. "Especially her thrashing around like that."

Ramirez winked at her. "When the job is done, let's get a drink and debrief."

Amanda nodded and smiled. "Nothing like a good debriefing."

Linc's eyes remained fixed on a spot on the van wall.

Amanda leaned against Ramirez and they looked at the information on the computer screen. Aside from the picture, the brief but detailed report said Diana Wynne, 42, had been born in Missouri, lived much of her adult life in the Pacific Northwest. She drove a 2016 grey Honda CR-V. She had two arrests for assault with no convictions, two speeding tickets, and a half dozen parking tickets over the past ten years.

There was an architect's blueprint that showed the layout of her 1100 square foot house when it was built 40 years earlier. With a Wells Fargo mortgage, she had purchased the bungalow for a good price shortly after the housing bubble burst in 2008. The description was consistent with what Lisa had described. One bedroom with a bathroom coming off of it, a small kitchen with adjacent dining nook, and a living room that was just off the front door.

Her father was deceased, her mother in a nursing home with dementia, and she had two sisters. She had a bachelor's degree in communications from Washington State University and had seldom lasted in a job for more than a year. She had worked as a waitress, whitewater rafting guide, and was currently an aerobics instructor who had competed in mixed martial arts and taught self-defense.

"Oooooh, she sounds tough," Amanda said sarcastically.

"Don't be cocky," Ramirez cautioned. "It sounds like she's got bigger balls than our target."

Vinnie had put the address into GPS when Kroll confirmed it with Lisa. "It's up on the hill near the hospital. We're about 45 minutes away if traffic don't get any worse." Amanda typed the address into Google Earth on the laptop and was rewarded with a clear view of the front of the small house as well as neighboring houses.

Ramirez took a couple of Tasers out of a black suitcase-sized Pelican case in the back of the van. He checked that they were charged and handed one to Linc. He took a few Flex ties and tucked them in his pocket. He tossed Linc a roll of duct tape.

Ramirez dug through the Pelican case. There were a couple of large magnetic decals saying "Johnson Creek Home Repair" with bogus contractor's board license number and phone number. Also, five syringes with methohexital, a powerful, fast-acting sedative with minimal side effects. It could knock a 200 pound man out in less than five seconds. The subject would be unconscious for at least an hour, then groggy for another hour.

There was a blue Portland Gas and Electric uniform, complete with reflective safety vest and clipboard. There was also a large fold up laundry cart, transponder, night vision goggles, tranquilizer dart rifle, 100 feet of rope and other gear. A box held wigs, mustaches and makeup for disguise.

Amanda took a Monadnock expandable baton out of her pocket and flicked it open to its full 21-inch length, then closed it, then re-flicked it.

"I wish we had time to do a dry run. Or know more about him," Ramirez said.

"We've improvised before," Amanda responded. "Remember that fat drug dealer we scooped up in Miami? He had guards with Uzis and didn't know what hit him."

"Lloyd's report is adequate," Ramirez said. "But how is the furniture really arranged? I don't trust what that Moreau said. Does Diana have a roommate she didn't tell us about?"

"Place looks small," Linc said. "A dog?"

"No mention of it," Amanda said.

"Lloyd would just know if it's licensed through the county or registered with AKC," Ramirez said. "And the gun would show up only if registered. How many guns you got?"

"Six," Linc responded.

"How many are registered?"

"Okay, I get your point."

"He's not telling us stuff. Particularly about this Lord guy."

* * *

Diana and Tom lay in her bed, naked, sweaty and quite content.

"I'd like to see your place sometime," she said.

"It's not much. Typical bachelor's pad. I'd have to clean for a week before you could visit."

"I doubt that. I suspect your place is neat and tidy. Minimalist. Am I right?"

He rolled on his side, facing her. "You're psychic."

"No, I just see you as a neat and tidy sort of guy. But I have been told I'm psychic. I think I'm just aware."

"What do you think about ESP?"

"Not sure. Inclined to believe it's possible. What about you?"

"Maybe." He hesitated, then quickly said, "We haven't done mindfulness together yet today."

Her hand drifted down his abdomen. "I thought what we just did was very mindful."

"Mindful and mindless, both in a wonderful way."

They snuggled up. "Your place is very nice," he said.

"Even though the first thing you did was criticize it."

"Not criticize, just make some suggestions."

He had suggested adding a keyed dead bolt to her back door, where anyone could smash out a pane and reach in and open it. As well as putting long nails through her sash window frames, nails that could be pulled out from the inside to let the window open. He had suggested trimming the tall, bushy rhododendrons in the front.

"They give me privacy," she'd said.

"But anyone could hide in there. Keep your curtains shut. It's a good practice anyway."

"You can be pretty paranoid, you know that?"

"Even paranoids have enemies," he joked.

But she had followed his advice. He had encouraged her getting pepper spray. She reminded him she could take of herself without a weapon. And she had a bow in the closet.

The bow was a special gift from her father. He had it made modeled on a Mongolian bow, smaller than regular bows, less cumbersome for someone her size. It had been hand crafted from Rosewood with fiberglass laminate. When she told him about it, she had gotten misty-eyed.

"Of course, I'd have to string it before I could shoot it," she said.

"That'd take way too long. And you could probably only get off a single shot, Katniss," Tom said. "Do you think you honestly could shoot someone?"

"I used to go hunting with my father. I didn't get buck fever when I killed my first. He insisted we go bowhunting, felt guns gave us an unfair advantage. Very up close and personal."

"But you never shot a human, I hope."

She shook her head and asked, "You ever killed anything?"

"Nothing bigger than a spider. You?"

"A deer's the biggest thing," Wynne said. "I'm not exactly a defenseless female." She clenched her hands into tight fists. He kissed the scarring on her knuckles. She stroked his face with her opened hand.

She asked, "How'd we get on such a romantic subject?"

"Freud said it was all about sex and death. Eros and Thanatos."

"Hmmm. I prefer the sex." She took him in her hand. "Besides, death you can only do once."

* * *

The rendition team drove up and down the block and found a place to park near an ugly 50s-era ranch house with a For Sale sign on the dried-up lawn. They were pleased Diana's house was somewhat isolated and the nearest houses were dark.

They sat in the van, with Vinnie in the driver's seat, playing the *Need for Speed* car racing game on his phone. Ramirez sat in the partitioned off rear, staring at the house through the darkened back window of the van. Amanda was next to him, quiet, attentive, occasionally brushing up against him in a supposedly accidental way. For her violence was an aphrodisiac. Their best dates had been after he'd beat up someone in a bar who she'd flirted with. Linc popped his neck and rolled his shoulders.

"No sign of activity at the house," Amanda said. "Her car is the only one."

"Hopefully he's there," Ramirez said. "If not, she'll lead us to him. Or be bait if necessary."

He went back to the Pelican case and took out an object that looked like three nickels welded together. "Let's get this transponder on the car in case we lose her. You want to do the honors or should I?"

"I'm getting restless," Amanda said. "I'll jog around the block, see if there's anything visible behind the house."

She had a bag with a couple changes of clothes. Since her role was often to be the distraction or first contact, she was used to different costumes. Many victims had stopped to give assistance to the helpless blonde standing by her seemingly broken-down van.

She slipped out of her jeans. Ramirez eyeballed her, Linc seemed to barely notice. She smiled at Ramirez, snapping the band on her pink thong. She donned jogging shorts. She didn't need to change her Timbers tee-shirt and was already wearing a sports bra and Nikes.

When there was no one on the street she hopped out of the van. She stood near the CR-V and made as if stretching. During one of her bends, she slipped the transponder under the rear bumper. One side was magnetic and it clung to the undercarriage.

Then she took off in a slow jog around the block.

* * *

Tom blinked a few times and suddenly looked distant.

"You okay?" Diana asked.

"Uh, sure."

"Something wrong?"

"Nah, nothing." He forced an awkward grin. "No complaints. You make me feel like a teenager again."

"Is that a bad thing?"

"What do you think?" He smiled more genuinely. "I just thought we were going on a hike today?"

"Too late for that. You disappointed?" she asked.

"I'll work through my grief."

"The weather is going to be nice this weekend. There's a couple special spots in the Gifford Pinchot Forest I'd like to share with you."

"Sounds great." He sat up in bed. "I'm starting to get hungry from the horizontal exercise. You want to go out to dinner?"

She leaned against him. "I don't feel like getting dressed. Portland restaurants are casual, but still..."

"You got something in mind?"

"I've got pasta and chopped meat and a secret tomato sauce recipe. You can make the salad. Maybe some garlic bread?"

"Sounds delicious." He had made omelets for lunch, which included doing a couple of sleight of hand tricks and having eggs come out of her ears and nose. "How about we shower then make the food?"

The shower turned into a half hour of mutual soaping, scrubbing, nibbling and squeezing.

In the kitchen she turned up the music. When Alice Merton began singing 'No Roots', she hummed and swayed her hips. By Natalia Kills' 'Wonderland', she was singing and dancing. He set down the garlic he was slicing and joined her. Neither of them was ever going to be on *America's Got Talent* but they were giddy as kids as they launched into Carly Rae Jepsen's bubbly 'Call Me Maybe'.

* * *

Amanda slipped into the front seat of the van, then climbed into the back. "Nothing much of interest," she said. "Good news is no one hanging out in their backyard or watering the lawn."

The sun was beginning to set, shadows darkening. A few cars drove down the street, a few people went into their houses as they returned from work. Vinnie kept an eye on neighboring houses. No signs of busybodies behind curtains.

"This waiting is the worst," Amanda said. Her blond hair was under a bushy red-headed wig that was topped with a yellow hard hat. Her blue blouse had Portland General

Electric embroidered on it, along with the square multi-colored logo. Over it was a reflective vest with PGE in big letters.

"What's the best part?"

"Everything else." She wet her lips with a quick flick of her tongue.

The sodium vapor streetlights kicked on as the sky darkened. But with numerous dense maples on the block, the light was limited.

Ramirez glanced at his Luminox SEAL watch. "Check your gear, ask any last questions. Ten minutes 'til showtime."

Chapter Six

"Uh, it's probably way too early to talk about this, but I'm not really interested in dating anyone else," Diana said. They were seated on the couch in her small living room, taking tentative sips of hot mint tea. Toshira Mifune, in a poster from *Yojimbo*, looked down with his fierce samurai glare.

"When you focus on something, you just focus on it. You don't like distractions."

"Yes!"

"In this case, that something is our relationship."

"Yes," she said more softly.

Diana wore a terrycloth robe, bare legs tucked underneath her. He was wearing boxers and a tee-shirt.

They had finished dinner and tidying up the kitchen. A remarkably comfortable domestic scene considering how short a time they had known each other.

"What about you?" she asked.

"You might be shocked to learn I'm not much of a ladies' man," he said. "Truth be told, I haven't thought about dating anyone since that night when you appeared as the Black Widow."

"It's kind of quick to be jumping into a committed relationship," she said hesitantly.

"Yeah, but..." He paused and looked as if he'd been hit. He winced.

"You okay?" she asked. "If you don't want to talk about it..."

Her doorbell rang.

He blinked again as she stood and went to the door. "Don't..."

"We can talk about something else," she said, peering through the peephole then reaching for the knob. "It's just someone from PGE." She was opening the door and saying, "Yes?" as he jumped off the couch.

The PGE worker, a redheaded woman, was stepping in, holding a clipboard and saying, "We have a report of..." when he threw the scalding tea at her face.

The redhead screamed and swiped at the hot liquid.

Diana gasped and stared at Tom.

An athletic-looking man tried to follow the PGE-uniformed woman in. Tom threw himself against the door and the intruder was knocked back.

The fake PGE woman snapped open a retractable club. She swung; Tom dodged. Her club shattered a lamp and knocked over a small end table.

Diana's reflexes switched on. She lashed out a roundhouse kick that caught the woman on the side of the head, toppling her back. The fake PGE woman lay on the floor groaning.

The door jamb shattered as the athletic guy and a tall, wiry man charged in. Both men had Tasers and fired simultaneously.

Wynne and Lord spasmed as 200,000 kilovolts hit them. They went down hard.

"Shit!" the wiry man said. He looked like a scary Abraham Lincoln, gaunt with chimpanzee long arms.

"Tape them up!" the athletic-looking man, the apparent leader, said.

Lincoln slapped duct tape around their wrists and over Diana and Tom's mouths. Then he taped their ankles together. He did it with the ease of someone who had done it many times before.

The fake PGE woman was seething, cursing, trying to get at the couple while the leader held her back and tried to calm her. He was someone who was used to being obeyed and equally clear that he had feelings for her. Only Lincoln was watching Diana and Tom. The couple was about 10 feet apart, leaning on the wall.

Tom made eye contact with Diana, then glanced down at the duct tape, wrinkled his forehead slightly, and mouthed "Watch me" under the tape, though he knew she couldn't see his lips. She gave a slight nod, wishing they had practiced the move he had described to her. The leader was focused on the fake PGE woman, distracted.

Lord wasn't struggling. He took a few deep calming breaths through his nose. The woman couldn't see him, her body blocked by the leader who had his hands on her shoulders and kept repeating, "Think of the payday, think of the payday." She continued to curse and demand that she be allowed to "cut his balls off as payback." The "his balls" clearly referred to Tom.

"Get them both sedated," the leader said over his shoulder to Lincoln. Lincoln reached into his small backpack.

Tom raised his hands over his head, flaring his elbows and pulling free, simultaneously falling sideways, rolling toward where the vase had shattered. With his hands free, he grabbed the biggest ceramic shard and sliced the tape by his ankles. Diana rolled toward him and he did the same for her as Lincoln shouted "Hey!"

He stepped toward Lord. Tom rolled as Lincoln shifted his weight to kick. Lord lashed out with the shard at Lincoln's calf. Lord sliced deep into where the Achilles tendon met the calf. Lincoln fell hard, screaming. Blood gushed from his leg. He passed out from shock moments after hitting the ground.

Then the leader charged. The PGE woman also focused on attacking Tom. Which allowed Diana to launch a sideways kick to the woman's knee that made a stomach-churning pop sound. An attack Diana favored.

The leader threw a punch toward Tom's gut. The leader was fast, barely any pause between thought and action. But Tom turned slightly so it grazed him rather than hitting his abdomen straight on. Even so, it bent Lord double.

Then Diana was on the leader, arm around his throat, choking. He couldn't pry her arm loose but slammed her back into the wall and loosened her grip. He threw her to the ground. But she did a skilled break fall and was up quickly, hands in front of her in a defensive position. He circled around so he could watch Diana and Tom.

The PGE woman was literally growling as she crawled forward like a kill-crazed animal. Diana shifted her attention momentarily and kicked her hard in the jaw. The woman fell flat, her red-haired wig covering her face.

The leader lunged at Diana.

She blocked and launched an elbow strike, which he parried and countered by trying a strike to her throat. Then they were on the ground, thrashing around, throwing punches at each other's head and ribs and trying to get a knee in. Their ferocity and speed seemed superhuman. Tom couldn't get close enough to the rapidly moving bodies to help.

Tom grabbed a syringe off the floor, popped the lid off and hurried over. Diana was holding her own but the leader was stronger and more trained in lethal combat. Her parries were less effective. When he pulled back his arm to punch her again, Tom was able to grab the arm and jab the needle into his deltoid. But the leader moved before Tom could get the plunger all the way down, getting only a half dose.

He stood and charged Lord, swinging wildly.

Two, three, four times he hit Lord, who wobbled. The drug slowed him, and Tom avoided the next few punches. Then Diana was on him again. She hit him in the floating ribs. Her blows and the drug finally took effect and he crumpled to the ground.

Diana and Tom faced each other. Her nose was bleeding, her lip split. Both were heaving.

"What the hell," she said.

"There's one more out in the van."

"How do you know?"

"I'll explain later."

"We should call the police," she said.

"No. Kroll's got too many connections. If we call, I wouldn't be surprised if it's intercepted."

"Who?"

"I'll explain everything. I promise. Right now, we just need to neutralize Vinnie and get away."

"Vinnie?"

"The driver."

"You know him?"

"No." Lord gulped. "Just trust me until we get out of here and I promise I'll tell you. It might not make sense but it'll be the truth."

"You have an idea for the driver?"

And he told her. They stripped off the fake PGE woman's uniform. She was taller and thinner than Diana, but people tended to notice big items, particularly when they are rushed or scared. Diana slipped out of her robe and into the work clothing. She wiped her face with a washcloth. The bleeding had stopped. She adjusted the red-haired wig, pulled the hard hat low so it partially blocked her face.

"How do I look?" she asked.

Tom nodded approval and handed her a syringe. "You got a Vise Grip?"

"Why?"

"After you sedate him, stick the key in the ignition and then break it off. Smash any electronics you see. We need to buy ourselves some time."

She nodded and walked briskly to the van. She banged her palm twice on the side of the van and Vinnie slid the door open.

She hit him with a palm heel strike to the chin before he even recognized it wasn't Amanda. Dazed, it took two more quick blows before he was unconscious.

Diana soon reappeared and Tom let her in.

"Any problems?" he asked.

"Not for me," she said, peeling off the wig and getting out of the too tight clothing.

Lincoln started to awaken. Tom gave him a shot of sedative in his sinewy arm. Diana put a clean towel over his wound and wrapped multiple strips of his duct tape around it. The bleeding had slowed but not stopped. His skin was clammy and an unhealthy color. The leader was actually snoring. The fake PGE woman looked like a broken doll. But she was breathing and not bleeding significantly. Diana threw the clothing on top of her.

"We've got to get out of here," Lord said.

"We can go to Lisa's place, I'm sure..."

"They probably know your friends, all the likely places. Certainly Lisa."

"Where then?"

"I don't know. I thought I was off the grid. I can't imagine how they found me and tracked me here."

"You want off the grid? I know places in the woods about 90 minutes north of here. Caves and thousands of acres of federal wilderness."

"Let's get out of town and sort it out."

She was heading toward her bedroom, beginning to gather gear, talking to Tom over her shoulder.

"I'll pack. We'll pick up some food. Plus warmer clothes for you."

"I'm going to give the leader the last shot. He only got a partial dose and he's the biggest threat."

"You know him too?" She stared, confusion and anger flitting across her face.

"I'll explain as soon as we get on the road. We don't have much time."

* * *

Kroll had been on his computer, working on the journal article, periodically checking the van GoPro.

He'd seen the woman enter, and the scuffle that ensued.

She glanced full face into the camera as she smashed it with the Vise Grips.

She couldn't see him but he'd seen her. Clearly.

He called Gunther whose plane was making its approach into the Hillsboro airport.

"A change of plan," he said.

Chapter Seven

Diana had loaded the car in silence. She stared straight ahead as she drove down the hill and got on the 405. "You going to tell me what the hell just happened?" she asked.

"You want the long version or the short?"

"The short version right now."

"When I was a teenager I was taken in to CIA and DIA funded experiments on ESP. The psychologist running them was Edward Kroll. I was one of the few who actually showed abilities. But the program was brutal in its own way. Eventually I ran. Have been running ever since. The feds shut down the program, in part when they found out what he was doing, in part because there weren't many real successes."

"So you've got ESP? Like you can move objects and tell the future?"

"That's telekinesis, which there's no real proof of, and precognition, which is questionable but some glimmers of a possibility. I actually have telepathy. Mind reading. That was how I could defend myself so well, knowing the attack they were thinking of."

She snorted in disbelief and drove for a few minutes in silence.

"We'll stop at the Fred Meyer's in Gateway district," she said, breaking the silence. "Get yourself a heavy jacket, socks, underwear and hiking shoes. I'm going to get us food."

One of her eyes was puffy. Bruising was starting under both of them. Her lip was split. Lord was hurting all over and had taken one tenth the beating she had.

"Uh, maybe some makeup to cover the injuries," he suggested.

She took her eyes off the road to glare at him. "It's just going to look like I'm trying to cover it up. It's not going to make the swelling go down." She turned her attention back to the road and spoke through gritted teeth. "You know what I'm thinking?"

"You're really mad at me."

"Wow. You are an amazing psychic."

They rode in silence, crossing the Willamette River, then I-5 until it connected with I-84 heading east. She pulled off in the Gateway district at the Fred Meyer. The mammoth store was like a Safeway had mated with a Target, a sprawl of efficient consumerism. She had a cap on her head with her ponytail pulled back. The big sunglasses she wore looked only a little out of place under the bright fluorescents.

They separated and he moved quickly through men's clothing, getting a Columbia Sportswear parka, a package of socks and briefs. Diana breezed by and took the socks and briefs out of his hand.

"Cotton? Really. You ever hear cotton is rotten?"

"No."

"Death cloth. It feels comfortable but when it gets wet, it stays wet."

She picked out polypropylene underwear and socks, plus a moisture-wicking top made of some fancy fiber. Getting a pair of good hiking boots took the longest. Still, they were out of the store in less than a half hour.

The small car was packed tight, with some of the food on the floor at his feet. She hit the accelerator and got them back on the freeway. He wanted to caution her to not call attention to them by speeding. But with her seething anger, he elected to sit quietly and hope there were no cops around.

After a long silence, he turned on the radio and tuned it to AM.

"What the hell are you doing?" she demanded.

* * *

Gunther Klimke hated flying commercial. Even in first class, it meant cramped shared bathrooms and breathing recirculated air. And more security with no chance to carry a weapon other than his custom 6-inch black ceramic Tanto knife in a custom sheath taped to his calf. The zirconium oxide blade was invisible to metal detectors.

But the privately-owned Cessna Citation jet had taken him right to Troutdale airport, with only one stop for refueling in Omaha. Kroll didn't own the plane, but somehow had access. Judging by the pilot's Russian accent, Klimke assumed it was connected with Kroll's shadowy Russian connections.

Born in South Africa, Klimke could pass as German, Dutch, or Australian. His parents had immigrated to the United States when they sensed apartheid was on its last legs. He had enlisted in the U.S. Army and served as a Ranger, then Special Forces. He was a 30-year-old captain when he decided the private sector offered more freedom and money. His passport showed stamps from thirty countries. Another 15 he had entered covertly.

A hulking Slav sat in the back of the plane, his blond hair trimmed in a straight-line buzz cut. With his blocky jaw, it gave his head a rectangular look. Klimke had exchanged few words with him. He said his name was Ivan. Judging by the way he smirked when he said it, Klimke suspected it was a *nom de guerre*. Ivan had a *Spetsnaz* tattoo on his considerable right bicep. Their logo looked like the bat signal imposed on rifle crosshairs. He had been told the man was along to help load the cargo and handle transshipment.

When the man now calling himself Tom Lord was picked up, he would be sedated, loaded into a special crate, and transported to Brooklyn. From there, a small boat would take him offshore to a Russian trawler. After that, Klimke could only guess. Although he had been with Kroll for almost five years, everything was on a need-to-know basis. Klimke gathered there had been a major clusterfuck five years ago in Hawaii. They'd nearly had Lord but the target had slipped away.

Klimke knew that Lord had been an ESP experimental subject. He was skeptical about ESP but didn't much care. Kroll paid well. The ex-soldier had been glad to get away from his work in West Africa, where he had seen people die from Ebola. He was fearless when it came to a sniper shot or IED explosion, but the prospect of dying slowly in a hospital terrified him. He'd seen both of his parents succumb, one to COPD, the other to melanoma. A noble warrior's death was his expectation, not withering away, helplessly attached to a half dozen tubes with nurses prolonging his bodily functions. He kept his 40-year-old body in top shape, running at least five miles daily whenever possible, coupled with an extensive core and upper body workout; eating all the fruits and vegetables you were supposed to but nobody did; not smoking; swallowing a dozen vitamins; and wearing a condom when he indulged with the occasional prostitute.

As Ivan drove their rented Ford Explorer from the airport to Diana's house, Klimke checked his Glock 43, a 9mm subcompact six shot weapon. Very concealable, durable, and accurate at close range. He owned a dozen other weapons. But gathering up Lord required subtlety, not the kind of firepower arsenal he'd bring to a shootout. "Never whack down a six-penny nail with a sledgehammer," a wise old sergeant had told him.

They pulled up in front of Wynne's house. Klimke got out and walked up to the white van parked at the curb. He couldn't see anything peering in the front window.

With his right hand resting on the butt of the Glock, he slid open the van's side door. Vinnie was lying trussed up on his stomach, hands bound behind his back with duct tape over his mouth. He had a patch of dried blood on his scalp. Uncertain who Klimke was but seeing the gun, Vinnie's eyes went wide.

"Stay quiet," Klimke commanded calmly, as if discovering a bound man in a van was a routine occurrence. Klimke climbed in, shut the door, and took the knife from the leg sheath. The razor-sharp blade sliced through the bindings.

"Keep your voice down," Klimke cautioned, waiting until Vinnie nodded before gently peeling the duct tape off the driver's mouth.

"Crazy bitch surprised me," Vinnie blurted out. "Hit me with a wrench before I knew what was happening. Then she smashed the shit out of everything." He pointed to the back, where the broken GoPro hung from the ceiling. The laptop looked like it had been a gorilla's toy. The screen on the dashboard was also shattered.

"How long ago?"

"Maybe 45 minutes, an hour. I'm not sure. I was out for a bit."

"How many inside?"

"Three. Ramirez, Amanda and Linc. I think the target and the crazy bitch took off. There was a grey Honda CR-V parked by the house. It's the 2005 model, the last year with the spare tire mounted on the rear door. MacPherson struts, 156 horsepower with a 2.0 liter-"

"I get it," Klimke interrupted. "Stay here. I'll call when I've confirmed the house is secure."

Vinnie climbed into the front seat, stretching cramped legs.

Klimke walked back to the Explorer. "I'm going in. You stay in the truck."

"I come in," Ivan said.

"Stay in the truck."

Ivan started to push open the door and Klimke pushed it shut. "Stay in the truck. Keep an eye out." Klimke didn't trust Ivan. No backup was better than an unknown commodity. To appease the Russian, he said, "All indications are there's nothing going on inside. I'd rather have you as sentry out here."

The Russian's look shifted to a flat-eyed stare and he nodded.

Klimke approached the door to the house cautiously. The Glock was tucked out of sight in his waistband. But his hand rested on the butt of the weapon. He saw where the door was smashed. He stepped off to the side to peer in. Three bodies on the floor. A two-foot-wide puddle of blood.

He slipped quickly inside. He leaned against the wall, gun in front of him in a classic Weaver two-handed grip. He went from room to room, checking it was clear before focusing on the trio on the floor. Klimke always carried heavy latex gloves. They served double duty by not leaving fingerprints and keeping him from contact with others' body fluids. He did a rapid triage. Linc had a well-executed field dressing on him. He had lost enough blood that he'd benefit from a transfusion, but he'd be okay. Amanda had the most damage, several broken bones, including a compound fracture on her thigh and a probable concussion. Ramirez had a dislocated elbow and a lot of bruising.

All three were groggy, slowly regaining consciousness. Amanda was holding her head and moaning. Linc stared blankly, drool trickling down from the corner of his mouth.

"There's a transponnnnnderrrrrrr," Ramirez said even before he was fully awake. Klimke had hired the team through Ramirez and knew the ex-soldier had a solid reputation.

"Where?"

"Her carrrrrrr. We have equipment innnn van to trrrrack itttt."

"Any electronics are pretty much gone." Klimke said, but he went back out to the van and confirmed his initial impression. He assessed Vinnie and found him safe to drive. He had him back the van up the driveway close to the front door.

He told Ivan, "We've got three casualties, two need to go to the hospital. The driver will take them. The leader is probably still operational. Or at least, he can answer questions."

Ivan nodded, got out of the van and stretched like he was indifferent to it all.

Klimke told Vinnie, "Take Linc and the woman to a hospital. Go to one on the outskirts of the city where there's less structure. They don't need fancy treatment. She'll need reconstructive surgery but that's after she's stabilized. Drill it into them they were in a car accident. If the police are called, just have them repeat the story. They have amnesia, not sure where the accident was. If the cops persist, get a lawyer. No one got hurt but them, there's no case. Our employer will take care of expenses." He didn't know whether Vinnie had been told Kroll's name, so he kept it vague.

Klimke glanced up and down the street. No indication any neighbor was aware what was going on. People minding their own business was a gift. Most were probably not yet home from work.

Back inside, Ivan prowled around the house. Ramirez was in the bathroom, throwing cold water on his face.

"Lord did this?" Klimke asked.

"It was like he knew we were coming in. He was too quick, man, something is fucked up there. But it was mainly that woman."

Klimke nodded. "I'm going to call in a sitrep. Then we'll see if the techs can locate the transponder."

Vinnie was helping Amanda into the van. Klimke had strapped up her broken bones but she was going in and out of consciousness.

Klimke went into the other room. Ivan hovered around, seemingly looking over Diana's belongings. Klimke was sure he was trying to eavesdrop on the call.

He connected with Lloyd Cutler. The ex-NSA expert's techies had been working since Kroll alerted them to the problems in Portland. They had vacuumed up every bit of data on Diana, adding to the considerable file on "Tom Lord." Using an SVR hack, they had accessed her Facebook, LinkedIn, and Instagram accounts. Through a backdoor option, they had reviewed her charge card record. The powerful computer in Cutler's office applied data analytics, drawing up probabilities and likelihoods of connections and actions.

Cutler had Klimke put Ramirez on the line. He asked a half dozen technical questions about the transponder. Ramirez had to check with Amanda, right before Vinnie carried her out to the van, for additional details. Cutler did a remote access hack on the laptop in the van, which still had some functionality. He was able to hijack the signal from the transponder.

"Bingo," Cutler said. "They're on I-84, nearing the airport."

"You think they're going to fly out?"

"Based on a quick review of the data, I'd say not. If he's in charge, probably a 30 percent chance. If she's in charge, maybe 10 percent."

"Where do you think they'll go?"

Through the phone, Klimke heard a keyboard's clicking. "Her comfort zone is in nature. They will get out of the city. Hide in the woods."

"You know where?"

"We're analyzing her Instagram pictures and most frequent locations logged by her phone's GPS now. There's a lot of pictures of Mt. Adams and Mt. St. Helens. A few of Mt. Hood area, some near Three-Fingered Jack, some by Mt. Jefferson. She likes the Cascade Mountains. But her current choices are limited by Lord's likely inability to keep up on the more challenging climbs." Cutler paused and typed some more. "She was operations director for the Mazamas. That's a top mountaineering club out there. She spends more money at REI than my ex-wife did at Saks. The psych profile indicates they may separate but odds are against it in the short run. I can see about getting a helicopter with infrared tracking in the sky in a couple hours. FLIR is right in Wilsonville and I've got a buddy there who's a VP."

"The fancy tech stuff is nice but I've got a better solution."

* * *

"Hear that clicking noise?" Tom asked when he had the AM radio tuned just right. "It means something is transmitting from the car."

"Should we put on our tin foil hats so we'll be safe?" she asked.

"If I was making all this up, who were those people back at your place? How did I know that woman at the door was not PGE and a danger?"

"The ones whose names you knew? Maybe fellow escapees from the asylum." She changed lanes smoothly. "Tell me more about this shit."

Lord did, starting with Kroll's recruiting him, through years in experiments. He described how his telepathy wasn't like other senses, often clouded, like trying to see through fog or pick out a sound when there was background noise. Lord told her about things she could check, like the 80,000 pages in CIA files that had been declassified, trying to help her understand the era.

"This guy's been pursuing you for decades and he hasn't caught you? Is that because of your superpowers?"

Tom didn't say anything. They rode in silence.

"I'm truly sorry I pulled you into my mess," he said. "He hasn't gotten me because it's ultimately just one man. He's brilliant, well connected and has money. But it's not like I'm really a fugitive from the government or anything. He's come close several times and I've escaped. Another part of it is he doesn't want his people to hurt me. Or more accurately, hurt my brain." Lord held up the damaged hand she had asked about. "This is how one of his goons tried to persuade me.

"Kroll saw his research as the next big step in human consciousness. He wanted to validate parapsychology. He wanted to see what kind of altered states could produce greater sensitivity. Whether it was orgasm, or LSD, physical abuse. There were times when he would combine all three."

"You mean..."

"Yeah, it got pretty weird for us."

"Us?"

"There was about maybe a dozen or so subjects at any given time. At one point he had us in a residential facility. An old orphanage in upstate New York. High security. To keep the curious out and keep us in. I got to know a few of the other subjects. There were penalties though if you got caught even telling one of the others your last name."

"Why'd you stay?"

"There were performance rewards. Severe punishments if you tried to leave. At first, it really wasn't bad. It got more and more twisted as he struggled to get results."

"Still, why didn't you leave?"

"I trusted him. It sounds stupid. Remember when I met him, I was still a teen. Maybe some Stockholm Syndrome stuff. Or the kind of psychological crippling that makes people stay in a cult. But when people talked about leaving, there were threats. Blackmail, financial ruin, hurting family members, ruining your future."

"Really? A big-name scientist, funded by tax dollars, doing such horrible stuff."

"Other programs have come out. Like MK Ultra, where they dosed people secretly with LSD. One scientist killed himself. President Ford personally apologized and they gave the family money. I got a settlement too. Was forced to sign a non-disclosure agreement. Even my telling you this is technically a violation of national security."

"Hard to believe," she said.

"That's not the worst thing Kroll's done." Tom sighed. "Let's take the next exit and go by the airport. There's a few hotels out there." Eager to change the subject, he told her his plan.

Chapter Eight

"They've stopped," Cutler told Klimke. "It's a hotel near the airport." Cutler had Klimke download the MobileSpy app, then patched through the results of the transponder so he could monitor the CR-V directly.

He had given Ramirez Vicodin and Ibuprofen. The rendition team leader was moving less stiffly. Ivan had gone outside and was making his own cell phone call. Cutler's team had done some quick research and Vinnie, Linc and Amanda were on their way to the emergency department at Tuality Healthcare in Forest Grove, at the edge of the metro area.

Diana's place looked like the crime scene it was, with a puddle of blood on the floor and toppled and broken furniture. Klimke made a few calls to his contacts and was put in touch with a firm that specialized in discrete clean-ups. If Diana were to return, there would be no evidence of her crazy story of being attacked.

Wearing a fresh pair of latex gloves, Klimke took Diana's underwear from the hamper, as well as rumpled sheets from the bed. He sealed them in a plastic bag.

With Ivan driving, Klimke riding shotgun and Ramirez in the back seat, they headed toward the airport.

* * *

Wynne and Lord had cruised by the airport hotels until they spotted one with a valet. The keyboard was next to the valet station sign and podium. Lord briefed Wynne on what she needed to do.

The valet on duty was a jug-eared 20-something with a perennially surprised expression. His eyes grew wider as the woman with a puffy blackening eye and a split lip hustled up to him and grabbed his arm.

"Have you seen my boyfriend? He's really big and he's really mad. He threw me out of the car."

"I'll call the cops, ma'am." He reached for his phone.

"No, don't. It'll be okay. He's going to check us into the hotel. Just don't make him mad."

"I really ought to call the cops. Maybe an ambulance. You look hurt."

Diana edged to the side and the valet naturally followed, keeping his attention on the panicked woman. He didn't notice as Tom casually sidled by and grabbed keys off the board.

Diana slipped away after a couple minutes, saying she was going to call her sister to pick her up. Tom pressed the key a few times and followed the beep to a 2016 silver Subaru Outback. Subarus, with their all-wheel drive, were as common as Starbucks in Portland. He drove it away and Diana followed in the Honda. They pulled off onto a side road and transferred the gear from the CR-V to the Outback. She parked the Honda in the long-term parking lot. They headed off in the Subaru with Lord driving.

Wynne said, "The valet was a decent kid. I hope he doesn't get in trouble."

"Assuming we get out of this, we'll make it up to him," Lord promised.

She nodded. "Assuming."

"Where are we going?"

"I'll navigate," she said. "Over the Bridge of the Gods to the Washington side of the river. Then to Wind River Road heading north."

* * *

"If we get stopped for speeding, it won't be good," Klimke said calmly as Ivan's lead foot kept them at 75, and up to 90 when traffic on the freeway thinned.

Ivan said nothing and didn't slow.

Klimke could think of no easy way to get rid of the Russian. As a military and paramilitary man for his whole adult life, Klimke hated it when there was no clear chain of command. He decided he needed the manpower if they had a large area to search. Klimke leaned back into the seat and slowly breathed in and out. It helped him to relax and sort out possibilities. He'd done it countless times before going into battle. Soldiers who didn't know him thought he was dozing. But his mind was doing rapid if A then B, then C calculations.

Cutler would be initiating electronic surveillance at Lisa Moreau's and a couple of Diana's friends, as well as her workplace. Cutler was also arranging through a reliable private investigation firm to have operatives watching those locales. If the couple went into the woods, he'd need Cutler to narrow down their probable destination.

Klimke decided to prepare for the forest option. He was a client in good standing of the Brokerage, an informal network of quasi-legal facilitators. It was the access that allowed him to impress Kroll, as much as his own knowledge, skills, and abilities. For boots on the ground and armament in the Northwest, he called Tang, a former Hong Kong businessman now based in Vancouver, British Columbia. He said he'd need a tracking dog and handler, plus a couple of men who wouldn't run to the authorities if laws were broken.

"I get back to you soon," Tang said.

They didn't discuss rates. There was a specific formula for the broker, based on urgency, skills required, and overall risk. Tang would negotiate rates with the strong-arm staff, and it would be resolved in a gentlemanly way. Violators of the rules faced ostracism from the system. And retribution if the break was severe and intentional.

The operators would be on hold until Klimke was certain they were needed. They would receive a retainer for their time, even if not activated. Klimke knew Kroll would not be pleased with the money being spent. But they were closer than they had been in years to fulfilling Kroll's dream.

Normally Klimke would have traveled with the equipment he needed. But this was supposed to be a simple pickup so he hadn't brought full gear. His next call was to the woman known as Ginger, based in Colorado, who ran a huge internet army-navy surplus market. Cabela's for operators. Her business had a covert and overt side. Every item she had ever supplied Klimke had been combat-ready.

He placed his order, paying the surcharge for overnight delivery. Night vision goggles, field packs and gear, MREs, camo clothing. He guessed sizes for Ivan and Ramirez. He didn't order any guns. He'd studied Ivan and Ramirez and hadn't seen any weapons but knew that a small concealable was hard to spot. He didn't trust Ivan. Ramirez, while a professional, might be holding a grudge over the decimation of his team. This was not a dead or alive hunt.

* * *

The Columbia River Gorge had basalt cliffs, dozens of waterfalls, views of the snow-capped Cascade Mountains, and hundreds of thousands of acres of forests, wildflower-covered meadows, rolling hills. Patches of leafy color were sprinkled in cliff sides covered with innumerable shades of green. But the couple's goal was escape, not sightseeing.

Diana sat battered and radiating waves of hostility. Lord was silent, wondering about suggesting they separate but unsure how she'd take it. His hope was to lower her risk. But would she see it as dumping her?

Lord let her know he didn't think going off into the woods was a great idea. He had three more fake IDs hidden in the vent at his apartment. If he could get back, he could slip away again. Not so easy for Diana. He could get her a basic fake ID package on the Dark Web. But how close were Kroll's team? And how did they find him this time?

"Make a left here," Diana snapped. Tom turned onto Wind River Road.

They drove through Carson, a town with a little more than a couple thousand people. The frequency of houses dwindled. Then farms and only a few of them. Then woods and a gentle rise in the road. Natural forests and tree farms, occasional areas of clear-cut where the earth was struggling to heal. The last sign of humanity they passed was an empty roadside stand with a hand-lettered sign saying, "We Buy Mushrooms."

"We're going to be taking a right a few miles up," Diana said. "Onto a forest service road into the Gifford Pinchot National Forest. Hopefully there's no trees downed."

"You've got a specific place in mind?"

"My father always told me in combat high ground was best. Or the opposite."

"The opposite?"

"Caves. The Vietnamese in Cu Chi. Saddam Hussein. Even Osama Bin Laden before he got the house in Pakistan. Hitler's bunker was just an artificial cave."

"Quite an illustrious group," Lord said, trying to joke and break the tension.

She didn't respond.

"There's dozens of lava tubes here, ranging from a few yards to miles long. Like Ape Caves by Mt. St. Helens. I have one in mind that isn't well known. It'll be cold if we need to hide. Probably mid-40s. I hope the coat you bought is warm."

"Should be. You brought your tent. Why a cave?"

"Did you notice the color of my tent?"

"Uh, red and gray."

"Gray with orange, visible from quite a distance. Good if you get lost or don't want a hunter to shoot at it. Not good if you're trying to evade people."

She had taken a paper map out of her backpack. She glanced at it as if to confirm something then folded it up again.

"You've been here before?"

"Several times. There's a bunch of defensible positions."

"You checked them out for that?"

She sighed as if explaining things to a child. "When I was a girl, my father would take me out in the woods and ask questions. Did I notice where to hide? Rocks to throw. Plants to eat, how to snare an animal, how to build a shelter or find water. How to make a man trap. How to survive."

"With all due respect, you call me paranoid? It sounds like your Dad might have had issues." Tom said. Regretting the words as soon as they escaped his lips, he began, "I mean…"

"He was a great man. A pioneer from the Green Berets. All the fighting skills of a top-notch soldier. Plus abilities in languages, medicine, construction, psy ops. A no bullshit army of one." She paused for a moment and looked like she wanted to hit Lord. "He taught me to take care of myself."

Her words hung in the air like a solid barrier.

"It sounds like he was a loving dad," Tom said, trying to make peace.

"My mom bought all three of us Barbies. I had him get me GI Joe clothing to dress mine. My sisters were more girly girls. I think that was when I became his favorite. Turn here."

He turned right off the paved Wind River Road onto a graveled forest service road. A sign pocked with bullet holes said Warren Gap Road.

"Forest service Road 65 is coming up soon," she said.

There was dense forest on both sides. The sun getting lower in the sky. The trees created a narrow corridor that grew darker with every passing minute. A tunnel of harsh shadows across the road.

Chapter Nine

The gravel road turned into hard-packed dirt. Progressively more and more rutted. Lord switched on the headlights and tried to avoid the deeper potholes. With limited success. When they bounced, Wynne flinched.

"You okay?" he asked.

She took Ibuprofen out of a small bag, gulped them with a swig of water from her insulated water bottle.

He said, "You really should take that with food. It can be hard on the stomach."

"That's the least of my concerns," she snapped.

They rode in silence for a couple minutes. She took a chocolate energy bar from her bag and offered him a bite. He took a nibble of the peace offering. She polished off the rest of the bar.

He slowed and the bumps were less jarring.

Seconds later, a raccoon ran across the road. He swerved. They bounced across a small ditch next to the road. He braked hard moments before they plowed into a big Douglas fir.

"Whew!" he said, clearly proud of his reflexes and not killing the raccoon.

"Do me a favor, the next time that happens, just drive straight. Unless it's a bear or an elk."

"Huh?"

"If it's a smaller animal, just hit the damn thing. It's about three miles further. Then we have a walk. Believe me the less walking we have to do, the better for both of us."

He slowly backed onto the road, not saying anything.

"Take the next left," she said.

The road sign was completely shot off, leaving just a wooden stake with a jagged top by the fork in the road. It was a creepy sight but also reassuring. Only someone who knew exactly where to go could ever find them.

* * *

Cutler had under retainer a team of hackers who operated out of a loft in a Greenpoint warehouse in Brooklyn. Two women and three men, the oldest was 24, the youngest 19. None had an IQ less than 140. They were skilled at social engineering and phishing as well as coming up with individualized malware, keystroke loggers and Trojan horses. Their multi-million-dollar revenue came primarily from opposition research and testing computer security for large corporations. When given a task they lived on Red Bulls, Doritos, coffee and doughnuts, working non-stop with a caffeine and carb driven ferocity. They idealized Cutler who had been a supervisor and mentor to two of them during his time at NSA.

The team studied Diana's social media and noted multiple cave images. But none of the postings had cave names or locations. Checking out spelunking websites, and with a few phone calls, they determined that keeping cave locations confidential was a big part of cave lovers' culture. Each of the five chose a target.

* * *

"This looks good," Wynne said, pointing to an opening between the trees. Lord pulled off the road and into an open area. There were a few stumps and downed trees. She took out her hatchet and went to work on branches that were a little thicker than her wrists. They dragged the cut wood until the car was partially covered. Someone driving by would only notice if they looked carefully. The couple smoothed out the dirt where the tires had left their mark in the mud.

They unloaded the gear and took out the two packs. He reached for the bigger one, but she took it out of his hands and swung it onto her back.

"How much hiking have you done?" she asked.

"Uh, a few overnight car camping trips. But a lot of day hikes."

"That's nice," she said with unmasked sarcasm.

She had an 80-liter red ripstop nylon pack. His matched hers but was half the size. It was designed for a woman. He fiddled with the straps but never got them really comfortable. They each carried their own sleeping bags—she carried the tent and her bow.

"Where are we going?" he asked as she began to move away from the car.

"Heading east, into Indian Heaven Wilderness. Midway between Mt. St. Helens and Mt. Adams." She walked ahead of him on the road, talking softly. "About 20,000 acres, fifteen lakes. Snow on the ground until late June. In the summer the mosquitoes make it more like hell than heaven. A month from now there'll be snow. This is the perfect time to visit."

She stepped off the road and walked on a narrow trail covered with fallen needles from the towering Douglas firs and the shorter Ponderosa pines. It was immediately much darker. She shone a small but powerful tactical flashlight ahead of them. No printed signs but clearly a trail.

"Watch out for roots and rocks," she said. She moved smoothly with the big pack. He twisted his shoulders, trying to adjust his without slowing down.

The trail climbed slowly. It took more effort.

Then they were at the top of a ridge in a clearing, looking out at three lakes and a dark sky bespeckled with stars. A half-moon reflected off the lakes.

"Beautiful!" he said. The awesome view was a stark contrast to the ugliness at Diana's house.

She shut the flashlight. "It is." She pointed up at the sky, identifying constellations. "Cassiopeia, that's the W. Orion and his belt over there. The Big Dipper. You could use them to point to Polaris, the North Star. I could navigate by the stars if I had to."

She gestured toward the lakes in front of us. "This is a volcanic plateau." She pointed back at Mt. St. Helens, silhouetted. There was a soft glow from the little crown of snow around the flattened top of the crater. "You remember in 1980 when she blew? Fifty-seven people died in the worst volcanic explosion in the continental U.S. There's about ten little volcanoes in Indian Heaven."

"Any active?" he asked, trying to not sound concerned.

She shook her head, turning the flashlight back on and pointing it ahead. "We've got another hour walking until the spot I have in mind."

They continued along the ridge line. A light drizzle softened the trail and they moved soundlessly.

* * *

The hacker Julie, who had the least piercings, had the greatest success. She found Wade, a caver whose personal website showed a strong narcissistic streak. She pretended to be working for a "famous Hollywood producer. I can't tell you his name, but if you've seen *ET* and *Saving Private Ryan* you can guess."

"I thought *Ready Player One* was great," he said confidently, and she knew she had him. She let him show off his knowledge of films for a couple of minutes then said, "We've got a project in development that will have multiple cave locations. Many are in the Northwest. But the photos of some were unclear as to location. If you can help us identify them, there's a stipend in it now and scouting work in the future."

"I'm your guy," he said. "Just send them to me and I'll get right on it."

True to his word, he reviewed the pictures and sent them back within an hour. With names and GPS locations.

* * *

"Is it much further?" Tom asked, breathing like an exhausted pack animal. Diana showed no signs of exertion.

"Only another mile. But it's several hundred feet of gain."

"How much have we done so far?"

"About 1,500 feet."

That didn't sound so bad, but then he realized, "That's like 150 stories."

When in a better mood, due to being in the place she loved so much, she'd throw out facts about the woods, the sky, nature in general. But then she'd think about why they were there, grow silent, and start going faster. With clipped, efficient movements that soon had Lord struggling to keep up.

They reached a clearing with a wooden marker that somehow she was able to spot in the dark. "Okay, we'll camp there."

* * *

Klimke mulled over heading out that night. If he had had night vision goggles, he might have attempted it. But following the plan of getting the gear and connecting with the trackers in the morning, while letting Ramirez have a night to recuperate, and having access to a helicopter reconnaissance, made the delay worthwhile.

* * *

Diana quickly set up the compact one-person tent. "It's going to be cramped," she said, like she wanted Tom to volunteer to sleep outside.

With the light drizzle, as soon as they stopped moving, he felt the chill. The temperature was in the mid-40s and dropping. She lay a pad down on the floor of the tent, which was three feet wide by the head, and tapered down a bit by the feet. About seven feet long. Two poles held up the durable polyester.

"If I felt better I'd see about hunting us something for dinner. Maybe raccoon," she said with a mirthless smile. "Raccoon is hard to prepare, can be really nasty if you don't prep the meat right."

"Really? You've eaten raccoon?"

"When my father and I would go out for a few days, we wouldn't bring any food. Berries, roots, snakes, squirrels. Anything was fair game."

"How about dogs and cats?"

"We never got that hungry."

After the tent was set up, they ate trail mix and energy bars. She put the food in a bag and hung it with a rope 50 yards away. He gave her a questioning look and she explained that bears would wreck a camp looking for food. "They're black bears, not really dangerous unless you get between a mother and cub. Or if they're hungry and smell human food."

"But our food is all sealed up. There's no meat."

"Bears will eat anything. They've got an incredible sense of smell. You want to trust your life to there not being a tiny rip in a bag? Or that some worker with food grease on their hand didn't touch the bag?"

They went separate ways to empty bladders and brush teeth. Tom was scanning the brush, looking for bears, and cougars, and wolves. He peed quickly and brushed his teeth back near the tent.

They settled in. She lay the bow and quiver down next to her, turned her back to him and they were pressed against each other, spooning. If they had been in a better mood, it could have been cozy. Instead, the tent felt cramped. They slept in the two layers of clothing they had been wearing, the pillow his folded up jacket. The sleeping bag was surprisingly warm. He passed out from exhaustion.

She got up early the next morning. By the time he was up it was well past dawn. The morning chill was worsened by dense fog, making the air moist as well as cold.

Diana was hunched over a small fire, roasting a rabbit on a stick. She had a small metal cup and had made instant coffee.

She shared her food.

"That's delicious," he said, and it was clear he meant it.

He got as close to the fire as he could as he slipped out of his clothes, changed his underwear and lower layer shirt, then got dressed. She had already changed. The fire was dwindling. She covered it with dirt, then a few rocks, leaving no trace.

They repacked their gear, she folded the tent up into a surprisingly small bag and they headed out.

* * *

The equipment arrived and Klimke inventoried it. Everything was in good shape. He gave Ivan and Ramirez their own gear and both men looked it over and approved.

"No guns?" Ivan asked.

"I don't want anyone accidentally killing the golden goose."

Ivan frowned.

Klimke turned to Ramirez. "You understand no weapon?"

Ramirez had grabbed a Taser and held it up. "Only this. If needed."

"Check."

They loaded the Ford Explorer and drove across the Columbia River, taking State Route 14 to the rest area where they had arranged to meet the trackers.

The trackers were standing next to a dark green, mud-spattered pickup that looked at least 20 years old. In the back were two golden brown bloodhounds, sniffing the air furiously and pacing around the metal bed of the 4x4. The men were clearly brothers, bearded, burly and clad in matching Carhartt's and Seahawks ball caps. The older brother, slightly more neatly trimmed, shook hands and introduced himself as Drew. He said his brother was Amos. Amos kept his eye on the dogs, barely glancing at Klimke and his crew.

"We gonna get going soon?" Amos asked.

"Real soon," Drew said. He was about 30, Klimke guessed, with Amos maybe three years younger. "We're looking for a man and a woman. They have something my employer wants. The man should be taken without any damage. The woman is expendable. She's also the far more dangerous one."

Ramirez gave an unconscious nod.

"Where they at?" Drew asked.

"Indian Heaven Wilderness."

"I been there," Amos said. "The girl pretty?"

"Why?" Klimke asked.

"Just wondering," Amos said.

Drew gave a little jerk of his head, indicating he wanted to talk to Klimke off to the side.

They drifted a couple of feet away. Amos was stroking the dogs, whispering in their big, floppy ears, getting them excited for the hunt. Though the animals clearly knew what was coming and were more than eager to go. Ivan and Ramirez stood silently, adjusting their packs and gear.

"My brother gets all his ideas off of the porn he watches."

"He better not let his thinking with his dick screw up this mission."

"Don't worry. He's the best tracker there is."

"Just make sure he does his job."

"We're on it."

Chapter Ten

Diana Wynne stopped at the top of the eroded 2000-foot volcanic crater. More and more of the multi-hued green landscape was becoming visible as the morning fog burned off. The temperature had climbed from low 40s to low 50s. With the exertion of going up and down the weathered volcanic cones, she opened her jacket.

Tom Lord puffed up the hill behind her. She knew she was moving at an aggressive, exhausting pace. There was no need to push so hard. She was convinced they were safe in the wilderness, part of her reason for coming here. Surrounded by the comfort that came only with nature, she was in a place she had hiked before.

When he'd make the crack about her father having issues, she had nearly lashed out. Just one smack to that stupid, grinning face of his. He wasn't grinning much now.

The hike reminded her of times with her father, him trotting along easily while she struggled to keep up. Well into his 50s, he still had the stamina to set a grueling pace. At the end of a run, or a couple days in the woods, he'd give her a hug and say, "Pretty good. For a girl." She would punch his rock-hard deltoids as hard as she could. He'd act like it had grievously injured him. She was convinced that nothing short of an armor-piercing round could've hurt his arms. There wasn't a day went by that she didn't miss him and the strength and feeling of safety he brought. Now she was with this doofus who could make a coin come out of his ear and had nearly gotten her killed.

What the hell was Lord's story? He had been a little wacky right from the beginning. More cute than crazy or dangerous. Then there had been the home invasion. Her home! He'd known the attackers' names, then had some cock and bull story about reading their minds. He'd told her that ESP nonsense before. She'd humored him. She didn't mind quirky. Many of her friends consulted astrologers before making decisions. One of her good friends was into Tarot and Ouija boards. Another dismissed western science and only treated her ailments with Chinese herbs and acupuncture. The city's unofficial slogan was "Keep Portland Weird." She didn't mind unconventional thinking and had hoped his odd beliefs would settle down as they got to know each other.

Some of what he knew seemed like telepathy. But he was an admitted stage magic buff. She'd seen David Blaine on TV "read minds" and do even more spectacular tricks. Know the card someone was thinking of and have it appear in their back pocket. Touch one person and have another feel it. Lord wasn't even half as convincing as Blaine.

On a flatter stretch, where he'd been able to catch his breath, he'd tried to make the case for ESP. She'd talked about the five senses and he'd interrupted.

"Actually there's more than five. That's just a cliché. Not counting ESP. There's proprioception, which is knowing where your body and its parts are. Like if a limb is lifted or not. There's sense of balance, sense of time, sense of distance and location. There's debate about some of them, like sense of hunger."

"Whatever. It's not like breaking the laws of physics around time and space," she'd responded.

"True. They're called non-local phenomena. You think we understand everything there is to know about physics right now? I'm sure everyone pre-Newton thought they did too. And pre-Einstein.

Maybe telepathy is just a type of communication we don't quite understand."

"It's too weird."

"I agree. So is a chemical that we don't really know how it works interacting with other chemicals to produce an electrical charge which travels to a membrane that vibrates which then disturbs molecules in a gas. Then reverse the whole process."

"What's that got to do with anything?"

"That's what we're doing now. A thought becoming speech and traveling to another person."

She glared at him. "Okay, so what am I thinking now?"

"How much you wish you'd never met me."

She grunted. "You don't have to be psychic to figure that out."

"I understand that completely. I wish I'd never put you in jeopardy."

"Okay, now I'm thinking of a number," she snapped.

"I can't do that. For some reason numbers just don't come through clearly. Emotions do. Shapes. Names sometimes, things like that."

"Okay, I'm thinking of a name."

Lord paused. "Lisa. Too easy."

She frowned.

He waited a moment. "Steve."

"No."

"Stefanie."

She was quiet and he knew he was right.

They did it three more times. He missed two of them.

"So you're sort of batting 50 percent," she said.

"In parapsychology studies experimenters were blown away when someone got 33 percent," Lord responded. "If someone is getting 100 percent, it's fake."

"Why?"

"No one really knows. I heard it compared to sports. Michael Jordan could sink a basket more than any other human. It's natural ability plus years and years of practice. But he doesn't sink every basket."

"He had five pros on the other team trying to keep him from sinking baskets."

"Even in practice, just shooting, no one sinks every basket."

"But a pro sinks better than 50 percent."

"It's a metaphor. Trying to explain something we don't really understand."

They had argued and then agreed that he wasn't going to convince her that it wasn't luck or a stage magic trick. She knew her skepticism was driven by resentment over his role in the attack.

She kept the pace relentless to minimize conversation.

Lord finally reached her and stood next to her, looking out.

"Nice view, huuuh," he said, breathing deeply. "What's the name, huuh, of the lake?"

"Can you read my mind and guess it?" she asked.

"Huuuh, Sally?"

"It's Lake Sahalee. But you could've seen that on a map. Coming up will be Lake Toke Tie, then Junction Lake."

"A lot of, huuuh, lakes, huuh."

"Yup. At least we passed where I wanted us to be last night."

"When?"

"You notice that pile of rock about a mile back?"

"I think so."

"There's a small cave under it. Would've been nice to have made it there yesterday."

"I guess," Lord said, continuing to heave.

"You ready to push on?"

"Couple minutes would be, huuuh, good."

"You don't want to pause too long or you'll stiffen up. We'll start moving again in five minutes."

"Huuuh. Okay."

* * *

"This is about as close as we can drive," Klimke told the men as they stood in front of the vehicles. Amos opened the tailgate of the dark green pickup and the dogs jumped down. They sniffed and made happy yipping noises. The game was about to begin. Amos got down and ruffled their wrinkly necks, stroked their muscular backs.

Then Drew went back to his truck and came out holding twin Remington .30-06s. The gunstocks were scuffed but the metal gleamed. Well used and well-tended weapons.

"No guns," Klimke said.

"That's bullshit," Drew said.

"There's five of us and two of them. I don't know you and your brother well enough to have you with guns."

"That's bullshit," Amos echoed.

Klimke just gave him a look and he went back to stroking the dogs.

"The people we after, they got guns?" Drew asked.

"No."

"You positive?"

"Positive."

Reluctantly he put the rifles back in the pickup, hiding them under a blanket and locking the door.

"What do you got to give the dogs scent?" Amos asked, clicking GPS collars onto the dogs and checking they were showing up on his cell phone.

"We got a ways to go," Klimke said.

"They'll hold it in their minds, make 'em want it more." He handed the bed sheet to Amos who brushed it against the dogs' faces. They inhaled deeply. Amos did the same with Wynne's underwear, then grinned like a naughty kid as he tucked the pink garment into his pocket.

"You know the part of the brain for smells is as big as a stamp in people. But in bloodhounds it's the size of a handkerchief," Amos said like a proud dad.

One of the dogs threw his head back and gave a full bugle. The other quickly matched him.

Klimke didn't like dogs. The idea of a slobbering creature you had to clean up after was as appealing as using a neglected latrine. But he had great respect for their superhuman abilities. He'd worked with SEALS parachuting with Belgian Malinois and police with German Shepherds tracking poachers in South Africa.

"We're ready," Amos said, letting the dogs loose. They bounded down the trail, ran about 30 yards, then waited for the humans to catch up.

The five men took off, their pace somewhere between a jog and a run. Drew and Amos had beer bellies but were more fit than they appeared. Klimke and Ivan followed. Ramirez brought up the rear. He was in good shape but still sore from his battle with Diana.

The dogs paused on the trail, stomping and pawing. They bugled in harmony and Amos grinned. "They got the scent." He bent to the ground and with his finger traced a shoe print. "'Bout a size 11. New."

"You really can tell that?"

Amos nodded, clearly proud. "See how crisp this edge is. Ain't been worn much, maybe never on concrete." He traced his finger along a smaller shoe print. "Maybe a size six. Been well worn. I betcha it goes with that thong."

The dogs made restless noises in the background.

"Anything else?"

"The girl is leading. They're going fast." He pointed to the long strides.

Klimke nodded. "Very good."

Amos and Drew both grinned.

* * *

It was the warmest part of the day. The sun was out and a light breeze blew. The light glittered off the surface of the lake

Diana stopped and glanced up at the sky.

"You hear that?" she asked.

Tom tried to control his heavy breathing. "Not really. What do-"

"Shhh."

He was quiet and listened again. A very faint unnatural sound. Like an insect buzz at first, then a little louder and it was clear what it was. A helicopter.

"We're between two of the Cascades Mountains. Not a good flight path. In all my hikes, there's only been one Forest Service plane flyover. That's once in about 15 times out here."

"Should we..."

"There's a tiny cave about a quarter mile ahead. Let's go."

The sound got louder as they ran down the trail. It was coming from the south, gaining on them. He stumbled but kept running. Adrenalin kicked over. The trail was mercifully downhill.

His foot caught on a root and he fell face forward. Fortunately, there was a layer of Douglas fir and pine needles. He stood quickly.

Then they were at a pile of rocks and Diana scurried into an opening the size of a stove. Tom quickly followed.

The copter passed overhead.

"Do you think they saw us?" he asked.

"Doubtful. We were under the trees."

They were just a few feet inside. Light spilled in. Diana played her flashlight across the walls. The chamber was about 20 feet deep, the floor strewn with rock fragments ranging from football-sized to one that could've blocked the doorway. If they could have moved it.

He leaned against a wall and caught his breath.

"We'll know soon if they saw us," she said.

"How?"

The noise of the helicopter had faded. There was a slight whooshing sound in the cave, air going from the opening they'd come in to some vent further back.

The helicopter noise began to grow again, like someone turning up the volume on a radio. They were doubling back.

"That's how," she said.

She had unslung her bow to enter the tiny cave. She spun the two ends and locked the risers into place. The bow was a little less than four feet, an inch and a half wide at its thickest parts. She attached a bow string by putting another string on the floor, attaching it to the ends of the bow, then stepping on it to pull the ends back. She slipped on a black leather three finger archer's glove. She took an arrow out of the quiver and slid the nock into the string. The whole sequence had taken barely a minute.

"You're going to use that against a helicopter?"

She answered with a glare. Holding the weapon loosely, she leaned against a large rock and faced the entrance.

"There's no real place for it to land around here. They could rappel down I suppose. We'll give it 10 minutes after we hear them leave. Then we've got to move."

The noise of the helicopter began to fade. "Maybe we should go now?" he asked.

"The entrance here is a natural chokepoint. Only one person can make it through at a time." She toyed with her bow. "They could deploy tear gas and force us out. That sounded like a small helo, probably more for scouting than transporting personnel." She had slipped into military speak she had learned from her father. "We wait. Then I'll creep out and reconnoiter. If it's safe, we'll keep going."

"Do you want me to..."

"Just be quiet. I'll let you know what I need you to do."

Chapter Eleven

Amos paused periodically to bend over, stare at the ground, and rub his fingers through the dirt. He said nothing but looked more pleased with each mile covered. He would snap his head side to side and sniff the air.

Klimke had written down the coordinates provided by the helicopter pilot.

"They just up and disappeared," the pilot had said over the radio. "But they showed up clear on the IR, heading in a northeasterly direction." The coordinates were consistent with the trail on the map. Getting confirmation from a forward spotter with infrared capability was reassuring. Controlling the air was always good.

"We believe she knows about caves in the area," Klimke said.

"Roger that. You need me to hang around? I can scope out the terrain for you."

"What's the capacity on your chopper?"

"It's a Safari two-seater, bubble front. About a 700-pound payload."

"You got anything bigger at home?"

"Got a surplussed Coast Guard Eurocopter HH-65 Dolphin. You know it?"

"Good short range. Quick. Yours have tracking electronics?"

"Negative. I use it to transport construction crews and gear. No need. The little gal I'm in is my spotter."

"There an LZ where you're at?"

After a moment's pause, the pilot said, "Affirmative. What do you have in mind?"

"We'll keep pushing on but they've got a big head start. Swap out your birds. Give us coordinates where you're at now and we'll meet you there about when?"

"Let's see, 110 miles an hour, dah, dah, dah, land this, takeoff that, 135 miles an hour coming back. Let's say between two and three hours."

"Check. Pick up rations and water for four men. Crates to keep the dogs contained. Some dog food too."

"Copy that." The pilot had the lazy drawl that Klimke associated with the best airmen. Klimke had been choppered out of a hot LZ more than once. He had a great respect for the unknown, unseen man he listened to. "Re-supplying is going to add about a half hour to my estimate."

"We'll need transport back. Four men, two dogs, plus the two lost campers we're tracking." Klimke doubted the pilot believed they were on a search and rescue mission, but the pilot had flown enough covert missions he probably had heard more flimsy stories. As long as they didn't get on board with recently shot bodies or a load of white crystalline powder he wouldn't care.

"Roger that. Back to base. All estimates are subject to weather. Over and out."

Klimke briefed his men.

"Them being in a cave is a good thing," Drew said. "Focuses the smell for the dogs."

"They don't need no help," Amos snapped.

"Of course not," Drew said.

"Be nice if we had flamethrower," Ivan said. He made as if he was maneuvering a flamethrower with his hands, while making a burning noise with his mouth.

"You know what I said about keeping the target in one piece?" Klimke said in a low, menacing voice.

Ivan forced a smile that suggested the opposite of mirth.

"I've got flash bangs and tear gas," Klimke said. "We take them with minimal damage."

The dogs were restless, and the men took off at a brisk clip. Klimke calculated that they should catch up with the couple by nightfall.

He wished he had had more time to plan the operation. He was surprised how far the couple had run. Lord was not known to be a fitness fanatic and was nearing 50. Even with an Amazonian girlfriend it was a lot to expect.

Klimke wished he had a solid team, not a wounded warrior, a questionable Russian and the unknown hound brothers. If the girl had to be killed, he might have to silence the brothers as well. But a double hunting accident wasn't plausible. Maybe dog lover accidentally shoots his brother, then commits suicide.

He had been prepared for a straightforward pickup and walked into a classic SNAFU. But like soldiers since the first troop that threw rocks, he'd make it work.

* * *

Diana crawled out of the cave, leaving her pack but taking her bow.

"Appears clear." she said and gathered up her gear. "I tried calling a friend who can help. No coverage."

"Your friend is out here?"

She shook her head, crawling out of the cave lugging the pack, then swinging it onto her back. Tom did the same.

"Not that far. East of Mt. Adams is the Yakama Reservation. I'll explain once we get moving. I also checked the map. There's some smaller trails we can follow."

She started off at her usual brutal pace. He was recharged enough from the break to be able to keep up.

* * *

Klimke saw the dogs circle and bugle up ahead. By the time they got to them, Amos was down on hands and knees, running fingers through the dirt. His fingers came up black.

"They built a fire here. This ash is less than 24 hours old. Want me to find where they camped out?"

"Not worth the time," Klimke said. "Keep moving."

* * *

"One of the tribal elder's daughters ran away to Portland," Diana said. The trail had gotten wider, looked a little more like something humans had etched out of the forest than the deer trails they had been on. "She got in with a bad crowd. This creep beat her, kept her drugged up, made her have sex with his friends so he could get meth. She managed to get away and press charges."

The ugly story seemed especially discordant in the beautiful natural setting.

"The DV shelter felt it was too high risk to keep her. They put her up in one of their safe houses with me as her roommate. The creep showed up. I subdued him. The prosecution was successful. I drove the girl home. The elder and the whole family were grateful." She paused and looked at me, with less fury than minutes ago, and smiled, "They had a little ceremony in my honor."

"That's awesome."

"The elder was amused that the creep wound up with the exact same body parts injured as the girl. The elder had quite the dry sense of humor. He said, 'The Creator works in mysterious ways.' Then he gave me a Native American name."

"Wow! Quite an honor."

Diana paused. They were crossing a small creek they had been paralleling. She took out the filter straw and took a few long sips. Then passed it to Tom.

As he was drinking, she continued, "For the two days I stayed there, everyone called me by the name. I was honored. Then I found out what it meant." She paused, he drank, and handed her back the straw.

"You want to use your ESP powers and tell me what it was?"

"I get that you don't believe me, want to test me. Now isn't the time or place. Let's just keep moving."

"Of course," she said cynically. "You want to know my nickname?"

"Sure."

"Crazy White Girl."

* * *

Klimke was impressed at how well the hound brothers and Ramirez were holding up. Amos was able to tell from the crispness of the tracks that they were gaining on the couple. The stride, particularly for the man, was lessening. "But if they keep it up at this pace, it's gonna be at least two days before we get to them."

"Then let's get moving," Klimke ordered, and they took off.

* * *

"I can't do this anymore," Lord said, in between gasps of air. He massaged his quadriceps, fighting off a cramp. The trail intersected with an unpaved forest service road. There were no signs, but it was clearly truck-wide. Not well traveled but not overgrown.

"We can take a five-minute break," she said. She took out the cell phone and tried again but got no signal.

"I've been thinking. I can follow this road. Just keep walking. You go off another way."

"You really think you can survive out here without me?"

"Not for very long," he admitted. "I'm sure whoever sent that helicopter will catch up. Maybe they'll even send the helicopter back."

"Then what?"

"They'll take me wherever they plan to take me. They won't kill me."

"I'm not going to leave you here. We can slow down a bit."

"I prefer that you go..."

"You know what you said when you stepped in to help my sister?"

"This is different. You've done more than anyone should."

"My father taught me all kinds of skills. But more important was the morality. You don't leave a buddy behind."

"I'm still your buddy?"

"I like you more than the assholes following us."

"I guess that's the best I can expect."

She checked the phone again. Still no reception. "It would make them happy to capture you. The last thing I want is to make them happy."

They hustled down the road, heading east, the ups and downs continuing.

The air felt colder, a slight breeze. Sweat chilled against their bodies. Nearly every time they crossed the creek, they'd take a few sips of water. "By the time you're thirsty, your body is dehydrated," she'd told him the first time.

"Your suggestion back there to give yourself up, how much of that was just wanting to quit and how much was a sacrifice to protect me?" she asked after another half hour of trudging.

He thought for a moment. "Probably about 50-50."

"Fair enough," she said. "I appreciate you not being a pure martyr."

The sun was beginning to go down behind them, creating hard parallel line shadows on the trees. They marched on in silence.

* * *

Klimke watched the Eurocopter Dolphin set down in the clearing, kicking up brush and loud enough that the men covered their ears. The copter was painted a light blue that blended into the sky. No longer the Coast Guard's classic white with broad red stripe. The pilot set her down smoothly and his co-pilot offloaded the supplies.

"Sit here, wait for our return," Klimke commanded.

The lanky pilot, eyes concealed behind green aviator sunglasses, nodded. "The meter will be running."

"Understood," Klimke responded.

"I brought gear for night flight, was scouting the route coming in. Not too many power lines, shouldn't be hard."

"I expect to be back soon."

* * *

The road continued to climb.

"We're going to go between Crofton Ridge and Snipes Mountain," Wynne said, checking her compass but not needing to look at the map. "The beginning of the foothills for Mt. Adams."

"Are we going to climb the mountain?"

"We don't have the gear," she said. "Ice axes, crampons, warmer clothes. I only have about 50 feet of rope. Maybe next time."

Her friendly teasing was the first time she had joked in a long time. She stopped and waved her hand for them to stand still. She closed her eyes, intently listening to something.

"All I hear is the wind in the-"

She held her finger to her lips in a "shhhhh" gesture.

Then he heard it too. The thump-thump-thump of a helicopter.

"Shit," she said. "There's no place for them to land in the last couple miles. But we better get off the road onto a trail." She checked the compass and map again. "About a quarter mile. Book it."

They had only gone a few hundred yards when she stopped again and listened. The helicopter noise had stopped. "They landed. Probably bringing in hunters."

When Tom heard the howl, he felt a primordial chill run down his spine. "Is that a wolf?"

"I wish." She spoke in a flat, quiet voice. Her shoulders sagged, her head lowered. "It's a tracking dog. A hound. We're screwed."

Chapter Twelve

Paris, France
2015

A few weeks after the debacle in Hawaii, Dr. Edward Kroll was glad to be at the conference in France. An excellent distraction. Great minds in cognitive psychology--experts on perception, memory, neurobiology, artificial intelligence, decision-making, learning, and motivation.

Kroll was on a panel to discuss motivation. At one point in his career, he would have been the keynote speaker. Now he had to accept sharing the dais with four other researchers—two MDS, two PhDs and a young twit who only had a master's degree. In the old days.

Kroll had been caught up in the 2014 scandals involving psychologists advising the CIA on the best way to do enhanced interrogation. The politicians and press were jackals tearing at prey. There was the forced testimony before a congressional committee. Fortunately, much of his work was classified and the results were never made public. But having political hacks question his methodology was an outrage. Worse still, grants had dried up. A promised chairmanship at Columbia University was imminent, then suddenly filled by a rival. A speaking engagement at UPenn was canceled when snotty, spoiled brats threatened to demonstrate if he spoke. Small consolation that scientific geniuses like Galileo were not honored in their time.

He had been through career ups and downs before. The aftermath of the Psychological Research Institute had been particularly ugly. PRI was named in Senator Proxmire's Golden Fleece award for wasting taxpayer dollars. Initially,

Kroll was fooled by reporters who seemed sympathetic. But when their articles came out, they made him sound like a crackpot. He had seen what the press did to astronaut Edgar Mitchell, who had tried doing an ESP experiment from space and received only ridicule when it was revealed.

The stupidity of the masses and their sensationalistic appeasers. A few interviewers had allowed his opinions to be heard.

"Even great minds in the past didn't know basics that today we take for granted," he'd said in an interview that ran on PBS. "Brilliant minds in Ancient Greece and Rome believed in the four humors. Even Hippocrates who is honored to this day. And the earth as the center of the universe was believed by the wise men so much that Galileo was convicted of heresy in 1633. It took only 300 years for the Catholic Church to acknowledge Galileo was correct. Atomic theory, quantum mechanics, so many paradigm shifts. In all sciences. When I was a young man, they only talked about the lymph system. The thymus and pineal gland were as vestigial as the appendix. Now medical researchers acknowledge the immune system as essential to our most challenging illnesses.

"My colleague David Eagleman uses the image of science as putting boards on a pier that stretches out into the ocean. Every year we add more boards. But the ocean is vast and limitless. As is the ignorance of those who do not want to search for answers but be content with what we know now.

He paused. The interviewer tried to ask a question but Kroll ignored her. "In my research I was going to prove non-local phenomena and advance human consciousness. To move beyond the primary five senses that is where humanity stalled in exploring the universe. Petty minds demanded instantaneous success. We were close to significant breakthroughs that would have advanced science. Instead, we took a giant step backward."

No point in stewing over past wrongs. He glanced at his notes. He would talk over his allotted five minutes. Let them cut into the foolish questions and answers that inevitably followed. Before his stroke, he wouldn't have needed notes. He could speak extemporaneously at length on any of the aspects of psychology he had studied. His CV was 16 pages, with hundreds of articles published in the most prestigious journals. He'd spoken at dozens of national and international conferences and been faculty at three different Ivy League universities.

It was an irony that his brain was the first organ to show signs of the betrayal of age. Why not his hip or even his heart? Some would have joked, behind his back, that the latter organ never got much of a workout.

In the second row there was a young man who reminded him of Jeremy Sherman. Not that he had a sure vision of what Sherman looked like. He'd had Klimke describe him in detail. Sherman, aka, Ian Martin, Dave Peterson, Steve Harris, Scott Johnson, Alan Wilson, Joseph Thaler, Thomas Lord. He'd often have the experience of seeing someone who looked like what he imagined Sherman did. He knew the phenomena was common for someone grieving a missing loved one.

He had loved young Sherman. Not in an unhealthy way, more the way a thoroughbred owner would love their prize-winning horse. But Sherman had betrayed him. He'd nurtured Sherman's gifts, albeit sternly, but that was necessary. Spare the rod, spoil the child.

Kroll knew that his actions with Sherman were in part driven by emotions, and he hated it. Emotions were messy, dirty things that diminished the accomplishments the prefrontal cortex could achieve. He was aware of the work of Paul Ekman on the universality of emotions and Joseph LeDoux and Antonio Damasio on how humans needed emotions for motivation and decision. But he had vowed that he would not be led around by them the way most people were.

But every time he thought of Jeremy Sherman, he could feel his pulse rise.

Sherman's elopement had been the beginning of the end of the program. Another one of the program's stars was so psychologically unstable, he had to have a watcher 24/7 after his second serious suicide attempt. A third very gifted subject sexually assaulted another subject. Managing a milieu loaded with often troubled teens and young adults was as challenging a task as the psychologist had ever faced.

But Sherman had proven exceedingly spoiled, running off and refusing to respond to repeated overtures. Despite considerable expense.

Then there had been the debacle in Hawaii. Kroll had been working through a private investigator, an ex-Navy SEAL in Oahu. The man had come with good references, excellent work finding and rescuing the brainwashed from the clutches of cults. The man had said his team "went a bit too far" in the attempt to corral Sherman. They had let him slip away.

Cutler had hacked Sherman's former girlfriend Leilani's account and he got a few details of what "too far" constituted. Idiots! Such an unfortunate misunderstanding.

He forced himself to refocus his thoughts, glancing around the audience. The small conference room was about two-thirds full. Maybe 35 people. A waste of his time. But the moderator was already at the dais, shuffling papers.

His gaze shifted back to the front row. There was a portly man, balding, bespectacled, staring at him. Gray hair with thick, dark eyebrows. Studying him the way Kroll studied his lab subjects. The man had a neatly trimmed gray beard, dark black eyes, and a suit that gracefully draped his ample frame.

Their eyes met and the man smiled as if he was an old friend.

Kroll prided himself on his memory for faces and was confident he had never seen him before.

The first speaker was presenting, a very attractive well-coifed woman. She had the rapt attention of the largely male audience as she spoke confidently and advanced through her PowerPoint presentation.

The man with the thick eyebrows didn't look at the screen or the presenter. He smiled amiably and stared at Kroll.

The professor had dealt with auditoriums full of bored college freshman and colloquiums packed with jealous rivals. Even aggressive congressional inquisitors. But the man's gaze was so intent Kroll had to work hard to stay focused.

The talk went reasonably well, with him only going about five minutes over his allotted time. The Q and A that followed was no more inane than most.

He came down off the podium and began heading toward the exit. A throng of gawky admirers surrounded the attractive doctor, asking her questions, offering her their business cards, asking for her contact email.

"Dr. Kroll?" The man with the bushy eyebrows had been waiting near the exit door. He kept his intense eyes focused on Kroll and extended his hand. "I'm Frederick Smythe." His voice was British but there was a vague hint of some other accent underneath. "I'm a big fan of your work."

"I'm not used to having fans," Kroll said crisply. "Are you affiliated with any institution?"

"A few. Most closely with Cambridge."

"Really? Do you know Professor Donald Harrington? In the psychology department,"

"I don't believe I do."

The name had been made up but Smythe hadn't taken the bait.

"Perhaps fan is too casual a term," Smythe continued. "Let's just say I'm very familiar and respectful of your work. Like the article you had six years ago in the Journal of Behavioral Analysis and Research on enhancing motivation in opioid addicts. Or the one in the Journal of Cognitive Psychology Research in 2018 on data processing in the default mode network via interaction with the amygdala."

"I noticed I had your full attention during the talk," Kroll said.

"Yes. Frankly, I'm here to chat with you about some possibilities. The chaps I work with are quite intrigued by some of your older work."

"If it is anything I did while under contract to the government, much of it is classified." Kroll had decided that the accent underneath the British was probably Russian. He had been approached by representatives of Russian, Chinese and Saudi governments in the past. He was wary of any hints of collusion or violation of nondisclosure agreements he had signed. Particularly after being nipped at by the politicians and press.

"Would you be willing to be my guest at a party this evening? We could continue the discussion later. I'm sure you would like to unwind after your talk today."

"Which of my older studies are we talking about?"

"You were a pioneer in parapsychology. Such a pity that your government and the universities were so short-sighted and permitted your efforts to wither on the vine." Smythe handed him a pale blue calling card on fine paper stock. An elegant script read Frederick Smythe, above a London phone number. Handwritten on it was an address in 3rd *Arrondisement.*

"I'll think about it," Kroll said.

He went back to his hotel room and held the card up, his hand hovering over the small garbage can. He hesitated. His flight back to the United States was tomorrow evening. He had planned a quiet dinner alone, catching up on journals he had brought. He doubted the articles would have anything of interest. There seldom was.

He read through one, confirming his belief, then showered and dressed in a different suit than he had worn to the conference. This was dark blue, custom Brooks Brothers he had purchased 20 years ago at Harrod's. People did judge a book by its cover. But fashion was conspicuous consumption for the masses. He had no interest in fleeting approval for the width of his tie or lapel.

He didn't want to dress like most of his academic colleagues who were often as sloppy in their attire as they were in their thinking. He believed in buying quality goods and making them last. Unfortunately, some were showing slight signs of wear. He had been forced to become more economical. The slowing of his career, some bad investments, and the pursuit of Jeremy/Tom had led him to become overextended. On paper, he appeared well off. In truth, he was facing giving up on capturing the most gifted telepathic subject he had ever seen.

He tucked two condoms and a Cialis into his pocket. Most of his adult sex life had taken place at conferences. Being away from home, in a hotel room, liquor poured freely. He had no desire for a serious relationship. But a night of experimentation, usually with a much younger woman, provided the release he needed.

The house was in the Marais neighborhood, which dated back to before the French Revolution, when nobility built their homes there. Narrow cobblestone streets and grand buildings. A few museums and posh hotels. He admired the classic lines of the chateau before ringing the doorbell. A surprisingly beefy butler answered, and said, "Dr. Kroll, welcome. May I take your coat?" His English was unaccented.

Kroll stepped into the entry hall, three stories high, a grand brass-railed staircase on one side, a large arched doorway into the main room behind it. Two stories high, with finely detailed gold filigreed molding around the ceiling. Large classic oil paintings on the walls. The enormous windows partially covered by equally grand flowing drapes. The feel was of a restored 18th century ballroom. Louis XVI and Marie Antoinette would have felt at home. But no one was wearing a white wig or a corseted dress. An upper-class crowd, judging by the amount of jewelry bouncing on pale or tanned decolletage. The men were largely in dark suits, with occasional flashes of color from more extravagant ties. About three dozen people, half filling the large room. Not counting serving staff who bustled about efficiently carrying trays with white or red wines and *hors d'oeuvres*.

Smythe bustled through the crowd with a brunette in her 30s on his arm. "This is Genevieve. I've been telling her about your work. She works with computers and has a fascination with artificial intelligence."

The woman was strikingly attractive in an understated way. Lustrous black hair, high cheekbones, minimal makeup. A string of elegant pearls resting above a fine bosom. A form-fitting black designer dress. Four-inch heels that made her nearly Kroll's height.

A waiter came and offered wine. Kroll took a glass of red, raised it in a toast to Smythe and Genevieve. He took a sip. A very fine Merlot. He nodded appreciatively.

"So, Genevieve, what do you do with computers?"

"In English, it is called neural networking." Her English, with a very light French accent, was as charming as the rest of her manner. "I have done much work with the facial recognition. As you are aware, it is not just a matter of programming since there are so many variables." She talked for a couple minutes about her research. Clearly not a tart hired to just stroke his ego, and whatever else, Kroll mused.

"But I am saying too much," she said, slipping from Smythe to gently hold Kroll's arm. "You must tell me about your work. Your studies sound fascinating."

The professor described some of his work to her. She joined him when he had a second glass of wine. When dinner was announced, they moved into a large dining room with a table set for 20. Places were set with fine silverware, candles burned in matching silver holders. The surface was covered by a white tablecloth, only the ornately carved wood legs of the table were visible. The chairs looked like they could be roped off as antiques and fit in a museum. About half the guests had disappeared, apparently invited only for the social hour.

The professor and Genevieve sat side by side at the table, her leg occasionally brushing against his, her hand patting his arm to make a point. There was another attractive woman to Kroll's left. They made brief conversation. She was "the friend" of an older gentleman sitting on her other side. She could have been his daughter, but Kroll presumed it was a *cinq a sept* relationship.

Kroll was no stranger to fine dining, but the meal was exceptional. *Galette* of finely sliced button mushrooms, Basque country trout with avocado and coriander flowers and *verjus* marinated *foie gras* dressed with hazelnut oil and turbot with baby spinach and sea urchins. He had lost track and stopped eating by the time they came out with *crème brûlée*, *crêpes*, and *profiterole*. After dinner many went back into the ballroom. A small group went into the library and clouds of cigar smoke wafted out.

"Would you like to see the upstairs?"

"But of course," Kroll said.

Genevieve moved confidently, her heels clicking on the marble stairs. Walking behind her, he could appreciate that her buttocks were as perfect as her breasts.

She opened the 10-foot high door and they stepped into the room. It was not a bedroom, more of an office. A small man sat behind a large mahogany desk. He was somewhere in his late 60s, balding with cold blue eyes, dressed in a gray suit that had the look of custom tailoring. As they first entered, Kroll thought for a fraction of a second it was Vladimir Putin.

"You are surprised?" the man behind the desk said.

"Not really," Kroll said. "For a moment I thought you were..."

"Yes, President Putin." Kroll could tell he was pleased by the comparison. "You are not the first." He gestured with his right hand to a red upholstered Louis Quatorze chair, one of a pair facing the desk, inviting the professor to sit. He gestured dismissively with his left and Genevieve exited without the slightest goodbye to Kroll.

"You were not expecting something different coming upstairs with Genevieve?"

"It has been my experience when a woman that young and attractive is so attentive to a man like me, particularly after this..." Kroll's finger traced the slight droop in his face due to the stroke. "...that she wants something. The question was only whether she would ask for it before or after *les rapports sexuel*. Or should I say *polovye snosheniye?*"

"You presume I am Russian?"

"Your English is excellent but you referred to President Putin. Not Russian president Putin. So I presume he is your president."

"The reports of your intelligence and perceptiveness were not an exaggeration," the man said. "I consider myself a citizen of the world. I am fortunate enough to consider him a friend."

"If I ask your name, would you tell me the truth?"

"You may call me Greg."

"For Grigory?"

He made the same dismissive gesture he had used sending Genevieve away. "I will call you Edward. Most men are quite charmed by Genevieve."

"She is charming. Bright enough to keep a conversation going, deferential enough to encourage my feeling special. And showing hints of a body that was designed for pleasure. The food, the wine, all of that is enough to get my dopamine flowing. With some adrenalin. And a dollop of testosterone. Which at my age is a tribute to her abilities. But you didn't invite me here and wine and dine me just to talk about Genevieve's charms."

"You Americans do like to, as you say, to cut to the chase? Very well. Your research is very intriguing."

"Most of the details on my work on enhanced interrogation have been made public. And I value my country enough to not share that which remains classified."

He repeated his dismissive gesture. "Edward, please, don't be silly. We have a different approach to questioning. Simply take several possible informants, slowly drown the first one in front of the others, then let the survivors sit for an hour. Let the interrogator go, have a cup of tea, read a newspaper. There is no need to waste time waterboarding. By the time the interrogator returns, the survivors will be begging to talk first. Americans can be so, I believe you say, namby-pamby."

Kroll nodded. Greg was clearly pleased with himself as he tossed out English slang. It led Kroll to believe he spent most of his time in Russia, speaking his native tongue.

"I am interested in your work on psychic phenomena. I believe it was a grievous mistake your efforts were shut down. I have been fortunate enough to look over your published and unpublished data. Particularly on the man you identified as Subject One. Though he was not your first, I believe you saw the most ability in him."

The professor nodded.

"Jeremy Sherman," Greg said, dragging out the name. "Many additional names since then. Yes, we have been monitoring."

"What specifically are you proposing?"

"I will fund your efforts to search for him. When he is located, if he cooperates, that would be excellent. Based on past history, it is doubtful. We can arrange for him to be shipped back to Russia.

We can motivate him to cooperate. Help him develop his abilities. Then perhaps learn how to train others to do what he does."

"Is it a matter of nature or nurture."

"Exactly. I suspect, and I believe it is your hypothesis as well, that as with so much in life, it is both. Lebron James was born with certain gifts. Height, hand to eye coordination, perhaps merged psoas and longer tendons in his legs. But if he hadn't spent thousands of hours on the basketball court, he might not be the man he is today." Kroll sensed Grigory's pride in knowledge of American sports.

"We believe our scientists could take your research a step further."

Kroll bristled. "You think they might have ideas I didn't consider?"

"Please, Edward, you were bound by certain constraints. Though you were more adventurous than many American researchers are."

Kroll wondered how much his host knew.

As if to answer him, Greg said, "The experiments with provoking different types of arousal were very creative. The targeting the hypothalamus in that manner. You might have taken it even further if it was not for small-minded bureaucrats."

Kroll had thought the exact same thing. He nodded. "But your people plan alternative approaches?"

"Your prime telepathic subject reported synesthesia with sight and sound when he was experiencing a telepathic connection. What if he was not bogged down with normal visual and auditory distractions?"

"If he was blind and deaf?"

"Yes. As a temporary measure, of course. If we found that it did accelerate his abilities, it might be necessary to make permanent. A small sacrifice for the good of science."

"An intriguing hypothesis."

"When it comes to fruition, we will fund an institute, perhaps in London or maybe here in Paris, named after you. The Dr. Edward Kroll Institute for the Study of Psychic Phenomena. We will be sure that credit is given where credit is due. The Institute will be funded through several cut outs, so there is not even the semblance of any government's involvement."

Kroll recognized the man was playing to his ego. But that didn't mean it wasn't a seductively appealing offer. He could imagine the brass plaque on the door of a 300-year-old building in the heart of London or the 8th *Arrondisement* of Paris. Scholars quoting the institute's research, him being described as the modern J.B. Rhine. But without the taint. "I'm interested."

"I am pleased. We can work out the details. Money can easily be transferred anonymously. But there will need to be a detailed accounting. Some people have taken advantage of our generosity in other matters. I am not interested in spending money on indulgences."

"I don't have any."

"The background check shows you to be a focused individual. We respect that. But as you know, people sometimes lose sight of their values when they know there is money available."

"I am not that sort."

Greg stood, came around the desk and the men shook hands. The little man had a powerful grip and he held Kroll's hand a trifle longer than was necessary.

"One last thing to seal the deal," Kroll said. "I took a Cialis a while back. I would hate to waste it. Is Genevieve available?"

Grigory smiled. "Go down to the third bedroom."

"I presume it is wired to record our activities. I would prefer it not be recorded."

"But of course," Greg said.

"I knew you'd understand."

After an hour with Genevieve, the woman slipped out of the room. Kroll assumed it had been taped. He wanted Gregory to know that he knew and was not intimidated.

The woman had made the right noises. He wasn't sure if she was acting. He didn't really care. If she was acting, she was good at it. He would expect nothing less.

His main thought as he said his goodbyes and exited the building was pondering how they would transport Sherman/Lord to Russia. And how much say would he have in how the Kroll Institute operated.

Chapter Thirteen

"The White Salmon River is nearby," Wynne said. "We'll walk in the water for a few hundred yards. It'll slow down them tracking us. Problem is, it'll slow us down too. Hopefully there'll be shallow spots and the current will be weaker this time of year."

First they heard, then they saw the 30-foot-wide blue and green swath cutting through the forest. There was a white froth in the middle as the river swirled around boulders.

Diana used her hatchet to make two walking sticks. She handed Tom the longer one. "The bottom's going to be slippery. Be careful."

She stepped into the water, sticking close to the shore, where it was shallowest. He stumbled a couple of times but avoided a dunking.

After a few hundred yards, the river was deeper, faster moving. They hustled out of the water when the river narrowed and they had to struggle to stay upright.

They dripped as they walked, making noisy sloshing sounds until their cuffs had emptied.

They heard another howl. Then a second. At least two hounds, coming closer. The river hadn't bought much time.

* * *

"I knew they couldn't stay in the river long," Amos said, pointing proudly to where the couple had come back on dry land. The drying water drops made their path easy to see. The dogs picked up the scent and took off. Excited, sensing they were closing in. The men sensed it too and they picked up the pace. Amos and his brother leading, the Russian right behind them. Klimke and Ramirez bringing up the rear.

* * *

"There's a small lava tube a few hundred yards ahead," Diana said. "I was thinking about it for overnight before they brought dogs. Now we just got to keep going."

"Maybe," he said.

"What do you mean?"

"Is there an entrance and exit or just one opening?"

"It's really one that lives up to the name. A tube. Only about 20 yards long."

"You willing to cut your paracord bracelet?"

"Why?"

He told her his idea and she surprised him with a kiss. It was more friendly than passionate, but still welcome.

They were surrounded by large rock outcroppings. Many the size of a bus. Dark gray and black, clad with moss and lichens. Awesome volcanic forces had shaped the landscape. Nature grand and cataclysmic.

The cave stood out nestled under a dozen or so lichen-covered boulders. There were beer cans, broken glass and an empty cigarette pack a few feet into the darkness.

Diana's paracord was black, which was perfect. She held the flashlight while he took her can of bear spray and removed the safety, looping the paracord through the trigger guard. There were large rocks lying on the floor of the cave. Diana cut pieces of wood that were somewhere between a large twig and a small branch.

He set the underwear and socks he'd worn on the floor. She did the same. The bear spray canister was nestled between two rocks, aimed a couple feet inside the door. They used the twigs and rocks to set the paracord as a tripwire. The cord was a couple inches off the ground.

"I feel bad for the dogs," he said.

"They'll live," she said. "Hopefully we will too."

They hustled toward the back of the cave. The enclosure narrowed, the ceiling six, then four, then two feet from the floor. They took their packs off and carried them. They climbed over more downed rubble. They laid the packs on the floor and pushed them ahead. They wiggled the last few feet and came out into the forest.

Diana checked the map and compass in the slowly failing light. He was taking out a flashlight and she pushed his hand down.

"Too visible," she squinted and figured out a route.

* * *

"Over here," Amos said. "We got 'em now."

The dogs' feet hit the tripwire as they rushed into the cave. A cloud of two percent capsaicin engulfed them. Right behind them, Amos took a face full. Both hounds howled in pain. Ivan had gotten a little, just enough to make him cry. But he did it silently and kept from rubbing his already inflamed eyes.

Klimke pulled Amos and the dogs out of the cave, holding his breath and squinting. He had a diluted brush with the capsaicin. As part of his military training, he had been required to run through a tear gas-filled Quonset hut. A nasty experience but by his third time through he could overcome the unpleasantness without panic. He dabbed at his face with a damp cloth while Drew helped his brother and the dogs.

"We're going back," Drew said.

"No. She hurt my dogs," Amos insisted.

"The dogs ain't fit for hunting right now," Drew said. "They can't smell worth a damn. Probably won't for hours."

"She hurt my dogs," Amos repeated.

"She's just fighting back, like any animal in a corner," Drew said.

"We're real close," Klimke said. "They're getting desperate."

"It ain't worth it," Drew said.

"Another $5000 each when we get them," Klimke offered.

"Ain't worth it," Drew insisted. Klimke could tell his mind was made up. Was it worth keeping Amos without his brother to rein him in? Could he track the couple as it got darker?

Amos had stopped wiping the damp rag on his face. His nose was still running. But he looked determined.

Drew was confident that he could find his way back. The dogs were still shnuffling and would be little help.

Amos scanned the ground and pointed. "This way."

The four men set off after the couple.

* * *

She checked the cell phone again but there were no bars. "Damn. We're not even that far from Trout Lake."

Wynne had been checking the map more as they followed a trail for a half mile, then got on a forest road, then back on a trail. Sometimes they moved on deer trails that were overgrown, with space not even shoulder width apart.

When she paused and used a branch to smooth out footprints they had made in the muddy soil, he realized she was following an erratic route to shake the men tracking them.

There were walls of the tall, evergreen Douglas fir and hemlocks. The understory was mainly maples, with some of the leaves beginning to change color.

He said, "I hate to suggest going uphill, but if we could get above the trees..."

She looked at him. "Brilliant!"

"Huh?"

She jogged over to an old growth Douglas fir, at least six feet in diameter. The branches lowest to the ground, not getting light, had withered and dropped off, leaving tiny stubs. The nearest real branch was about 20 feet up.

She took an arrow and tied rope just behind the steel point. Then she moved a few dozen feet out from the tree, unslung the bow and aimed just above the branch.

The arrow got tangled in the leaves and didn't wrap around the branch she was aiming for. Not the lowest, but the next one up, about four feet higher. About six inches thick nearest the trunk. On her second try, the arrow passed over but got stuck in the greenery. Her third shot did what she wanted. The arrow passed through the leaves and came back down

She retrieved it and removed the rope. She tied a butterfly knot near the end, then did a bowline on a bight, creating two loops that she put her legs through. Her left foot went into the butterfly knot.

"Okay, here's where you come in," she said to Tom, handing him the far end of the rope. She put her gloves on, walked up to the tree, and put her fingers in a crevice in the bark. "Pull when I say."

"Are you sure you want to do this?" he asked.

"Our best chance is to connect with Marvin."

"Marvin?"

"Marvin Whitehorse."

"That tree looks like it's about 100 feet high."

"Taller than all the others around it," she responded, beginning her climb.

She pulled up with her arms, lifted her legs to her chest, then had Tom pull, then pushed up with her legs. Moving like a giant inchworm. It took her five minutes to make it to where she could stand on the lowest branch. She pulled the rope up and tossed it above her, looping around a branch eight feet above her and the trunk of the tree. Then she continued her climb.

Tom alternated between worriedly watching her and worriedly scanning the woods for signs of their pursuers.

He could barely make out her movements through the understory. The tree had narrowed to no more than a foot thick. She looped a length of rope around the trunk and tied herself in with two half hitches. He saw her finally stop and take out her cell phone.

A couple of minutes later and she began to descend, carefully tying around a branch, lowering herself, then repeating the move when she was secure another six feet or so down.

She looped it around the lowest branch and tossed the standing end down to him. She rappelled down the final 20 feet, standing on the trunk and walking, her body parallel to the ground.

"That was amazing," he said.

She shrugged. "My father taught me how to do that improvising with the sleeves from a jacket. It's easier with a rope. And someone to belay you." She smiled. "I got through. Good news, bad news. He's getting his son and a few buddies to meet us at the edge of the reservation and escort us in."

"The people following us won't be easily discouraged."

Diana's grin, particularly with her bruised and puffy face, was almost scary. "Unless they're bringing a half dozen tanks and attack helicopters, I'm not worried. You don't mess with the Yakama, particularly on their turf."

"What's the bad news?"

"The bastards coming after us must have a damn good tracker. I could see them in the distance when they went through a clearing. They're coming our way."

Chapter Fourteen

"I saw four," she said. "Three were wearing black tac vests. One wasn't. If I had to guess, he's the tracker, someone they picked up locally. I didn't see long weapons but couldn't make out detail at this distance. No idea what they have on their backs."

"How far were they?"

"I'd guess less than a mile. But that's a straight line. I'd say they have to walk twice that to get to us, if you remember how many curves there's been in the trail."

"I remember."

"We're less than four miles from the reservation border," she said. "But there's the same problem. That's as the crow flies. Probably closer to six realistically."

Almost as bad as the lung-busting pace were the changes in temperature. Four degrees colder for every thousand feet of elevation. But changes in elevation also meant less trees, more wind. He'd be sweating enough to peel off a layer going up a hill, then need to put two layers on at the top. Even with moisture-wicking fabric. She had warned him about heat stroke versus hypothermia.

They were moving at the old heart-pounding clip. After a half hour largely going uphill, they stopped and polished off the last of the GORP. And sipped deliciously cold water from Hole in the Ground Creek with the Lifestraw.

"I don't, huuh, think I can, hhuuuuuh, keep up this pace, huuuuuh, for too much longer, huh, huuh," he said.

She unslung her bow and the small quiver and stood it against a tree. Then she took off her pack, grabbed a few items from it, then stuffed them in his pack.

Wynne removed her pack and hurried off the trail. She laid her pack down, including the tent, and then piled brush on top so it wasn't visible. Back on the trail, she stared where she'd hidden the pack, nodding her approval. "Now, give me the one you've got."

"I can do it," Lord said.

"I can handle the pack better. We'll go faster if you've got no extra weight."

"Maybe we can ditch both packs?"

"If we spend another night here, we'll need the food, and the space blankets. The hatchet for cutting wood, and as a weapon."

When he peeled the pack off, he stood straighter and tried not to look relieved. She slipped the pack on, adjusted the sling, bow and quiver and they took off.

* * *

Having skipped a day's march thanks to the helicopter, Klimke's team hiked at a near jog. They couldn't run due to possible booby traps. But Amos now was alert for any signs of disturbance in the trail that could mean a tripwire. Klimke doubted that there would be more—strategically the benefit of setting another one would take more time than the couple could afford. Anyone who could so artfully rig a trap like that probably had a good tactical sense. He held grudging respect for Wynne.

Ramirez straggled behind, clearly hurting from his injuries. But then Amos would pause to study the ground for a couple minutes, giving the tough ex-soldier a chance to catch up.

The tracker had been helped by the light drizzle which made the hard-packed dirt more communicative. But when they reached a fork in the trail, with no apparent marks going either way, Amos went down on hands and knees. He rolled dirt between his fingers, lay on his side studying a mark from a different angle, and sniffed the soil.

"Got her," he said, waving them to a barely noticeable dirt trail. "She thinks she's so smart, covering the ground up." The trio joined him. Amos pointed to a gap, a few missing twigs on a tree, then footprints about six paces down the trail.

"The man was here. Pretty recent, based on how crisp those marks are. His pack probably caught on the tree, then he stepped down hard as he pulled it out."

"You're sure it's them?"

"The shoes match the ones we've been following," he said, sounding offended at being questioned. "Look!" He bent again and pointed.

Klimke didn't see anything until he ran a finger along a faint line. "That's her footprint. We got 'em."

* * *

"Want me, to, huuuuuuh, carry the pack, hhhhuh?" Tom gasped.

"Don't be ridiculous," she said, without slowing her pace. Despite her carrying the extra weight, she remained in far better shape.

His foot hit a root and he went down hard. He broke the fall with his hands. His palms were raw from little rocks on the trail. He brushed the rocks off. No bleeding. But his pants knee was torn and darkening with blood.

She dug into the backpack while he pulled up his pants leg. She wiped the scrape with antiseptic then slapped a gauze strip on, then taped it in place. It hadn't taken very long but she said, "We're not going to outrun them to the rez."

"My offer stands. They're not going to kill me. I can't say what could happen to you. Please go."

"No way. You don't leave a comrade behind."

"I've been downgraded from buddy to comrade?" he joked.

She didn't smile. "That spot up ahead, we're at the edge of the lava bed. I can be off on the side, hidden by trees. When they're exposed, I'll take out the tracker."

"Kill him?"

"Hopefully not. Put an arrow in his leg."

"That sounds pretty risky. If they have guns..."

"It's risky because I'd rather shoot for the main body mass. I'm not sure how protective those vests are. It could bounce off or be a kill shot."

She moved faster, increasing the distance between them.

Deep trenches, shallow ruts and mounds of broken rock created eerie shapes in the fading light. Vestiges of a flow from thousands of years ago. Bushes, small trees and patches of ferns and moss broke up the harsh field of jagged black and gray rocks. A low crater was visible at the north end. Around the edges of the flow, about the size of four football fields, lodgepole pines and alders and other greenery fought for life in the cracks.

"You keep going," she commanded, setting the pack down.

"What? What about the leave no comrade behind?"

"I'm going to get off a couple shots then catch up with you."

"Maybe I can..."

"Go!"

She headed one way and he went the other.

* * *

Amos studied the trail leading to the lava bed. "Damn rock is hard to read," he said. "If my dogs were here, they'd follow them no problem."

"They seemed to be going pretty straight," Klimke said. "We'll just keep going and hope you can pick up the trail."

"Lava beds are tricky. Got magnetic ores. Screws up compasses. Lots of little holes you can break an ankle in."

"You saying we shouldn't go this way?" Klimke asked.

"Might have to. But it'd be better if I scout around the-"

He screamed and fell to the ground as an arrow embedded itself in his groin.

The other three men dove for the ground, trying to shelter themselves by the largest boulders they could find. None of the rocks were more than a couple feet high.

Amos yowled in pain.

"You see where it came from?" Klimke asked the other men drawing his gun.

"About two o-clock, a clump of pines," Ramirez said.

Klimke was confident that Lord was not firing the bow. There was no report of him having that skill and the woman had been described as an archer. But was he standing right next to her? If Klimke missed her, would he be putting a bullet in the prize?

Another arrow whistled by, catching Ivan in the shoulder.

Klimke fired. A double tap where he estimated the bow had been. He waited for another arrow. The only sound was Amos thrashing around and screaming in pain, his groin dark with blood. Klimke believed he had hit the woman. But there had been no cry of pain and the image of Amos with an arrow protruding from his groin was a strong deterrent to advancing.

Lying a few feet away, Ivan pulled an arrow out of his vest, leaving a big hole in the black Kevlar. There was a trickle of blood. "Nice vest," he said. He pulled it aside. The arrow had made a shallow cut.

"Think you can crawl off to the right, get to the tree line and outflank her," Klimke whispered. He kept the Glock aimed where the arrow had come from. "I'll provide covering fire if needed."

Ivan nodded and began crawling rapidly across the rough ground.

"You take care of Amos," Klimke said to Ramirez. He tossed him the first aid kit. "Know what to do?"

"Of course. The one in Ivan's shoulder was a broadhead. Assuming the same in Amos, I cut off the shaft, leave the head in."

"Don't cut my shaft," Amos said between wails.

"Not your shaft, the arrow shaft," Ramirez said, muttering "dimwit." The arrow was high on the man's thigh. He couldn't tell yet if it had hit the tracker's testicles. At first glance, it seemed like he wouldn't need a tourniquet. If the arrow had hit his femoral artery, he'd bleed out pretty quick. Ramirez pulled on latex gloves, hoping Amos wouldn't be too squirrelly. He'd knock the tracker out if he had to.

Under most circumstances, Klimke would have laid down preemptive covering fire and advanced himself. But he was concerned about hitting Lord with a stray shot.

* * *

Diana lay on the forest floor, pressing her hand where the bullet had grazed her thigh. She tried to stand but fell hard. It felt like someone had hit her in the leg with a baseball bat. What had her father told her about wounds? He had three Purple Hearts. She tried to remember but was foggy with pain.

She heard someone approaching. She slid the remaining arrow from her quiver and slipped it underneath her. Her right hand held the shaft, six inches below the razor sharp broadhead.

The attacker was approaching quickly. She kept her breath shallow, hoping the attacker would assume her dead. His tac vest would weaken the arrow's damage. She planned to go for his throat.

Shooting the tracker from a distance had been harder than she had thought. Part of it was due to her eye being swollen. But most of her difficulty was shooting another human being.

She had missed the mid quadricep spot she was aiming for. Ironically, where it had landed made it even more psychologically intimidating.

Now she was getting ready to kill someone close up. Him or her. No real thoughts about him other than either he or she would be dead within seconds.

As he loomed over her, she rolled on her good side, away from the injured leg. She jabbed the arrow toward his neck.

Tom swatted it sideways and made a shushing gesture with index finger to his lips.

With the adrenalin strength that allows grandmothers to lift cars off of toddlers, he hoisted her on his shoulder in a firefighter's carry and made his way through the woods.

Chapter Fifteen

Wynne held the bow in her left hand, her right grabbed tight on Lord's belt. He set her down after a few hundred yards.

Lord looked back and saw her bleeding leg had left a blood trail that didn't require a skilled tracker to follow.

At a fork in the trail, he leaned her against a tree in a dense grove of big leaf maples and took the arrow from her.

"What're you gonna do?" she whispered. He cut his left sleeve, then ripped it off and applied a crude pressure dressing to her leg.

She stared as he brushed the arrow across his bared forearm and a line of blood quickly appeared.

"Magic!" he said, flourishing his hands with an exaggerated wave. "Which way do we need to go?"

Uncertain what he was up to and struggling with her pain, she said, "Right. About two more miles."

Lord nodded and went a few feet down the left trail. Then he squeezed his arm until a few droplets of blood hit a rock in the trail. Jogging a dozen more yards down the road, he did it again. He repeated the move a few times, put a strip of cloth around his own arm to act as a pressure dressing and hustled back to her.

"Let's go."

* * *

"Just wait here," Klimke said to Amos, who leaned against a rock, his pants cut down to his legs. A wooden stub was poking up from his groin, next to his penis. The arrowhead was embedded in his testicles. Ramirez had done a skillful job wrapping the wound with antibiotic soaked gauze and tape. He'd given Amos a fentanyl patch and the tracker was glassy-eyed but quiet.

"When we catch them we'll have the helicopter pick us up and get you to a hospital," Klimke said, leaning over the man and patting his shoulder. "It's not a bad wound, you'll be fine."

"My balls," Amos cried.

"Don't worry." Klimke patted him again and stood up as Ivan ran up.

"They got away," Ivan said. "I found two sets of prints. You hit *suka*. Bigger footprints only then. But a blood trail."

"*Suka?*"

"The bitch."

"Let's go."

They progressed slowly due to increasing darkness. And the image of what Diana's arrow had done to Amos. The men instinctively kept their hands near their crotches.

The temperature was dropping.

They weren't equipped for a night mission, but Klimke guessed neither was the couple.

He had one big advantage. He took out his night vision goggles and turned them on. The world for him turned green. But a bright and clear green.

They came to a fork in the road and the blood trail was clear. They headed left.

* * *

Lord and Wynne moved awkwardly down the road, like an extended three-legged race under a darkening sky, with relentless pursuers, and stretching for miles. He had to shorten his stride, she had to lengthen hers. They struggled to move in a coordinated manner. After about a quarter mile, they found their rhythm. They seemed to take turns stumbling, with the other one keeping them upright and on course. It was a sign of Diana's injury that she was barely matching him in brisk walking.

"Thank you," she said softly.

* * *

Klimke had lost the blood trail. He circled right, then left. The other men bent and squinted but even with flashlights couldn't see blood. They were careful to not shine their light anyway near where Klimke was scanning since they knew the brightness would be painful through the night vision optics.

Klimke took out a map and studied it, his finger tracing the route they had been on, up to the last fork in the road.

"Let's backtrack," he said.

"You think they went different way?" Ivan asked.

Klimke held up the map and pointed. "Look, they were following pretty much a straight-line northwest. At that last fork, they headed northeast. What if they figured out she was leaving a blood trail, stopped it, and doubled back?"

They went back to the fork and studied the ground.

"Here!" Ramirez shouted, when he found a couple of Tom's footprints in the moist earth.

"Clever bitch," Ramirez said.

"Or clever bastard," Klimke responded. "He's thrown hunters off his scent dozens of times in the past."

* * *

Diana flinched with every step but didn't complain. They didn't even pause to study the map, hoping that the trail they were on was the right one.

"I think it's through that grove of trees and two more hills," she said. "Then only about a mile." They were in an open area, brightly lit by the moon.

Tom's head snapped up right, tensely alert, scanning.

"What's going-"

He interrupted her question by shoving her hard. She bashed into a rock.

"What the f-"

A piece of the rock flew off, almost as if she had chipped the hard basalt. The sound of the gunshot came a fraction of a second later.

"Don't move," the sinewy blond man with the gun ordered, pointing his weapon at Diana but looking at Tom. His eyes flitted back and forth between the couple. But it was obvious he was talking to Lord. With her injured leg, and having hit the rock hard, Wynne lay still and glared at the gunman.

"The girl is expendable, and you know it," Klimke said. "Cooperate fully and she doesn't get hurt."

There were two men standing behind him. One was the leader from the raid, the other a big man with a blocky head and close-cropped hair.

Tom was distracted, his head twisting, scanning the tree line like a dog picking up a faint scent.

"It's you who better put your gun down," Lord said to the blond man.

"Really?" Klimke asked. "Why?"

A red laser dot appeared on his stomach and traveled up to his forehead. He had seen it move and could only imagine where it rested.

"We have only one fancy rifle with a laser sight," a man in the darkness yelled. "The other guns are all scoped. But my friends can hit a chipmunk at this distance." He rode up until he was visible on the top of the hill, lit from the west by a few weak rays from the dying sun and from behind by the bright moon. He was tall, slender, with a red bandanna tied around deep black hair. He was out of pistol range but well within rifle range. There was a grove of alders along the crest of the hill. Barely visible, another Native American stood with his gun resting on a tree branch and aimed at Klimke. Next to him was a third man, also with a rifle aimed at Klimke, Ivan, and Ramirez. A fourth man was standing on the other side of the man with the bandanna. He also held a rifle, aimed casually, confidently at the trio who had been tracking Lord and Wynne. It wasn't clear who was in whose gunsights. The Russian set his knife down, Ramirez set his Taser and knife down. Klimke kept his gun on Diana.

Klimke shouted, "We're federal marshals. These two are fugitives." He slowly reached into his tac vest and took out a US Marshal's badge.

The man with the bandanna nodded his head and grunted. "White man speak with forked tongue."

"Huh?" the Russian said.

"I always wanted to say that." Bandanna smiled. "You're full of shit, blondie."

"This is federal land," Klimke insisted. "You're off the reservation and we're going to take them in."

"Lecturing Native Americans about who owns the land is not a good bargaining strategy," Tom said, *sotto voce*. "Particularly with a rifle laser dot on your forehead."

"Shut up, Lord." Klimke snapped.

"Just saying." Lord was giddy with relief.

"This is over, Klimke. Stand down," Lord said, trying to sound commanding.

"How'd you know my name?"

"Ramirez is thinking your name. So is the big Russian. They're practically screaming that it's time to walk away."

Klimke fought the urge to turn around and look at the men, keeping his gun aimed at Diana.

Slowly he lowered it. Diana, who had used the rock to stand, glared with a ferocity that made it clear if she had the gun, he'd be dead.

"Good," Bandanna said. "Now set it on the ground slowly and take four steps back. You other two, any other weapons?"

They shook their heads.

"Tom will check," Bandanna said. Diana had told his name when she'd called.

Lord warily approached the big Russian. Standing three feet away, Lord said, "You're wondering about grabbing me in a choke hold and negotiating with the men with guns."

The Russian stared but neither confirmed nor denied.

"Put your hands behind your back, fingers intertwined. I'm going to go behind you, so the men with the rifles have a clear shot if you move. Understand?"

"Understood," Ivan said. Tom patted him down, finding a foot-long dagger which he confiscated. He then repeated the maneuver with Ramirez, who was glaring at Tom as angrily as Diana was looking at Klimke.

Lord gave Bandanna the thumbs up sign when he was done with the frisk.

"I'm taking the night vision gear as a donation to the tribal fund," Bandanna said. "You can make it back to your camp by moonlight. Any problems with that?"

Klimke shook his head.

"If you do anything stupid like try and double back, remember you're going to be bringing sticks and rocks to a gun fight. Go!"

Klimke and his two men turned and walked away. Posture erect, not looking back, with as much dignity as defeated warriors could muster.

Bandanna came down the hill, his riflemen staying in position. He went to Diana and assessed her wound. "You up for an hour or so horseback ride?"

"Sure. Thanks for coming."

He waved his hand dismissively and turned to Tom. "I'm Frank." He shook Tom's hand. "Let's get her up the hill." Diana scooped up the bow she had dropped. Frank glanced at it, nodded approval and showed Tom how to grab his left wrist with his right hand, while he did the same, then he grabbed Tom's right wrist with his left, and Tom did the same with him. Their hands formed a rough square, a seat that Diana lowered herself into. She draped the bow across Tom's shoulder then used her hands to hold on.

They moved up the hill where one of the riflemen, who had slung his weapon over his shoulder, inspected her wound. He carried in his pack a well-stocked first aid kit. He smoothly cleaned and dressed her wound. One of the other riflemen joined them and the five of them headed down a narrow trail the other side of the hill. The fourth man stayed in position, watching where Klimke, Ramirez and the Russian had headed off.

"See you back home," Frank said.

The man staying behind nodded.

They walked a quarter mile, with one of the rescuers replacing Tom as part of Diana's chair.

"Save your strength," Frank said when Tom tried to rotate back in. He said the same thing to Diana when she asked to walk.

The trees grew denser overhead, the trail darker. Moonlight barely filtered through. The point man moved swiftly, not running but with as little hesitancy as a New Yorker on an empty sidewalk.

Then they were in a clearing with four tethered horses happily grazing. The sun was gone, the dark brown and black shapes lit by moon light. One horse had a few white patches that glistened. All had western style saddles and the glowing sheen of good care.

Frank climbed up on a big roan that whinnied as he settled in. He left one stirrup empty. He offered a hand to Diana who swung up easily and settled in behind him.

One of the other men waved Tom over. "I'm Joe," he said. He grabbed the pommel from the saddle, put a foot in the stirrup and swung up easily onto the black horse.

"I'm Tom. Thanks for saving us."

He didn't respond, merely extending a hand to help Lord climb up. Lord tried to mimic the move he had seen Diana do, putting his foot into the stirrup, grasping the hand, and climbing up. The horse moved and Tom fell back. The horse shook its head as if refusing to have him climb aboard.

"You ever ridden before?" Joe asked.

"Once, at a dude ranch when I was 14."

"Shit," he muttered. Joe got off the horse and after a couple of tries was able to boost Tom into the saddle. Then he climbed up in front of Tom. "Hold on like your life depends on it. Because it does."

The other two men on horseback were already out of sight. Lord hugged him as they followed.

"Bounce gently with the horse. Don't be stiff," he cautioned.

Lord tried but couldn't seem to get in sync with the big beast. The horse knew it and gave an occasional head shake and annoyed whinny. Joe patted its mane.

After a while it seemed a little better. Lord clung to Joe's back and leaned in as tightly as he could without restricting his breathing.

The horses weren't galloping but weren't walking either. They seemed to be as comfortable with the trail as the men had been. Aside from occasionally getting swatted in the face by a branch, the ride went smoothly. Soon the trees thinned out and Tom saw a small house up ahead.

Chapter Sixteen

As Klimke walked back to where Amos lay, he debated killing and burying Amos in the forest. But then he would also have to kill his brother. He didn't know who else knew about them joining him on this FUBAR mission. Extracting Lord from the reservation would be as tough as kidnapping an Iman from a mosque in Yemen. Not impossible but not like a simple urban grab in a busy city.

Klimke called for the helicopter to pick them up. Then he leaned over the wounded tracker. "You've got a choice. Either you swear to never say anything about what you've seen to anyone or I kill you right here and you don't have to worry about it." Klimke's cold fury over the failed mission enhanced his menace.

"I won't say nothing."

"If I ever hear you did, and I have ways of knowing these things, I will kill your brother and your dogs in front of you. Then you. As slowly as I can. It will last for days. Understand?"

"Yessss, sir." Amos said.

"You had a hunting accident. That's it. Your medical care will be taken care of. You will be paid. Got it?"

"Yesss sir."

The Eurocopter HH-65 Dolphin helicopter arrived in a few minutes and lifted the men out. They landed at Pearson Airfield in Vancouver, Washington. The small one-time military airport was now a municipal airfield, with tall yellow and green corrugated metal hangars. Four rows for 150 planes. But far from full. There were a half dozen small planes, a six-seater the largest, parked on the asphalt. The airport was under the jurisdiction of Portland International Airport but with minimal bureaucracy. And no TSA, air marshals or airport cops snooping about. Klimke arranged for Amos to be transported to the nearby Southwest Washington Medical Center. The mercenary was glad it was an arrow and not a gunshot wound. The ED doc wouldn't be obliged to report it to the authorities. As long as Amos kept his mouth shut.

Klimke walked a few dozen yards from where the helicopter had powered down. He could see the old Army Air Corps hangars in the distance. He let his gaze pan across the airfield. No threats. A couple of windsocks fluttering feebly in the weak breeze. Two men standing near a Piper Cub chatting. A man and a woman going over a checklist outside a Cessna Turbo Stationair.

Klimke called Drew and let him know that he'd be fully paid, and his brother had had a non-lethal hunting accident. Telling anyone anything other than that would "result in my having to track you down. That wouldn't be pleasant for either of us," Klimke told him. He believed that Drew didn't need as forceful a message as Amos had. And his fury had cooled.

Drew agreed to keep his mouth shut.

Klimke dreaded making his next phone call the way most men dreaded going into battle. It wasn't often he had to give a complete failure of a sitrep to a commander. Particularly a boss who had never been under gunfire. Kroll was a ruthless fighter. But his combat involved scathing articles in academic journals or undercutting a rival in a university's psychology department meeting. He would not understand the feeling of surviving a lost battle, the bitter victory, the regret and relief of being alive coming in alternating waves.

"I hope you're calling with good news," Kroll said.

"No sir. He got away." Klimke gave a concise rundown of the failed operation.

"Do you know how much this has cost so far?"

"No sir."

"My estimate is more than a quarter million, when you figure that you want me to pay the medical expenses of all these people."

"Yes sir. We don't need disgruntled survivors out there."

"What do you plan to do now?"

"I'm thinking we need to stand down."

"You know where he is and you want to give up?"

"It's a large area. Hostile territory. His protectors will be on the alert."

"You can't get him?"

"It would take a well-organized operation. A well-equipped squad, a helicopter to deliver them. Good intel on exactly where he is. Some plausible deniability and willingness to deal with possible legal consequences. Frankly, I think the costs outweigh the benefits. He'll resurface somewhere."

"I'll have Lloyd get on the intel and have him predict how long Lord will be there. Lloyd is quite good at his job."

The last sentence was a dig. Klimke saw Cutler as a desk bound nerd who couldn't survive a night in a campground. Cutler saw Klimke as a dangerous Neanderthal. Klimke knew that Kroll believed the rivalry enhanced motivation.

"I'll put together a plan," Klimke said."

"Do that. And if it's not too difficult for you, factor in costs."

"Yes sir," Klimke said between gritted teeth.

* * *

The next few days were a blur. With a lot of time sleeping. The house on the reservation had three bedrooms. Diana and Tom shared a full-size bed in one, Frank's parents in the other. The third bedroom was empty. From dribs and drabs of conversation, the couple learned it belonged to the young woman Diana had helped. Who had disappeared again about six months before their arrival. It was clear she was not to be talked about. But the room was ready if she returned.

None of the rooms were very big, the furniture was worn, but the house had a warm, homey feel. The living room merged into the dining room. There were always people dropping in. Some people were introduced as cousin or uncle but unclear if it was an honorific. Or maybe everybody was related, even if only distantly. Joe was one who came by and remained his surly self. He came with his wife, who was equally uncommunicative.

Part of the homey feel came from the constant cooking smells in the air. Even if Tom hadn't been ravenous after a couple days of minimal eating it would have been a mouth-watering fog. All the differences from the past few days were sources of pleasure. The bliss of a long, hot shower. Not having to be constantly moving. Nor worrying about weather conditions. Being surrounded by friendly people. And of course, not worrying about being captured.

The first day Mary--Frank's mother, Marvin's wife, and the creator of the delicious smells--came and gave Lord an ointment for his aching legs. He was also painfully saddle sore from his ride with Joe and the big black butt-bruising horse that he learned was named Flower.

He took the ointment and rubbed it in. After a few minutes, his lower body felt better.

"Is this a traditional Yakama medicine?" he asked.

She shook her head. "Tiger balm with marijuana. High CBD."

There were lots of moments like that, where he was culturally awkward but insanely grateful.

Diana slept. Mary put salves on her leg wound, not the Tiger Balm, but with a lot of aloe. She gave Diana a poultice for her face. The bruising faded over the course of two days.

Lord had hoped that their time being chased in the wilderness, including carrying her, would bring them closer. But if anything, Diana was more distant. He wondered if she didn't like being helped. Or was mad that the pursuit was because of connecting with him. But he was tired of apologizing, tired of her not believing about the ESP, tired of her bullheaded independence, tired of her temper.

A typical conversation was when she asked how he responded so quickly when she was playing dead then tried to stab me with an arrow.

"Are you sorry you didn't stab me?" he joked.

"Was there a movement I made that gave it away?"

"No. I read your mind. Sorry. It was kind of like checking your neck for a pulse."

She wrinkled her nose briefly, her disbelieving face. "Really, so what else was I thinking?"

Annoyed at her tone, he said, "You were thinking about what your father would have done in a similar circumstance."

"Hmmph. That's amateur psychology. You know I think about him a lot. There's nobody who would be better at an ambush."

"You also were blaming yourself for taking the second shot, thinking you should have moved after firing."

She was silent for a moment and glared. "Maybe. But again, any amateur shrink would know when things go wrong, I might blame myself."

"What about my pushing you to safety when I felt the thoughts of Klimke? Moments before he fired?"

"You probably have very acute hearing. He made a noise and you realized it subconsciously."

"Okay, I'm done," Tom said. "I'm tired of trying to prove myself to you. Believe what you want."

He left the house, walked a few hundred yards to a clearing and started doing *tai chi chuan*. It was a sunny, crisp day and it felt glorious to move. The aches in his legs translated into increased awareness. He was on a slight hillock, with a view that stretched miles in every direction. There were a few houses in sight but mainly trees, other hills, and a sky as blue as he had ever seen. With puffy white clouds that were scudding rapidly across the sky.

"Tai chi?"

Frank had come up behind Tom. He was standing a dozen yards away, respectful of Lord's space.

Tom felt a strong bond with Frank. Not surprising since he had saved Lord's life.

The two men had spent much of the previous night outside Whitehorse's trailer, seated in white plastic lawn chairs, smoking a little weed, with him talking about Yakama history including the 1855 war against the United States. Frank told Tom about the language, *ichishkiin Sinwit*, and how there were conflicting beliefs about what exactly Yakama meant, ranging from pregnant ones to black bear, to runaways, to people of the narrow river. He talked bitterly about his parents being sent to boarding schools and having their language beaten out of them. He told Tom about Mt. Adams, which whites named after President John Adams, but his people called *Pahto*, which meant "high up." They chuckled over that as they shared a joint.

Lord was never a big drinker. Or pot smoker. He didn't like losing control. Alcohol or marijuana increased the chances of making a mistake. And when he'd been in Kroll's program he'd been forced to take numerous drugs, mainly psychedelics.

"I always talk too much," Whitehorse said. "My father jokes that my mother must have slept with an Italian. Indian humor."

There was a long silence.

Lord said, "I appreciate your openness."

"That's just 'cause you and Diana are feuding."

"How do you know that?"

"We've about 10,000 people on 1.2 million acres. With surprisingly little privacy. That's one thing I liked when I lived in Portland."

"When was that?"

"I went to Lewis and Clark Law School. Kind of ironic, huh? Lewis and Clark aren't exactly heroes for my people. But then again, my people call me an apple."

"An Apple?" Lord asked, thinking it a compliment. "Like a Mac? Computer smart?"

He snorted. "Red on the outside, white on the inside. I was sent off to learn the law, come back and fight for more rights. But it's easy to sell out. How many successful rappers live in Compton?"

Tom didn't get the point he was making at first. The pot weakening his focus.

"I came back to the reservation." He took another hit and passed the joint to Tom. "With reservations." He laughed without humor. Lord laughed uncomfortably.

"I had developed a taste for Thai cuisine, a different bar every night, pale-skinned blond women."

Tom took a hit on the joint. They were both quiet for a long time.

"I had gotten a scholarship. The tribe paid the rest. And we're not exactly rolling in the big bucks out here. There was no way I couldn't come back." He sighed. "I'm being groomed to be a leader. One of the youngest on the tribal council. The most successful battles against white men were fought in the courts. Fishing rights, land rights, self-governance versus state control."

"You're not happy here?" Lord asked.

"It's not about being happy. You whites and your individualism. You don't understand responsibility to the tribe. Doing what you are meant to do."

"I don't know what I'm meant to do."

It was as intimate a moment as Tom had ever had. He felt like he needed to share part of himself he hadn't talked with anyone about.

"The last woman before Diana was Leilani Palakiko." Tom said her name slowly, savoring each syllable. "In Pahoa, on the Big Island of Hawaii. Pahoa is one of those places where half the people are running from something. Everyone minds their own business. Plus it's beautiful. You might've heard of it when there was that eruption by Kilauea in 2018?"

"I don't think so."

"There's acres and acres of lava flows. Patches that look like a moonscape. But the tropical greenery keeps pushing in."

"Some of that in Indian Heaven. Not the tropical greenery part." Whitehorse laughed and Lord joined him.

They were quiet, listening to the night wind.

Frank's eyes drooped. "Hawaiian women are beautiful."

Frank's being in a cannabis haze made it easier to talk.

"I was working as a cell phone salesman in this storefront that we shared with a tax prep business and a realty firm. Leilani came in to get taxes done. On April 14th. I flirted with her. Asked her out. She said her family would have a fit if they knew she went out with a *haole*. But she did. And after six months we were living together in a small place with a view of the Pacific. Palm trees blowing in the wind. Banyan trees, monkey pod trees. Coconut trees you could pluck breakfast from. Sit on the lanai with a fresh cup of Kona coffee grown just a few miles away. Wearing clothes only if you wanted, no one in sight. Away from everyone else. You could pretend you were on your own tropical island. As close to paradise as I'd ever found."

Tom got lost in the memory. Frank grinned as if he was experiencing the memory with him.

"They found us. I'm still not sure how. Four big guys crashed in. The middle of the night. Our privacy meant no neighbors to hear. I managed to hurt one of them. But then one of them connected. I went down, woke up handcuffed. They told me I had to go with them. Cooperate with the experiments. The goons didn't even know what the experiments were. One of them kept eyeing Leilani. They took her in the other room.

"I heard her fighting. I begged, I pleaded, I promised I'd do what they wanted. They were out of control. I read their minds. I was supposed to be unhurt, just scared. They were mad because they didn't like a white guy with a Hawaiian woman. I let them know I knew they had exceeded their mandate. Which was stupid.

"The leader told me to not even think about reporting it to police. One was actually a top cop's son. The leader took my hand in his. He said he heard I liked to do sleight of hand. Then he bent my finger back until it snapped."

"That sucks, man," Frank said. "Was it the blond guy who was chasing you here?"

Lord shook his head. "No. The guys who did it were huge. They dumped me in the room with her. She was also handcuffed. My hands were behind my back, so I couldn't pick my lock. I was dizzy with pain but picked hers. Then I told her how to get me out of the handcuffs. It's not that hard. Just a shim on the ratchet part, a push in.

"The goons were arguing about something in the other room. We slipped out the back window. I kept apologizing as we stumbled down the mountain. She told me she never wanted to see me again. I said we should go to the police. She refused, kept repeating she never wanted to see me, that her family was right, she should never have been with me.

"I stole a boat and got over to Oahu. Then the mainland. I tried reaching out to her. One of her brothers called me, threatened me, told me to never try again. I hired an investigator a few years ago. She's supposedly happy, married to a local guy, a couple of kids. Living in a nice part of the island."

The two men sat in silence, the sun going down, a strong breeze bringing the smell of drying grass and cows.

"Is that why you took on the creeps when you first met Diana?"

"Probably part of it."

Their talk had gotten both deeper and less coherent as they continued to smoke.

"So why were the big guys after you?" Whitehorse asked. "Aside from you being a non-Hawaiian?"

"That's a long story," Tom said.

Frank nodded and didn't ask anything more. Eventually Tom made his way the few hundred yards back to the bedroom in the house. Diana barely stirred as he slipped into bed next to her.

* * *

Cutler had called Klimke and asked for a detailed description of the Native Americans who had ambushed them. Klimke couldn't provide much. He guessed ages and height/weights, described the leader as best he could, including speech patterns, speculation about IQ, even that he had a sense of humor. He heard Cutler tapping away at a keyboard as he answered questions.

Working with Tang, Ginger, and the helicopter pilot, Klimke had put together a plan. Equipment and personnel. Ivan and Ramirez were bonus operators. He wanted a cushion this time. He still didn't completely trust Ivan, but the Russian had proven himself as having grace under pressure. Klimke had a rough cost projection for Kroll. But he needed intel as to where Lord was hiding.

"You didn't give me much," Cutler said when he called back.

Klimke fought the urge to say, "Fuck off!"

"But I dug deeper on Diana Wynne. She was involved in a domestic violence case with a Yakama woman about four years ago. The woman comes from a respected family, the kind that would have the resources to mobilize four armed men on short notice. There's a high probability the leader was a man named Frank Whitehorse. The victim's brother. I'll send you his driver's license photo for confirmation. There's low probability the family would be stashing Lord somewhere else. I have the coordinates of the parents' house. Frank lives on their property, a couple of relatives within a mile or so. With military age males."

Klimke checked his e-mail. The photo of Frank Whitehorse showed he was most likely the leader. He called Cutler back and verified it.

"Looking at probabilities, I think they'll be leaving the reservation within three to seven days of arrival. We're on day four."

"Got it."

"Dr. Kroll wants your team ready."

* * *

The morning of the day after Tom's heart-to-heart with Frank, Tom was doing *tai chi* when he saw Frank watching. He stopped but Frank said, "Finish, it's nice to watch."

Lord completed the third set then walked to where Whitehorse stood.

"Cool," he said, nodding his head. "You got to respect the older cultures. The Chinese, the Jews, the Greeks. In the United States, if a business is 20 years old, they boast about it."

They started walking, but away from the house. Tom could tell Frank had something he wanted to talk about. But Whitehorse digressed into an intellectual riff, quoting Joseph Campbell on mountains in religion. The Chinese had *Kunlan*, Jews had Mt. Sinai, Greeks had Mt. Olympus. "And we have *Pahto*. It gives you power to look up at such towering strength."

They had climbed a few hundred feet.

Frank said, "I try to imagine what it was like a thousand years ago. Hell, a few hundred years ago."

"I've got the feeling there's something else you want to talk about."

"A Skamania county sheriff was hassling a cousin. He accused him of shoplifting from a store in town. The cop was asking about a white couple, who they were staying with. My cousin said he made up a story, but I don't know. My cousin is the kind who would talk if he was scared."

"There's no mystery. Kroll's people know I'm here."

"Kroll?"

Lord filled him in on the full story. Whitehorse nodded along without challenging the idea of psychic abilities.

"My father would never ask you to leave," Frank said. "It is a matter of honor. But the men that were after you are not going away."

Lord recognized he had deluded himself. Like a fugitive on vacation who believes he can live his life at a resort, walking on the beach and enjoying sunsets, indifferent to the outside world. He had hoped it would last longer. "What should I do?"

"You seeking Native American wisdom? My people got screwed over from Maine to California, from Florida to Washington." He gave one of his bitter laughs. "I've got my tribe. For all the good and bad that entails. Only you know what you need to do." He turned and walked back toward his battered Toyota pickup. As he climbed in, he yelled to Lord, "Just don't sign any treaties."

Tom did 15 minutes of *qigong*. It was hard to focus on the movements, hard not to ponder the next step.

He went back to the house. Diana and Mary were talking. They stopped when he entered. Mary went into the kitchen, leaving Diana and Tom alone in the living room.

"You and Frank were talking a long time," Diana said.

"Yeah." Lord hesitated, then blurted, "We should head back to Portland."

She nodded. "I was thinking the same thing. I can reach out to some of the women in the DV program. There are safe houses. It's not a permanent solution but it'll give us some more time."

He had expected resistance and was pleasantly surprised they were in agreement. "At least we don't have much to pack."

She didn't respond to his attempt at humor. "Do you have any ideas?"

"Yes. I've got to put together a tribe."

Chapter Seventeen

Considering how difficult life had been, the next few steps went surprisingly well. Mary drove them to where the Subaru was hidden. It started smoothly, a reminder of just how short a time they had been on the run.

They were able to get within a mile of where Diana had stashed her pack and retrieve it, none the worse for wear. He convinced her that using her phone was not safe. In a strip mall grocery on the edge of Vancouver they bought a couple of burner phones. She used one to make a few phone calls and was given an address in Beaverton.

They rode I-205 across the Glenn Jackson Bridge then got off in northeast Portland. He found an Outback that matched the one they had stolen—not hard in Portland—and swapped out the license plates.

Lord took a half hour of unnecessary turns, waiting until a light was changing to scoot through intersections, circling blocks a couple of times, pulling over and parking for a few minutes. A basic surveillance detection route. No vehicle seemed suspicious. They drove to his apartment. He circled the block a few times. Nothing out of the ordinary.

He wore a Seahawks ball cap pulled low and big sunglasses. Diana stayed ducked down since they were more identifiable as a couple. She voiced her annoyance and skepticism repeatedly but honored his request.

"You know the woods a lot better than I do," he said. "But in an urban setting you need to trust me."

"Well, how come they found you?"

"I don't know. Just trust me. Please."

She muttered but remained low.

After a half hour of watching from the car, he spent another 15 minutes walking around the block. He changed caps and sunglasses and took off his jacket. Still no sign of watchers.

He went up to the apartment. The layer of Rice Krispies he kept under the mat was untrampled. He let himself in and did a quick inspection. None of the objects that would have been irresistible to an intruder--like his computer-- showed any signs of movement. He had aligned the laptop perfectly with the edges of the table and left a sheet of paper casually draped over a corner of the keyboard. They were exactly as he had left them.

He went to the duct and took out his RF bug detector. He swept the apartment. No beeps or squeals indicating a transmitter. He retrieved his fake ID—three new identities.

He knew with a fake ID, you have to find a birth certificate that matches your age and race. Then make sure the name and ethnicity fit where you're trying to hide. Birth certificate leads to social security card and driver's license. Bills at an address, library card, credit cards to build history. Keep the credit cards active with small purchases, monthly ones like a Pandora membership. Order goods a few times a year, have them delivered to an address you can watch to see if anyone is alerted. The ultimate harvest is a passport. Mail in the paperwork, use a dummy address, and keep fingers crossed that a Department of Homeland Security squad doesn't show up with the little blue book. It had taken lots of work, but two of his identities had clean credit cards and passports.

The brief visit to his apartment was revitalizing. But Diana's zinger stuck with him. How had they tracked him?

They rented a Toyota RAV4 and ditched the stolen Subaru after wiping it down for prints. He called the police non-emergency number, speaking with a nonsense accent and talking through a few tissues, and told them where it could be found.

As they left downtown, Diana told him there were a half dozen secure residences scattered around the Portland metro area, used for domestic violence survivors who couldn't stay in one of the shelters. The houses were only for special cases since they required individual staffing 24/7. Diana had worked at several--guarding women like the Whitehorse daughter--when there were pending court cases or other exceptional circumstances.

She had made it clear that if a case came up, the couple would have to leave immediately to make the residence available.

The safehouse was a blue clapboard ranch-style structure, about 60 years old. It was the size of the Whitehorse home but had neighbors a dozen feet away on either side. She said the neighbors were led to believe the house was an Airbnb property. There were no obvious signs of excessive security—only a gated, four-foot-high cyclone fence as well as motion detector lights on all sides. The door had steel bars but none of the windows did. There was a sign for an alarm system.

There were no shrubs that anyone could hide in near the home. The garden was well maintained but sparsely landscaped with a parched lawn, like most of the other houses around it. With the slight variations, it was clear one developer had put up all the buildings. Probably as quickly and as cheaply as possible.

The low frills look continued on the interior, where everything had come from Ikea, including the attempt at making it homier by putting up wall art. When the couple opened the door, the place smelled mildly of Febreze. There were cans of tuna, beans, soups as well as boxes of pasta, tomato sauce and other staples in the cabinets, TV dinners in the freezer, but no perishable food in the refrigerator.

There were actual little signs it was not someone's home. The little sign by the sink said, "Do not leave dirty dishes." Another little sign next to the alarm panel detailed the procedure for turning it on and off.

After they had settled in, she said, "Were you just being flippant back on the reservation when you made the comment about putting together a tribe?"

"No. Talking to Frank sparked an idea. Doing two things I had done unsuccessfully in the past. But doing them together."

She looked at him quizzically.

"You asked if I had ever fought back. In my twenties I decided to try and find some of the others. A few were dead from what seemed like natural causes. The internet wasn't what it is now. It was harder to find people. Plus Kroll had discouraged us connecting with each other, made us distrustful. Penalized anyone who tried to get deeper with anyone else, claiming it could contaminate results. No fraternizing among 'the subjects.' When we ate in the small cafeteria, conversation was forbidden. You could get written up and lose privileges if you chatted. Some people earned points by snitching out others.

"About 10 years ago, I tried getting the media interested in the story. *The New York Times, Washington Post, 60 Minutes.* I worked my way down, reached out to dozens of media outlets. It got to the point where I was tired of being laughed at by a cub reporter at the *Iowa City Daily Dog Catcher Gazette.*"

"I understand their skepticism," she said stiffly.

"But if I could get a few people now to confirm the story, hopefully there'd be a willingness to investigate. Post

Harvey Weinstein there's recognition that a private citizen with massive resources can do as much to bury a story as the government. In this case, the government also has an interest in details not getting out."

"Have you tried the Freedom of Information Act?"

"Yes. I got a 'no records' or 'all records destroyed.' You know when Richard Helms had everything from MK Ultra shredded, a lot of other edgy programs were made to disappear."

"MK Ultra?"

"The CIA's mind control program. They did a lot of the crazy stuff even before Kroll. "Hypnosis, sex, drugs, borderline torture. Civil liberties were not on their list of priorities."

Her face showed a mixture of disbelief and disgust.

"You said Lisa was a computer whiz? And I know you want to let her know you're okay. I'm willing to get her on board."

"I'll call," Diana said, picking up her phone.

"No. I'm sure they've got her lines monitored. Probably most of your friends, employers, family. We'll drive by her house tonight to see if there's any physical surveillance."

"If there isn't, I can finally let her know I'm okay?"

"No. Tomorrow's Halloween. It'll be a perfect time to reach out to her. Carefully."

"You really think they even know we're not on the reservation?"

"I wouldn't be surprised."

"How? Does he have an army of psychics tracking you?"

"I'd appreciate it if you'd knock off the sarcasm," he said. "Kroll has tech people that do top notch data analytics.

They were able to guess we'd go to the wilderness and pinpoint where. They crunch huge amounts of seemingly unrelated data and develop probabilities. What are the odds we'd go someplace new versus someplace familiar. Who would we contact. I'm sure they know about your DV work and are nibbling away at that network."

"People know not to talk. Lives are at stake."

"You ever hear the quote from Ben Franklin that three may keep a secret if two of them are dead?"

* * *

"They're no longer on the reservation," Cutler reported.

"I'm glad," Klimke said.

"You should be. I ran some projections. You had a 27 percent chance of succeeding with an extraction there."

"It's nice you have such confidence in me."

"You knew it too."

Klimke didn't respond. "Any leads?"

"Nothing solid yet. There's a 92 percent chance they've returned to Portland. We've increased surveillance. Multiple likely contact points are being monitored. If they do go there, there's an 86 percent chance they'll use her domestic violence group connections for safe housing. One of our investigators has gotten a volunteer position at the crisis line. She's forwarded the shelter addresses but there are apparently additional housing sites that are more closely guarded. We're trying to figure out how they're funded and hack the database. But I'm getting into details you don't need to know."

Cutler was showing off and Klimke knew it. He didn't take the bait.

"Ivan should take the jet back to the east coast," Cutler continued. "You can keep Ramirez with you if you think it necessary."

"I will. He's a proven commodity."

"Whose failure is what set us down this path."

Klimke was going to respond to his desk bound "brother" but held back. "Ramirez is motivated. He wants to see the mission ultimately succeed."

"You're in the field. It's your tactical decision."

"Glad that's recognized."

"Either Dr. Kroll or I will get back to you if there's a change in strategy."

Cutler hung up and Klimke muttered obscenities into the mouthpiece.

* * *

Diana and Tom spent the afternoon shopping, buying groceries, hair dye, the weakest power reading glasses, sunglasses, reversible jackets and multiple caps for both of them. Though Tom paid for them, Diana complained about the purchases as a waste of money. At a Halloween store he bought a bushy mustache and a surprisingly realistic beard.

"With the mustache you look like a gay porn star from the 80s," Diana joked. "The beard makes you look like a *Duck Dynasty* fugitive."

"Sometimes the best thing about a garish disguise is that it is garish," he explained. "People will notice my mustache but not eye color, height or other things that are harder to change. Which reminds me, we should get me lifts and you high heels. And contact lenses for both of us with different colors."

She was even more reluctant about cutting and dying her hair. Tom reminded her that the attack on her house and the relentless pursuit through the forest "was not just my paranoia."

That evening, Wynne drove the Toyota to Moreau's house. Wynne had most of her far shorter blond hair tucked into a hat, the reading glasses low on her nose so they didn't interfere with her vision. Lord, now with neatly trimmed graying black hair, had bought a toy periscope and was ducked down in the rear seat.

After they circled the block, Diana said, "I saw two vans. And a woman sitting in that car halfway down the block."

"Good job. You ever notice those vans here before?"

"I don't recall. But I can't say I made a real effort to remember her neighbor's cars in the past."

They parked at the end of the block and watched. After about a half hour, one van left. The other, a late model silver GMC Savana remained parked across the street and a few doors up from Moreau's house in what was a perfect surveillance spot.

Lord studied the van, then looked it up online.

"See that plate-sized convex window on the side."

"Yes."

"That's customized. For surveillance vehicles."

"Interesting," Wynne said. "But that woman is still in her car on her cell phone. She's been there a godawful long time."

Lord lay on the seat and closed his eyes. They were parked four houses away from the woman. A couple houses further from the van.

"What are you doing?" Diana snapped.

"Focusing. Please be quiet. If you can." He regretted his verbal jab, but his patience was wearing thin. It was hard to read minds at a distance. He had to filter out others' thoughts.

"She's not a watcher. Or at least not a professional," Lord said.

"You're sure?"

"Reasonably sure. It's never 100 percent. Particularly under conditions like this."

"What about the van?"

"Too far. But there is someone in the back of it."

"What're they thinking?" she asked skeptically.

"Too far away. And they're not in a state of arousal. It's like listening to a very faint radio signal."

"So what's your plan?" she asked.

"Do you know whether she tends to go out on Halloween? Or leaves her house dark to not be bothered?"

"I do know. She stays at home, loves to hand out candy. She told me it was her favorite holiday."

"Excellent. Mine too."

Chapter Eighteen

Guy Fawkes drove with Pennywise the clown in the passenger seat. Fawkes wore his black cap, his large conical hat on the back seat. And the sharp-chinned white plastic face with upturned mustache and thin vertical beard. Stephen King's grinning, sadistic clown, with slight feminine curves, had strapped her cleavage down with KT tape. She wore a baggy yellow coverall with puffy blue and white shirt beneath it. White gloves on her hands.

"You've got the signs?" Lord asked, adjusting the Fawkes mask

"Yes," Wynne said, pressing down the red flame-like hair attached to her mask.

"You know the plan?"

"We've only gone over it 20 times."

"Okay, okay," Lord said, recognizing his own anxiety.

They drove down Moreau's block. He had swapped out the license again, in case Kroll's men had a plate reader attached to the silver GMC van to alert them to repeat traffic.

It was nearing 8 p.m. Dark, no rain. The surge of trick or treating children with parents had passed. Now it was the slightly older crowd, teens who didn't have a party to go to or were being ironic and enjoying a cynical revisit to their childhood. Or pumpkin smashers out for tricks not treats.

The silver van with the custom window was parked across the street, a few houses from Moreau's home. This time the sign on the side said, "Rose City Home Improvement," with contractor's board and phone number and "No Job Too Big or Too Small." Lord wondered if it was a peel off or magnetic temporary sign.

"You know the drill?" Lord asked again, as they sat in the car up the block.

She sighed. "Let's just get it done." She had a half dozen pieces of paper. He had a dozen eggs and $150 in ten-dollar bills.

They waited. A few trick or treaters passed. Lord and Wynne ignored them.

"Okay, this is it," he said, spotting three gangly teenage boys. They were loose-limbed and looked like they were struggling with growth spurts. He got out of the car and approached the trio.

The apparent leader was dressed as Michael Myers from *Halloween*. One buddy was a cape wearing vampire. The third was a zombie. They eyed him suspiciously. Lord guessed they were about 15 years old.

"*V for Vendetta* was way cool," Myers said, referring to the movie that popularized Lord's masks. "But you're old to be out."

"You guys want to earn some quick money?" Lord responded, facing Myers, their clear leader.

"What d'you have in mind?" Myers asked.

"I ain't doing nothing illegal," the zombie said.

"I get that." He showed them the eggs. "You see that silver GMC van up the block. There's a guy in there who's trying to steal my girlfriend."

"What's he doing in the van?" Myers asked.

"He thinks I'm inside the house with her. He's waiting until he thinks I'm out then he's going to knock on her door."

"That sucks, man," the vampire said. "I had a girl that was screwing around on me too."

"She was a bitch from the start," Myers said.

"Bite me," the vampire said.

They started bickering and Lord interrupted. "Guys, guys, there's twenty bucks a piece for each of you if you egg his van. He might chase you. You guys fast?"

"I'm on the track team," Myers said.

"I just never tried out," the zombie said. "I'm fast."

"Me too," the vampire said.

"Make it thirty and we'll do it," Myers said.

Lord counted out the money and Myers pocketed it.

Guy Fawkes kept two eggs for himself and gave them the carton. He was hopeful that the surveillant would be stiff-kneed and chunky from lots of time sitting watching targets. And that he would be unprofessional enough to be distracted by the vandalism. While street surveillance remained a challenging art, with all the modern technology and remote electronic possibilities, sitting in a van for hours would be a task for the low man on the totem pole. Hopefully burned out and lethargic.

The trio of villains swaggered down the street. Tom a dozen paces behind them. They hesitated and he wondered if they were going to take the money and run. The zombie threw the first egg. His buddies quickly followed. The eggs hit the van with a loud thud that must have startled whoever was inside.

Tom watched from behind a bush. He threw one egg, making sure to spatter the small window in the back of the van.

The van door slammed open. "What're you assholes doing?"

A mustachioed man in his 50s jumped out of the van. Despite his impressive gut, he took off after the egg throwers. He was way too slow to catch the adrenalized young men who had a good head start.

Lord watched Pennywise walk up to Moreau's door and ring the bell. He was glad Diana was moving quickly. The surveillant would quickly realize he didn't have a chance of catching the vandalistic villains.

Diana waited until Lisa answered the door. Moreau, dressed as a bumble bee, had a big bowl of chocolate candies. She was reaching in to give one to Pennywise when the clown held up her first written sign.

"Don't say anything. Act like I'm just another trick-or-treater." Next to the words was a heart with arrows and the initials LM and DW. It had been a joke between them one night when they were bonding over being disgusted with men.

Lisa froze.

"What the..."

The next sign said, "It's Diana."

Lisa's eyes went wide.

"They're listening. Maybe watching," the third sign read.

Lisa regained her composure, nodded. "Ohh, aren't you the scary clown."

Diana nodded back. She handed Moreau a slip of paper with more detailed instructions.

Lisa read the paper and said, "That's so nice." She handed Diana two miniature Kit Kats and a Hershey bar.

Diana nodded her thanks, her grin hidden under the Pennywise mask. She walked away as Lisa closed the door.

After less than five minutes, the mustachioed surveillant was back. He quickly wiped down the round custom window. He glared both ways before climbing back in the van, leaving the rest of the egg remnants smeared on the side of his vehicle.

Fawkes and Pennywise got in the car. After 15 minutes, Lisa shut her lights, indicating trick-or-treaters were no longer welcome. Tom and Diana waited.

There was no obvious indication that Moreau was slipping out of the rear of the house, climbing over her backyard fence, and calling a cab. She would not use Lyft or Uber, paying the cabbie cash to avoid a credit card trail. Getting picked up by the driver a half dozen blocks from her home.

The surveillance van remained parked.

Tom and Diana peeled off their masks. Diana's tight latex mask had left her hair sweaty and plastered to her head.

"Nice job," Lord said.

Diana gazed at the mask in her hand. "So creepy. I never understood why people liked clowns."

"I would've preferred you as the Black Widow."

She gave an exasperated sigh. "Just drive."

They headed toward the rendezvous point.

Chapter Nineteen

The Washington Park Archery range was theoretically open until 10 p.m., when the park closed. The range had ten wooden structures holding bales of hay wrapped in a tough fibrous white plastic with printed targets on them. There were no lights, but the white seemed to glow in the night from city light reflecting off clouds. The targets stretched from five to 77 yards at the far end of the tree-lined field. There were orange posts marking the firing line plus decapitated orange road cones to hold arrows. Far from elaborate. But it gave an excuse for Diana to carry her bow.

Tom was hidden behind a toppled log on the hillside below the range, a dozen feet back from the curvy two-way road that led to the site.

Diana was in the wooded area on the hillside south of the range. She had hiked up the nearby Wildwood Trail and found a spot dense with foliage. Vine and big leaf maples, rhododendrons, and towering Douglas firs over a rich mix of bushes and ground cover. Fifty shades of green. With her bow, she wanted to command the high ground.

The couple arrived nearly a half hour before Moreau was due. There had been no suspicious traffic. One man walking a Pekingese with pink bows in its hair. A couple that paused every few dozen yards for a kiss and a grope. Three slow-moving cars that continued on, probably looking for a romantic site in the wooded 400-acre park.

The note had told Moreau to take a cab to the MAX light rail stop near the zoo. She could walk the less than 3/4 of a mile on the tree-lined road and see if there was anyone around. One side of the road, the back of the zoo, was secured with a cyclone fence topped with barbed wire. The other side led up steeply to the Hoyt Arboretum.

Diana saw her first. She used her burner phone to text Tom, "Robin."

Tom texted her back. "Hood," the agreed upon signals for all clear.

Moreau reached the parking area. No one else in sight.

Wynne hurried down the hillside. Lord was slower in his approach, still looking for Klimke and his team. Lisa saw Diana and ran to her. Tom was still a dozen yards away as the women hugged. Lisa cried. Diana fought back her tears.

"I thought you were dead," Moreau said.

Diana responded, "I've been so worried about you, I wanted to talk to you sooner but things got... complicated."

"What happened?" they both said simultaneously, then laughed and hugged.

"You go first." Again they spoke simultaneously. They laughed and hugged once more.

Diana went first, recounting what had happened. Tom was impressed with how concise and accurate her recitation was.

Then Moreau asked, "You didn't get my warning?"

"What warning?" Diana responded.

Moreau told her about her kidnapping and torture, how she had said more than she wanted but tried to hold back as much as possible. "There's parts I can't remember. Parts I remember too much. Flashbacks, nightmares. Messed up in my head with stuff that happened when I was a kid. I just want to kill those fuckers and make it right."

Diana hugged her friend. "I'm so, so sorry."

"It's not your fault. I shouldn't have let it happen."

"I never got your message," Diana said, shaking her head slowly.

"They must have done a man-in-the-middle hack." The first words Lord had spoken. The women looked almost surprised that he was there. "Electronically mimicked a cell phone tower and caught your signal."

"So they got to us through you," Diana said to Tom, her words so soft they were barely audible.

"I'm sorry," Moreau said. "I was just looking out for you."

Wynne turned to him with an expression Lord hadn't seen before. Sadness, vulnerability, regret.

"Oh my god," she whispered.

"What?" he asked.

"All this time I was hating you for screwing up my life. But it was me who screwed up your life." Her voice quivered slightly, "If you hadn't met me, you would've been safe."

Moreau said, "You didn't know what I was doing. It ain't your fault."

"Still..."

"Hey, this isn't about blame," he said. To Diana, he added, "I fell for you. I have no regrets." Turning toward Lisa, "You were acting to protect your friend. Acting out of concern, out of love. You didn't mean to poke the bear."

Both women stared at him, expecting a harsher reaction.

Diana came close and gave him a warmer kiss than she had in days. "You're amazing."

Lisa said, "Hey, when you're done with magic man, I'll take him. There ain't many out there like that."

"No need to wait until she's done. We can have a *menage a trois*."

Both women stared at him. When Tom grinned, Diana smacked his shoulder. Hard enough to hurt.

"Okay, okay, just kidding." He laughed; glad the tension had been broken. He turned to Moreau. "Diana said you're a computer whiz." He took out a paper with a list of names. "I need to see what you can find out about these people. Credit scores, criminal history, family problems. The more info the better."

She glanced at the dozen names and took the paper. "Shouldn't be a problem."

"Getting any intel is going to be harder than you think. Some of them may have tried to live off the grid the way I have." He gave a quick history, telling her about the experiments he had been forced into.

"I've heard about the government doing crazy shit like that. I just didn't know whether to believe it," she said. "It's hard to know what's paranoid crap and what's really gone on."

Diana nodded vigorously.

Moreau asked, "Why do you need the info on them?"

Wynne was about to speak and he cut her off. "I'm just hoping to get a critical mass, gather data."

Diana looked at him, about to mention the plan to talk with the media. He cut her off again, talking directly to Lisa. "You're under surveillance."

"I was gonna ask about all this cloak and dagger shit," Moreau said.

"There's an excellent chance your house is bugged. Anything you do on the computer is probably being watched. You're at the top of the list for who she would contact."

Moreau reached into her purse and took out a small Taurus 9mm G2S Luger. "After what happened I got this. They mess with me again, they're dead."

He shook his head. "A gun gives a false sense of security. You say 'stop or I'll shoot' and they don't stop. You hesitate. They don't."

"I don't hesitate," Moreau said. "I see any of these motherfuckers, I'm pulling the trigger."

"That's fine against some street punk. But these people are professionals. You won't get a chance to..."

"You saying I should just give up? Roll over and let them get away with it."

"No. The best way is to be cautious. Be careful."

"So I'm supposed to be looking over my shoulder the rest of my life?"

"Look, I don't want things to get any worse for you."

She put the gun back in her bag. "I can take care of myself."

He could tell there was no point pushing. "You know about the dark web?" he asked.

"A little."

"How about TAILS?"

He could see from her expression that she didn't.

"These computer geniuses love oddball names," he explained. "TAILS works with TOR. The Onion Router. It's a covert operating system. You need to download it on a public Wi-Fi. Don't use it at your house. There's probably a bug. Maybe a keystroke logger. Or even a video feed. Or your Wi-Fi hacked. The same precautions at work." He gave her a brief tutorial on accessing the web covertly.

He gave her an email account username he had set up with ProtonMail, a Swiss company with servers buried in the Alps that offers free encryption.

"If you open a message in there, type in text edit and then switch it to white print. Then type some innocuous message above it. The bulk will show up as a blank draft. I'll know to switch to black or some other color if I see any message in there."

"You don't want me to just send you the results?" Moreau asked.

He was disappointed. She really didn't get the pervasive nature of the threat. "No. When you've got someone like Kroll and his people after you, there's no such thing as secrecy on the internet. Everything requires extra steps. Even then there's no guarantees."

He gave her a disposable phone. He cautioned her to use it only in a safe location and only use it to call them. With urgent updates or in an emergency.

Diana had been watching, listening. As Tom explained procedures to Moreau, it was clear that Wynne wasn't really understanding the details. But Moreau was. She seemed to have absorbed the rapid orientation to getting better privacy. The plan was for her to do the above the line research, accessing the tens of thousands of databases on the web, while Lord did the social engineering, below the line, that involved deceit.

"The best thing you can do to fight back is carefully research these names. Emphasis on the word carefully. If they suspect you know, they'll come back to question you. Or worse."

"You really think they're watching me? Bugged my place?"

"There's a high probability. Please leave the bugs in place. Go about your life with no seeming changes. Other than covertly doing the research."

"So if I have a guy over, I shouldn't care if they're listening to us getting it on?" she asked with a scowl.

"You're best off not socializing for a bit."

She was unconvinced.

"Make sure it is a guy you really, really know. I'd say anyone you've met since you were kidnapped is suspect. Male or female. Friend or lover. Has any new person suddenly cropped up?"

She hesitated. "There was a delivery guy. Cute. Hitting on me pretty hard. I gave him my number, supposed to go out this Saturday."

"Don't," Tom said, more forcefully than he intended.

"Guys are hitting on me all the time," she boasted.

"Please, Lisa, don't." he said seriously.

"I agree," Diana chimed in. "You got any old boyfriends circling the airport?"

"Always," Moreau said with a grin.

"Stick with them if you absolutely have to go out," Tom said.

She frowned. "I've been going to a quarry and practicing how to shoot. I know it ain't a matter of being a marksman. Just get it out quick and squeeze without shaking." She mimicked shooting someone. Holding the weapon increased her confidence.

"Lisa, please, listen to me," he said. "If you get in a gun fight with them, you're going to lose."

She shook her head. "Your style is to run. I don't play that way."

He worded it slightly differently, repeating himself several times. He tried it as a command, a request, a plea. No change in her attitude.

"Hey girl, I think he's right," Diana said. "I've seen these bastards. They're the real deal. We only got away from them because we were lucky."

Lisa tucked the pistol back in her bag. "Well, I'm lucky too. If they come at me, I'm gonna have the element of surprise."

The women talked for a few more minutes as they walked to where the couple had parked the car. Lisa was as stubborn as Diana. Maybe more so. They gave Lisa a lift to a spot at a New Seasons market a few blocks from her house. She agreed to do a brief shop and return with groceries. Hopefully it would seem like the watcher had just missed her leaving and not like she had snuck out. The goal of evading surveillance is to make them feel they lost you, not you lost them. It would be in the watcher's interest to not report the lapse.

After they dropped Moreau, Wynne asked Lord, "Why didn't you tell her what we planned?"

"Need to know."

"This isn't some spy operation. She's my friend. My best friend. She's taking a risk for us."

"I get that."

There was a heavy silence in the car. "What you were saying about guns, it was similar to the way my father spoke."

"Really? I figured him for pretty pro-gun."

"He had very mixed feelings. Too many untrained jerks. It's a serious commitment. He said only the well-trained or psychos could use a weapon quickly. Most people were in more danger of shooting their foot, their dog, or having the gun taken away from them by a bad guy."

Lord said, "I regret contacting her. I'm afraid she's going to get swept up again."

"She's tougher than you think. Smart too."

"I know. Hopefully I'm wrong."

Chapter Twenty

Back at the safe house, Diana said "I feel terrible."

"Me too. I'm worried about Lisa."

"Not just that. My anger against you. You didn't deserve it."

"Yes and no. You didn't have people storming your house until you met me."

She leaned in to give him a kiss. She pressed against him. He quickly responded. She reached down and held him.

"I think I may have psychic abilities," she said, gently stroking him. "I have a feeling I know exactly what's on your mind."

"I'm going to make a joke about crystal balls if we don't get horizontal pretty quick."

Their lovemaking passionate, explosive. The joys of make-up sex.

Lying in bed afterwards, she rested her head on his shoulder and said softly, "I want to apologize for all the cynicism about your ESP."

"You believe?"

"Sort of. There's just too many times you've done things that couldn't just be a trick. Like saving my life twice. I've always thought ESP was bullshit."

"I knew you were going to say that."

She looked at him for a moment, then saw his "Just kidding" grin.

"I mean it. It's like being an atheist and suddenly thinking 'hey, there is a god.'"

"I'm not requiring you worship me. But if you wanted to..."

"You do that when things get serious, make a joke. I'm trying to get you to understand how hard it is."

He resisted the urge to make a joke about being hard and kissed her gently. "Thank you. Sometimes it's difficult even for me to know what ESP is and what is just regular senses. I've gotten good at reading cues. Stuff other people might not notice. Like eyes dilating when someone is interested. Or micro expressions. Even quivers in the voice. Coupled with reading thoughts. It's like watching a movie with subtitles. I get info on a few different levels. Sometimes it's more confusing than helpful."

She nodded.

"When I was a kid, before I recognized I was different, I thought everyone could do it. I think of it like a sense of smell. Sometimes it's clear that the food is rotten. Sometimes you can't really tell. You have to taste it."

"Not a real attractive metaphor."

"But it's like smell in that some people are better than others. Or you can tell there's a barbecue but no idea what kind of meat is cooking. Some get trained to be good at it. Like people who work making perfumes."

"Perfume is better than rotten food," she said with a smile.

He smiled back and they kissed. "Maybe I should work on my explanation. How about it's like some people have perfect pitch. Some are tone deaf. And the vast majority are somewhere in the middle."

"Better. But in this case most people are tone deaf. You're one of a very few with perfect pitch."

"Not perfect. That was one of the few good things about being with Kroll. At least a few of the others had the gift. Or the curse."

"You really think of it as a curse?"

"I've always felt like an oddball. Very much alone. And it put me in Kroll's sight. I'm not complaining. It's who I am. But I can't say I'd wish it on anyone I liked."

"Didn't it give you an advantage?"

"Sometimes yes, sometimes no." He could tell she wanted more. "Okay, so my father was a big football fan. Johnny Unitas and the Baltimore Colts. He used to toss the football with me from when I was a little kid. I got a pretty good arm. In high school I decided to try out for quarterback. I'm on the field, dropping back into the pocket, and I get flooded by thoughts from the defensive linemen. The kindest one was probably 'Rip that motherfucker's head off and stomp on his nuts.'"

She chuckled.

"Needless to say I froze up. I tried a second time, even worse. I slunk off the field."

"Awww."

"And when I was first dating, I still couldn't really control it. The more aroused I got, the more I was listening in on the girls' mind."

"That could give you an edge. A sensitive guy."

"I would've made out better if I had made the football team. Maybe just because they were high school girls, or the girls I was with, but the thoughts were of previous boyfriends who were cuter, or worrying about how they looked, or if they could get me to take them on an expensive date. Only a couple seemed to be into the date as much as I was. Ultimately it felt sleazy to be reading their minds. I developed my own code of ethics."

They snuggled closer. He told her, "I want you to know I will always respect your privacy."

"I know you will. Though you can pretty much bet that whatever is on my mind, I'll be telling you. Actually, there is something else I've been wanting to tell you. Something else that got pushed into the background when I was scared and so angry with you."

He waited.

"I love you."

He hugged her. "I love you too."

"You don't need to say that."

"I don't need to. I want to."

They cuddled and the world was wonderful.

The next few days were like first love, bobbling around with that special glow. Even when things didn't go that well. She wanted to check in at work. He had her call from a burner phone. She told them she had a family emergency and would be out for a week. One gym was understanding, the other made it clear she was easily replaceable.

He worked on building her a couple of false identities. Kits were available on numerous sites on the Dark Web. The problem was lack of honor among thieves. A false identity might have been stolen years ago and used multiple times, with the real owner alerting authorities a long time ago.

Many sites delivered painfully obvious papers despite the slick-looking products they showed online. Their primary market was teens looking for fake IDs to buy alcohol. Only the most indifferent club bouncer would let them pass. But he had a couple of solid sites. Connecticut and Florida were two states whose driver's licenses were more easily forged, with easier to mimic holograms.

He took several pictures of Diana with a neutral background and uploaded them, then transferred money from one of his secure accounts and paid for the papers in bitcoin. The license would be shipped to a PO box a few miles from the house.

Diana had a daily two-hour workout. She had gotten back into her routine, which was exhausting just to watch. A mix of yoga, Pilates and lots of punches and kicks. Plus a five-mile run. Not a jog, a flat out run.

He always scanned the street before she took off. Exiting the house was one of the riskiest times. She agreed to his condition that she significantly vary her route every day. As well as the time she went. The first day he had tried going with her. He was quickly reminded that he was a four-times-a-week-for-an-hour-at-the-gym guy and she was as fit as a professional athlete. She was only gone for less than 45 minutes. It was better for both of them for him to tolerate his anxiety. Denying her a full workout was like keeping a border collie in a crate for hours.

Much of his time was spent at various cafes with a cheap 32 GB laptop he'd purchased. Though he didn't have access to the extensive paid databases that Moreau did, he searched for information on the eleven names he had.

He hadn't seen Lisa's cyber skills in action, though Diana had raved about them. Wynne was computer literate but not savvy. She might have been easily impressed. Moreau had seemed to know her stuff. She had quickly picked up what he had explained that night at the archery range. But better a little redundancy than trusting someone else who might miss something. As Mark Twain had said, not double-checking facts on the internet was begging to be a victim.

Mainly he had relied on services that had spiderbots, aggressive web crawlers that snarfed up data from a multitude of public sources. The process was as simple as putting in his account name, typing in the target's name and waiting a few minutes as 15 billion records were scanned. Local, state and federal civil and criminal courts, property records, voting records, public utilities, private business records, the criminal justice system, and social media profiles. The reports would include hard data and correlations e.g., target lived in such and such middle-class neighborhood where residents tended to make $60,000 median income.

When Lord had as much data as he thought he could gather legitimately, he switched over to social engineering. Going into trickster mode appealed to the magician in him. A little deception to lead the audience to believe what they wanted to believe. He spent hours creating new online identities with innocuous email usernames.

But he had no intention of bilking anyone, catfishing, or being a troll. If everyone who lied about their age, weight, occupation, and appearance on the web was banned, there would only be a handful of people allowed in cyberspace. At least that's what he told himself.

He spoofed the email feeding it into one account, despite the different names that could appear in the recipient's inbox. He was spear phishing. He already knew a bit about the targets. He wanted to know more. Things that they thought were private but still out on the web.

On the intimacy front, he spent time, using his bogus email as a foundation, to set up accounts on OKCupid and Plenty of Fish. He didn't want to waste one of his credit cards for the paid sites. He created a couple of men and women of varying ages and descriptions. He chose pictures from multiple sites of ordinary looking people and uploaded them. Then answered a couple dozen questions on each one. He would modify his profile as needed, e.g., if his target was an avid stamp collector, his profile would include details about his passion for philately.

About half the people had varying degrees of activity on Facebook. He set up two bogus Facebook accounts with a profile of two different females. Tiffany was 40 and worked with computers doing freelance social media marketing. Jane was 60 and contemplating early retirement from her job as a librarian. They both enjoyed birding, gardening, and reading. The details weren't very relevant—he just wanted them to be non-threatening.

On the first day, he befriended multiple Facebook friends of the targets. By the next day, he had 39 new "friends." It was like ringing all the doorbells to an apartment house you wanted to get into. Then he made a friend request to the targets. Most saw that he was friends with their friends and gave him access.

He repeated the process for Instagram, Twitter, and Linked In. He was starting to get a feel for his fellow subjects. At least to the extent you can ever really know someone based on their cyber face.

When not staring at the computer screen and vacuuming up details of his fellow subjects' lives, he got back into doing his daily *tai chi*, as well as 40 minutes daily mindfulness. Diana would join him for one of the two 20-minute sessions. Usually they were islands of calm in the turbulent emotional sea. But sometimes it was near torturous to sit still.

His insomnia was at its worst. He would get up after 30 minutes of trying to sleep and do all the sleep hygiene stuff. Read a book that didn't interest him (there was a mini-library at the house, with many weathered romance novels), do an unpleasant chore (the bathroom had never been kept as clean) or endlessly practice coin and card tricks.

Diana sometimes awoke. The first couple times she came out to the living room and asked if he was okay. After reassuring her he was just restless and didn't want to wake her, she'd go back to sleep. Sometimes he would sit in the chair in the bedroom and just watch her sleep. He didn't want to seem like a weirdo, but it was the most soothing activity. When she slept her face would relax into a smile.

Every six hours, even if it was the middle of the night, he would check the email account he had given Lisa. He logged in and went to drafts. She had followed instructions and there would be a draft with blather at the top. "Hi Uncle John, Hope you're doing well. Things okay here, but work has been tough. Blah, blah blah." He'd go to colors and click red. Her message would be below the blather.

"Nothing yet. How u 2 doing?" He'd write back some variant on "We're doing fine, everything quiet. How about you?" She'd respond, usually with an angry tirade against their pursuers.

On the fourth day, there was a message. "Close to done. Will call soon."

Chapter Twenty-One

While waiting for Lisa's call, he reviewed the information he had.

The last time he had tried to approach his fellow test subjects he had been younger, somewhat impulsive, confident that he was in the right and justice would prevail. He had located three. Two of them were now dead. They had both been in their 60s when they died. One from cancer. The cause of the other's death was not mentioned. After lots of web searching and awkward calls to hospitals, funeral homes, and family members--often getting rebuffed--he was reasonably confident their deaths were due to natural causes.

The obituaries indicated a fairly normal life for one. "Much beloved wife and mother," died in her New Jersey home surrounded by family and friends, survived by husband, two kids, five grandkids. Long employment as an accountant. Suggestion to donate money to the Leukemia and Lymphoma Society or the Sierra Club in her name.

For the other subject there were signs of a more troubled life. Divorced four times, nine kids and stepkids, had lived in a half-dozen towns and cities, no mention of his employment. With no cause of death noted he wondered if it was suicide, cirrhosis, or accidental overdose. Death by despair. At least someone had done the obituary. Hopefully there had been a service if there were people who cared about him.

The one still alive was Joan Martin. She'd been one of the younger subjects and he remembered her as smart, sarcastic, fun to be with. She was also telepathic. They'd had a few voiceless chats. Fumbling with miscommunication as neither one was very skilled.

He had located her in Pennsylvania back then. She had been working in a clothing store in a Scranton mall. He had showed up at her workplace after sending messages twice to an email address he'd secured. She hadn't responded. He presumed it was an account she didn't check.

She was unhappy to see him. She had gotten the messages but had no desire to connect. She reluctantly agreed to talk for a few minutes.

They had gone to the mall's food court. Over barely drinkable coffee she told him she'd worked hard to put her time in the program out of her mind. She still had telepathic moments, but they were few and far between. She was grateful for that. Very firm in her desire to limit contact. She ended the talk after 15 minutes.

Now it had taken a couple hours of work to find her since she had remarried and taken on her husband's name. She was now Joan Hendrickson, living in Raleigh, North Carolina. According to Zillow, their house was worth $732,000. Her public Facebook pictures showed her as quite content with husband Bob, her three kids, and two Golden Retrievers. They had an RV and traveled all over the country. Lots of happy family snapshots in the best touristy locations.

He was debating reaching out again to Joan Hendrickson.

There were eight remaining subjects. He had a spreadsheet with the names, locations, family and friends, and a miscellaneous, which is where he included things like what they were interested in, financial status or criminal histories, if they had any. Three of the subjects did not have anything listed in Spokeo or Been Verified. Either they'd opted out, or deliberately gone off the grid. Leaving seven possible people to contact, if he included Joan.

* * *

The phone rang and he grabbed it.

"Lisa?"

"I got mainly good news," she said. She was talking softly, her voice had an odd echoey quality. "I'll get the bad news out of the way first. Of the 14 names, there's three I can't find. I'm guessing they're like you and covered their tracks. I'll keep at it but I ain't optimistic. They've got common names. You know how many Tina Browns there are? Plus the marital name changes."

"Don't worry about it," Tom said. "There's 11 left. That's more than enough."

"That's the other bad news. Six of those 11 are dead. Which is higher than you'd expect based on actuarial data. American men typically live to about 80, women a few years more. None of these folks made it past 70. They ain't dying in the prime of life, but still. I looked into all of the deceased and there were none reported as a homicide. Two suicides which is statistically high, one fatal car accident. Which again is unusual with all the safety gear in cars nowadays. Two died of complications of AIDS in the nineties. The others all seemed to be pretty natural causes."

"No indications of foul play?"

"Nothing jumps out. It's possible that people lived edgier lives," she speculated. "More health risks of all sorts. Smoke and drink, Hep C, drive without seat belts, get more dangerous jobs."

"Possible."

"There seemed to be a disproportionate number of gay or lesbian subjects," she said.

"That makes sense," Lord said.

"You saying they are more sensitive or something?"

"No. It was more about family attitude at the time. Sexual minority kids would be rejected by their families. By the time Kroll had the place in upstate New York going, he was looking for people on the fringes. Runaways or older people without families or connections. The last thing he would've needed was to be holding some Senator's son against his will. I was one of the few who wasn't marginalized."

"Makes sense as far as the deaths," she said. "Like you said about yourself, it's not in Kroll's interest to see you dead."

"Yes and no. I was his star subject. Lots of others turned out to not have statistically significant ability. He kept some who he had hopes for around for a while. Others he kept around as controls. He still wants me for testing. Probably three quarters of the others would be more of a nuisance to him. Any articles on others going public?"

"Nada. But I'll keep digging." She rattled off names of the deceased, which included the two he had researched. He told her about Joan Hendrickson. She verified what he had learned, but added that Joan was now a devout Methodist, had a hobby of scrapbooking, and might be having an affair with a guy named Rick. He didn't ask her how she knew.

"I need to go to bed," she said. "Got to be up for work at the crack of dawn tomorrow. But I had to let you know. I'll send the report before I hit the hay."

"Diana was right. You know your stuff. Just keep being careful."

"Why do you think I'm calling you from the bathroom?"

"I'm glad to hear that. It only takes one slip."

"I've cleared my browsing history, done stuff through TOR and new email addresses. I could've done a lot of this much quicker at work. But I didn't."

"I'm really glad you're taking precautions. Do you finally believe what I've told you?"

"I do. That delivery guy I told you about. He showed up at the New Seasons where I shop. Said it was a coincidence, kept pushing to go out. I took his number, told him I'd call. But there's something wrong about him. I know what's normal horny and what's creepy. Maybe he's just a random serial killer type." She chuckled. Tom didn't.

"You should check into a motel. I'll give you a clean credit card number."

"No way am I running. That's the way you handle your shit. Not me."

"Please, Lisa..."

"Don't waste your breath. I'm sleeping in my own bed. With my gun handy. I got an alarm put in. Particularly after I found the bugs in my apartment."

"What?" Lord tried not to gasp.

"In the smoke detectors."

"You should've told me that first thing."

"I know what you're going to say. That's why I'm talking quietly and calling from the toilet. I went over the bathroom carefully and didn't find anything."

"What else did you do?" he asked, squeezing the phone so hard his knuckles were turning white.

"I left the bugs in place."

"But they probably heard you poking around."

"I made like I was cleaning up. Ran a vacuum first. I kept it running for background noise when I climbed up and fiddled with the detector."

"Is the silver van still parked across the street?"

He heard her getting up.

"Don't go to the window!"

After a pause she returned to the phone. "Don't worry, the room is dark. I didn't bring the bright cell screen with me," she whispered. "If there's someone in the street they can't see me. I know some about taking care of myself." She was quiet for a few moments. "No silver van." She was talking softly with the echo sound. He presumed she was back in the bathroom. "There's a big black SUV parked a few houses up. Facing away from my place. I first saw it a couple nights ago. At first, seemed like probably a neighbor just has a new car. But I think there's someone in it. The windows are tinted. But they could be eyeballing my place in their mirror."

"Can you slip out the back again, get a cab, go to a motel?"

"Like I said, I'm not running. It could be nothing anyway."

"They've clearly made you a top priority. You're not safe."

"I'm going to get off and send you the info."

"Lisa, wait please..."

But she had disconnected.

Diana had heard Tom's side of the conversation and he filled in the details.

"Can you talk with her, convince her to hide out somewhere at least for a few days?"

"She prides herself on not taking shit from anyone," Diana said.

"But if she keeps–"

"I can try talking to her but don't get your hopes up. The harder we push, the more she's going to say no."

She called but Moreau didn't pick up. "She probably went to bed, like she said she was."

"You don't believe she's in danger?" he asked.

"Sounds like she's being careful."

"These people are professionals. No amateur is going to beat them in the long run."

"What about you?"

"I'm not confident Kroll won't win in the end."

"See, that's why you are always running, afraid to fight back."

"Now isn't the time for this discussion. I need you to do everything you can to get her to go into hiding. Even stop the searching."

She saw how serious he was. She sighed and sent Lisa a text. "Call me. 911."

After 15 minutes there was still no response.

"She must've gone to sleep," Wynne said, a hint of tension in her voice. "We should too."

"In a bit."

She gave him a kiss. They hugged. More evidence of the relationship's deepening. They could disagree without her getting sarcastic and his withdrawing.

He sat in a chair, the phone next to him, playing with coins. His hands weren't as nimble as they had been before Hawaii. But he still could do the basics smoothly. He stared at the phone as if his gaze could make it ring.

After about an hour, Diana came out of the bedroom. "You planning on coming to bed?"

"In a bit."

"You said that a half hour ago." She sat next to him. "You're really worried about her?"

He nodded. She leaned over and hugged him. "Babe, me too. Maybe your paranoia is rubbing off on me. I think we have to stop by. Or would that create more problems?"

"The physical surveillance probably stops when they see the lights go out. But the bugs are still in place. If we ring the doorbell in the middle of the night, they'll know. Even if you held up a 'don't say anything' sign."

"I have the key."

"Not with her having a gun and being on edge. It would be doubly tragic if she shot you."

They sat on the couch and both looked at the phone.

"Maybe if we went there and parked," he suggested. "Keep watch on her house. We can follow her to work tomorrow morning, maybe get her to pull over and you talk with her."

"Sounds like a plan," she said.

"Not a good one, but maybe we'll think of something better on the way over."

Chapter Twenty-Two

Moreau's home was only a couple miles from the safe house. A quiet residential street, a couple blocks north of Beaverton-Hillsdale highway. As the rain started, he had to adjust the windshield wipers from intermittent, to regular, to rapid.

"Okay, once we get to her block, we find a parking space and sit tight. Any traffic this time of night will cause attention," he said.

"Agreed."

"If we see the light is still on in her place, text her we're outside. Tell her to meet us where we last met in a half hour. Slip out as quietly as possible."

"Got it."

They heard sirens as they got closer.

From a half dozen blocks away they could see the flash of red and blue lights. Bright colors reflected off dark, slick pavement.

A police car blocked Moreau's street. Yellow "Crime Scene" tape was strung across the fence to her house. A half dozen official-looking men and women stood in front of the building. They huddled under the wide eave and sought shelter from the rain under the striped metal awning over the porch. Forensic techs and detectives chatting, just another night's work. The couple saw the flash of a camera inside the house. Grim lightening.

They parked and Diana started to get out of the car.

He grabbed her arm. "No. We can't go any closer."

"We have to find out what happened," she insisted, her voice quivering.

"There's nothing we can do now. Kroll's people are probably watching."

"I've got to know if she's okay. I don't see an ambulance."

As if to answer her, the white Multnomah County Medical Examiner van, with caduceus in a circular blue field on the side, drove up. The police car blocking the street moved momentarily out of the way. The medical examiner's van parked in front of Moreau's house.

She stared blankly.

"We've got to move. You okay to drive?" he asked, getting out of the car and getting into the passenger seat after she nodded.

"Where to?"

"Any direction but toward where we're staying."

She looked at him quizzically but headed north. The safe house was to the east.

He took out a phone, looked up KGW news, scanned the website for staff names, then typed *67 and called the Portland Police Bureau main number. "Hi, this is Mike Winters, KGW news team 8 assignment editor," he said. "We're getting a lot of calls about a major police response in Raleigh Hills. I'm getting ready to dispatch a crew."

"Hold on please," the operator said.

"Sgt. Washington, central division. Who am I speaking with?"

Tom repeated his bogus intro.

"I don't believe I've worked with you before," he responded.

"That's right, sergeant. I'm new here," Tom said cheerily. "I'd been working for CBS in the Tri-cities area." Lord sounded casual, confident, maybe even a little bored.

"So what can you tell me about what's going on? Should I be sending a crew out? Hate to get the crews soggy in this rain."

"I can give you the blotter information. Our officers responded a half hour ago to multiple shots fired. They found a female dead at the scene. The apparent resident of the house. Her name will not be released pending notification of next of kin."

"Any suspects?"

"We are exploring multiple possibilities," he said. "We'll be putting information out soon. You need to speak with our PIO for any additional details. What did you say your name was?"

Lord ended the call. He felt sick.

He was using a dime to pry the back off to take out the battery when the phone rang. He had already gotten a couple of spam calls on it. But when he looked at the number, the last four digits were the same as the street address of the facility Kroll had run in upstate New York.

He pressed the green answer button. "Yes?'

"Thomas, how are you?" Kroll's deep, controlled voice.

Tom's throat tightened. "What do you want?"

"You know what I want. For all these years. The best for you."

"Bullshit."

"No need for vulgarities."

"You want the best for you," Lord told him.

"For both of us," Kroll said. "And for humanity as well."

"Is that him? Kroll?" Diana asked. Before Tom could respond, she snarled, "I'm gonna see you dead, you fucking bastard!"

"I presume that is Ms. Wynne," Kroll said through the phone. "Quite a formidable scrapper, I've heard."

"Did you kill her?" Diana demanded, trying to grab the phone. Tom held on to it and waved for Diana to stop.

"Not me," Kroll responded. "I understand Ms. Moreau brought it on herself. My associates just wanted to question her. She pulled a gun. Severely injured two of them, I might add."

"You're blaming her?" Diana shouted. "She should've let you fuckheads torture her again?"

"My concern is ultimately the greatest good for the greatest number," Kroll said calmly. "But this isn't the time to debate morality. It would be most helpful if you would come in and-"

"I hope they die! I hope you all die!" Diana yelled.

She blew through a stop sign. A car swerved to avoid them, the driver leaning on his horn. She skidded on the wet asphalt but regained control before she hit anything.

"Careful there," Kroll cautioned, hearing the horn and squealing tires. "You've got precious cargo."

"Why are you calling?" Tom asked.

"I'm asking you to work with me again. I can set you up in a nice place. There are so many intriguing issues to explore. Like the impact of aging on your ability. Do you believe you are better or worse than when you were young?"

"I'm not interested."

"Shall we get together and talk? Before there's any more collateral damage. If you care about Ms. Wynne, you'll meet with me."

"Fuck you!" Diana yelled. In the tight confines of the car, her shout was painful. Her rage was like a force of nature, like standing in a field with lightning striking a few feet away.

Tom said flatly, "I'll think about it."

"Decide quickly. I've been patient for a long time."

Lord disconnected the call. "Pull over," he told Diana.

"Are you going to meet with him?" The emotion she'd been displaying just moments before seemed compartmentalized, her tone stoic now.

"No. I just wanted to buy us time. Though I doubt me pretending to consider his offer will really delay him."

Tom pried open the back of the phone, removing the battery and the SIM card. He tossed the phone, the battery and the SIM card all a few blocks apart.

"Let's go to the house."

She nodded and began driving.

"They'll draw a line from Lisa's house to where the phone was last pinged," he said. "It's going to take at least a few minutes to triangulate the cell phone towers and pinpoint us."

"I get it." She stared ahead at the road.

"I'm sorry about Lisa."

After a long silence, she murmured, "She died a warrior's death. She would rather die fighting than go on the run…and probably die anyway. You're absolutely not planning on surrendering, are you? Her death can't be for nothing."

"I'm not. At this point, I'm afraid you know too much. I still have a value to him. If I were to disappear, he'd want you to disappear too."

Chapter Twenty-Three

Klimke had done a thorough site-sensitive exploitation search of Moreau's home, forwarding all the cyber material to Lloyd Cutler for dissection. The mercenary had checked out the burner phone, providing the information to Kroll and allowing him to make the call to Lord.

"She took good basic precautions," Cutler had said after going over the hard drive that he had accessed remotely. "She used AxCrypt but made a few telling mistakes. There's definitely been search activity. The very fact she has worked so hard to conceal her footprint says something."

"What did she find?" Kroll asked, standing over Cutler's desk. The ex-NSA man peered at two large monitors barely a foot from his face. Both had black screens covered with letters and numbers, unintelligible to Kroll but seeming to have meaning for Cutler.

"I can't tell yet," Cutler said, tapping at one of the keyboards. "Klimke is overnighting us the laptop itself. I can pull more data off of that. The mole we planted at the domestic violence agency came up with a list of their properties and which are occupied."

"You found them?"

"I just received the list. It's encoded. I have one of my techs working on it."

"How long?"

"I gather it is not a very sophisticated encryption."

"Hurry him up."

"Doctor, it doesn't work that way. I have my best code breaker on it. She was with the NSA for 10 years. She's working as quickly as she can. We'll hear soon."

Kroll paced around the office. He caught himself and sighed. "A pity my conversation with Jeremy or Tom or whatever he's calling himself didn't go better. He's gotten more obstinate as he's gotten older. That Diana woman has been a bad influence," he said. "What's your hypothesis about what they are looking for?"

"Either specifics about you currently or the experiment he was part of."

"That's a no-brainer. For what purpose?"

"If it is you, he is looking for vulnerabilities, ways to counterattack."

"Obviously. And the experiment?"

"To contact others. Maybe try and get some investigative agency or reporter interested in the story."

"Turning any rocks over is not in the government's best interest."

"Sometimes a new administration likes to embarrass the old," Cutler suggested.

"Any scandal is not worth the possible blowback."

"Or New York State wanting to embarrass the federal government?"

"Possible but doubtful."

"There's always some reporter looking to make a reputation."

"With a questionable decades old story? ESP is seen as being as far out there as séances and UFOs," Kroll said. "He tried before and got laughed at."

"If I had to guess, I'd speculate that Lord is trying to identify other subjects and go public," Cutler repeated, trying to not sound impatient. Kroll's tension was contagious.

"They've all signed non-disclosure agreements and been compensated. Those that needed to be warned about consequences were silenced long ago. Besides, being linked to the project would be embarrassing for many."

"I'm just speculating," Cutler said. "What do you want me to do?"

"Get me more information," Kroll snapped and strode from the room.

Kroll was frustrated with Klimke and Cutler. The Russians were putting more pressure on him. He had sensed a shift from Moscow, less enthusiasm. Constantly reminding him that he was going over budget and producing no results, just near misses. They would not authorize the resources to look into multiple people in multiple states.

Moreau, with Lord's encouragement, had been up to something. Could it be trying to find connections between Kroll to the Russians? Small-minded people could not appreciate the sacrifice he was making to move parapsychology forward. Tolerating the arrogance and mistreatment by the Russians. Wasting his time on a manhunt instead of publishing papers.

Genevieve had been made his contact. He recognized that she was his handler, periodically meeting for updates. Her mission seemed to be to goad him and keep him in line. He did not know if she was a French woman who had been recruited by the Russians, or native Russian who spoke French and could pass easily as Parisian. It was clear she loathed him.

Their last meeting was in a Russian restaurant in Brighton Beach at the southern end of Brooklyn. They had met face to face once before in Montreal, another time in Italy. Always in a Russian neighborhood.

They had dined in a restaurant on Brighton Beach Avenue, where the subway screeched and screamed overhead every few minutes. When they entered, the puffed-up tuxedoed *maître d'* initially saw Kroll and told him, "We closed." Even though they were clearly open with other customers sitting and enjoying their borscht and vodka. Always vodka with the Russians.

Genevieve had fired off a burst of Russian that had rocked the *maître d'* back. He waved them in. They were seated and given attentive service. The waiter was a muscular Dolph Lundgren lookalike who flirted with her. He had asked in Russian what her relationship was with Kroll.

She told him the psychologist was her mildly demented uncle and she had taken him out from the nursing home where he lived to enjoy some fine Russian food.

After the appetizers, Kroll had said, in Russian, "You know I understood what you said?"

She popped a *pelmeni* dumpling in her mouth, licking her lips sensuously. Kroll knew he had as much of a chance of having sex with her now as he did with the Queen of England.

He had asked, "Was it necessary to say I was in a nursing home?"

"As good a story as any," she said with an unpleasant smile.

She had pulled similar embarrassing moves in the past. Usually referencing his feebleness to someone waiting on them and talking about adult diapers or his other alleged biological problems. The psychologist had contacted Grigory, requesting a new handler. Nothing changed. Keeping her in charge was part of their keeping him in his place. The Russians were not subtle.

She set her phone down on the table and tapped an app she had used in the past. The app activated a jamming device and recorded the conversation. He had previously asked if it broadcast their conversation in real time to Moscow. She had ignored his question, responding with a condescending smirk.

She had relayed word from Grigory that they were upset about his mounting expenses with lack of results.

"If you do not produce Mr. Lord within 30 days, project is over. You will refund all monies given you."

"What? There's no way I could come up with that without selling my house, my savings, my-"

"Not our problem," she said dismissively.

Kroll was aware he had used a similar strategy with the subjects in the studies at PRI. Most of them were judgment-proof with negligible assets. Fear of financial ruin had been just one of many ways he kept everyone in place. Fear of physical assault, revealing sexual peccadillos, drug use or other crimes. Even if the crimes had been set up.

She had reported that their man with Klimke felt the mercenary was doing a competent job but was being outmaneuvered by Lord and the girl. "Your soldier has good tactics. But you are the general, responsible for the strategies of the battle."

"I can't make field decisions for him."

"As I said, not our problem." She slid another dumpling into her mouth and made a "Mmmmmmn" sound as she licked her fingers, staring directly into Kroll's eyes. "Our people have checked out your assets. You will be able to cover costs and have a few thousand left over for basics. Very basics."

Lost in the unpleasant reverie, Kroll caught himself pacing in the hall outside Cutler's room. When Cutler's phone rang, the psychologist hurried in.

The computer expert was grinning as he made a note on a piece of paper. "Very good," Cutler said into the phone. He held up the paper, showing two addresses. "He's at one of these."

Chapter Twenty-Four

Kroll called Klimke and gave him the two addresses. "You must act swiftly."

"Understood." Klimke had expected the call. He'd had weapons delivered. Including four H & K 9mm semiautomatics that had been illegally modified for a screw-in silencer. He was field stripping and cleaning the weapons when he received the order. He had been out in a quarry near the coastal range test firing the weapons. H & Ks were as dependable as you could get. But he lived by the code of never trusting anyone else to pack your parachute. No weapon was guaranteed until he had personally stripped it down, inspected it, and fired 200 rounds through it.

"I can have a team ready within a half hour." Ramirez was on standby alert.

"Ivan needs to be with you," Kroll said.

Klimke wondered whose rule that was but knew better than to ask. The role of the Russians in Kroll's life was not to be discussed. In truth, Klimke had been favorably impressed with the big Russian, though he felt there was always a hidden agenda. Though that was the way he felt with most Russians. And most people.

"The rules of engagement are somewhat different," Kroll said. "The girl is a problem. Kill her unless it is necessary to use her to compel his cooperation. The rest of the plan is the same. Sedate and crate Lord and a plane will pick him up. You and Ivan will escort him back here. Further shipment will be handled on this end."

"Check," Klimke said, and ended the call. Klimke had, through the broker Tang, connected with another ex-military man, Roger Courtain. Courtain was an ex-SEAL who worked as a bank guard in downtown Portland and was eager for any job that offered more challenge and better pay. Shooing away intoxicated homeless people from the front of the bank provided most of his daily excitement. He looked forward to the very rare times when one of them would act up. He was 5'10" and slender, with about 10 percent body fat. But only someone out of touch with reality would be foolish enough to get aggressive with him.

Within a half hour, the four men were heading toward the address they had been given.

* * *

Moreau's reports were well-organized, clearly written, with just a little hint of the snark that she showed in every interaction:

*Ray "Shorty" McGuire, 66-year-old Caucasian male. A few arrests on misdemeanor charges, none in the past 30 years. Assault, disorderly conduct, drunk driving. GED diploma. Vietnam combat veteran with Purple Heart. Retired stunt man with multiple injuries, including more than a dozen fractures, dislocations, concussions and muscle tears. History of opiate addiction with no indications of current use.

Moreau had information about his bills and credit (barely getting by, credit not good with a FICO score of 485). He didn't post on any social media but posted to some of the more paranoid right-wing blogs. Worried about the Trilateral Commission revoking the 2nd Amendment.

He had lived in a half dozen locations, most recently on a 10-acre farm on the outskirts of Palmdale. His wife was deceased and he was estranged from his four children.

Lord had a vague recollection of him from PRI as being tough, standoffish. Older than most of the participants in the program, he was one of the few they were testing for psychokinesis.

*Hector Vasquez was 55 and lived in East Los Angeles. Now a Catholic priest with a storefront congregation, he had been convicted as a youth for arson, burning down the home he had been placed in after his mother died. His father was in prison. The conviction had been reversed but Moreau wasn't clear why. Obtaining details on a juvenile record was no simple feat. Vasquez had done prison time for armed robbery in his 20s. He had turned to religion and apparently been genuinely reformed. Moreau noted no hints of scandal. Well respected in the community. His Facebook page offered homilies, links to his web page that had sermons on it, as well as pictures of congregational activities.

Lord remembered him for having multiple homemade tattoos and being in the precognition program. They had chatted a few times, nothing very significant. Lord probed his mind once, not finding the meanness he expected. Mostly just sadness.

* * *

Klimke thought of all the things that were wrong with the mission as the big gray van with an Amazon logo on the side was parked a couple houses down from the address he'd been given. Too few men was his primary concern. Ideally he would have six for the raiding party, plus a driver. And there would have been time to scout the house for at least a day, getting a feel for the rhythms of the neighborhood. At least he had gotten a full set of supplies, anticipating the assault. Aside from the silenced weapons, he had a two-foot pry bar, flash bang and smoke grenades, a drug kit to sedate Lord, Tasers, handcuffs, small explosive charges for breaching, and a laundry cart. The cart would be used to transport Lord. Hardly inconspicuous but less obvious than over someone's shoulder.

He hoped he wouldn't have to do a forced entry as the noise would increase the chances of being observed. If they did go that route, all the men had balaclavas and a second set of clothing.

Klimke also had ordered a handheld infrared scope. The scope was military grade with five power zoom and high resolution. He played it across the building. Two warm bodies inside. One big, one small, in the kitchen. They looked like an eerie ghostly reddish-orange silhouette against a blue green background on the screen. Flares of red and orange came from what Klimke presumed was the stove.

The house was a single story with a low cyclone fence. A sign from an alarm company in the front yard. Neatly trimmed shrubbery. Security lights under the eaves was all that distinguished it from surrounding homes.

Klimke had timed the approach carefully. It was after 7:30 p.m., so those coming home from work should be indoors. More than two hours past sunset. The night would be chilly, which would keep random pedestrians to a minimum.

Ramirez used a slingshot to take out the streetlight.

They didn't see Wynne's vehicle. Running the plates on the cars parked near the house would have been a waste of precious minutes. Klimke presumed the couple were smart enough to park at least a block away.

Courtain was given an empty cardboard box, a light blue jacket and matching cap with an Amazon logo on it. He was an untested commodity but the only raider who Lord and Wynne hadn't seen. He would walk up the front steps and peer into the house. If he was able to confirm the target, he would raise his right hand. The other raiders would then swiftly approach the house. Klimke joining him at the front, Ramirez and Ivan at the back door. Ramirez also was responsible for the left side of the house, Klimke for the right if the couple tried to escape through a window. A few seconds exposure. Hopefully no one would be looking out their window, no nearby dog sounding the alarm, or dog owners deciding it would be a good time to take Fido for a stroll.

Courtain opened the gate and walked up to the front steps. Through the infrared scope, Klimke saw the larger figure come out of the kitchen and move toward the door. Picking an object up off the table. Holding it like a baseball bat. Not what Klimke expected—he presumed Wynne would be the more aggressive one.

There must have been a sensor on the gate, or an electric eye beam.

"Get ready," he said to Ivan and Ramirez. The ex-SEAL had his gun tucked into the small of his back. But there were strict orders to not shoot Lord.

The door swung open. A big woman stood there, bat at her side. She was at least six foot and had puffed up gray hair that made her look six inches taller.

"What is it?" she demanded.

"I've got a package for Christa Hines."

"Who?"

"Christa Hines."

"No one here by that name," the woman growled.

Courtain feigned looking perplexed, then read off the address.

"You're two blocks off," the big woman said.

"Oh, you're right. Sorry to disturb you."

Courtain walked to the van. The woman watched until he was back inside. She glared up and down the street then shut the door.

"Whew," Courtain said once inside the vehicle. "She reminded me of a CPO I had during Hell Week." He started the van.

"Would have been fun to see you try and take her down," Ivan said.

"Maybe for you," Courtain said. Ramirez and Ivan laughed in a release of tension.

Klimke just said, "Let's move out. We've lost time here. The sooner we get to the other house the better."

"ETA in 15 minutes," Courtain said after checking Waze.

* * *

Lord had his own impression of Joan Hendrickson. Moreau had confirmed what he had learned. She was a financially stable upright member of the community. But Moreau had speculated she was having an affair. He wished there was some way to ask her what she based that theory on. Of course, he wished that she was around for many reasons.

Diana sat next to him. Seething. Anger seeped out of her pores. It was like trying to focus while sitting next to a tiger. He wanted to comfort her. And run away.

He scrolled down to the two final subjects:

*Sean Sinclair was a disbarred attorney living in Chicago. Divorced twice, no children. Lived in a pricy part of the Windy City. Successful and sleazy, a high-priced fixer. That was consistent with the person Tom remembered. Sinclair supposedly was good at projecting thoughts more than receiving them. Kroll had had great hopes that his best transmitter and best receiver would have the best results. The times when they had been paired with him, they had done anything but connect. Kroll had tried forcing Sinclair and Lord to cooperate but telepathy was like love, or trying to fall asleep. The more you forced it, the less likely it was to happen. It was a sign of Lord's desperation that he was willing to approach the man.

*Chris Pruitt was in Rapid City South Dakota. Teaching science at the high school. Recognized multiple times as a teacher of the year, particularly for her physics classes. Two young adult children. Married 20 years, husband a reporter on the Rapid City Journal. Good FICO score, house in a prosperous neighborhood. The summary was stunning. Pruitt had been among the most unhappy people Lord had encountered. She would've fit better in a locked psych ward than at PRI. But reading about her change, Lord understood why.

Lord had been most impressed with Moreau's research and finding Chris. He had been unable to find her. But when she turned up in Moreau's report, it all made sense.

"We've got to do something," Wynne said.

"We are."

"Something active."

"You want to go for a run?"

"No. I want to get the bastards that killed her. I want to hurt them like I've never hurt anyone."

"The best thing we can do right now is finish up reading what she left us. I'm already getting some ideas."

"Like what?"

"Well, two of the subjects wound up in LA. Getting there is a couple days drive. Then maybe cross country to check on the other ones. Driving has the least chance of hitting Kroll's tripwires."

She nodded. "Going public isn't enough."

"Let's cross that bridge when we come to it. Can we finish reading?"

"You read. I'm too restless."

"I've got an idea."

"What?"

"Let me finish reading," he said, not wanting to be distracted. "Then I'll let you know."

* * *

On the short drive to the second house, Ramirez, Ivan and Courtain bantered, insulting each other's intelligence, looks, bravery, and sexual prowess. Klimke had seen the patter countless times before. There was a bond having faced a combat situation together that allowed insults that would have led to a bloody fistfight anywhere else. Ivan and Ramirez had been to battle together and Courtain was allowed to join them due to calm facing the baseball bat-toting woman.

Klimke's mind was elsewhere, thinking of what could go wrong. And countermeasures. The fact that Courtain had apparently tripped some sort of alarm at the other house made him presume the same protection would be in place here. Was it necessary to avoid it? Courtain was, after all, ostensibly just a delivery man with a package. Though it was getting late for any legitimate delivery.

Klimke took the cardboard box and cut a nickel-sized small hole in the front, and a fist-sized hole on the bottom.

"What you doing?" Ivan asked.

To answer, Klimke put his hand through the hole in the bottom, then used the other hand to pass over the Taser. He rested the front of the weapon against the hole.

"Nice," Courtain said.

"Put the H & K inside the box," Klimke instructed. "If the man answers, Taser him. Grab the gun immediately. Be prepared for the woman. Have you ever shot a woman?"

"Yes. Teenager. She had a bomb vest on," Courtain said unemotionally. "I detonated her from 100 yards."

Klimke nodded. "Think of this woman as having a bomb vest on."

"He ain't exaggerating," Ramirez chimed in. "She disabled one member of our raiding team, put an arrow in the balls of a tracker."

"You not mentioning her kicking the *kakat'sya* out of you," Ivan added.

Ramirez gave him a nasty look. "She's one of the best hand-to-hand fighters I've ever met. If she had another couple inches and ten pounds, I don't know how our fight would've turned out." Ramirez thought about Amanda, wondered how she was doing. His mood worsened.

"She very cute," Ivan said. "Not like Al's girlfriend back at last house. Makes it harder to..." Ivan used his right hand to mimic shooting someone. "She's pretty enough to be St. Petersburg girl."

"Pretty like a cobra," Ramirez said to Ivan. "I wish you'd gone head-to-head with her. See what it's like."

"I go head-to-head with her maybe she not be so quick to fight." Ivan patted his groin.

"Gentlemen, we arrive in five minutes. Everyone clear on your roles?"

Nods all around.

"Just to be clear, minimal force with him. Take her out quickly. If we can get in and out under five minutes, we'll be in good shape."

* * *

Cutler's main computer pinged. A special sound rarely heard. His hands played across the keyboard like a virtuoso pianist. He called Kroll.

"Sherman, or Lord, or whatever he's calling himself made a mistake. He used an old identity to charge an inquiry. Then a couple of plane tickets."

"What was he researching?"

"You. That's why he hit my tripwire. Plus I had an alert for the old name."

"Why would he use an old name?"

"He's probably running out of identities. This one has been dormant long enough that he thinks it's safe."

"Where's he headed?"

"Chicago. Should we pull Klimke back?"

"No. Maybe they can get them at the house. Procurement will be harder at the airport. But we're in a better position than we've been in years." Kroll wondered why Chicago. He had approached Rush University and University of Chicago about parapsychology research. There had been several meetings but nothing had come of it. Was there something in those contacts that Lord was focusing on?

* * *

Klimke and his team parked a few residences up from the second safe house. It looked strikingly similar to the other home. Klimke wondered if it was the same developer, or just a cookie cutter pattern that had been popular in the 1960s.

He took out the infrared scope and studied the house.

No signs of activity.

"Shit!" he muttered.

"What?" Ivan asked.

Klimke instructed Courtain to deliver the package. But the men knew even before he rang the bell and got no answer that the couple was gone.

Chapter Twenty-Five

Klimke was at the wheel, driving a steady nine miles over the speed limit on the freeways as they raced across town. Lord's flight was due to take off in 90 minutes. He assumed the couple was taking a car and not mass transit, meaning they would get out in a parking garage. Which one? Since they were being rushed, most likely the short-term lot nearest the terminal. Would they dare to just abandon the car at the curb?

Cutler had given them the particulars. "Alan Wilson" was flying to Chicago on Alaska Airlines. Gate D2.

Klimke had them stop at the Target near the airport. He bought two carry on-sized duffel bags, four ball caps, and three pairs of lightly tinted sunglasses. He bought a shirt, shoes, pants underwear in his size and had Courtain do the same. Ivan was behind the wheel as they drove the short distance to the airport. Klimke and Courtain cut tags off the freshly purchased clothing. On the X-ray machine, only the shapes, not that they were all unworn, would show up. He quickly packed the duffel bag after giving the men the caps and sunglasses. He had his own special glasses, provided by Cutler that would scramble any facial recognition software. The sunglasses and caps would make it a little harder to identify his operators. Klimke knew that airports were infested with overt and covert video surveillance equipment and they probably would be identified. That was a problem to be dealt with later.

His team had small radios with flesh-colored earpieces and wrist mikes. Ramirez and Ivan would be waiting outside the metal detectors and could carry guns.

As they pulled onto NE Airport Way, Klimke told the men, "If we assume they are together, we need at least two to get them. If you need to show a gun, do it cautiously. If there's resistance, sedate one, loudly say you're a doctor, say the other one is in shock, announce there's an emergency infirmary by the garage that you're taking them to. Let us know ASAP so we can swarm them. We'll have the van at the curb. If they've split up, get the shot into him, announce that your friend always gets nervous before flights, drank too much. Watch out for her.

"I'll always be near a fire alarm. If things go to shit, I'll set it off. If I'm involved in taking them down, any of you can do the same. Or we'll set down one of the duffels and call in a bomb threat. Know that you will be picked up on closed circuit TV. And there's undercover air marshals all over the place besides TSA."

The plan was rotten. An excellent chance of getting swept up by airport security. They were too far along to give up.

Klimke and Courtain hurried to the Alaska counter and bought tickets on the flight to Chicago. Ridiculously expensive last-minute tickets. Klimke had a fake ID but Courtain had to use his real driver's license. They needed the boarding pass to get through the security line. If the couple boarded the plane, it would be the last chance to get them. Klimke hadn't yet figured out how.

Klimke and Courtain separated so that if one was caught, the other still could make it through. They were lucky in that the security lines were low. Klimke had his ceramic knife strapped to his leg. He had a white armband in his pocket with a Red Cross on it. He had a blue armband that said, "Security" but figured that would be a risky cover at the airport.

The TSA agent by the scanner whispered something to the agent next to her and Klimke was diverted to the side.

Klimke maintained his polite smile as the stern agent studied him and said, "There are no toiletries in your bag, sir. Can you explain?"

The mercenary allowed a sad expression to creep across his face. "I realized that when I got to the airport." He flashed an embarrassed smile. "I had just gotten a call about my aunt. She probably won't make it through the night. I rushed out without thinking."

The agent studied Klimke, allowing his intimidating stare to linger on the mercenary. Klimke had been glared at by AK-toting, drug-addled teen soldiers at middle of nowhere checkpoints in war-torn countries. His body language remained relaxed; his pulse rate didn't increase by a single beat.

The TSA agent gave a dismissive wave and said, "Good luck with your aunt."

"Thank you," Klimke said, taking his bag and hurrying off.

Courtain, who had drawn a less zealous TSA scanner, took a position lounging on a seat near gate D2. The hope was that Ivan and Ramirez would spot the pair in the garage and be able to intercept. They had radios to notify Klimke and Courtain. But if the couple made it by Ivan and Ramirez, whether coming in a different way or by force, Klimke would hopefully catch them as they made their way to the terminal. Courtain, the only one they hadn't seen, would be the backstop. The plan was sloppy but Klimke was gambling on the fact that airport security was designed for keeping malefactors from getting past security and approaching the airplanes more than keeping malefactors from going the other way.

"See anything?" Klimke said into his wrist mic, inside the terminal. He was talking to Ramirez, positioned near the van in the garage.

"There's a couple coming. Possible."

After a minute, Ramirez said, "Not them. No other probables currently in view."

"Watcher two?" Klimke asked.

"*Nyet*," Ivan said.

"Keep an eye on the stairwells as much as the elevator. Maybe even more so. They've got to be on the alert."

"This not my first roadshow," Ivan said.

"Roadshow?" Klimke asked, figuring the radio had distorted Ivan's words.

"Roadshow. Like with broncos."

"That's rodeo."

"That what I meant," Ivan said.

"Just stay alert," Klimke said and clicked off.

Klimke positioned himself between the TSA screening point and gate D2. There was enough general activity and varieties of individuals that he hoped he and his men didn't stand out.

He scanned faces, looking for Lord or Wynne. A few times there were false positives, duos of roughly the same size and shape. He assumed Lord and Wynne had changed the easier aspects of their appearance, like hair.

"Will Alaska passenger Alan Wilson please go to a white courtesy phone," the mellow woman's voice announced through the overhead speakers.

"Did you hear that?" Klimke said, turning away from the security checkpoint and speaking into his wrist mic. He did not want to call any extra attention to himself.

"Roger that," Courtain said.

"I'll watch the phones by the odd numbered gates, you watch the even numbers," Klimke said.

"Will do," Courtain said.

Klimke saw Courtain get up slowly. Very professional. No sudden moves unless absolutely necessary.

"What is going on?" Ivan asked through the radio.

"The name our target is using was just paged."

"Should we come in?" Ramirez asked.

"No. Stay put. This guy is the king of distractions. You'd have to buy tickets first anyway."

A few minutes passed with Klimke and Courtain on hyper-alert. No one looking anything like Lord or Wynne approached the white phones mounted on the walls near the gate.

After 20 minutes, when the page had been repeated twice, Klimke walked to a phone and picked it up. "Hello?"

"Who's this?"

"Alan," Klimke said.

"Not very convincing, Klimke," Lord said.

"What's going on Tom?"

"I just wanted to say hi."

"Time to stop playing around. Turn yourself in. Then we leave the girl alone."

"If she heard you call her a girl, she'd be quite annoyed."

"Where are you?"

"Not at the airport, I suspect you've realized." Tom took a deep breath. "If you get Kroll to back off, I will go quiet. Diana and I have split up. I don't want her in jeopardy. She was too much of a loose cannon. I can promise that I won't give the good doctor a hard time."

"I can relay word. Though it would be better if you would tell him yourself. Face to face."

"Frankly, I'd rather stick my dick in a hornet's nest."

"That's a firm no?"

"You're very perceptive. Let Eddie know I'm going to lose myself. Leaning toward Los Angeles but maybe San Francisco. Take care now."

The connection ended.

There was a part of Klimke that was glad the operation had failed. A snatch of two people at the airport was more than high-risk. Klimke knew he was a more skillful soldier than covert operator. He had learned enough of the murky skills of civilian special ops. Surveillance, evading laws, using extreme levels of force if necessary. It was better than running high risk operations with ill-trained troops in germ-infested developing nations. But first and foremost, he was a soldier. Which meant following orders.

He radioed his team and headed with Courtain toward the parking garage,

His cell phone vibrated, the third time in the past half hour. The same New Jersey number came up. Kroll, wanting an update.

This time he picked up and told the psychologist what had happened.

There was a long silence. "What do you think?"

"He probably was lying about everything other than not being at the airport."

More silence.

"I'll be in touch." Kroll hung up more abruptly than Lord.

"We stand down," Klimke said to his team.

* * *

"Why'd you tell him we were going to Los Angeles?" Diana demanded.

They were back on the road after stopping in a Walmart by Eugene. They had bought a bunch of snacks and a radar detector. The snacks were for both of them, the radar detector was mainly for her. She did not respond well to his requests to slow down. He hoped their fake ID would hold up if they got caught in a speed trap.

"It's a double reverse. They assume I'm lying, so I tell them the truth."

Diana looked skeptical.

"Trust me, I know the way Kroll thinks. If it seems too simple, he'll look for complications to find."

"What about the stuff about us separating?"

"That was pure bullshit."

"And me being a loose cannon?"

"Should we stop in Medford?" he asked.

Wynne cocked her head.

"How about just a cannon?" he asked.

"Hmmmph."

He turned on the radio. Tom Petty's nasal twang came through the speakers, telling the world how he won't back down. Lord turned up the volume and began to sing. After a few choruses repeating how he was going to stand his ground, Wynne seemed to soften.

"It's a good thing you didn't try to include singing in your stage act," she said, with the barest hint of a smile. Her first in days. "You want me to take a turn at the wheel?"

"Nah. I'm good. Why don't you get some sleep." He shut the radio.

"I keep thinking about Lisa, about our time together," Diana said. "She was a special person."

"She was. You want to talk about it?"

"Not now." Diana took a jacket out of the back and rested it against the window. The freeway was smooth beneath the tires. Within a few minutes she was asleep.

He was sad about Moreau's death. She had paid the ultimate price for her curiosity and well-intentioned concern for Diana. He forgave Lisa but complex conflicting thoughts and emotions swirled as the miles passed. He felt anger at her actions, guilt over the outcome, and sadness for the loss of a life, particularly someone who meant so much to Diana.

He envied the way Diana slid effortlessly into sleep. A knack he never had. But he made the insomnia work for them. They passed Roseburg, then Grants Pass, and Medford. The tank was near empty when they stopped at a gas station near Ashland. He convinced Diana to stay low in the car. He kept the cap pulled down on his head to avoid the inevitable security cameras. The clerk, who had been watching a video on his phone when they pulled in, made it clear by his terseness that he was annoyed at the interruption.

Tom paid for the gas and bought a couple of Red Bulls and a few energy bars. He used the painfully foul bathroom. When Diana said she wanted to go, he encouraged her to hold out for the next rest area. The clerk would pay more attention to an attractive woman getting out of the car. Or maybe not. It probably didn't matter. Tom wanted to leave as few footprints as possible.

He knew Diana often saw him as paranoid and maybe he was a bit excessive at times. It led to a few squabbles. Like when she suggested connecting her phone to the car via Bluetooth so they could listen to music.

"Really?" he'd snapped. "Haven't you listened to anything I've said? Why don't you just send Kroll your cell phone with all the information on it?"

She'd responded with silence and after about fifteen minutes, he'd said, "Sorry. My response on the Bluetooth was a bit over the top. I'm a bit overtired. And tense."

She reached over and squeezed his thigh. "Apology accepted. You've got a right to be tense."

He fought back tears of joy and gratitude. Whew, this fatigue was making all his emotions too near the top.

They stopped in the Siskiyou rest area a couple miles south of town. There were three trucks and a few cars parked. While Diana used the facilities, he swigged a Red Bull and ate two energy bars. Diana had an energy bar. She offered to take the wheel but he told her he was good to go. He doubted he could sleep.

Back on the freeway, she quickly dozed off.

As he drove on, the caffeine battling the fatigue, he deliberately fidgeted to reduce the hypnotic sedation of the road. He didn't want to disturb her with his usual strategies of blasting fresh air on his face or cranking up the radio. He took pleasure in glancing over and watching her sleep, proud that she seemed to be trusting him more.

Singing to the radio reminded him of being in Diana's house, when the two of them had sang and danced, with no idea of what was to come. Barely a month ago.

He knew one other way to ensure he would stay awake. He allowed himself to go back into his memories of intense times with Dr. Kroll.

Chapter Twenty-Six

Upstate New York
June 1993

The area south of Rochester was hit hard by the recession. Kodak was in sharp decline, staggering toward bankruptcy.

The Boys and Girls County Home Orphanage had been progressive when opened in 1920. Children from all over Upstate New York were referred. Some had been orphaned, many were just too much for their parents to handle. Over the decades it had deteriorated into a sprawling disgrace. By the 1970s, the shuttered institution was known best as a place where teens would covertly get drunk and homeless people would find squalid shelter from the cold winters.

Unemployment was a sensitive issue, so when Dr. Edward Kroll told politicians he would be buying the long-abandoned building and hiring about thirty local people--with the possibility of later expanding his operation--he received a tax break and a royal welcome.

A few area residents were suspicious, with rumors the site was going to be a germ warfare facility. But most were thrilled, particularly if a family member got a job there.

Kroll engineered a multi-million-dollar renovation. Due to the collapse of the Soviet Union a year earlier, the Defense Intelligence Agency had generous amounts of black funds, covert cash that needed to be spent. The facility, renamed the Psychological Research Institute (PRI), opened without fanfare in June 1992.

About one quarter of the main building looked like a small hospital, with an infirmary, exam rooms, an EEG machine, an MRI suite, and a lab for weekly blood workups.

Aside from monitoring brain function, the psychologist tracked data on blood counts, organ function, hormones, neuropeptides, and inflammatory marker levels. All the small, sparsely furnished "treatment rooms" had one-way mirrors.

The rest looked like a small college, without classrooms. There was a gym, a rec room with big screen TV, and a cafeteria. A few outlier buildings included a garage for service vehicles, the separate security office, and a dedicated building that housed the MRI machine. There were magnetic field warning signs 25 feet out from the structure.

The doors to the ninety-square-foot private dorm rooms locked from the outside. Security was handled by a team brought in from out of the area. The force, armed with shotguns, patrolled the grounds. High-tech motion detector electronics bolstered the ribbon wire-topped cyclone fence around the building. The few neighbors—no one lived closer than a quarter mile away—complained that it was just one guard tower away from looking fully like a prison.

The jobs paid well above local wages. Everyone, from initial construction workers to maintenance staff to techs, was sworn to secrecy with non-disclosure contracts stressing that any disclosure could be a breach of national security, punishable by both jail and substantial fines. All that leaked out was that federal government work was being done there.

The teen who would one day be Tom Lord, but then went by his given name of Jeremy Sherman, was the star pupil. He spent close to a year there, far longer than any other subject. Of the 15 dorm rooms, no more than 11 were ever filled long term in his time at PRI.

His favorite experiment was the *ganzfeld* where he was put in a large, shielded room with a recliner and an EEG machine. A tech squirted goop on his head and put a red bathing cap-like thing on. It had more than 100 wires coming out of it. Then she gently taped spheres, like half a ping pong ball, over his eyes.

He was told to just say whatever came into his head. Free associating. It went on for a half hour. For ten minutes of that time another tech in a nearby room was looking at a randomly chosen ViewMaster reel and focusing on a randomly chosen image on that reel. Subjects ranged from a scenic tourist spot like the Taj Mahal, to a classic TV show like *The Munsters*, to historic scenes of Plains Indians killing a buffalo.

After Lord's free associating, he would go through three reels, essentially 21 pictures, and see if there were any that he felt had been transmitted to him. He wasn't told results but could sense the enthusiasm.

There were groups of young men who rotated in for short stays. Based on their age, their close- to-the-scalp haircuts, their excellent physical shape, and their tendency to answer questions with a "Yes, sir" or "No, sir" everyone presumed they were military. No other participants questioned them and they didn't volunteer information. Instead of name, rank and serial number they would give name, where they were from, and a superficial interest when engaged in conversation. "I'm George from Boston. You like the Patriots? They're good but I love the Red Sox," as if working off a shared script. The deepest they were willing to go would be to comment on the weather. "Yeah, it's cold but we get much worse in Boston." After a month to six-week rotation, the presumed military men would be gone.

A primary hope for the Defense Intelligence Agency was that the subjects, who had been drawn from all branches of the armed services, would be able to be trained to use psychic powers. They had been screened and found to meet basic criteria. In interviews, some had reported unusual ways of knowing.

Civilian subjects could leave whenever they wanted. But Kroll had ways to persuade those he wanted to stay.

* * *

Jeremy had a crush on Belinda, the relentlessly perky blonde who would prep him for many of the tests. He learned small details about her—she was 19, just broke up with her boyfriend, lived with her parents and two siblings in a crowded house in nearby Henrietta. A high school graduate who hoped to go to community college and become a nurse. She was full-figured and accidentally brushed against him quite often. When she leaned in close with her top open a couple of buttons, Sherman saw enough of her that the memories lingered when he was alone in his room at night.

One evening, as she was about to leave, she asked if he'd like to meet after work in the woods behind the garage. There were a few picnic tables and a barbecue pit. Jeremy, who would one day be Tom, quickly agreed.

"But you could get in trouble," he said, knowing that there were rules against "fraternization between staff and subjects." In limited conversations with other subjects, Jeremy had learned that several of them came through the foster care system or juvenile justice. They were not averse to breaking rules. Thus the doors that locked from the outside and heavy security force. To keep them in line as well as keep nosy intruders away.

A freelance reporter had snuck in. Word was that he had been roughed up by security, his camera broken. Lawyers had warned the newspaper he worked for that trespassers would be aggressively prosecuted and could even be shot. No one else had ever breached the perimeter. Word had spread through the gossip grapevine which was as strong within PRI as within any institution. Which meant that it was as quick and pervasive as the internet would soon be.

Jeremy had a rigorous schedule at PRI. The day Belinda approached him had been particularly grueling. Hours spent doing mental exercises, from mindfulness to problem-solving, coupled with being paired up with those believed to be good senders and those who were "normals." Then there would be extensive debriefings, where he'd have to describe his thought processes in detail. He thought of it as describing the indescribable. But Kroll and his assistants were relentless.

The thought of what might happen with Belinda in the woods seemed like a fantasy come true. He half-believed she wouldn't show up. When she did, with a six pack of Genesee, he struggled to not reach for her immediately.

She had a backpack with the beers and handed him a brew. They polished off one and started in on a second. Jeremy was not a big drinker—no alcohol was allowed for subjects—and he started feeling woozy. Strangely so. Colors were brighter. And simultaneously darker. Noises louder, smells more intense. The beer tasted more beery. His sense of touch had him feeling the fabric rubbing against his skin.

Then her hand was resting on his thigh. Other senses lost their power. She was telling him about how much she enjoyed working with him. But there was a noise in the background, the sound he associated with danger.

Her hand was higher on his thigh. The danger warning blurred. He swayed. They were next to each other on a picnic bench. He leaned in and began running his hands over her back, her butt. They kissed. Tongues dancing, probing. Gently nibbling her ear, nuzzling her neck. He clumsily unhooked her bra and his hands went under her blouse.

Her hands had run over his groin, then unzipped him. She was stroking him the way he rubbed her, gently, roughly, gently, roughly.

"Hey! What's going on over there?" One of the security guards was fast approaching. Henry was broad-shouldered, thick-necked, scowling. Ten years out of the Marines but he had kept his close-cropped haircut.

"I didn't want to," Belinda said, seeming to be fighting back tears.

"What?" Jeremy yelped.

"He was forcing me to do it," she said.

"That's not-" Jeremy began.

"Shut up, you pervert!" Henry said. He closed the distance quickly and swung his big hand, slapping Jeremy's face.

"Wait, wait, this isn't-"

Henry swung again. Jeremy knew what he was going to do and dodged the blow. Henry went to cuff his face again. Jeremy dodged it. Henry tried to punch him in the gut. Jeremy anticipated and moved away. The scuffle went on for several minutes, with Jeremy dodging and Henry getting more and more aggressive. And tired. But then the ex-Marine connected with a slap to Jeremy's ear. Jeremy yowled in pain. Henry stepped up his attack. Within a few seconds, Jeremy was lying on the floor, gasping for air and trying to not whimper from the pain.

Belinda stood watching. Jeremy, curled up, entered her mind as he tried to figure out what happened; his dizziness hindered him, but he sensed sadness and guilt.

Henry handcuffed him and brought him into the security office. Gray metal desks and chairs. Clipboards and wanted posters. A wannabe police station. One entire wall was covered with a dozen closed circuit TV monitors.

Jeremy tried to speak. "We were just-"

"I know what you were trying to do," Henry said. "Get a minor drunk and rape her."

"What? She's not a minor. "

"She's 17."

"She told me-"

"Shut up, you pervert."

"I didn't know. She bought the beer."

"Bullshit. She's a minor."

Kroll came into the security office. "What's going on?"

"We caught this bastard trying to rape Belinda out back. He was getting her drunk, groping her, making her wank his Johnson when I caught him."

"That's not what happened," Jeremy said. "She had asked me to meet her. I was just-"

"Don't say anything more, Jeremy," Kroll said firmly. "Henry, please release him into my custody."

"Yes sir, Dr. Kroll."

"You can take the handcuffs off him. He's not going anywhere. And I don't believe he is a danger. Right, Jeremy?"

Jeremy nodded.

Henry uncuffed him, whispering under his breath, "I should have killed you, asshole."

Kroll handed him tissues and Jeremy realized his nose was bleeding. The blood almost seemed to glow. His pained sensations remained more intense. Colors too bright, sounds too strong.

They went in through the rear entrance and up to Kroll's large corner office on the second floor of the building. The second floor was largely given over to the more medical facilities, and larger bedrooms for Kroll and key staff.

Jeremy sat in a stiff-backed chair facing the psychologist's massive wooden desk. They waited a few minutes while Jeremy sat with his head tilted back. The bleeding stopped. Jeremy tossed the wad of bloody tissues into a waste basket Kroll provided.

"Before we talk, I'd like you to humor me," Kroll said gently. "Remember our first real meeting, when we went through the Zener cards?"

"Of course."

Kroll took out a deck and they went through it. Three times. Kroll was his usual non-committal self.

"Feel better?" the psychologist asked. The tone was of assessment, not sympathy.

Jeremy had been so focused on trying to read Kroll's mind he had relaxed. Telepathy with Kroll was always challenging. The psychologist had a lack of emotion that muted signals. There were always twists and turns, maybe this, maybe that, like walking through a dark labyrinth.

"Yes." Jeremy began sputtering rapidly. "She told me she was 19. That's just three years younger than me. She invited me there, I didn't even know she was bringing alcohol. My head's fuzzier than it should be from a couple beers. I don't know how but I think she drugged me. Maybe LSD. She was the one who put her hand on my thigh first. She-"

"I believe you," Kroll said with a firm paternal tone. "But I do not know how the Monroe County district attorney and the upstate courts will feel about it. They're surprisingly provincial."

"She's got to admit it."

Kroll shook his head. "She wants to protect her job. Her reputation." Kroll steepled his fingers. "I think I can get it resolved. Reassure her there will be no repercussions. I can educate her how difficult it would be to go through a whole proceeding."

"Really?"

"I'll talk with Henry too. He was overzealous in his breaking things up. He could face losing his job for using excessive force."

"You'd do that?"

"I'm not supposed to have favorites." Kroll smiled his usual uncomfortable grin. "But let's just say I appreciate all the hard work you've done in the program."

"Thank you, thank you."

After that Jeremy had been even more willing to push himself. To work longer days than anyone. To willingly undergo near torturous sessions. He was administered LSD and psilocybin. He consented to electric shocks to see if pain and stress enhanced his abilities. He masturbated under supervision in the lab and then was tested to see if orgasm heightened awareness.

He had less contact with Belinda, who was reassigned to work with other subjects. On the rare occasions when they interacted, she was more formal, distant, eyes averted.

With her betraying him, he felt no social contract to not go into her mind. He picked up guilt and shame connected with lying. No surprise. But then one day another word bubbled up when she was applying gel to his scalp in preparation for an EEG.

Set up.

At first he thought it was referring to her setting up the experiment.

Then he recalled that she hadn't appeared surprised when Henry had appeared. The emotions he'd sensed in her were sadness and guilt. Not fear or surprise.

Henry had been careful to not punch his head. Only slaps above the neck. Jeremy knew that Kroll was very concerned about head trauma and its possible impact on abilities.

Jeremy didn't say anything. But he used his abilities to scan the other subjects. He found proof when he accessed Dashawn. Dashawn was a couple years younger, an extroverted teen who seemed super alert. Jeremy deduced that he was being studied as a sender. Jeremy sensed a peculiar clarity of thought. An internal loudness.

There had been experiments with implanting ideas. Even some real-world trials. The CIA about 15 years earlier had tried using magician and media savvy psychic Uri Geller to implant ideas in a Russian leader's head. Inconclusive results, but it had kept President Carter enthused about the possibilities.

One day he was talking sports with Dashawn in the hallway and Belinda walked by. She ignored the two young men. But Dashawn had the clear thought of "bitch set me up."

Jeremy struggled to control his response, to not blurt out a question.

"She's a good-looking woman," Jeremy said.

Dashawn just grunted. "Don't go there."

"What do you mean?"

"That skank be trouble."

"How?"

A security guard stepped up to the two men. Jeremy was amazed at how quickly he had appeared. "Hey guys, what're you up to?"

"Just shooting the shit," Dashawn said.

"Aren't you due for a blood draw?" the guard said to Dashawn.

"Not for another 15 minutes."

"Okay," the guard said. But then he stood there and there was no more chance to chat.

Jeremy never saw Dashawn again. The word was that he had requested to leave and been discharged. He had seemed quite content in the program, aside from his anger with Belinda. Jeremy was surprised. Dashawn was one of the foster care system young adults. While PRI was institutional, it was clearly better than a lot of places he had been.

Jeremy had avoided Henry since the night he had been caught by the guard with Belinda. Now he actively sought him out.

"I've got a question, Henry," he said, catching the big guard while he was walking the perimeter with no one else around. "What were you doing back there when you came across me and Belinda?"

"I was on patrol."

Lying.

"I've never seen a guard patrolling there."

"It's none of your business where we go, dickhead" Henry shoved past Jeremy, nearly knocking him to the ground.

More lies. Way more agitated than he needed to be.

Belinda wasn't in that day but Jeremy planned to confront her on her next time in.

The next day, Henry was gone. The official word was he had gotten another job in Schenectady. Belinda never came back to work.

Jeremy thought about leaving. He had a college degree and then a gap in his resume. What could he tell potential employers? He was prohibited by his non-disclosure statement from telling anyone what he had been doing. He hadn't realized what a trap it was when he first agreed to stay at PRI.

He stopped volunteering for the more uncomfortable experiments. He did the absolute minimum as far as participation.

Only a few days after this change in attitude, Kroll called him to his office.

"How are you doing, Jeremy?" Kroll asked.

"Okay."

"I've received word that you are less enthusiastic about your work."

"I've been here longer than anyone else."

"Yes. And the program has treated you well."

"Mostly." Jeremy concentrated, probing Kroll's mind.

"You're trying to read my thoughts, aren't you?"

"What makes you say that?"

"I've studied the video tapes of your sessions for hours. There are certain furrows you get in the corrugator muscle on your forehead. A special kind of concentrating you don't show when, for example, you work on one of the math puzzles we give you."

Jeremy tried to relax his face.

"Feel free to poke around," Kroll said. "Find anything of interest?"

"No. But I never feel like I'm getting anywhere with you."

"You've tried before?"

"During the exercises."

"Never at other times?"

Jeremy was silent.

"Of course you have," Kroll said. "Quite natural. I take no offense. I'd be more bothered if you hadn't. That would mean you weren't interested in my thinking."

"Belinda's gone."

"Who? Oh yes, that girl you were caught with."

"She wasn't a girl."

"She was a minor."

"She looked older. She told me she was 19."

"There's no point in rehashing this."

"I read her mind before she left. She was older."

Jeremy sensed a ping in Kroll he had never felt. A vulnerable fraction of a moment. A tell. The psychologist had been caught in a lie.

"Where did she go?" Jeremy asked.

"I believe she is going off to college."

"It's June, hardly a time to start school."

"Perhaps she's beginning with a summer session. I don't keep track of staff's comings and goings."

Jeremy sensed the psychologist's tell again.

"How about Henry?"

Another tell.

Kroll leaned forward in his chair. "You're wrinkling your corrugator again. What are you finding?"

"You're lying."

"How can you say that?"

"I just know it."

"What do you see? Or hear? Are there other senses in play?"

"This isn't an experiment. You lied to me. And I'm not the only one. Dashawn. Fred. Chris."

Jeremy bluffed rattling off the names of some of the other long-term subjects he had had minimal contact with.

For the first time, Jeremy sensed Kroll's anger.

"You've become unappreciative of all I've done for you."

"Done to me. I want to leave."

"You know there's a 48-hour cooling off period. We will have to tally your bill."

"What bill?"

"It was in the papers you signed initially. If you leave before you are discharged, you're responsible for room and board. A hundred dollars a day is quite reasonable. But it does add up for someone who has been a guest as long as you have."

"A guest?" Jeremy shouted.

"Please lower your voice. Hopefully we can work past this little breach in our relationship. There may also be ramifications as far as your college tuition. You had a free ride at Yale but if you fail to fulfill your obligations with PRI, that bill comes due too. Good schools cost money."

Jeremy stormed out.

Later that day, one of the unsmiling security guards presented him with papers to sign to formally request release. Attached was a bill for $42,534. For room and board and various itemized expenses, like treatment in the facility's infirmary, laundry, and the field trips he had gone on. The bill was due within 90 days of discharge. Jeremy had virtually no assets and no credit.

He stayed but his participation in the experiments lessened further. He deliberately guessed wrong. He was written up several times for infractions—talking to other subjects, gathering information. He scanned minds freely, gathering names, data. He was careful with the way he wrote things down, finding the few spots at PRI where there weren't video cameras.

He decided he would run away without signing the discharge papers. He wasn't sure what that meant legally but hoped he could argue that he had signed it unknowingly in the beginning. Signing an agreement the second time would weaken that argument. He realized how scared he was of Edward Kroll. The psychologist clearly believed Jeremy owed him.

After studying the routines and physical grounds for several days, Jeremy began probing minds to find a way to escape. His most successful interaction was with Bill, the oldest guard, who was probably in his early 50s. He had slicked back, dyed black hair, a handlebar mustache, and a perennially angry expression.

"I bet it wouldn't be hard to sneak out of here," Jeremy said one afternoon when they were together outside, with no one around.

"Yeah, that's what you think," Bill said with a sneer.

"Every puzzle has a solution," Jeremy said, trying to avoid the forehead wrinkle that Kroll had identified. Not that Bill could probably pick it up.

"Says you, smart guy. No one gets away without Dr. Kroll knowing. If they get away, it's because he's decided they're not worth the effort."

Bill was in some ways a perfect subject to read. Not that bright, very linear, concrete thinking. There wasn't a lot going on in his head. Unlike Kroll, where it was like playing 3D chess in a dark room with distracting noises.

As Jeremy suggested the idea of escape, Bill thought of vulnerabilities. Short staffed on holidays, only one guard on duty from midnight to 6 a.m.

"I bet they don't even have very sophisticated electronics," Jeremy said.

"Shows what you know. You think you can trick me into telling you." Bill folded his hairy, muscled arms across his chest. "No way, dirtbag."

But as he'd thought about it he had inadvertently told Jeremy.

A week later, on the night of the fourth of July, Jeremy used his lock picking skills to slip through the gate, avoiding where he knew the electronic sensors were, and walking on dark country roads, then more brightly lit suburban streets, to Rochester. His backpack held clothing and a couple books.

He wanted to get as far away as quickly as possible. But he had barely a hundred dollars and he didn't want to have to show the ID required to fly. He did not want to bother his mother, who was struggling with serious health problems and expenses. His dream had been to help her out, not be more dependent. Or worse, pull her into trouble with Kroll.

Using cash, he bought an Amtrak ticket to New York City. He got out at Grand Central Station and walked across town, checking for surveillance. It was morning. Kroll was probably just noticing his absence.

Times Square was in transition. As a kid, Jeremy had gone on a field trip to New York. He remembered Times Square for XXX porno theaters with movies like *Fox Holes* and *Centerfold Slut*. With posters that the guys in his junior high school class stared at and made clueless raunchy comments about.

But of as much interest to Jeremy were the tourist trap dives with sun faded "Going Out of Business" signs that were probably as old as he was. They sold various crappy knick-knacks, postcards, knockoff watches, newspapers that you could have printed with your name in the headlines, and various forms of fake ID. There was a sign above the ID card display that stated, "Cards For Amusement Purposes Only."

Many were obviously silly, like the one with "FBI Special Agent" in big letters, with "Federal Bra Inspector" printed smaller beneath it. Other ID cards looked like press passes, police department identification, and driver's licenses. He bought licenses that said they were from Utah and Wisconsin, reasoning there was less chance anyone looking at them would really know what the license looked like.

For a few additional bucks, the hunchbacked old man behind the counter took his picture and typed in the name he gave on the licenses. Thus Alan Wilson was born.

Jeremy kept repeating the name "Alan Wilson" as he walked south on Eighth Avenue, until he got to the Port Authority Bus Terminal. While parts of Times Square were showing signs of renovation, with big, clean corporate businesses replacing sleazy massage parlors and porno theaters, the bus terminal was as scuzzy as he remembered it. Aggressive panhandlers stepped over passed out drunks who lay in puddles of urine. Litter, grime and slime on most surfaces.

He moved quickly, buying a ticket to Atlantic City on a rundown bus that belched a black cloud as it took off for the tunnel to New Jersey.

The Atlantic City casinos were more tacky than posh but an improvement over the scenes in the crotch of New York. Jeremy resisted the temptation to show off his cardistry. As part of his sleight of hand skills he had an impressive array of cuts and flourishes. But the last thing he wanted was to look skillful. He had been a fair to middling poker player, not even understanding all the terms like "flop," "bomb pot," and "river card." But he knew the ranking of hands and had a rough feeling for the odds.

Sitting at the table, he studied his hand, working to keep his face neutral. Around him the players and the dealer were equally impassive. He couldn't read their minds as far as specific cards but it wasn't hard for him to know who was tamping down their enthusiasm with a straight and who was debating whether to go all in with a bluff on a busted flush.

Within three hours, he was up $5000. He left when he had doubled it. He treated himself to a room in the casino's five-star hotel, ordering the surf and turf special from room service. The luxury was bedazzling after his Spartan years at PRI.

After three nights, when he was up $35,000, there was a knock at the door. The purple color and unpleasant squeal of danger was evident but not as intense as it could be. He wasn't expecting anyone and peered through the peephole. Three burly men, all wearing blue blazers with the hotel's name and the word "Security" embroidered below the chest pocket.

"Yes?" he said through the door.

"Mr. Wilson, open the door. We have the master key. We're knocking as a courtesy."

He scanned them and confirmed they were who they said they were. He opened the door and they entered. The leader, with a shaved head and a fire plug physique, introduced himself as Mr. Castellano. He had a neutral expression. Two burly assistants stood behind him, glowering at Jeremy.

"We've checked the identification you gave on check-in. It's bogus."

"I've paid all my bills in cash."

"We've noticed some irregularities in your play. We've studied the tapes. We're not sure what you're doing but you're banned from the casino. And tomorrow we want you to check out."

"I'll take my business elsewhere."

Castellano rubbed his eyes with his index fingers in a parody of crying. "The other casinos in town all have your picture. You're toast in Atlantic City. We don't care if you rip off the Indians. Or the assholes in Las Vegas. But I will tell you that if you wind up in the Las Vegas black book, someone might take you out in the parking lot and provide strong motivation to leave town. We're nicer here." Castellano gave him a grin that was anything but nice. "That's why we're letting you stay overnight. Customer satisfaction."

Jeremy didn't want to call attention to himself. He wasn't sure at what point security would call the police. He hadn't committed any crime, as far as he knew. But he was sure Atlantic City cops would be friendlier to the gambling industry than a stranger taking money out of the town.

He slipped out in the early morning hours, cautiously aware that he was carrying enough cash to make him a very desirable target. He was followed to the train station. He recognized one of the men who had been backing up Castellano. There was no thought of robbery in his man's mind. Jeremy was partially glad he was being watched.

At the train station he bought a ticket to New York and another to Baltimore. He headed to the New York bound platform, with the security man watching. When the train pulled in, blocking the surveillant's view, Jeremy scurried up the stairs to the Baltimore bound platform, hurried on the train and sat where he couldn't be seen through the window.

Jeremy knew better than to return to his old neighborhood. It was amazing how many fugitives were caught doing just that. He applied for a job at a mini-mart two communities away from where he'd grown up. The neighborhood was run down, the store what cops called a "shop and rob." He stayed in a nearby hotel that catered to people who couldn't afford first and last month's rent or pass a credit check. They were happy to take his cash.

Each month he had to dip into his savings a little, since the store provided a barely livable wage. But the manager soon noticed that whatever shift Jeremy worked, the store tended to make the most money. Jeremy was better than most of the staff in that he showed up sober for all of his shifts.

He was soon the assistant manager.

The next big advance came when he caught a minor with very good fake ID. She was fidgety and he scanned her mind even as she was adamant she was 18 and able to buy cigarettes and beer.

"Who is Mr. C?" he asked her after a scan.

"How'd you know?"

"Just tell me."

She sputtered for a couple minutes but he threatened to call her parents. Or the police. She glanced both ways. "I got the ID from him. He said it was guaranteed."

"I want to talk with him."

"He can't know I told you."

"I promise."

Three days later, with Jeremy $400 poorer, Alan Wilson had a real-looking Virginia driver's license. Plus a driver's license with his photo and the name "Scott Johnson." He had been working in the mini mart for six months and gotten a debit card. He applied for a credit card from the same bank. He got it, with a credit limit of $1000. He didn't care about how much he could charge. Paying cash for everything kept him largely off the grid. He was more interested in the credibility the card offered, whether getting a hotel room or a rental car.

Jeremy had taken precautions, being sure to tip everyone. Reasonably, not so generously that they wondered where his money was coming from. One evening the desk clerk told him, "Hey, there were a couple guys around looking for you. They told me to not tell you. "

"Thanks," Jeremy said, slipping him $20. "What'd they look like?"

"Cops. That's why I'm telling you. I hate cops. Two big guys. White. Clean shaven. Hair cut short. Acted like they owned the place. Wearing sport jackets. Pretty sure one had a gun under it. Couldn't tell about the other. They said they'd be coming back tomorrow."

"Okay. I'll be checking out. Prep my bill." Jeremy gave him another $20.

"I ain't gonna ask what it's about. I been there myself." The second $20 disappeared. "You been a good guest. No noise, no smoking. No obvious drugs, no hookers in your room. No busting my balls. I can give you another room if you want. Tell 'em you left."

Jeremy considered the offer. He had settled in. There was a comfort and familiarity. But he doubted his pursuers could be fooled. They were probably from Kroll. Could they force him to go back? They didn't sound like the casino security men. Were they on to the Alan Wilson identity? He'd have to start over again as Scott Johnson, get a job without having any references, build credit, stay under the radar. Shit!

He hurried back to his room. He was only aware of the cloud of danger when he stepped inside. Strangely, not the usual color, more of a greenish mist. The sound was like waves on the ocean.

One intruder pushed the door closed behind Jeremy as he tried to pivot and escape. Another was seated in the dark room, on the edge of the bed. Aside from a menacing bulk and different color sports jackets, they were nondescript near lookalikes.

"We're not here to harm you, Jeremy," the one wearing a gray sport jacket said.

"Or maybe you prefer Alan?" the one wearing a navy-blue sport jacket said.

"What do you want?"

"You ran away from PRI nearly a year ago," Gray said.

"I'm not going back."

"There's nothing to go back to," Blue said. "It closed about three months ago."

"Really?"

The one in blue nodded.

Jeremy scanned the man and learned it was true. As was their stated desire to not harm him. "What do you want?" Jeremy repeated.

"To help you," Gray said.

"How?"

"It has been brought to the government's attention that you were inadvertently wronged while taking part in the experiments. We're here to make it right."

"You work for the government?" Jeremy asked. "Let me see some ID."

The agent in blue took out a card that showed he was an employee of the Defense Intelligence Agency. The name on the card was Richard Smith. The gray-jacketed one produced a similar card. The name on his card was John Jones.

"Is that real ID?"

"It is real in that it was issued by the DIA. You're asking if those are our names. Our names are not really important," Jones said, tucking the card back into his pocket. The gun in his shoulder holster had been briefly visible, as had the gun in Smith's belly holster.

"We'd like to help you move out of this dive," Jones said.

"Take me into custody?"

"No, no, no," Jones said. "Provide you compensation for your time at PRI."

"Do I owe anything?"

"Nope," Smith said.

Jeremy scanned them and from what he detected, they were still telling the truth.

"How much are you offering?

"Two hundred thousand dollars has been approved," Jones said, taking papers from his pocket. "We need you to sign for it. The money will subsequently be transferred into the account you designate. Acceptance includes a non-disclosure agreement under the National Security Act of 1990 which has severe penalties, up to and including imprisonment, for any breach. Do you understand?"

"Yes. How did you find me?'

"Sources and methods are something we don't discuss," Smith said.

"If Uncle Sam wants you, he finds you," Jones said. "We can offer you a false identification packet. You don't meet criteria to go into the Witness Protection program but we utilize related services on a limited basis."

"Why would I need it?"

"We have information that Dr. Kroll is still fixated on you," Jones said. "He's been de-funded but has considerable resources. The government believes it best to help you avoid him."

"You can keep Alan Wilson," Mr. Smith added. "And Scott Johnson."

"How'd you know about that?"

"Sources and methods," Smith said. Jones bobbed his head.

"I'd like to think about it."

"You've got two minutes," Jones said. "It's a one-time offer. If you do go public about PRI you still would be prosecutable for violating national security. And federal accommodations are even less charming than this." He gestured to indicate the shabby motel room.

The two agents waited, silent and motionless as statues.

Jeremy heard horns honking, muffled voices, sirens and other muted big city noise outside.

"I'll take it," Jeremy said.

"A wise decision," Jones said as Smith handed Jeremy the papers and a pen.

Chapter Twenty-Seven

By the time they reached Weed, despite his best efforts, Tom's eyes were drooping. He had been driving for almost seven hours. They stopped in a gas station for the car, and a fast-food joint for themselves. Tom debated getting coffee and pushing on but knew he was at the point of being more of a danger than an asset behind the wheel.

Diana took over. As she adjusted the seat and mirrors, he curled up in the back seat and put a jacket over his head. Now the goal was to push the emotional thoughts out. Part of the goal of mindfulness practice. He focused on his breathing and soon fatigue overcame him.

They passed through the Shasta Cascade region, paralleling the mountains that went all the way to Canada. Then into the Sacramento Valley. The sun glinted off high-tension wires paralleling the road, the artery of energy that allowed Los Angeles to become the megalopolis it had become in what was once the desert. Views of sprawling irrigated farmland and stretches of as yet unclaimed desert. With occasional large towns not quite big enough to be called cities.

She drove through the notoriously steep Grapevine, to the Tejon Pass, connecting the Sacramento Valley with Southern California.

Tom awoke a half hour from Palmdale. They got off I-5 at California State Route 138, the two lane Pearlblossom Highway that followed the northern edge of the San Gabriel Mountains in the western portion of the Mohave Desert.

"Do you recall what I told you about Shorty McGuire?" he asked.

She briefly took her eyes off the road and gave him an annoyed glance. "He's a 66-year-old widowed Caucasian male who lives alone on a small farm about five miles outside Palmdale. Survivalist. He was among the oldest at PRI. You knew him but he was kind of a cranky loner, even back then. Vietnam war combat veteran. Legal trouble when he was young. Wandered around the country, landed in LA where he became a stunt man, did various low-level jobs, then retired out here. Most likely armed and the most dangerous PRI subject we'll be approaching."

"Wow! Concise, accurate, hit all the key points."

"You want me to trust you and I'm getting better at it. I expect you to trust me as well."

"Agreed."

She drove for a bit and he said, "We can stop at a motel and you can sleep if you want. Or just re-charge."

"I'm okay," she responded.

"If you don't want to do this, now is the time to speak up."

"Are you thinking of giving up?"

"No."

"Because if you are, I will take you out in the middle of the Mohave and leave you without water."

"It's better to use positive reinforcement. Like promise to take me to a motel room and make sweaty monkey love for hours when this is done."

"Maybe I'll do it beforehand to get you dehydrated before I leave you in the desert."

"You do know the way to a man's heart."

She drove on. They were both pleased that they could squabble and banter and not lose their connection.

He said, "You know David Hockney used this road for a photocollage."

"I'd be dazzled if I knew who David Hockney was."

So he told her about the English artist. She was most impressed that one of his works had sold for nearly $50 million. Then he told her about the Palmdale-Lancaster area, it's booming aerospace industry on the edge of the desert, how Palmdale got its name from German Lutherans in 1886 who thought the Joshua trees were palms. And the Palmdale bulge, where the scar of the San Andreas fault zippered across the landscape.

"You've been Googling," she said.

He nodded.

"It reminds me of when I was first getting to know you. Any quiet was filled with facts, facts, facts."

"And still you stuck with me."

"It can be annoying. But for some reason I found it cute. You find out anything that will help us with Shorty McGuire?"

He looked down. "Not really."

"Well, if conversation with him lags, I'm sure you can lighten it up with some fascinating facts."

"Are you being sarcastic?"

She started humming, "I Won't Back Down."

He joined her on the chorus, then said, "Get on Redman and keep heading east. Then north on 100th Street. If we hit Edwards Air Force Base, we've gone too far."

They rode for a bit and she said, "You got any other facts you'd like to share? Annual rainfall? Were there conquistadors here?"

"The only other fact is there is no one else on earth I'd rather be going to talk to a gun-crazed survivalist with than you."

"Aww. If there was a motel around I might just take a detour and spend some time decompressing with you."

"Not just to dehydrate me and leave me in the desert?"

"Only when you run out of facts. Which is probably like getting to the end of the internet."

"So Wi-Fi is a priority."

They continued the back-and-forth, enjoying the distraction.

The strip malls with ubiquitous franchises petered out, as did the all too similar housing developments. The small homes, most in the Spanish style with orange tile roofs and adobe walls, became smaller and more spread out. Occasional clumps of hardy native plants replaced the bright green of watered lawns. They reached an unmarked dirt road. He told her to follow it for a half mile.

There were deep potholes and she focused on the driving. He gazed out the window.

Houses were even further apart, more run down. Some had two or three parked and cannibalized vehicles baking in the sun. The most intense color came from sun-bleached blue tarps.

Most of the homes were trailers. A few small houses. No mini mansions but lots of cheap land. The same attraction that lured aerospace to the area. The houses were a quarter mile or more apart.

"This is it," Lord said. It was the only property encircled by a six-foot-high barbed wire fence.

"Maybe he's got a herd of cattle," she said flippantly.

"Stowed away in a hidden underground barn that doubles as a fallout shelter."

McGuire's stark property was dotted with random piles of rocks and clumps of Joshua trees. Closer to McGuire's trailer was white and black sage and antelope bitterbrush providing a bit of color on the gray-yellow ground.

The double-wide trailer had an adjacent wooden beam and post structure with a huge blue tarp draped over it.

About halfway up the driveway was a metal gate. Signs warned *Keep Out, No Soliciting, No Trespassing, No Hunting. Protected by Smith and Wesson* were tacked to a wood post.

On another post was a small, weathered intercom box.

"What do you want?" a gravelly voice growled from the box as they pulled to a stop near it.

"Mr. McGuire, I don't know if you remember me. My name is Jeremy Sherman. I was with you at PRI a long time ago."

His response was indecipherable.

"Can we come in and talk?" Tom asked.

"You here from the government?"

"No."

"You'd say that even if you were."

"I promise we're not. Please let us come in and talk face to face. If you're not interested, we'll be gone in five minutes."

Seconds passed.

The lock on the gate buzzed and they drove toward the house.

Chapter Twenty-Eight

"He's going to be pretty paranoid," Lord warned as they drove slowly toward the house.

"You don't need to be psychic to figure that out."

"Just let me do the talking."

They passed by a couple of small metal boxes by the side of the road.

"Perimeter alarms," she said.

"I wonder what other kinds of protection he has. Land mines?" he half-joked.

"Probably not. But I wouldn't go walking out in the brush without a metal detector."

Then they were at the door. A solid steel barrier with a small peephole that looked like it belonged on a fort.

Ray "Shorty" McGuire opened the door and stepped back, a short-barreled shotgun in his hands. He stood far enough back that he could hit both Tom and Diana with one blast.

"You got one minute to tell me your business," McGuire snapped. He was barely 5'8", more gristle than anything else. He looked to be in his 70s, though they knew he was younger. Short cut gray hair, blue eyes glaring.

"I was at PRI," Tom said rapidly. "Kroll has been hounding me for years. I've been on the run but decided now to fight back. I want to get a bunch of others who were there to come forward, go to the press with me, and get him punished. Or at least get him to back off."

"And why is that my problem?"

"I, I figured you might have had a hard time too," Tom sputtered. "He's done bad stuff to a lot of people."

"The world's a tough place, sonny boy. It ain't my problem."

"But don't you care that-"

"I don't give a tinker's damn," McGuire interrupted. "You think going to the Jew media is gonna clear things up? They got their agenda. They like his type."

"Is that a Mossberg Raptor you've got there?" Diana asked the scowling senior.

"What?" McGuire responded. "Yeah. You know about it?"

"Twelve gauge. Raptor grip. Fourteen-inch barrel. The savvy types get around the gun-hating feds by having a longer stock."

McGuire's face remained impassive, the gun unwavering, but Lord felt the hostility within the ex-stunt man lessen.

"So what do you want from me?" McGuire asked Tom.

"Uh, like I said, I'm planning on going public about what Kroll did. I'd like to get your account. Have you come forward with me." Lord was regretting they had come. Between the gun being waved and McGuire's lack of appeal as a witness, the costs outweighed the benefits.

McGuire gestured with his shotgun toward a couch in the living room. The furniture was worn but clean. A well-groomed calico cat sat on the arm on one end of the sofa, looking indifferent as Wynne and Lord sat at the other end.

"I used to have a couple dogs, three cats. Ginger's the last survivor. I figure at my age it don't make sense to be taking any critters in. Except the chickens. And I make sure they got a short life expectancy."

The comment about murdering chickens was the first non-hostile communication by McGuire. The couple responded with awkward chuckles and nods.

"You really think anyone cares about shit you went through 30 years ago?" Shorty turned to Diana. "Pardon my French. I ain't used to having a lady around since my wife died. And that was in 2010."

"Sorry for your loss," Diana said. "Don't worry about cussing. I grew up on Army bases."

"Yeah? Which ones?"

"Bragg mainly. But also Benning, Carson. In Germany at a couple."

"Your old man was career Army?"

"More than career. He loved it. Colonel Charlie Wynne."

McGuire's jaw dropped like a cartoon character showing surprise. "Holy shit? Gotta Wynne? You're his daughter?"

She nodded, pleased at how impressed Shorty was.

"Prove it!" McGuire demanded, his scowl returning.

"You want to hear his full military career? He helped found Special Forces. Two Purple hearts in Vietnam. Silver Star. Combat cross. Would go out running with his men though he was better than twice their age. He thought some of the MREs actually tasted good. He told me a lot of times after you've been out in the brush with nothing but bugs, you get a taste for processed mystery meat. There's a reason why his troops were nicknamed 'Snake Eaters.'

"He could've been a general if he didn't speak his mind," she continued. "Like getting in a congressman's face who was on a bullshit fact-finding tour. The congressman complained about accommodations and then was critical of my dad's troops. He wouldn't take some chickenshit civilian criticizing his boys. You want to hear a list of battles he was in? It'll take a while. Nam Dong, Lang Vei, A Sau, Ben Het..."

"You could get most of that stuff off the internet or outta books." Shorty stared at her, curious but distrusting. "He teach you to shoot?"

"A little."

"Let me show you something." McGuire picked up the shotgun but held it loosely at his side. They walked through the living room into one of the two small bedrooms. Their host moved slowly, with a bit of a limp.

The bedroom was surprisingly neat and tidy, though Tom doubted Shorty had any visitors. No bed. The walls had posters from several action movies that had gone right to video. Lord guessed McGuire had appeared in them. A bookshelf held Louie L'Amour, Mickey Spillane, Tom Clancy.

The ex-stuntman opened the shade and pointed out the window.

There was a small hillock, with a three walled roofless cinder block structure. The missing wall was on the side nearest the trailer. Inside the open U shape structure was a wooden frame. Stapled to the frame were three targets. A silhouette target flanked two sheets with black bullseyes.

McGuire turned a hand crank and opened the window. One wall was dominated by a locked floor-to-ceiling gun cabinet. He fiddled with the combination. Lord saw at least four rifles inside the cabinet.

Shorty opened a drawer at the bottom and took out a pistol. "A Beretta. Good for small hands. But still got stopping power."

"Replaced the M1911 Colt. My father didn't approve."

McGuire grinned. "Special Forces guys hung onto the Colt. I didn't think the Italians could make a good gun. But they did."

He handed it to Diana. "Think you can hit the target?"

She handled the gun cautiously. "One thing I remember for sure. Treat every gun like it's loaded."

"Of course I keep it loaded. What's the point of having a gun if it ain't loaded?"

She continued to handle the gun awkwardly, pointing to various parts. "This is the safety, right? It's on?"

"Yup. Just slide it in and the firearm's ready to use." He set a second clip down on the small table near the window. "If you don't hit the target with the first clip, I got plenty more bullets." McGuire was clearly struggling to not smile, enjoying a chance to share his private gun range with someone. Lord was amazed at how quickly he had gone from belligerent to welcoming host.

"Thanks." She stepped to the window, rocking from side to side, hefting the weapon. She moved into the Weaver stance, gun extended, arms forming a triangle. She looked stiff, like someone mimicking a pose she had seen on a TV cop show.

Three shots. Pause. Three shots. Pause. Three shots. Pause. After fifteen shots. The gun stayed open.

Looking out the window, the targets all looked intact.

"She's not used to the gun," Lord said defensively. "The targets are pretty far out too. Most handgun battles are just..."

"Holy shit!" McGuire repeated.

As smoothly and artfully as Serena Williams with a tennis racket, Diana released the clip, put the fresh one in, and racked the barrel so it was ready to fire.

Tom looked at the targets again. He hadn't been able to see clearly since it was dark behind the black centers. But when he squinted and stared, he saw that the centers of all three targets were chewed out by bullets.

"You are Gotta Wynne's daughter," McGuire said like a teenage girl introduced to BTS.

Tom just stared at her. "I thought your father was against guns for civilians?"

"He said if he could collect them all and melt them down, he would. But since he couldn't he wanted me to know how to use one."

McGuire was staring at her too. "Honey, if I was 20 years younger, I'd kill your boyfriend here and run off with you."

"Well, I'm glad you're not younger then," she said, setting the gun down. "He's my guy."

"Women never did have much good taste. I used to tell my last wife that. Why she stayed married to me, I'll never know."

He set a small fan in the window. It blew the cordite-scented air out into the desert.

"You two hungry?" McGuire asked.

"A bit," Diana responded before Tom could say no.

"Killed a chicken a couple days ago. Stopped laying eggs. You ever kill a chicken?"

She nodded. "My father told us if you're going to eat meat, you should know where it comes from, how it gets to your plate. But I was the only one of his daughters able to actually kill a bird."

McGuire nodded his approval, then turned to Lord. "How about you?"

Lord shook his head.

McGuire snorted and said, "I figured. I can show you how. Hatchet makes it pretty quick. You ever hear the expression, 'running around like a chicken without a head'?"

"Yeah."

"It's a bitch when that happens." Shorty stared at Lord with a smirk.

Then Shorty limped into his small, efficient kitchen.

"Can I give you a hand with anything?" Diana offered.

"You can set the table."

"Anything I can do?" Tom asked.

"Just stay out of trouble," Shorty responded.

Lord sat down in the nook area while Diana set the table. He took out a couple of coins, rolled them through across his fingers.

McGuire brought out three six-inch hoagie breads, loaded with slices of chicken. He set out bowls of lettuce, tomato, Swiss and cheddar cheese, onions, and pickles. "Who wants ketchup, mayo, hot sauce?"

They made their own sandwiches while he set Budweisers, Cokes, and bottled water on the table.

"Damn, that's good," Diana said after she bit into her sandwich.

Lord did too, fighting the image of the decapitated chicken. A literal head game by Shorty and he refused to give in to it. The sandwich was indeed delicious.

Shorty talked. Tom had seen it before in various sales jobs, when a lonely person, frequently elderly, got an audience. The couple learned that Clint ("He insists that no one call him Mr. Eastwood") was an absolute gentleman who ran an incredibly efficient set. Jackie Chan and Jet Li were "really sharp, decent guys, even though they're Chinamen." Jason Statham was "a little taller than me but "a tough cuss who was willing to really go at it in a fight scene." Unlike some of the other martial arts stars who were surprisingly "delicate flowers."

"How'd you come to Kroll's attention?" Lord asked when it seemed like McGuire had name-dropped halfway through IMDb.

"I'm the seventh son of the seventh son. You know what that means?"

"Special powers," Lord answered. "A healer?"

"Some people say," Shorty responded. "When I was a kid, they had me dowsing. You know what that is?" Shorty emphasized the word "that" and Tom felt like he was being tested.

"You use a stick or bent wires to find things in the ground. Water, some people say gold."

"I wish it was gold. I had a knack for finding water. Maybe I just knew instinctively how to read the land, tell people where to best put their well. But growing up in Kentucky, you got a lot of Southern Baptists say it's the devil's work. They don't give a hard time to the Holy Rollers with their snakes and talking in tongues. Made me get away from that religious B.S. Part of why I hit the road."

He told them his story, which was consistent with the information Lord and Moreau had gathered.

"Never made the Green Beanies," he said to Diana. "I was a Lurp. Long Range Patrol. Go into hostile territory and whack suspected VC or even an NVA officer. I did stuff that I still dream about. Not good dreams."

He told more war stories, then his transition to civilian life. He didn't sugarcoat his dark times. "I got addicted to heroin in Vietnam. Had some shrapnel hurting me and it was a way to cope with that. And with seeing friends get their heads blown off. I came back and kicked the Big H after a few months. Bounced around doing odd jobs. My time at PRI. Then I wound up in the City of Fallen Angels. Got hooked on heroin again after a few bad stunts."

He started to tell more Hollywood stories but Diana gently interrupted. "Tom's told me about PRI. What was your time there like?"

"I'd been in a lot worse places. In Vietnam. County jails around the country. Or when I lived in shooting galleries with scumbag junkies. Places where you could get killed for a fix."

"So you had psychic abilities?" Diana prompted.

"Stuff did strange things when I was around," McGuire said.

Tom was about to press for details but let Diana lead since she had better rapport with Shorty.

"What do you mean?" she asked.

"The weirdness started when I was a kid. Something would just fall off a shelf when I had a temper tantrum. Lots of times folks thought I knocked it off. But then they started seeing that I was on one side of the room and the shelf was on the other. It wasn't something I was trying to do. You can imagine what them self-righteous Baptists thought."

Lord nodded. "Part of why you had to leave."

"Yup. That, and I was a little asshole. Never fit in, started swiping stuff when I was in first grade. School only went to sixth grade and I barely made it through. Fist fights, stealing, using the Lord's name in vain. I was as glad to get out of there as they were for me leavin'."

McGuire took his dishes into the kitchen. Wynne and Lord followed. Shorty piled his dishes in the small stainless steel sink then limped into the dining room. Wynne brought hers in and set them down on top of his. Lord made a strategic decision to stay in the kitchen and rinse dishes, allowing Diana to sit with Shorty in the adjacent living room. With the running water on low Lord could clearly hear what was being said.

In the kitchen, Lord was amused at the older man's verbosity. Though still a bit impatient. Diana skillfully redirected Shorty when he began digressing, which was often. "So tell me more about what you called spontaneous psychokinesis?"

"I first heard the term from Dr. Ed. Back in Vietnam, there was times I was walking on a trail and a booby trap went off when I was maybe ten feet from it. Word spread. I got stuck walking point every patrol. That's the kind of shit that ability got me."

"Dr. Kroll knew about this?" Lord asked, the dishes washed and no excuse to not join them. Diana and Shorty were sitting on the couch. Tom pulled up a rattan-seated wooden chair.

"Yeah. Not sure how. It mighta been in my military record." He looked a little annoyed that Lord had intruded on his conversation with Wynne.

"So what did he have you do at PRI?" Diana asked.

"The tests started with trying to get me to move a ball bearing out of a little notch. Or a paper clip balanced on the edge of the table. Dr. Ed would rile me up, or calm me, or give a drug. Lots of blood tests and crap like that."

Lord nodded. "Me too."

"I said I wanted to leave and he sweetened the deal. Gave me a few Percocet every now and then. Let me go off site and hook up with women in Rochester." Shorty had been talking to Tom. He looked over at Diana, embarrassed. "I was young, not married or anything."

She patted his hand again. "Nothing to be ashamed about."

"You ever have results?" Lord asked.

"With the women? Sure." Shorty answered sincerely.

Lord nearly laughed at the misunderstanding, but McGuire was serious and always on the verge of anger. "No, in the lab."

"Sometimes. But Old Dr. Eddie said I had deliberately banged the floor or shook the table. He bolted everything down, had me on a cement pad."

"Did you bang the table?"

"Might've. But there was a few times where I was sitting there concentrating for hours. 'Til I broke into a sweat. And then it would move. The doc said too many faked things, didn't trust me. Then he had me with a random number generator where I was just supposed to be tweaking molecules to make certain numbers appear more than statistically significant."

"How'd that go?" Diana asked.

"Never really anything. I just couldn't get into staring at a machine. I did better with small objects. The doc insisted. He got to be more and more of a dick. Threatened me, like saying I had stolen the drugs from the infirmary and he would have me arrested if I didn't cooperate."

"What did you do?"

"That dipshit security couldn't keep me locked up. I'd been in combat, man. A fucking Ranger," Shorty said. "Sorry hon, I just keep cussing."

"I don't give a shit," Diana said.

Shorty snorted and laughed hard. He turned to Lord. "You better treat this lady right. If I find out otherwise, I'll track you down and slit your throat."

"That's very nice," Lord responded. "But if I don't treat her right, I think she'll slit my throat herself."

Shorty hesitated, then laughed hard again. Diana joined him. Then Tom laughed too.

"Maybe he does have possibilities," Shorty said. "I'll tell you a secret." He paused. "Maybe I'm just a crazy old man with a brain baked too long in the desert. But I've been spending hours trying to move a paper clip. Sometimes it does. Just a little bit." He looked at the two of them with a flash of vulnerability. "Now you probably think I'm nuts."

"No," Lord said.

"No nuttier than I thought before you told me," Wynne said.

McGuire looked at her and then they both laughed. "How about you two stay here tonight? The couch opens up into a bed."

They had barely noticed the dusky skies outside. Diana looked questioningly at Tom.

"I was planning on us getting a motel in LA, closer to our next contact," Tom said. "Get to him early in the morning."

"Another one from PRI?" McGuire asked.

Tom nodded.

"Would I know him?" McGuire asked.

"Probably not," Lord said. "I'm trying to respect everyone's privacy, not giving out anyone's info to anyone else until we confront Kroll." Lord didn't want to mention that their next contact was a Latino man. Things were going well with McGuire and he wanted to keep the bigotry tamped down.

"Fort McGuire is safer than anywhere in LA," McGuire bragged. "The city's a damn jungle."

Wynne sensed the elderly stunt man's loneliness and looked at Lord.

McGuire looked at Wynne.

"We can't just impose on your hospitality," she said. "How about we take you out to dinner in Palmdale?"

"Nah. I got plenty of food in the freezer," McGuire said. "Got things I want to use up. You'd be doing me a favor. It ain't every day I get Special Forces royalty dropping by."

"Ah, knock it off," Diana said.

She nodded and McGuire beamed.

Hours passed with Shorty telling them war stories and Hollywood gossip. Diana fired off the second clip from the Beretta.

Dinner was venison with potatoes and a salad. The conversation was dominated by Shorty, and tidbits about which male action stars had fathered children out of wedlock, actresses the stunt man had slept with, as well as various and sundry drug scenes he'd seen--and sometimes participated in--on sets. He mentioned he'd had two minor heart attacks. His doctor had told him he should live close to a medical facility.

"Hell, I'm never gonna live in town again. I like it out here. Less than a mile from the San Andreas Fault. When Mother Earth decides to shake her booty, ain't gonna be nothing left to worry about."

He asked Lord about the coin handling he had seen him do earlier and Lord did a half dozen tricks. Then Shorty got out a deck of cards and Lord did another half dozen, mainly predicting which cards had been picked.

McGuire scratched his head, perplexed. "How much of that was ESP and how much was tricks?"

"Hundred percent tricks," Lord said.

"You any good at cards other than tricks?"

"Poker?" Lord asked.

McGuire grinned. "Nickel a point. Seven-card Texas hold' em, high-low, five-card stud, Omaha, whatever you want. Dealer's choice as far as if anything's wild."

"You boys gonna cut me out of the game?" Wynne said with an exaggerated pout.

"I'm happy to take your money, little lady," McGuire said. He got out a carousel of chips and dealt everyone in.

With a lot of banter, they began a low stakes game. After 90 minutes, Lord had all but cleaned out the other two. Shorty was scowling. "You reading our minds?"

"Cross my heart and hope to die, no," said Lord.

"Impossible for us to lose that big if you ain't."

"Since we're just doing it for fun, I'm donating all my earnings back to pay for dinner," Lord said, sliding the money toward McGuire. "And I'll tell you how I did it."

He paused. Diana and Shorty leaned forward.

"You both have tells," Lord said. "Picked them up by mindfulness more than mind reading."

"Like what?" Wynne demanded.

"When you have a good hand, you get a quick micro-expression frown," he told Diana. "When you have a bad hand, you force a smile and push back from the table a bit. Shorty, you squeeze your cards tighter when you have a good hand. With a bad hand, you rub your nose or have a slight squint."

"Sonofabitch," McGuire muttered. "I never knew."

Shorty glanced at his watch. "It's an hour past my usual bedtime. You can go for a walk and enjoy the stars, if you'd like. I can tell you where the booby traps are outside. None of them would kill ya, but you'd be spending a few days in the hospital."

"Nah, I think we'll stay in," Lord replied quickly. "We drove straight through, haven't gotten much sleep."

Shorty made up their bed.

McGuire gave Diana a hug. He shook Lord's hand with a two-handed grip, saying, "You're all right. Not as big an asshole as you seemed."

"Thanks," Lord said, thinking, "And right back at ya," but wisely just smiled and headed to bed.

* * *

Shorty made Diana and Tom a hearty breakfast with freshly laid eggs, toast, sausage, and coffee. There wasn't much to pack and they began their goodbyes.

"I've got something for you," Shorty said to Diana, going into his gun room. He brought out an oak box and handed it to her. Inside, resting on red velvety fabric, was a subcompact handgun.

"What's this?" Diana asked.

"A pistol," Shorty responded with a big grin. "I thought maybe you'd seen them before."

"A Walther PPS. Nine-millimeter," Diana said, taking it out of the case. "Designed as a concealed weapon, a carry gun."

"Like James Bond?" Lord asked.

Shorty gave him a condescending smile. "That's a Walther PPK. This here is a nice lady's gun. This beauty was a present to my wife for our fifth anniversary. "I'd like you to have it."

"I can't accept that," Diana said.

"Hey, you're going into Los Angeles. I should give you a bazooka and a machine gun."

Diana looked almost teary-eyed. So did Shorty. Tom's preference would have been to not take the gun but he had learned when it was best to be quiet.

"Really?" Diana said.

"Let's go out back and put a few rounds through it," Shorty said.

They stood ten feet from the target and Diana went through a clip. Seven shots, with one in the chamber.

"Light trigger pull," Diana commented.

"I modified it. My wife felt it was a bit stiff. At less than five pounds pressure now."

"Low recoil."

"You like the grips?"

And so they chatted about the weapon, Diana put another 50 rounds through the gun. The holes in the target got tighter and tighter.

"Very nice," she said.

"Guns are like women," Shorty responded. "Even if they seem the same, they're all a little different."

"Couldn't the same be said about men?" Lord asked.

"Nah. Men are like clubs. They're all the same blunt force instruments," Diana said, giving Tom a peck on the lips. "Except you, honey."

She turned to Shorty. "This gift is very sweet but I can't accept. It was your wife's. Don't you want to keep it?"

"I'm gonna die soon enough. My no-good kids will probably sell everything. Hell, two of 'em are anti-gun nuts."

The aging stunt man got a small, weathered brown leather belly holster and slipped the gun in. He kissed the holster and handed it to Wynne, along with two more clips loaded with 9mm ammo.

"I will cherish this," she said.

"It's a damn gun," Shorty responded. "Don't make a big fuss." He turned to Lord. "You must have something going for you to have a woman like this in your corner."

"I've got something for you," Tom said to Shorty. "But no sentimental value. It's a prepaid phone. Use it to contact us if there's an emergency. And I'll use it to reach out to you when I need your help. Please don't use it for anything else."

"I got a Jitterbug I use every once in a while. Not many people I need to call." He pocketed the phone and gave Diana a long hug. He shook Tom's hand. "Now get outta here and be careful. There's lots of nuts out there."

Chapter Twenty-Nine

If they could have cut through the San Gabriel Mountains in the Angeles National Forest it would have been a straight shot south. But the mountains that form the basin that is Los Angeles forced them to head indirectly toward their next destination, eventually ending up on the East Pomona Freeway.

Lord drove while Wynne muttered a continuous litany of threats and insults at Los Angeles drivers.

"Idiots got to drive while talking on their cell phones," she spewed. "Look at that one, he's texting. Or that one putting on makeup. Barely staying in her lane. I wish I could fire a warning shot over her dumbass."

"Honey, I think you spent a little too much time with Shorty," Lord said gently.

"Maybe. But look at that idiot over there?" she pointed to a Mercedes driver with a cup of coffee in one hand, a cell phone in the other, controlling the wheel with his elbows. "Is there a state law that you have to be stupid and on your cell phone before you can drive here?"

They passed under the big Whittier Boulevard metal arch that served as the official gateway to East Los Angeles. With the densest Latino population in the country, signs in English were the minority, and even then there was always a Spanish translation. *Aguadienteria, Bzcoteria, Carniceria, Cerveceria, Drugeria, Verduleria.* Brightly colored signs, with green, white and red predominating.

Aside from heavy bars on most windows, it looked like a thriving middle-class community.

"He lives in the back of the church," Lord said as they drove down the crowded street.

"Are you going to quiz me on his background? The gang banger, armed robber arsonist turned priest."

"Not necessary. I trust you."

She squeezed his hand.

La Iglesia de la Bendita Madre was housed in a block of stores off of Kennan Avenue. The corner store's large side wall was painted with a commanding mural of the Virgin Mary holding the Christ in her arms. Unlike many other walls, there was no graffiti on it.

They knocked at the battered wooden side door and it was opened almost instantly.

Father Hector Vasquez had slicked-back black hair with gray streaks, a droopy mustache and eyes so dark a brown they seemed black. There was a tear tattooed next to his left eye. He had deep lines in his face and a world-weary gaze that would have been intimidating if not set off by a gentle smile.

"Welcome, please come in," he said before Lord could introduce them.

Wynne and Lord stepped inside. A short, narrow hallway led to a small living room that was sparsely furnished with a cheap table, chairs and sofa. The only decorations on the pale green water-stained walls were a large cross and a picture of Jesus, with blood dripping from his crown of thorns. A ceiling fan swiped unsuccessfully at the warm air. An even smaller room, previously a closet, was visible through a doorway. There was a neatly made twin-size bed inside.

Through the other doorway, arched and much larger, they could see the main room. There were a few weathered wooden pews and about 75 well-worn folding chairs. A large statue of an emaciated, bleeding Christ on the cross dominated one wall. There were shelves filled with prayer books. A modest altar with lectern was at the far side of the room. Several rows of votive candles in glasses rested on a couple of wooden tables on the far wall.

"You've come a long way," Vasquez said. "Can I offer you something to drink? Coffee, tea, water?"

They accepted a couple of glasses of tap water and sat on the couch.

"You were expecting us?" Lord asked.

"I wasn't sure when," he answered. "Now is not a good time. But it is the time the Lord chose and so it is the right time."

"Do you know why we're here?" Lord asked.

"You need help," Vasquez responded.

"I suspect most of the people who show up at your door do," Wynne said dryly.

"That is true. But most of them do not come from my past. And from far away. I help my parishioners as best I can."

"You know who we are?" Wynne asked.

"Not exactly. The messages are seldom that clear. I suspect it has to do with Dr. Kroll. PRI?"

"Yes," Lord said. "I was at PRI with you many years ago."

"Did you recognize him?" Wynne asked the priest.

"Maybe. He's gotten older," Vasquez said with a smile. "The years do that, don't they?"

"Just what do you know?" Wynne demanded.

"Diana, please," Lord said.

"No, no. Your girlfriend is impatient and that is fine. She is a woman of action. I like people who are direct. You need my help with Dr. Kroll. He has been a dark presence in your life all these years. You want that to end."

"That's a logical conclusion," Wynne said. "Why did you say this is a bad time?"

"I believe people are coming to kill me."

"What?" Wynne said loudly, skeptically. "Who?"

"Who and why is a long story." Vasquez sighed. "With all due modesty I must say I am respected in my community. Through the grace of God I have been able to help many people. I have access to funds through anonymous donors. If someone needs an operation and can't afford it, funds are available. If someone is working hard at their business but suffers a setback, a no interest loan appears."

"Who is the good Samaritan?" Wynne asked. "Is it some drug dealer trying to buy into God's good graces?"

"Ahh, perhaps you have heard of Jesus Malverde?"

Wynne and Lord shook their heads.

"The patron saint of drug dealers. An unfortunate popular myth among poor people with little hope. Just the way the *narco corridos* are played. The ballads to drug dealers. The myth of Robin Hood runs strong. Supposedly brave men who steal from the rich and give to the poor."

"Addicts are hardly rich," Wynne said.

"I agree. But we have a saying, it translates as 'Poor Mexico, so far from God, so close to the United States.' Many feel that if gringos want to ruin their lives, why not feed your family with their foolishness."

"You support the drug dealers?" Wynne snapped.

"No! I stop them whenever I can. I have succeeded many times. But there are always new young men who want the quick buck, the expensive cars, the flashiest girls."

Lord studied the priest. He had the saddest smile Lord had ever seen. Like he had witnessed centuries of suffering in a single lifetime. But there was something about his calm presence that seemed to even be impacting Wynne. Though her words were still hostile, her body had lost some of its tension.

"I struggle with what I do," Vasquez said. "I have warned several dealers when they were going to be killed by rivals. But I have never told anyone when I know of a police raid."

"How exactly do you know?" Wynne asked.

"Things come to me in dreams. At PRI, I did barely above average as far as predicting. The dreams can't be forced. Dr. Kroll tried to force my abilities with drugs."

"I can't believe this," Diana said, softening. "I'm still struggling with telepathy. You think you can tell the future?"

"I do not claim to understand how events that have yet to come enter my mind. One time Dr. Kroll was trying to explain the theory, the fluidity of time, the flow back and forth and fixed points in the universe. Like eddies in a river. Non-locality he called it. I still do not comprehend his explanation. But I don't understand a computer, yet I can still use it."

"You were talking about a Good Samaritan," Wynne said. "Who is this donor? And the people who want to kill you?"

"In my dream, a man came who could read minds." He looked at Lord. "Go into my mind and tell her the answer."

Vasquez exhaled and stared at Lord with a calm smile.

Lord closed his eyes and focused. A wave of warmth came over him, a gentle golden glow, soft noise, almost musical but indistinguishable.

"It's you," Lord said. "You have dreams about companies, invest in the stock market."

Vasquez beamed. "Exactly right."

"You mean you could make a fortune?" Wynne asked, looking at the surroundings that could only charitably be described as modest.

"I have. And I spend that fortune wisely. Discreetly. If word spread I would be besieged. Maybe banned from investing by the SEC. Imprisoned for insider knowledge. Kidnapped and tortured by cartels to launder money. Or locked up as a mad man."

Diana suddenly stiffened, aware that she had lowered her guard in response to the priest's gentle demeanor. "How could you set fire to the building where they took you in?" she asked. "There were children."

Vasquez leaned forward in his seat and locked eyes on Diana. "I dreamt of the fire before it happened. I went to the house mother and warned her. She dismissed me, punished me. Two days later the building burned down. She told the arson investigators about my warning. It gave them a prime suspect.

"I had been a bad kid. Nothing big. Shoplifting, graffiti, curfew violations. But even my attorney thought I was guilty. Legal Aid, overworked, skeptical to the point of indifference. Used to dealing with disreputables. I was sent to prison. I was a little punk, scared out of my mind. Of course, I had to affiliate. *La Eme* or *Nuestra Familia*. *La Eme* was more urban, *Nuestra Familia* from rural areas." He rolled up his sleeves, his arms covered with crude prison tattoos.

"I never heard of *La Eme*," Wynne said.

"The Mexican Mafia. Most of the gang had never even been to Mexico. And there was no real connection with the Italian Mafia. Other than greed and a willingness to be violent."

"How'd you get from there to here?" she asked.

"Through the grace of God. I found Christ after getting pulled into a fight in the yard at San Quentin. I was thrown in solitary. A trustee smuggled me in a Bible. I was struck by the story of Joseph. His dreams foretold the future. For his gift, his brothers sold him into slavery. Eventually he became one of the most powerful men in Egypt, adviser to the Pharaoh. Not that I aspire to such heights." Vasquez got up and refilled their water glasses. "By the time my two weeks in the hole were done, I was ready to give myself to the Lord." He smiled at Tom. "A nice name you have chosen."

Lord smiled back. "I read that you were cleared of the charges."

"I had served ten years. There was a good lawyer who heard my story, believed me and my faith in our Lord Jesus Christ. He used his own money to have the case investigated. He found proof that the fire was actually caused by faulty wiring. That the owner had known about. The whole case was covered up since the owner of the property was a big donor to the governor at that time."

"What happened to him?" Diana asked.

Vasquez shrugged. "I don't know. It does me no good to carry hate in my heart. I was released and drifted around. My application to become a priest had been denied. Even though I was declared innocent, I had a ten-year gap on my history. And not much of an employment history before prison. Dr. Kroll had heard of the case, apparently. That is how I wound up at PRI.

"PRI wasn't a bad place for me. But when Dr. Kroll realized there was no real way to force my dreams, he discharged me. My guardian angel must have been watching because I was seriously thinking about going back and rejoining a gang. No real opportunities. But the bishop in Los Angeles decided they needed priests willing to work in tough areas. This church is about a half mile from where I grew up."

"That's an amazing story," Lord said.

"What about the people who want to kill you?" Wynne asked.

"You have heard of MS-13?"

"The Salvadoran gang," Lord said. "Very brutal."

"Why you?" Diana asked.

"There has been conflict with the gang in this neighborhood. They want to take over dealing. They cannot get to the leaders of the gang," Vasquez explained. "As I said, I am well regarded here. Killing me would send a message. No one is safe."

"Have you told the police?" Lord asked.

Vasquez chuckled. "They don't really care as long as violence doesn't spill out of the neighborhood. I have given sanctuary to men who are wicked. Through God's grace, some sinners have changed their ways. And if I told the police I had a dream, they would only laugh harder."

"When did your dream say they would be here?" Diana asked.

"After you arrived."

"Then we should get out of here," Lord said, standing up. "You can come with us." He took a couple of steps toward the door. Wynne stood as well. The priest slowly followed. They were standing near the arched doorway that led to what would be called the nave in a free-standing church.

Vasquez shook his head. "This is my community. I will not run."

"If we leave, does that mean the reality doesn't play out the way your dream said?" Wynne asked.

"I don't know."

"You're willing to stay here and die?" Wynne asked.

"It will happen sometime. In my dream, I survive."

"And us?" Wynne asked.

The rear door banged open. Three young men, none older than 20, charged in. Two held automatic weapons, short-barreled Mac-10s. Ugly, stubby weapons with protruding silencers. The third held a machete. They were thin, wearing t-shirts and tight-fitting jeans. They looked like countless young men the couple had passed on the streets on the ride over. Except for extensive tattoos visible on their bare arms, necks and faces.

The one with the machete had devil horns tattooed on his forehead. In case the message wasn't clear, *El Diablo* was written under his collar bone in a flowery script. Another had a tattooed black widow spider on his right cheek with webbing going down his neck. Tarantulas on each arm. The third had *Santa* on his left jaw and *Muerte* on the right. Written in a bold Gothic script. The top of a skull wrapped in a shawl was partially visible on his chest.

Vasquez and his guests took a step into the nave, instinctively moving away from the danger.

"Don't move!" El Diablo shouted.

All three froze and raised their hands in a gesture of surrender.

"You the priest with the visions?" *El Diablo* sneered as he approached. He was the oldest, skinny with the bad skin, bad teeth and the jitters of a meth addict. Bobbing up and down as he spoke.

His two accomplices looked like brothers, equally twitchy. *El Diablo* waved the machete, pointing the large blade at Vasquez. Spiders aimed his gun at Vasquez. *Santa Muerte* aimed his weapon at Lord. Though if they started spraying, Diana was close enough that she would be hit. They didn't recognize that the petite woman was the biggest physical threat. The holstered gun was hidden under her loose shirt.

"I start with your right arm," *El Diablo* said, gesturing with the machete. "Then your left. See if you still alive when I get to your legs."

Lord looked over at Wynne. Their eyes met. She gave a subtle nod. Lord knew she was ready.   "Hey guys," Lord said. "We were just here for that confession thing. I wonder if we could leave and you settle things up without us."

"What?" *El Diablo* exclaimed. "You think you just gonna walk out of here?"

"No harm, no foul," Lord said, smiling but wiggling his fingers nervously. The twitchy-eyed gunmen glanced at his hands.

"I cut you up first, *maricon*," El Diablo said.

"We're not even Catholic," Lord continued. His fingers seemed as jittery as the gunmen. "We just heard good things and figured we'd stop by. I guess it's not the best timing."

The distraction gave Diana the extra fraction of a second that she needed to draw the Walther from the gun at her waist. Three shots in Spiders, three shots in Saint Death. Death managed to squeeze the trigger and thirty-two 9mm rounds sprayed around the rectory. Even with the silencers, the noise of the shots echoed in the confined space.

El Diablo raised his blade and lunged at her. She put two shots into him and the gun locked open. Empty. Still he charged. As *El Diablo* passed Lord, his rage focused on Wynne, Lord stepped forward and shoved him with all his strength. The mix of adrenaline and years of doing push-hands sent the Devil flying. *El Diablo* looked like a wire work stuntman in a Hong Kong martial arts movie as he smashed into the wall more than a foot off the ground. He slid to the floor and thrashed around, trying to get up. He nearly stood, then fell as he slipped on his own blood.

One of the shots from the Mac-10 had hit Vasquez. There was a growing dark red spot on his chest.

He wobbled over to his dying attackers. "Would you like last rites?" he offered.

"Fuck you," the Devil said before spewing a string of words in Spanish clearly reiterating his feelings.

Spiders was dead, *Santa Muerte* was barely conscious. Vasquez made the sign of the cross over them.

"We better get you to a doctor," Lord said to the priest.

The door swung open. Diana cocked her arm to throw the pistol but held back as a middle-aged Latina woman rushed in. The woman hurried to Vasquez, taking a gauze pack out of her bag.

"I'm a nurse at County USC emergency," she said to Diana, ripping off Vasquez's shirt and gently pushing him onto the couch.

Diana lowered her gun.

As Vasquez lay back, he said to Lord, "You better go. Police will be here soon."

"He'll be okay," the nurse said. "I've seen worse."

"How did you know what..." Wynne began.

With great effort, Vasquez raised his hand. "The Lord works in mysterious ways." He smiled. "I also asked neighbors to keep an eye open. Go now. When it is time, I will come."

Lord took out a burner cell phone and slipped it to Vasquez. "If you need to contact me, in an emergency."

"Like this," he said with his weary smile, waving his hand to indicate the gang members lying on the floor."

"Hopefully this is a once in a lifetime occurrence," Lord said. "It's also for when I need you."

The door opened again. An elderly man and woman hurried in. The woman joined the nurse in helping Vasquez. The grandfatherly man tugged Diana's hand and led them out the door. He led them down a block, then up a driveway, into a backyard, then another backyard. They moved quickly in the rear from house to house. He seemed to know where there were no fences, no dogs. He moved surprisingly quickly for someone who no doubt was well passed his 70th birthday.

More screaming sirens. Louder and louder. LA County Sheriff's Department vehicles screeched by on the street. But the trio was out of view. They passed under the Pomona Freeway. Then they were by Bella Vista Park. *"Llave?"* the grandfatherly man asked.

The couple looked perplexed. The man took keys out of his pocket and pointed to them.

Lord handed him the car keys.

"Espere aquí!" the man said, holding up his hand in a "stop" gesture, then pointing to the ground. He hustled off down the street.

"I'm pretty sure that means wait here," Lord said.

It felt strange to be standing waiting by the park, watching young men playing soccer, couples at the picnic tables, mothers pushing baby carriages. A *mariachi* band practiced in another corner. Moments away from the carnage and death at the church.

"I can't believe we got there just before the killers," Diana said. "And Vasquez seemed so calm about it. If I didn't have Shorty's gun, we'd be dead."

"Or if we got there a half hour later, we would have found his body. Or we could have left Palmdale earlier and gotten out before the killers. Maybe it's all just the multiverse, different possibilities. This happens to be ours."

"Too weird," she said.

Fifteen minutes later, the grandmotherly woman drove up, parked, and handed Lord the keys. She walked away without saying anything.

Tom noticed Diana's hands were shaking as they climbed into the car.

"You okay?" he asked.

"I never shot anyone before. Never killed anyone. I feel every nerve ending. But I feel disconnected. I'm horrified but so glad to be alive. I can't describe it. ...I had no choice, right?"

"Of course not. You saved our lives. Is there anything I can do?"

"Just get us the hell out of here."

Chapter Thirty

They headed northeast, navigating the Los Angeles freeways until getting on Interstate 15. Lord drove and Wynne switched through the radio dial, trying to catch news about the shootout they had just survived. She settled on KNX 1070.

When the story came on, details were sketchy. Three suspected gang members dead, the priest wounded but expected to live. No suspects in custody. Police were actively pursuing leads.

"*Suspected* gang members?" Wynne snorted. "None of them looked like they could work anyplace other than a meth lab."

"I'm just glad Hector is okay," Lord said.

"Me too. I was thinking what would have happened if Shorty hadn't given me the gun."

"That was amazing shooting."

"Two out of three were good. That devil guy would've cut me bad if you hadn't shoved him," she recalled. "Or actually, calling what you did a shove doesn't do it justice. He looked like he was hit by a freight train."

"It's *fa jing*. When you use *qi* in a power burst. Besides you had already softened him up with a few shots."

"He was so hopped up, he could have kept swinging. Like Shorty's chicken without a head," she said. "You stepped in. You could've had your head sliced off too."

Lord shrugged. "At least it wouldn't be a vital organ."

"You don't need to joke. Thank you."

"Pleased to be of assistance, ma'am."

She squeezed his thigh, noticing the blood spatter for the first time. "Are you okay?"

"The blood's not mine. Either devil's or the priest's. Hopefully the devil."

They took turns driving, gazing out the window, and dozing. Lord researched their destination when not at the wheel. He read Diana the bubbly Chamber of Commerce prose: "Nestled among the pines of South Dakota's beautiful Black Hills and six breathtaking parks and monuments is a vibrant city beckoning to be explored.... The Gateway to Mount Rushmore...Gateway to the Black Hills...Gateway to the Badlands."

"Quite the gateway," Wynne said.

"Forty-two presidential statues, a short drive to five national parks. Cathedral Spires of Custer State Park, Crazy Horse Memorial..."

"You want to forget about Chris Pruitt and just go hiking?" Wynne asked sarcastically.

"Okay, okay," Lord said, swiping at his phone. "Let's see, Rapid City High School, home of the Eagles, 363 students, 31.86 teachers, the 13, 363rd largest high school nationally, which puts it at about the halfway point for size. I wonder what the .86 teacher looks like."

"Tom, if I didn't love you, I would shove you out of the car. On the freeway. That whole speech you gave before about how the interstate system is actually the Dwight D. Eisenhower National System of Interstate and Defense Highways, developed in 1956 for I forgot how many billion and how many tens of thousands of miles..."

"It's up to 48,000 plus now. And..."

"Please stop. I know it's your way of trying to regain control, make sense of things. Sometimes it's cute. Sometimes, let's just say it's not cute."

"Okay. I'll Google Earth her house and the school. I'll stay focused."

"Thank you."

After about four hours of driving, they stopped in the outskirts of Las Vegas. Tom bought an electric screwdriver in a hardware store. They drove into town and searched for cheaper casino parking lots, ones that didn't have video cameras covering every square foot. Tom stole four sets of plates from CRVs. He managed to get two plates from Nevada, one from Utah, and one from Wyoming. States they would be passing through. If a cop ran them, they'd match the model. Though not the VIN, if the officer took it that far.

He had them both wear sunglasses and ball caps, with Diana's hair tucked up tight and barely visible. They changed outfits. He put on a fake mustache and had Diana puff out her cheeks with balls of cotton in her mouth.

"Is this really necessary?" Diana asked.

"Yes. Kroll's eyes are everywhere. He probably knows I headed to Atlantic City after escaping PRI. One logical conclusion would be that I would go for a fortune in Las Vegas. This city is loaded with closed circuit cameras and undercover private security."

She harrumphed. "I thought what happens in Vegas stays in Vegas."

"As long as you don't piss off the casino owners by taking money out of the place. And if you think there's no mob presence here anymore, you probably believe that Disneyland is run by Mickey Mouse."

"I sorta feel bad stealing license plates from people," Diana said.

"I'll send them money orders for $100 for the aggravation of going to DMV. It won't make up for what they've lost at the casino."

They mingled with throngs wandering The Strip. The street was clogged with honking cars. The sidewalks also filled with pedestrians enjoying the balmy 70-degree weather. The couple treated themselves to a meal at the Bacchanal Buffet at Caesar's Palace.

"So weird, seeing all these people just living their lives, eating, gambling, laughing," she said, as she tugged at a crab leg. "A few hours ago..." Her voice trailed off.

He patted her hand under the table. "How you holding up?"

"Pretty good. All things considered."

"Eat, drink and be merry," he said. "Tonight we'll be sleeping in the state that's the exact opposite of Nevada. From the excess of Vegas to the repression of Salt Lake City. Let's pig out on a couple of desserts. After that, you want to see me use my abilities?"

"Of course."

"We have to be careful. But it'll be good to replenish our cash," he said. "I've done this periodically over the years. Always cautiously."

Over the next five hours, they went to the poker tables at Caesar's and Bellagio on the Strip, then the Golden Nugget and Binion's in downtown. They left $11,400 richer.

"Is this why money isn't an issue for you?" Wynne asked as they got into the car.

"I also did well with bitcoin. The secrecy of it appealed to my paranoia. I figured I wouldn't be the only one wanting to cut the banks out and stay off the grid. I put about $2,000 in, which was almost all my life savings at the time. Late 2010. I started cashing out when it topped a million. I've got a frugal lifestyle. You never did see where I lived, did you?"

She shook her head.

"Let's just say I'm comfortable with a minimalist approach. Still, the money goes out so I make a trip every now and then to the casinos."

"But you lost sometimes."

"Of course. Did you notice the pit boss start to hover at the Nugget?"

"That scowling guy with the blond toupee and the big nose with broken blood vessels?"

"Yup. They've got eye in the sky cameras hidden in the ceilings at all those places. Watching for card counters, card markers, anyone colluding with a dealer. Do you know much about poker?"

"Not really."

"Okay, when I had a straight, that's a good hand. Normally someone would keep betting. I folded because I knew that woman with the red hair two seats over from me had a killer hand. She did a great job masking her excitement. I had watched her play and knew she was skilled, not an amateur excited by two pair. She ultimately showed a full house, which would have beaten me. There were a couple times when I went all in on a bluff since I knew no one else had anything better. Also the way I sit down, make money, and get the hell out. I'm sure there's surveillance people right now looking over tapes, wondering about me. It's time to get out of town."

They had many hours and thousands of miles to talk. Despite his best intentions, Tom sometimes bombarded her with unnecessary details. She would make a zip your lip gesture and he'd stop. When she was more annoyed, she'd make a throat slitting gesture. He told her about ESP research, how the EEG was first developed by someone looking for psychic connection, or the 2013 Duke University study where rats demonstrated telepathic connection when wired with electrodes. And how Duke was the birthplace of parapsychology research, with J.B Rhine in the 1930s. But significant research had been done at Stanford Research

Institute, Princeton Engineering Anomalies Research Lab, UCLA, University of Arizona, Cornell, University of Virginia.

Occasionally they went deeper, to discussions about life and death.

"I suppose I should feel guilty," Diana said. "Or proud. Or angry. But I just feel kind of numb."

"Your mind is digesting something it never had to process before."

"I remember asking my father how many people he killed. I was about 10. At first, he said he didn't know. He'd tell me a lot of times shots would come out of a clump of trees and he'd shoot back. The shooting would stop. But over the years I kept persisting. He'd say, 'not as many as a pilot does on one bombing run.' But I was a curious kid. Persistent too. I didn't get that the topic was something he wasn't happy to talk about.

"He'd divert me with sayings like 'being a good soldier doesn't mean dying for your country, it means helping your enemy die for his country.' A few years before he passed, he finally told me the number. Face to face, he had killed 29 men. Twenty-nine sounds like a little and sounds like a lot. He admitted that some of their faces came to him at night. Of course if you count all the lives taken by the men under his command, there'd be thousands of deaths. He told me that he saw mainly faces of buddies who had died."

Tom would encourage her to talk but he allowed long silences when he felt she needed them. She'd ask how he was doing with the killings and nearly being killed. He told her, "My main emotion is gratitude that we made it out safely. At the same time, I wish we had never been there."

During a long stretch traveling north through Nevada, skirting the edge of the Mojave Desert, she said, "It's not like

I haven't been in fights. I've knocked people down, knocked people out. I've seriously hurt people."

"Like those creeps when we first met."

"For them, not seriously enough. But there's something about death. Knowing that they are just no more. What do you think happens when people die?"

They talked about their beliefs, and then transitioned into how ESP often got thrown in with séances and psychics who supposedly talked to the departed.

"That's when you get too many scammers involved," Lord said angrily. "People preying on grief, taking money from loved ones who just can't let go. The phonies make it hard to do legitimate studies. Every time a con artist is exposed, the hardcore skeptics can go 'see, look, it's all bogus.' But that's like looking at some televangelist con man creep and saying there's no good in religion." He told her how Houdini, The Amazing Randi and other magicians were obsessed with using their skills to debunk psychic scammers.

They talked about the general and the specific, the past and the present. With little talk about the future.

"I wish I could tell Shorty what happened," Diana mused. "I suspect he'd be thrilled."

"You know we never can."

"Of course."

"And we should start getting rid of pieces of the gun. Drop a part as we go over a river or leave a small part in a rest stop trash can until it's all gone."

"The firing pin is probably most damning. I didn't get a chance to collect shells after they ejected," she said.

"Hopefully Hector's helpers did."

Diana took the gun out of the holster and held it gently in her hands. "It did its job." She field stripped it, breaking the weapon down into slide, guard rod, barrel, grip, and clips. She wiped everything down with a rag.

"Your father would've been proud of your shooting," he said as she stared fondly at the pieces of the weapon. She laid the pieces on the floor in the back seat, under the rag.

"Maybe. But he would've given me a hard time for not dropping the Devil. Two out of three isn't good enough when the third's got a machete." She paused. "Unless you've got a ballsy boyfriend who's willing to step up."

* * *

Cutler had come to dread his interactions with Kroll. His boss had never been pleasant. As the pressure from the Russians had increased, he'd become even more abrasive. Despite all his years working with the psychologist, Cutler didn't know details of Kroll's Moscow relationship. Which was not an issue for someone who had been a long time NSA employee. Need-to-know and compartmentalizing were the norm. But whatever grip the Russians had on Kroll, it was tightening.

Kroll had a standing order that he wanted to know details of any significant life changes for any of the PRI subjects. This meant that Cutler's internet alert system—his own proprietary variation on Google alerts—was frequently pinging. If anything was published, pretty much anywhere, he would pick it up. Birth or death notices, journal article published, businesses opened, employee of the month, lawsuit filed, teacher of the year, marriage/divorce, even a subject's child winning a sports trophy.

There were 21 survivors being tracked. Most of the information he didn't bother to pass on. Some were false positives. Jeremy Sherman chose common names. Most of the Alan Wilson stories had to do with a publicity-loving low-level

Minneapolis executive who was frequently featured in Chamber of Commerce press releases. Dave Peterson's namesake was a petty criminal, nicknamed "Dirty Dave," who often turned up on the police blotter in Louisville, Kentucky. Another alias was shared with a trophy-winning fisherman in Miami who fancied himself quite the Casanova. Cutler was fed up with pictures of him with a dead marlin and yet another young woman in a bikini, standing on a dock, grinning.

But this ping was more significant.

Kroll was in his office editing an article for the *Trends in Cognitive Science* journal. The psychologist was trying to keep busy, to not think about Jeremy and the deadline from the Russians.

Cutler knocked gently on his open door.

"Yes?" Kroll said, not looking up from his computer.

"One of the PRI subjects was shot several times."

"Who?"

"Vasquez. The priest in East Los Angeles."

"The one with the gang affiliation," Kroll said. "Why should I care?"

"There were initial reports that a couple was seen in the area shortly before the shootout."

"Jeremy and that woman?"

"Possibly."

Kroll swiveled in his chair and stared at Cutler. "You said initial reports?"

"Yes. A nearby shopkeeper told investigators he saw a couple going in shortly before the shooting. Right age, general physical description, not Latinos. When the homicide detective returned to question the man, the store owner was much less certain. Other supposed eyewitnesses muddied the waters. Multiple descriptions. The person or persons who killed the hit men range from looking like LeBron James to

Danny DeVito to Jennifer Lopez. Varying races, numbers, genders, ages, weights."

"You're not giving me helpful information."

"My investigator spoofed being a journalist doing an in-depth piece on MS-13. The hit men were meth heads, known enforcers. Sounds like one shooter took out all three of them. Same gun, all from the same general spot. The cop described it as amazing shooting."

"That doesn't sound like Jeremy."

"No, but it could be the woman."

"Could be. Possibly. Conflicting reports," Kroll snapped. "I'm not impressed. I need solid information. Not wild speculation."

"Yes sir. I'll keep on it," Cutler said, looking down as he walked back to his office. His gut told him it had been the couple at the shootout. He decided to assign one of his best diggers to get more information.

* * *

All the parts of the gun were gone, separated by hundreds of miles, by the time they reached Sulphurdale, Utah. They pulled off the freeway and walked into the Fishlake National Forest. Though the sun was setting, Wynne wanted to see Pando, a giant quaking aspen that is the largest and oldest living organism on earth. She let Tom look it up and he told her the trees were 80,000 years old, 106 acres and 13 million pounds.

"The bad news is, it's dying," Lord read. "They blame drought and overgrazing. But fire suppression may be part of it too. The fires would kill off the conifers, which are the aspen's big rival. The tree would stay growing underground even as the earth got scorched."

They stood in silence, staring at the acres of white-trunked, yellow-leafed trees. A gentle breeze and the setting sun made the fluttering leaves look like they were on fire.

When she was confident no one was around, Diana buried the leather holster like it was a beloved pet. Tom knew to be quiet as she tamped the earth down.

They got back onto the freeway and drove up to the Sundance Resort northeast of Provo. They ate in The Tree Room, with 20-foot-high ceilings, Native American art from Robert Redford's private collection, and artfully prepared American cuisine. They each ordered a glass of wine, a feat not possible in much of Utah, and enjoyed a candlelight dinner.

"Someday I'd like to come back and spend the night here," Lord told her.

"That's fine," she said, though he could tell she was disappointed they weren't going to stay.

"If we wanted to check in, they'd want credit card and ID," he explained. "What we have should hold up but I prefer to not leave any sort of paper trail."

She stroked his hand on the table. "I understand."

"We'll go someplace smaller, not as nice, but less likely to have a firm corporate check-in policy."

She tenderly held his hand. "There's a part of me that's enjoying this Bonnie and Clyde adventure. Not a typical road trip."

"Hopefully we have a happier ending than Bonnie and Clyde."

They drove a half hour and found a motel that Tom said looked perfect. Ten units, with just four cars in the parking lot. Well-kept, simple amenities. A large, weathered sign boasting of being AAA selected and having a continental breakfast, cable TV, Wi-Fi and an outdoor swimming pool. It was dark but a couple of teens were hanging out by the pool, making loud, playful noises.

The man behind the counter didn't look happy. He was somewhere past 60, could have been 80, slender with rheumy eyes. The office smelled of cigarette smoke. A large basket on the floor held two curled up gray cats who didn't stir, even when the bell on the door rang loudly as the couple entered. A TV played in the room behind the small front office.

Lord filled out the paperwork while Wynne thumbed through the wire rack holding brightly colored brochures for local attractions. Zip-lining, river rafting, skiing, snowboarding, paleontology museum, a water park.

"Smoking or non-smoking room?" the man behind the counter asked flatly.

"Non-smoking."

"Smart. I wish my wife had done the same. The prophet Joseph Smith made it clear in the Words of Wisdom."

"What did you say?" barked a gravelly female voice from the room with the TV.

"Nothing, dear," the owner responded.

He whispered, "Disgusting habit. Going to kill her someday."

Tom nodded.

"Credit card?" the man asked.

"Sure," taking out a Visa with the name Steve Talley on it. "But listen, the little woman went a little crazy in Las Vegas. Shopping while I was in the casino. The card is probably maxed out." Tom took out a wad of cash and paid in full for the room. "If there's any problem, I'll pay for everything with good old American greenbacks."

"I hear you," the clerk said. "I'm giving you the room at the far end. Those teens can be a bit noisy. If you look out the back window it's got a nice view."

Tom and Diana checked into the room which smelled mildly of industrial cleaner. The space was tidy, with a queen-size bed and clean bedding. The lithographs on the wall showed mountain scenes, and the bathroom was nicer than expected.

"Shower together?" Lord suggested and she agreed.

They savored their time under the hot water.

Wrapped in towels, they sauntered into the bedroom.

"What's that talk about 'the little woman going crazy?'" Diana teased.

"I wanted to bond with him."

"You couldn't just rave about the Utah Jazz?"

"It seemed more natural. Would you prefer being my better half? Or ball and chain?"

"I just don't like you sounding like 1950s patriarchy."

"But you are a little woman," he said playfully. "What would you like-"

She had yanked away his towel and shoved him to the bed before he could complete the sentence. Her own towel fell to the floor and then she was naked astride him on the bed.

"What would I like? Well, your talk made me dissatisfied. You're not going to get to go to sleep until I'm satisfied. That could take a while. You up for it?"

"I think you can see I am."

They stayed up later than they should have but neither had complaints.

As they were dozing off, Lord murmured, "My little woman" in her ear.

"My just big enough man," she responded and they snuggled closer.

Chapter Thirty-One

They headed east, stopping for breakfast and gas on the outskirts of Salt Lake City. The diner was clean and quiet and they found a booth a comfortable distance from other customers.

"You haven't really said much about Chris Pruitt," Wynne said. "Just that Lisa did a great job figuring out where she was. What was so hard?"

"When I knew Chris, it was short for Christopher. Now it's Christina."

"Ahhhh. That would be confusing. Though not as bad as it was for her."

"He, er, she was very troubled. There was at least one suicide attempt. And cutting. I was freaked out at the time but it makes more sense now. Chris was clairvoyant. Remote viewing. That actually was the highest priority for the program. I know Kroll kept testing me, hoping I had that ability. I never did. When I read the declassified stuff later one CIA official described it as like a human spy satellite that could see through walls.

"There were a couple of physicists at Stanford who were big on the idea. And when the U.S. found out the Soviets were working on it, there was this psychic cold war. I had the best telepathy results but I know Kroll was most hopeful about Chris. He, ah, she would've been kicked out if not for that."

"You keep saying 'he.' Do you have a problem with her?"

"No. I just think of her as a him. Trying to recalibrate."

"Better get your pronouns right before we meet her."

"It's hard to reconcile the info from Lisa with my image of Chris. He was miserable. I dipped into his mind once and the disconnect was super intense. Lisa's info has Christina as the happy housewife of South Dakota. Successful teacher. Beloved stepmom to two kids. I never would've figured her for moving out of the city. Truth be told, I figured he'd be dead by this time."

"She."

"My memories are of him."

"Focus on using she. A slip up could be hurtful. How did she get to South Dakota?"

"The last trace I could find of her, she was working as a waiter in New York."

Diana gave him a scolding look.

"Waitress. But she was somewhere in transition, so I don't know what to say," Lord said. "Look, I'm trying. She was wait staff in NY. At a coffee shop on the upper west side. I found one psych hospitalization for a suicide attempt. Then she disappeared. I presumed she was dead. Lisa somehow found her and was able to backtrack. Working at another restaurant, as a woman, apparently off the books, she met a Columbia School of Journalism student named Randall Pruitt. They fell in love. She followed him as he moved around the country, working at several different papers, career on the rise. He had aging parents in Rapid City, gave up a rising star position at the St. Louis Post Dispatch and went home. With his wife."

"And she seems to have fit right in?"

"Chris was from a small town in Nebraska so that wasn't hard. I don't know how the transgender thing played out. But I'm sure we'll find out. I've been thinking this whole time how to approach her. I'm not really sure how."

"You don't want to call her beforehand?"

"No. That element of surprise is important."

"I don't know," Diana said, shaking her head. "She's not going to be happy to see you."

"I don't want to give her a chance to run. Or get a few cowboy neighbors to ride us out of town." Lord dipped his toast in his eggs and ate. "We've got about 10 more hours' drive time. Shall we see if we can make it to Rock Springs, Table Rock or Point of Rocks? We can stop and see the Natural Corrals Ice Caves. It's an archaeology site, known for Native American buffalo kills. Bring back memories of our time in Indian Heaven. Or maybe you'd prefer the Wyoming Frontier Prison tour? It's another hour or so up the road."

"You've been Googling," her tone somewhere between annoyance and amusement.

"Part of my trying to figure out when best to approach her. We might as well take a break on the road rather than hanging out in Rapid City."

"That makes sense," she said. "Let's just see how it goes. I'll take the first shift driving. You keep thinking about the when and how of approaching her."

* * *

Cutler knocked at his boss's partially open door.

"What is it?" Kroll snapped.

"News about Lord and Wynne."

"More definitive than last time, I trust," Kroll said.

"Yes."

Kroll crooked his finger indicating for Cutler to enter.

"What do you have?' the psychologist asked.

"Absolute confirmation that it was them in Los Angeles. My investigator convinced the shop owner that no authorities or people in the neighborhood would know what he said. Then she had a sketch artist do images of the two people the shopkeeper had seen." Cutler took out the drawings.

Kroll squinted at them. "This could be them. Of course, this could be a thousand other couples. These are after all rather generic images."

"I decided to have her go up to see Ray McGuire in Palmdale. He's the former stunt man who has been a fringe survivalist for many years."

"I know my test subjects," Kroll said tersely. "Shorty. Former addict, very questionable psychokinesis test subject. Had he seen them?"

"He threatened my investigators. They identified themselves as FBI. He said if they didn't have a warrant, they better get off his property. He started quoting distorted laws and waving a gun."

"They learned nothing other than confirming he's on the fringe?"

"From him, yes. But they found a neighbor who saw a couple visiting him a couple days ago. He never had any visitors. This neighbor has lived there 15 years. The couple fit the description of Lord and Wynne. This neighbor admitted it was unusual enough that she watched them through binoculars. They were shooting at the target range he has off of his trailer."

"This is decent circumstantial evidence," Kroll said. "Did your investigators go back?"

"They felt it was too dangerous. And the couple was long gone." He didn't tell Kroll about another card he had to play. He didn't want to seem to fail again in his boss's eyes.

"Even if it is them, all we know is they were in Los Angeles and then near Los Angeles."

"I have more." Cutler took out two grainy head shots. "There's different kinds of cameras in public areas. Ones from law enforcement are hardest to hack. But there's some that are traffic cams, or even webcams just to show the curious the weather. Very easily hacked. Some are even deliberately open to public viewers."

Kroll waved his hand impatiently to indicate Cutler wasn't divulging any news.

"I had a hunch that they would go to Las Vegas," Cutler continued. "We know he has done that before to replenish his cash. We've always been a couple steps behind him."

Kroll looked at the head shots. "Again, it could be them, or could be a similar couple."

"I ran it through my facial recognition software. There's an 82 percent chance it is them. Very good odds."

"Are they still there? Do we have more specifics?"

"Using traffic cams I was able to learn that they are in a relatively late model gray Honda CRV. It was a Nevada plate, but I was unable to get the number. They left the city heading northeast. We're working to narrow it down."

"Going into the heartland. You are convinced they are contacting other PRI students?"

"Yes."

"Let me know as soon as you have more specifics. And alert Klimke."

* * *

Salt Lake City was in the northeast corner of Utah, Rapid City in the southeast corner of South Dakota, so most of the drive was in Wyoming. Montana, just to the north, was the Big Sky state. But the description certainly could apply to Wyoming.

Every car on the road was either an SUV or a pickup. Most had gun racks in the back. Some had guns displayed.

"Getting a gun here probably wouldn't be hard," Diana mused.

"I suspect you'd have to show residency. But I could Google..."

"I bet you could," she said, and they drove on. "If we meet up with those bastards, I'll blow their heads off."

Lord looked at her, surprised by the vehemence. "If we need to kill to defend ourselves, that's one thing. You're talking about executing people."

"They executed Lisa."

"We don't know..."

"If Kroll didn't pull the trigger, he's still responsible."

"We can't..."

"You've said they haven't tried to kill you since you're the prize. I'm collateral damage. And like I just said, they killed my best friend."

"It's not like they haven't made my life hell. For years. After shooting those guys in self-defense you were all shook up. Now you're ready to be judge, jury, executioner."

"I've been thinking about Lisa a lot. What her final moments were like. Let alone that they had tortured her before. And how they tried to kidnap you and kill me in Indian Heaven."

"So you kill Kroll and anyone with him? Any witnesses?"

"I'm just saying that I will if I have to."

"What if we can get them to back off?"

"That makes everything okay for you? All the years you've been on the run, all the people they've hurt."

"No. But if you start executing people-"

She held her hand up in a "stop" gesture. "Let's just enjoy the view."

The deep blue sky had a few postcard perfect white cumulus clouds, giant puffballs. There were barbed wire fences with occasional tumble weeds pinned up against them by the wind. Other areas were delineated by split rail fences, the wood baked gray by the sun. Huge expanses of land. The prairie. Small groves of trees. Herds of black and white cattle, an occasional horse. An infrequent house. Corrals. Rocky low rolling hills, mountains off in the distance.

Stops for gas, food and bathrooms were brief and kept to a minimum. Diana relaxed, she extended her right hand and Tom took it in his left and gently squeezed.

They avoided talking about Kroll and his men, focusing on the beauty of the scenery. Lord spewed out facts about the Native Americans, the wildlife, the state history. They debated the merits of surprising Pruitt versus giving her notice that they were coming.

Ultimately, Lord decided on a compromise. Rather than just drop in on Chris Pruitt, he called her when they were a couple exits from Rapid City.

"Chris, this is Jeremy Sherman. I don't know if you remember me, but I was at PRI with you."

"Oh." There was a long silence.

"I'd like to come by and talk. I'm less than 15 minutes away. If it wouldn't be too inconvenient, it's very important."

"I imagine so. I presume you weren't just visiting Mt. Rushmore and decided to drop in. I've worked hard to distance myself from my past."

"I understand. Just hear me out. Please."

An even longer silence.

She finally said, "You have my address, I presume?"

"We get off the freeway at Deadwood Avenue, then on to Tatanka Road."

"Yes. I'll see you soon."

After she disconnected, Diana said, "Seems like you made the right decision, giving her a bit of notice. She didn't sound happy. But she didn't tell you to piss off."

"My presence must be very jarring," Lord said.

One of the burner phones began to chirp. Lord checked the caller ID.

"It's Shorty," he said to Diana as he hit the button to accept the call.

"Hey Shorty. What's going on?" Lord asked.

"I was debating whether to call or not. But I figured better to be safe than sorry. A couple days ago these two assholes showed up and flashed ID saying they were FBI, looking for you."

"What?"

"Don't worry, I didn't tell 'em anything. Chased them off the property."

"What did they look like?"

"A guy and a gal." McGuire described them.

Neither sounded like Klimke or his men.

"You sure you didn't say anything about us?"

"I told them what I would have told them even if I thought they were real feds. Come back with a warrant if you want anything.'"

"Thanks."

"How's it going?"

"Pretty good," Lord said. "Talk later." He disconnected.

Lord turned to Diana. "Did you hear?"

"Yes. You were pretty abrupt with him. I'm sure he wanted to talk."

"I do too. But phones are just not secure."

"Really? You think Kroll has capacity to listen in on everyone's phone calls?"

"No. But someone in a car with a good amplified parabolic mike can pick a conversation up from 500 feet away. Or more likely they can bounce a laser off a window from much further and listen in on any conversation in the room. Hopefully they're not still watching Shorty."

"I don't know if you're paranoid or if I should worry more."

"Probably both."

* * *

An hour later, Cutler hurried into Kroll's office after a quick knock. Kroll could tell his usually sedate tech man was excited.

"I knew it," Cutler blurted out. "They're in South Dakota. About 15 miles west of Rapid City. One of your subjects, Chris Pruitt lives there. She's the only one in South Dakota or within 500 miles of their locale."

"This sounds like it isn't just a computer projection. That you're sure of where they are?"

"Absolutely. Hard data. While McGuire was talking to one of my agents, the other one managed to drop a reader next to the fence. It mimics a cell phone tower, like a Stingray Interceptor and can pick up a phone signal from 100 yards. I've personally developed the equipment to miniaturize. The device is no bigger than a paperback book."

"You didn't mention that before?"

"I wanted to be sure I'd get helpful data."

Kroll nodded. "Good work."

"The bad news is I've spoken with Gunther and he said the nearest operatives he could locate are in Chicago. Two hours away by private jet. At least an hour to mobilize them. I did some analytics, based on the amount of traveling they've done, going from McGuire to Vasquez to Pruitt, factored in with their apparent direction, the number of other subjects he may be aware of, and-"

"I doubt they will be staying in Rapid City," Kroll said.

Cutler sensed his boss's frustration at having good intelligence but not being able to act on it.

He silently watched Kroll calculate.

"They could conceivably steal a different vehicle or decide to shift to Amtrak or Greyhound. How likely is it that their destination is Chicago?"

"Better than 92 percent."

"As I recall, we have only one former subject left living there."

"Correct."

"Laying the trap nearest to the bait is the most logical move. Alert Gunther to fly to Chicago to intercept them."

"Will do, sir."

Kroll directed his attention to his computer and tapped an inquiry into Google Maps. "The drive to Rapid City is about 20 hours." He leaned back in his chair and steepled his fingers. "Assuming they stopped to sleep and didn't drive straight through, and there were no adverse driving events, they should be reaching the subject about now.

"Get me Pruitt's phone number. Perhaps I can gather some additional information that will help us locate him."

"We certainly have biographical leverage on her."

"That we do," Kroll agreed.

Chapter Thirty-Two

The house was a sprawling ranch-style, about 50 years old, freshly painted. Well landscaped. Thriving small plantings along the sides of the long driveway. The door to the two-car garage was shut. The driveway forked to the front of the house, and another unlandscaped stretch to a small barn in the distance. A big lawn and what looked like considerable undeveloped acreage behind the house. Part of the land was set off in a football field-sized horse corral.

They parked near the front door. The only security evident was a small doorbell video camera.

The couple was hypervigilant as they approached, struggling with memories of the bloodbath in the church. They had continued to process that gruesome experience, each in their own way. Lots of prolonged silences. The driver drove and the passenger stared out the window. The beautiful scenery continued but neither one absorbed much of it.

A second after Tom pressed the doorbell button, the door opened.

"Please, come in," she said graciously. Her voice was soft, a little deep.

She was skillfully made up, showing off deep brown eyes. No sign of stubble. A little bit of cleavage in her clingy dress. Definitely a woman's body.

She seemed to know what Tom was thinking. She smiled with the look women get when they seem to be 500 years ahead of men in evolution. "It's been a while, Jeremy. Would you care to introduce me?" she asked, turning toward Diana.

"Christina Pruitt, Diana Wynne."

"I've always dreaded someone from my past coming here. But that doesn't mean I can't be polite." She turned back to me. "Please come in the other room. I was just taking a pie out of the oven when you called."

A sliding glass door at the far side of the room opened onto a deck that poked out into the wide-open spaces behind the house. Two walls were dominated by animal heads: deer, elk, a black bear, cougar, mountain goat, antelope, big horn sheep and bison. With some repeats, there were close to 20 taxidermized eyes staring into the room.

Christina came out of the kitchen with three slices of pie and small pitchers of lemonade and iced tea on a serving tray. "I have soda or tea. Coffee if you'd like?"

"This will be fine," Tom said.

She sat down, crossing her legs gracefully. She handed them small plates and they ate. Apple rhubarb pie. Tom said it was as good as any he had ever eaten. Diana nodded in agreement.

"Going through the process I went through to get here, I appreciate being a woman more than many cisgender women do," she said. She daintily nibbled a piece of pie. "Do you know why I agreed to see you?"

He shook his head.

"You were nice to me back then," she said.

"I don't recall doing anything special."

"Let me rephrase it. You weren't mean to me. I went through a lot of cruelty, a lot of abuse. By the time I got to PRI I was a wreck. Even there, the cruelty continued. Dr. Kroll ran a tight ship but bullies find a way." She turned to Diana. "But Jeremy was different. He treated me with decency. That was an unusual experience. You know who else also treated me like a human being?"

Diana and Tom shook their heads.

"Dr. Kroll. I know he was intrigued by my abilities. We spent hours just talking. That man is so brilliant. We talked a lot about physics. Einstein's spooky action at a distance. Neuropsychology. Non-local consciousness. Astral projection. Schrodinger's non-locality and entanglement. Fluidity of time and space. Out-of-body experiences. Quantum mechanics. He gave me books and articles to read.

"A lot of trauma survivors dissociate. When you're a kid being abused and your body is trapped in a terrible situation, it's a skill to be able to send your mind elsewhere. I had that ability but in a way most other trauma survivors don't. I could report back specifics. He had me mind travel to a Soviet missile base. I described things in detail that no one could have known. Verified by satellite scans. I was one of the few who had multiple types of ESP. Remote viewing. Clairvoyance with some precog abilities. Dr. Kroll said I showed incredible promise. But the psychological trauma was just too much. The government was pushing him, he was pushing me. You know about my suicide attempts?"

Lord nodded.

"I was one of the last to be discharged. They gave me some hush money. I started investigating gender confirming surgery and going through the process. Lots and lots of time and money. There's so many things you take for granted, like every step you take. Women's hips are different. The worst thing a person in transition can do is start walking with a hip flounce like a truck-stop slut.

"But you know what—even during those hellish years I never had any doubts over whether I was doing the right thing. I chose to keep a variation of my dead name, Christopher. To never forget. Not that I ever really would." She smiled sadly. "Would you like more pie?"

"Maybe just a little piece," Tom said.

"An even smaller one for me," Diana seconded.

Christina got up and went into the kitchen, returning with two slices. "I haven't ever really told anyone about this. Randy knows, of course, and we've talked some. But I never wanted him to know about the old miserable me. Though I think he does and is just too much of a gentleman to push. We met when I was about halfway through the process. At first we were just friends. Then it became much, much more. Married coming up on twenty-two years." She smiled to herself and almost blushed.

"His sister has been wonderful. The Pruitt family owns one of the biggest agricultural equipment supply companies. She married into a family that controls three of the largest ranches in the area. She's a queen bee. When she threw her arm around me at the annual family barbecue and introduced me as her new sister, the little hens that might have pecked at me fell into line."

"I wondered what it was like as an outsider here," Diana said.

"You've got small-minded types. But you find just as many in the big city. They just talk different. Like people in Manhattan who made fun of people from Brooklyn until Brooklyn became hip and now they can both rag on the other boroughs. They call New York the melting pot but it sure isn't from what I saw. You've got just as much racism, sexism and bias as anywhere else."

"But more LGBTQ," Lord said.

"True. I have to go to Minneapolis for my OB-GYN. I wouldn't want a local doctor anyway. They would probably be able to keep a secret but I never know if their office staff would gossip. It's small enough that there's one degree of separation between most folks. It's not San Francisco. There's one gay bar in Sioux Falls, no place here in town." She paused, taking a bite of pie and a sip of iced tea.

"Dr. Kroll had nurtured my interest in science. It was too late for me to get a doctorate and become a scientist, so I got a teaching degree. If I could pass my passion to others, particularly girls, it would give my life meaning. And I also keep an eye out for girls or boys who might be struggling with their sexual orientation or gender identity. Nothing obvious, but I let them know that the time will come when they have more control over their lives. And there's nothing wrong with being attracted to whoever you're attracted to."

A car door slammed. Chris looked questioningly toward her front door.

"Get down," Tom shouted, jumping up and pushing Chris to the floor. Diana grabbed a fork and moved to next to the door, the side that swung open. Lord scrambled to get to the other side, against the wall, ready to jump into the fray.

"Who do you think-" the big man bellowed as he charged through the door.

Diana tackled him and had him down on the floor, fork at his throat.

"Stop! Stop!" Chris screamed.

There was no one behind the solo intruder and Tom shut the door. The big man lay on the floor. No weapon in sight.

Diana paused.

"That's my husband," Christina shouted, pulling herself up with the help of the coffee table. The remaining pie pieces and all the beverages had spilled on the hard wood floors.

Diana untangled herself from Randy Pruitt, keeping a wary eye on him as they both stood.

"What the hell is going on?" Randy snapped.

"Sorry," Tom said. "We're a bit edgy."

"A bit edgy? Psycho is more like it," he said. "This is my house, my wife."

"We thought you might have been someone else," Diana said.

Chris went into the kitchen and got a roll of paper towels. She began cleaning up the mess on the floor. Her husband stared at Lord and Wynne, arms folded across his chest. He was 6'4 and at least 250. Probably a football player in high school. Dark black hair with streaks of gray. Strong nose and cheek bones. A hint in his stern features that there might have been a Sioux ancestor. Dressed in jeans and a plaid work shirt, he looked more like a cowboy than a reporter. Which probably was a good thing in South Dakota.

"I thought you'd be in Pierre until late," Christina said to him.

"The hearing got put over," Randy responded. "I was going to surprise you. Then you called and told me about this guy coming over. You sounded stressed. So I burned up the road."

Tom apologized again.

Randy went into the kitchen and got a Lord Grizzly beer from the refrigerator. He downed half of it in a couple of swallows.

"Why are you bothering my wife?" he demanded, alternating between glaring at Diana and Tom.

"Honey, I told them they could come over," Chris said. "Unless he's changed significantly, Jeremy is a good person."

"Hmmm," he said, plopping down into a recliner that faced the couch. He took another gulp of beer.

"Can I help with the cleanup?" Tom asked Christina.

"No, no problem. Let's just sit down and talk."

"You got no business coming here," Randy said. "Then roughing up my wife and me."

"We never touched her. You were coming in hot and I sensed it," Tom said. "We're sorry for any trouble. We wouldn't have come all this way if there wasn't a really important reason."

Diana sat down next to Tom on the sofa. She kept her eyes on Randy, as if expecting him to make a sudden move. She had a forced smile on her face.

Christina sat on the love seat that matched the sofa. "Please continue," she said to Tom.

Lord told them everything.

"I think I remember Shorty," she said. "A gruff, tough little fellow, even back then. Kind of standoffish."

"He hasn't changed much," Tom said.

Tom thought for a moment of telling them what they had been through in East Los Angeles, but instantly recognized it was a dumb idea. They were fugitives from a triple homicide. Didn't want to make Chris and Randy accessories. Tom didn't identify Vasquez, only mentioning that they had stumbled into major trouble when they went to see a former PRI subject who lived in East Los Angeles.

When Tom told him about the attack at Diana's house and Moreau being killed, Randy shifted from protective husband to interested journalist. He got up and got another beer. This time he offered Tom and Diana one. Diana accepted. Randy brought Christina a large glass of chardonnay.

"We haven't asked about your abilities," Tom said to Christina.

"Funny how that goes," she said. "As I went through the transition process, as I became more and more comfortable with my body, the visions stopped. I've tried several times but no luck. Dr. Kroll reached out to me too after PRI. But when he found out I had lost my abilities, I never heard from him again. It's a trade-off I didn't anticipate. But I'm glad I did."

"Would you be willing to talk about your PRI experiences to a reporter?" Tom asked. "Maybe someone Randy recommends."

"No," Randy snapped. "There's no way we could keep things private. The news would come out and it would destroy her life."

"Don't worry about me," she said.

"It would impact me too. And the kids. The whole family."

"Are you saying you'd be ashamed?" she asked.

The two locked eyes. Their love was palpable. It was clearly something they had discussed before but never really resolved.

"If you want to do it, I'm with you," he said. "If people don't like it, fuck 'em and the horse they rode in on."

"I appreciate that." She went over to her husband and gave him a long kiss. "But I do know what it would mean. I wouldn't take it lightly. I'm not willing to throw away the life we've built here."

"What about people being open-minded?" Tom asked.

"I've suffered enough. Adjusted to the stealth lifestyle. I don't think I'm willing to confront Dr. Kroll. He was largely a positive force in my life. Even though I know he was doing it for his own interests. I'll think about it. Maybe Randy can help you find a sympathetic reporter."

Her mind was made up. Tom had seen enough deals go south when a salesperson pushed too hard. Diana saw Tom focusing and spoke for a bit, trying to change Chris's mind. No luck.

Tom was concerned about losing Christina and Randy as possible allies and shifted his approach.

"I understand," Tom said. "If you change your mind, I'll give you a number to call." Turning to Randy, Tom said, "It would be too obvious if you broke the story. There could be blowback on Chris and you. Is there someone you trust?"

He nodded. "Esteban Rodriquez. He's at the New York Times. I met him back in J-school and we've been in touch over the years. A rival then, a buddy now. He did a big story on fracking about two years ago that I helped him out on with local sources. He's solid, good instincts and as persistent as a terrier with a bone. The story you told is great but you're going to need more proof to get it past him. And his editors."

"Maybe Christina could confirm some stuff to him off the record?" Tom asked.

"Maybe."

"There's documents available through Freedom of Information Act requests. About 80,000 pages on ESP research but Kroll's stuff is still classified or was shredded. He was mentioned briefly at some of the congressional hearings on CIA excess. But you have to be able to read between the lines. The Congress people were more interested in grandstanding than uncovering the truth."

"Nothing from back then is going to be that damning," Randy said. "Interesting history but not much more than that. It's about his fanatic pursuit of you up until the present. You mentioned possible Russian involvement? That'll make them sit up and take notice. Maybe if Esteban can find some other current evidence, you'll have something the editors won't shitcan."

"We'll keep at it," Diana said.

"Good! If there's one thing I learned," Christina said, "It's don't give up."

Chapter Thirty-Three

"That was intense," Lord said as they got onto I-90 heading east. Although it would be a main city on ramp at a busy time of day, there were no cars waiting. Traffic must've been as unusual a phenomena for residents as silence was for New Yorkers. "She needed to talk as much as Shorty did. I'm glad she trusted us enough to open up."

"Even though she won't confront Kroll with you," Diana responded.

"But it's a good lead on a journalist. And she might change her mind. I felt her ambivalence."

"I understand her not wanting to rock the boat. She's made a nice life for herself."

Lord nodded. "You want to do anything touristy? We're not coming back this way I suspect and it's a long drive to Chicago."

"And after Chicago what?"

"North Carolina. Maybe by train. This driving is wearing me down," he said.

"I can drive."

"Sitting in the passenger seat is almost worse."

"You can surf the web." She had a Mona Lisa smile.

"We go in and out of cell phone service. I'd say we could switch to a train but there's no stops anywhere in South Dakota. And nothing in southern Minnesota. We'd have to go up north to Minneapolis, add on a few hours."

"You've been Googling."

"Guilty as charged. Though technically I've been using Duck, Duck Go to reduce my footprint."

"I'm getting cabin fever," she said. "Or whatever it is when you spend endless hours on the road locked in a car with a Google junkie." Her smile made it clear she was kidding.

A big brown road sign announced they were nearing the Badlands.

"How about we stop there?" he suggested. "You go for a run, I do some *tai chi*, we recharge. It's a fine tradition. Teddy Roosevelt came here after his wife died giving birth. Actually, he went to the North Dakota Badlands. How that name developed is interesting. The French, the English and the Native Americans all talked about it in a similar way. There's all the grasslands, the prairie, and then these desolate but beautiful rock formations.

"My gosh, tell me more," she said with an amused sarcasm.

He launched into an explanation of the geology, of hoodoos and caprocks, buttes and pinnacles.

How relentless erosion in the already stark landscape led to crumbling soil and changing features. He told her how the area used by the Lakota Sioux for ghost dances was turned into an Air Force bombing test site during the Korean War. Leading to a legacy of warnings about unexploded ordnance.

Soon the park appeared and he stopped talking. They both gawked at the view, like the Grand Canyon but with less color and sharper features.

"I know I'm not the first to say this, but it looks like another planet," Lord said.

The heat of the day had passed. The temperature had cooled to 50 degrees and they could feel it dropping further as they parked in the south unit lot. Diana changed into a running outfit. They kissed and she sprinted off on a trail that was sparingly marked with yellow poles.

He watched her quickly grow smaller and then disappear around a spire.

Tom took the short Window Trail to the top. From the lookout point, he had a view that was more than spectacular. He could see a few other people, solo hikers and couples, spread out in the huge park.

He found a flat spot, did a few stretches and a *qi*-enhancing warmup, then began to do the first set.

Despite all they had been through, and the challenge that he knew was to come, life was good.

* * *

"Hello Chris, how have you been?"

She instantly recognized the psychologist's deep voice.

"Fine," she said, fighting to keep a quiver from her response. "How are you?"

"Doing well, thank you. Your visitors are gone," he said confidently. Making it clear he knew. Kroll had waited until he estimated that Lord had moved on. He didn't want her warning him.

"Yes, yes."

"It must have been quite a surprise to see Jeremy and his girlfriend."

"Yes."

Kroll made a note on a pad. "JS still with DW."

"I presume you realize it is no coincidence my calling so shortly after their visit."

"Are you watching me?"

"Think of me as like Santa Claus, very aware who is naughty or nice. Now, Jeremy made a request of you, didn't he?"

"Yes."

Kroll was pleased at her compliance. And honesty. He wanted to keep her in a "yes set" mode.

"The request involves his interactions with me," Kroll said. "Am I correct?"

"Yes."

"He's unhappy that I've been trying to work with him all these years. I'm concerned he's become somewhat paranoid. But I still would like to help him. Where is he going?"

After a moment's hesitation, she said. "I don't know."

"Chris, I fear that you are not telling me the truth. You've built a very nice life for yourself there. Beloved wife, respected teacher, popular member of the community. But it's built on a lie. How do you think people will feel if they find out? Some might just hate you for being transgender. Others will be angry and feel deceived. You would lose your job. Randy could too. Your stepchildren shamed. Maybe a rock through the window. Or worse."

Chris gulped, fighting down a wave of nausea.

"Did you see *Boys Don't Cry*? Such a very moving story. And so tragic," Kroll said softly. "None of that needs to happen. I only ask you tell me exactly what he said and where he went."

"I, I did a lot of the talking."

"But I'm sure he didn't visit you just to chat," Kroll said. "Please tell me exactly what happened before I need to start sending old pictures and background to people." He rattled off the names of her principal, fellow teachers, several neighbors. "I'm sure your husband's employer won't run an article. But it is so easy to spread information now even without a newspaper. People can be so cruel on social media. Who do you think is the biggest gossip? Mrs. Lattimore? Mr.

Wilbur?" he asked, naming her next-door neighbor and the owner of the grocery where she shopped.

Chris was gasping for air, fighting back a panic attack. "He told me you'd been harassing him, making his life miserable. He wanted to go to the authorities with several people, try to get media interest."

"It's an old story. Not very credible as well. When you say several people, who did he name?"

"He didn't. But it sounded like they were on the West Coast."

"Did he ask your husband to write about it?"

"No. Randy refused even before he did. Randy said it would ruin our lives here."

"Your husband is a wise man. Now the biggest question. Where is he going?"

"He didn't say. Honestly. I swear."

"I believe you, Chris. If I find out you lied to me, I will deliver that lump of coal. You might wake up some morning and find your phone flooded with hate messages from people who you thought liked you. Which way was he heading?"

"Back toward the freeway."

"One last question. I presume you haven't had any of your abilities return?"

"No."

"So sad," Kroll said, and disconnected.

Pruitt dropped her phone, hurried to the bathroom and threw up into the toilet.

Chapter Thirty-Four

Klimke was in business class, heading from Los Angeles to Chicago. Ivan was a few seats away—they had bought the tickets last minute. Not that he was a buddy that Klimke cared about sitting next to. Rodriguez or Courtain would have been preferred travel companions. But neither of them would be on the next stage of the op.

It was a sign of the shift in the situation that there was no private plane, no bringing in his own team. Kroll had informed him that there would be operatives assigned to him in Chicago. The good news was that they would have their own weapons and provide the hardware Klimke requested. Not that getting illegal guns would have been hard for Klimke in Chicago. About as tough as getting a good hot dog. Though the thought of eating a hot dog from a street vendor repulsed him.

Another change was that Diana Wynne was no longer acceptable collateral damage. Kroll had said that she needed to be kept alive to be used to compel Lord to cooperate. Klimke understood what that meant. She could be damaged physically but Lord would remain uninjured. At least physically.

During his years as a mercenary Klimke had sometimes been present when a family would be tortured in front of the actual target to get information. Or to send a warning to other potential opponents. The method was ugly and he had avoided it as much as possible. He wished it hadn't been necessary. But shit happens. He was dependable. And more often than not, on the right side. Like guarding ships against Somali pirates. Or rescuing hostages from Boko Harem.

Asking ethical questions was a pastime for philosophy professors. Was it right that he'd trained and assisted Botswana troops in catching and killing poachers? If they'd been brought to trial, punishment would have been minimal and they'd been back killing elephants within weeks. But the poachers were starving Basarwa tribe members trying to feed their families.

He had no idea how many people he had killed. But he reminded himself everyone had done things in their life that they regretted. He pulled his thoughts back to the mission at hand.

Cutler had sent him an information packet on Sean Sinclair. A disbarred lawyer working as a fixer. Living in a posh neighborhood. Klimke was tasked with setting the trap. He would have three men added to his team. A decent size, but it meant working with operators he didn't know. The message he had gotten was that he would not be in tactical command, just an observer and consultant.

He had been in a similar position many times when operating in Africa, the Middle East and South America. It was important for the locals to run the show, no matter how ill-trained they were. Though Kroll hadn't outright stated it, Klimke deduced the rendition team were Russians. Which would mean ex-*Spetsnaz*, *Dzerzhinsky* Brigade, or various Special Operations Forces units. He presumed like Ivan they would be skilled, ruthless operators. Never a question of courage. More of a concern about heavy handedness. The Russians he had worked with were always quick to kick in the door, without bothering to see if it was unlocked.

Kroll had made Klimke's role clear. Develop a plan that would allow for minimal use of force or detection by authorities. Klimke was to make sure the target was safely handed over at a dock in Brooklyn within 24 hours. With multiple potential drivers, they could do the 12-hour drive without any significant stops. The gear that would be waiting included drugs and syringes to sedate the couple and a special crate to house their unconscious bodies. Based on the destination, Klimke presumed they'd be transferred to a cargo container and then shipped out. Outgoing cargo was not searched anywhere near as zealously as incoming loads. Russia would be the one presumably worried about drugs or bombs being smuggled in. And Klimke suspected the Russian government knew exactly what the cargo would be.

Klimke studied his iPad looking at the information from Cutler. The computer geek was confident Lord would continue to drive to Chicago, which gave them about 12 hours.

Klimke focused his attention on Sinclair, who lived alone in a high-rise condo overlooking Lake Michigan. He had more girlfriends than Chicago had winter storms. No pets. No registered firearms. The building had a doorman 24 hours a day, secured parking beneath it. Did it make sense to put pressure on the bait and wait in his home or snatch Lord before he even got there?

The ex-soldier closed his eyes, seeming to doze. Various scenarios of how Lord could arrive and the best way to scoop him up played out in his mind. He saw the main problems as Lord knowing they were coming before they got in place, Wynne's fighting skills, and Lord's ability to get out of most restraints. Surprise and quickly sedating them was essential. Kroll had told him something about the bait that made the success far more likely. Klimke had an idea for the operation that was outside of anything he had done before. He smiled at the thought.

Anyone looking at him would have thought he was a happy traveler, calmly thinking about his destination. Which ultimately, he was.

* * *

Diana and Tom rode in quiet bliss. They debated finding a motel in Pierre but instead just gassed up and pushed on. A heavy rainstorm swept over the road. They had to slow to 20 miles an hour. The windshield wipers made a dent in the downpour, but visibility was barely a few dozen yards.

The heavy rain made them stop in Mitchell. They found a restaurant still open near the Corn Palace. The Corn Palace was decorated with murals that had the earthy colors of dried corn and grains. The building looked like a psychedelic mosque. Tom offered to tell her about the restaurant but she patted his leg and asked, "What's bothering you?"

"Are you psychic?" he asked, smiling.

She smiled back. "A little. I can predict the future. When we settle into a motel room, I foresee that we will find a way we can relax." The couple kissed. Long but not long enough.

They got soaked just making the sprint from the car to Longhorn Bar and Grill.

A little bell tinkled as they entered the restaurant. There were a few other patrons, lone men who looked like truckers. More male patrons were in the dark bar, visible through a doorway with a genuine western saloon split swinging door. Tom scanned everyone and found no threats.

The restaurant was country rustic, with four-seat tables covered with red-checked tablecloths, slat backed chairs, simple wood wainscoting, and walls covered with photos of local celebs. Like the car dealership owner who had been captain of the 1999 winning football team. Last year's winner of the Major James Stampede rodeo bronc riding event. And several decades of Miss Corn Palace beauty queens. All the photos were autographed. The vibe felt authentic, unlike the corporate restaurant chains that presented the same pseudo-country face in hundreds of locations.

They sat at a table where Tom could face the door.

"Do we get coffee and drive through the night, find a place near here, or just go a couple hours more?" she asked.

"A little more than three hours to Rochester, Minnesota. It's the third largest city in Minnesota," he said. "The Mayo Clinic is based there. It was founded as a stagecoach stop in 1854 by-"

She raised her hand in the stop gesture. "You were going to tell me what's bothering you."

"I've been thinking about Joan Henderson."

"Whether to drive all the way to North Carolina or reach out to her by phone?"

"No. About using the info Lisa gathered to put pressure on her. That she's having an affair."

"You afraid it's not accurate?"

"Not questioning whether it is right. But is it the right thing to do? From a practical standpoint, if Lisa learned it, Kroll's people can learn it too. Which means if Joan helps me it'll blow up on her. But even more than that, blackmailing someone is not who I want to be."

"Even though she seems to be the most normal, the most credible of any of the ex-PRIers that you found?"

"Yes."

"Even though it could be your best chance to push back on Kroll?"

"Yes."

She rested her hands on the table and leaned into them, staring at him. "I don't know if I'd be as noble, but you are a very special man."

"Shucks."

The food came and they tore into it. The friendly waitress voiced approval over their enthusiasm. She told them about home-baked cookies and they ordered a couple for the road.

By the time they headed out, the rain had let up.

"We go for three more hours?" he asked, sliding behind the wheel.

"That'll give me time to think of a special way to distract a special man."

"Just keep an eye on me that I don't speed too much."

They kissed again and he started the engine.

Chapter Thirty-Five

As they checked out of the motel, they were putting off the kind of energy that made the matronly woman behind the motel counter ask if they were on their honeymoon.

"I wish," Lord said.

Diana looked at him with a pleasantly surprised expression.

"You make a real cute couple," the clerk said.

They exchanged flirty looks and laughed.

Time and miles passed pleasantly.

* * *

"You are Klimke?" the stout man with a shaved head and a bushy beard asked, approaching the ex-mercenary as he retrieved his luggage from the baggage carousel.

"I am."

"We have car outside," he stated in monotone.

The bearded man saw Ivan, nodded, and fired off a few words. The two Russians shook hands. Ivan got his bag from the carousel and they followed the bearded man to the curb. A black Hummer, with a driver, was waiting. To Klimke, the driver looked like a clone of the first man to make contact.

They pulled away from the curb. Ivan and the first bearded man chatted in Russian. They talked like old friends and Klimke wondered if they had served together or just shared a common military experience.

Klimke heard his name and the word "Indian" in rapid-fire Russian. Whatever Ivan said, the other Russians eyed Klimke respectfully.

* * *

Diana was driving and they were passing through Madison, Wisconsin when Lord made the long-delayed call to Joan Henderson.

"What do you want?" she demanded after he identified himself and asked, "How are you?"

"Uh, I was wondering if you'd be able to help me."

"You're going to try and talk with Kroll? You want the same thing as before?"

"Yeah."

"The answer is the same."

"I got a couple other PRI subjects. I was hoping that-"

"You can hope all you want. I'm going through a bad divorce right now. I don't need any more crap to deal with. You understand?"

"Do you think-"

"Clean up your own shit by yourself. Goodbye. I'm going to block this number. You call me again, I'll have you arrested for harassment."

She disconnected.

"Sorry," Diana said, patting his leg.

"I am too. And glad I wasn't banking on her."

There was more traffic on the road now, not just pick-up trucks, SUVs and long-haul tractor- trailer rigs. Even an occasional Prius. They crossed the Mississippi River at the Wisconsin-Minnesota border. They transitioned from the Midwest into the Rust Belt. Less farms, more industrial sites. Some clearly in a state of disrepair, some still functioning.

There was less banter, more silence. When not driving, Lord fiddled with the radio, never seeming to find the music he wanted. But there was less Christian rock or county and western. And an occasional rap/hip hop station.

"Have you figured out what you're going to say to Sinclair?" she asked.

"Of all the PRI people we've approached, he's the one I probably had the most time with," Lord said. "But I don't feel like I know him. He was a conniver."

"How?"

"Sucking up to the guards, to Kroll. He got special privileges. How he connived is hard to nail down specifically." Lord paused. "Somehow he never got punished for it."

"Did you scan him?"

"I was in experiments where I was supposed to. Lots of thoughts about how great he was, as well as thoughts about how inferior everyone else was. He was sex-obsessed, but I suppose a lot of us were. Kroll did his best to keep the sexes apart but ultimately it was a coed institution. Lots of young libido."

"Were you able to read his mind?"

"When paired up we did a little better than average on tests." Lord frowned. "He used to call me 'Mr. Sensitive.' He seemed to have a chip on his shoulder unless he wanted something. There's evidence that if you dislike someone it's harder to scan them."

"So if I want to keep my brain safe from you, I just have to piss you off?"

"It's more complicated."

"I still struggle with believing this psychic stuff."

"Heck, so do I."

"Did you just say heck? Did passing through the Midwest turn you into Opie?"

"Golly gosh, I hope not, ma'am."

"I think 'ma'am' is more far west."

"Shucks. I'll just drop a few F bombs and you'll know I'm still a city boy."

"I suspect they drop F bombs outside the east coast."

After a pause that lasted 10 miles, she asked, "You think he'll cooperate?"

"I have no idea," Lord said. "If it is somehow in his best interest, yes."

Then the silhouette of Chicago loomed against the sky. The Sears Tower. The Trump Tower, the Aon Center, the John Hancock Center. Four of America's eight tallest buildings. Serious traffic. More and more aggressive. It was past 8 p.m., the rush hour dwindling. Not as bad as the east coast. Just the consequence of a few million people packed into a relatively small area.

The radio announcer on the classic rock station they were listening to—in between Joni Mitchell and The Rolling Stones—warned that they were expecting the second snowstorm of the season. But he said he was embarrassed to even call it a storm, with no more than two inches predicted.

"In Portland that would shut the city down," Diana said, shaking her head.

"For a few days," Lord added.

They chatted about adverse weather they had encountered, hurricanes on the East Coast, heavy rains and mudslides in Los Angeles, tornadoes in the Midwest. Then they laughed together over the superficiality of chatting about the weather.

"I guess we've spent too much time together," he said.

"Yup. Maybe just drop me at a corner and I'll catch a cab."

"I can if you would like," he said seriously. "I still feel bad about dragging you into this."

"They have to account for what they've done to Lisa. And you. And me. If you decided to quit right now, I'd still go after them. So shut up and keep driving."

Chapter Thirty-Six

They circled the apartment building twice. Just off of North Lake Shore Drive on East Grand Avenue. There were enough other cars that they figured they would not be conspicuous as they moved slowly through the canyon of tall buildings. No one in the sluggish traffic seemed to pay attention to them. Diana driving. They both scanned the streets. No suspicious pedestrians. Everyone moving along as it got darker and the temperature continued to drop.

"His building has a doorman," Lord said.

"I saw. Big dude in a red uniform. Hard to miss. Underground parking with a key card reader."

"I saw that too. With a security video camera covering the entrance as well."

"Can you hack the garage entry?"

"Possibly. These new electronic gizmos can be a bit tricky. Some are ridiculously easy, others surprisingly difficult. I'm not sure the field the video camera covers. If it's wide angle, it could pick up activity by the reader."

"You think we should just do it straightforward? Go up to the doorman and have him announce us?"

"As a last resort." Lord took out his iPhone and tapped keys.

"You going to Google something?"

"Maybe another time. I'm looking for the packet Lisa sent me. She had a *Chicago Magazine* article from a couple years ago, a profile of Sinclair. Assuming he hasn't moved, it might help us pinpoint where he's living. I'm betting there's no names on the individual doors." Lord scanned the article quickly. "Okay, it raves about the view from his 27th story condo."

"Does it say how many units on the floor?"

"No." Tom fiddled with a picture of Sinclair, spreading his fingers to enlarge it. Sinclair was standing with a floor to ceiling window behind him. "Look out his window. There's no other tall buildings nearby. So at least that window is probably facing out toward the water."

"Nice. That certainly narrows it down some."

"Let's circle one more time then park. I've got an idea."

* * *

Randy Pruitt had helped his wife up off the bathroom floor and into bed. She stared at the ceiling. He debated calling the family doctor. Treatment for anything that wasn't routine could lead to a detailed exam, which would reveal Chris's secret. He wished he could consult with her. She was 75 pounds lighter and 10 inches shorter than him. But she was the stronger of the two. She was a survivor who once she made her mind up was unstoppable.

He took her temperature. No fever, though she was sweating and looked overheated. He put a cold compress on her head and gently stroked her.

"Are you okay honey?" he whispered.

Her eyes snapped open.

"They're in trouble," she said.

"Who?"

"Jeremy. Diana."

"Jeremy?"

"Tom's original name." Chris had a stare he hadn't seen before. Not really seeing him. Like she was focused on something far in the distance.

"How do you know?"

Her attention shifted from the distance to his face. Her expression was so intense that even though he knew she bore him no malice, he nearly recoiled.

"I just do," she said flatly.

* * *

Tom crouched down behind a row of five-foot boxwoods near the garage entrance. Trying hard to not shiver. Diana was in a doorway up the block. He suspected she was as chilled. Neither of them had brought good winter wear.

A black Escalade rolled down the short ramp, pausing by the key card reader. A hand reached out. Tom ducked back behind a big bush as the driver swiped the card over the reader. A low beep and the red LED turned to green. The car rolled in. He snuck in behind it, invisible to the security camera. There was another camera just inside the door and he dodged to the side, using the bulk of the entering vehicle to avoid the monitor's peripheral vision.

Tom hid behind a parked Audi. The garage was filled with late model, high end vehicles. Mainly German, with Porsches, BMWs, Mercedes, Audis. A few Teslas, Range Rovers, Lincolns. Most of the cars in the six-figure range. Gleaming chrome and radiant colors. The SUVs looked like they had never been exposed to dirt.

Lord called Wynne. "There's an electric eye beam to allow drivers to leave without a key," he said quietly. "But if I trip it to let you in, it'll be obvious if anyone is watching the camera."

"You really think they're that alert?"

"Probably not. But let's wait and see if there's another car in the next few minutes. People are still coming home from work. Just sneak in in their blind spot. There's another security camera just inside, so juke right as soon as you enter."

"Gotcha. But let's not wait more than a few minutes. I parked the car in a lot. I'm close but freezing my butt off here."

"It's such a perfect butt, we can't let that happen," he joked but she'd already disconnected.

Four minutes later a blue Porsche Panamera 4 pulled up to the reader. Diana had to duck low to hide behind it, but she was inside and next to him within seconds.

They walked confidently to the elevator. They looked like they could be tenants. Being a couple, Caucasian, well past their teens, and dressed reasonably well would've assuaged all but the most diligent security guard. An alert guard might wonder how they suddenly appeared in the garage. But low wages and staring at monitors for hours at a time in a building where there was little threat would not make for vigilance.

The elevator had a regular button, not a key card, but that momentary lucky break was washed away when they got inside the car. A keypad was mounted just above the button panel.

"Shit!" Diana said.

Tom leaned over and kissed her, whispering in her ear, "There's a small camera mounted up high to the right. The elevator might be miked. Don't worry, I got this." The elevator was probably programmed to just go to the first floor, with private access only above that.

"Did you forget something, honey?" he asked more loudly.

"Damn, we should've picked up wine."

"Oh, he'll understand we had to rush to get here," he said sweetly. "You're such a cute ditz, my little sugar plum."

"When we get that bottle of wine, I know just where I'm going to put it," she said, giving him a smile loaded with mock menace.

Lord positioned himself so his back was blocking the camera's view of his hands. Using his lock pick set, he poked in the firefighter's override keyhole. The door shut. He pushed the button for 27.

Chapter Thirty-Seven

Randy Pruitt had never seen his wife as frail. She was trembling so hard it almost looked like she was faking it. She staggered to the phone Lord had left for her.

"Jeremy, it's a trap. Get away."

Randy looked at her expectantly when she hung up.

"It just went to voicemail," she said.

* * *

One can tell a lot about a building just by its hallways. Narrow hallways mean builders are using every bit of space. The claustrophobic feel is the price of frugality. This hallway was eight feet wide, more than any building code demanded, artfully lit, very clean. No surveillance cameras. The residents must've figured their privacy was more important. No barbarians should be able to breach the outer defenses.

There were only two possible doors for condos having the right view. Tom leaned against one door and heard a child complaining loudly about some injustice. Probably not enough caramelized sugar in the *crème brûlée*. Behind the other door was silence. There was the chance Sinclair wasn't home and they'd have to wait. If he was out of town, and according to the article he traveled quite a bit, the couple was screwed. This whole entry would just be a trial run.

"He's more likely to open the door for an attractive woman," he said softly as they stood near the entry to his place.

"If you're trying to make up for calling me a ditz, that's a decent start," she said.

"When you were talking about stowing that wine bottle, I presume you meant in the pantry."

"If that gives you comfort, you can believe it."

They exchanged a quick kiss and she knocked.

* * *

Klimke and the Russian team sat in the Hummer parked in the rear of the garage. They had watched Lord and Wynne come in and go upstairs. The Hummer had third row seating. The big car was filled with big men and the faint smell of sweat and gun oil. No one was wearing tac vests or camo. Guns, Tasers, handcuffs, knives and blackjacks were hidden. In small backpacks. To an unwitting observer they could've been a rugby team going to a game. Lots of testosterone but no overt signs of menace.

"I do not understand why we not grab them when they come in," the Russian leader said.

"This'll be smoother. They're not in a public place. Wait for the signal."

Klimke heard grumbling and mumbling from the men. They were not used to listening to a stranger. Once the operation started, Klimke knew he'd have to take a back seat.

The commander snapped off a few quick words and the muttering stopped.

Klimke was pleased. Not just at getting his way, but that the team had discipline. You could judge a whole army by watching how a sentry performed guard duty. Dozing, smoking, chatting on a phone all meant it was a force ripe to be overrun. These men knew when to shut up and stay focused.

* * *

Diana knocked and a mellifluous voice said, "One minute."

In less than that time the door opened.

"Well, hello," Sinclair said.

Up close and in person, Tom could see traces of the Sean Sinclair that he'd known nearly 30 years ago. In the packet Lisa had sent he looked fantastic. He had filled in, overshooting his ideal weight by more than 25 pounds. The article had said he was a gourmet and a "charming man about town." He had the air of a sybaritic Roman emperor. He was Tom's age but looked younger. His icy-smooth forehead and lack of jowl was evidence he was well known to a plastic surgeon.

He smiled at Diana, then saw Tom and looked momentarily confused.

"Jeremy?"

Tom nodded.

"A pleasant and perplexing surprise. But please, welcome to my humble abode." He opened the door wide and beckoned them in.

Both the surprise and the pleasure appeared genuine. The barest hint of anxiety, which was to be expected with a stranger, and near stranger, showing up at his door.

The living room was dominated by a giant L-shaped leather sofa that faced the floor to ceiling windows. The lights of the city made the lightly falling snowflakes glow like little stars. Lake Michigan was a dark expanse. Cars streaked by on Lake Shore Drive North, 27 stories below. He saw Lord looking out the window.

"The view is what sold me on this place. This condo costs way too much but I love it. And you only go around once, right?"

"The view is beautiful," Tom said. Sean was very much the charming host. Soft jazz played through hidden speakers.

Abstract modern art on the wall. Sleek furnishings that looked custom made. No smudges or handprints. The layout by a designer with good taste and generous funding. Black and white with clean, cold lines.

"Let me get you some treats to nibble. And a glass of wine. I've got a fruity and aromatic *Riesling* or a light-bodied but impertinent *Pinot Noir* open. With a host of other options available."

"We don't want to impose," Tom said. "I've got a request I'd like to make and then we'll be out of your hair."

"It'll be nice to catch up on things." He locked his eyes on Diana and smiled lecherously. "And to get to know you."

"I'll have the *Riesling*," Diana said.

"Me too," Tom chimed in.

Sinclair bustled into the kitchen, a large open space just off the living room. There was a mammoth Sub-Zero refrigerator-freezer, white marble counter tops, and a dozen pots hanging from a wrought iron contraption above the counter. Wood blocks on the counters holding miscellaneous tools. Ladles, spatulas, tongs and whisks, and more exotic cutlery. Knives ranging from a few inches to more than a foot. It looked like it could be the kitchen for a high-end restaurant. Sinclair bustled away, clearly pleased to entertain them.

Diana and Tom exchanged an amused look, then stared out the window.

Sean returned in a few minutes with a silver platter loaded with four different types of crackers, as well as *edam, gouda, brie* and a couple less recognizable cheeses. He said one was *cacio bufala.* "It's made from buffalo milk, which is richer than cow's milk." Another was "Jersey Blue, which was from the UK but is now made in Switzerland. It's got an earthy flavor, a fudgy texture." He then waxed poetic about the various crackers. "But I'll tell you a secret," he paused, conspiratorially, "I get most of them at Trader Joe's."

They ate and sipped wine. It was all delicious, they told him so, and he talked more. There were several times he paused when Tom tried to get him on track, but Sean quickly digressed. Shorty had been driven by loneliness, Chris by a shared secret. Sean was driven by ego, talking at them, a monologue more than a dialogue. Sinclair closed his eyes and savored a mouthful of cheese, washed down the *Riesling*. "You know what I do?"

Lord and Wynne shook their heads.

"I don't believe you," he said with a smile. "The Jeremy I knew was such a nerd, always looking things up. Google must be a godsend for you."

Diana fought back a smirk.

"I did read a bit," Tom admitted. "You were an attorney. You still work in the legal system, making deals."

"Crass people would call it a fixer. I think of it as a facilitator."

"What exactly do you do?" Diana asked, emphasizing "exactly."

"Well, I'm hired by attorneys who don't want to get their hands dirty. That lets me be covered by attorney-client privilege. All sorts of things well within the law."

"Sorts of things?" Tom asked. Not wanting to challenge Sinclair but annoyed by his bluster. And the way he kept eyeing Diana.

"Let's say there's a big chemical company that's dealing with local resistance. I spread a little wealth around to the mayor, some of the powers that be. Make it clear that the company may close the plant, all those jobs lost. Hire a few scientists who come up with alternative theories for any health problems. If some family starts making too much noise, we enhance financial motivation to go along. And make it clear if they say anything bad, they'll be dragged through the courts in a messy slander suit that will expose every skeleton in their closet." He rolled his wine around the glass, sniffed it, and sipped. "Everyone has skeletons in their closet. Thank goodness."

He refilled the couple's glasses and encouraged them to try different cheese-cracker combinations.

"Or in a criminal matter. Let's say there's a detective who wants his kid to get into a good college. And can't really afford the tuition. I help the kid get into the school, pay the bills, and when the detective takes the stand his testimony is a little weak. He doesn't lie, just he doesn't perform well. But his son gets to find his dream at University of Whatever."

Lord could sense Sinclair was thinking about Diana in his mind. His thoughts went from PG to R to X. Mentally undressing her then re-dressing her provocatively.

Tom blinked a couple times to clear out the images, focus on where they were. Diana looked at Tom questioningly, picking up on his distraction and strange looks at her. Sinclair didn't seem to notice.

"So exactly what brings you here?" he asked finally. "Something to do with PRI?"

"Kroll has been after me for decades," Tom said, fighting back anger at Sean's lewd thoughts about Diana. Tom filled in what had happened with Lisa and the raid on Diana's place. It was hard to stay focused and not lash out at Sean.

"You were his *wunderkind*," Sinclair responded. "So serious, so desperately wanting to please him. I suppose we all did. He was really disheartened when you eloped. He gave us others more attention." Sinclair smiled at Diana. "They always had more interest in the receivers than the encoders. It pissed me off then."

Lord was feeling a bit groggy. He had finished the first glass of wine and barely taken a sip from the second. He needed to stay focused. The long hours on the road were catching up.

"If you join with me and talk about PRI, it'll have more clout," Tom said. "I have a couple others who will join us."

"I might be able to do better. Did you ever file a police report?"

"No. I tried in Hawaii and got nowhere. They treated me like I should be wearing a tin-foil helmet. Kroll still has connections and looks super reputable."

"Have you ever talked with an attorney about a civil suit?"

"A long time ago. I approached a couple of lawyers who felt it was too weak a case." The words were surprisingly hard to get out. He scanned Sinclair again. It took effort but images of Diana had been replaced by thoughts of money. Greed. Tom ate a couple more cheese and crackers, hoping to dilute the alcohol.

"I know a lot of hungry litigators. It will take cash for an initial retainer, but they'll do it on a contingency basis. With your allegations filed in court papers, the media might bite. No risk of a libel suit if they're reporting filings. Lawyers get a fee and some publicity, reporters get a story, you get your version out there. A win, win, win situation."

Lord wanted to respond but it was too hard to move his lips.

Sinclair paused and studied him. "After you were gone Kroll recognized the importance of senders. It has stood me in good stead. I can put a thought in a target's mind, like what life would be like if he took the money. Or how bad things could get if he didn't. Not everyone is receptive. Some people you could hit them over the head with a club and they wouldn't receive. Others hear me loud and clear. Of course, you are more aware than most, right Mr. Sensitive?"

Tom was swaying now, harder to stay upright. Diana had sagged into the couch.

"It's not like I can make people do what's against their will. Sort of like hypnosis without words. Power of suggestion. Just plant an idea and see if it grows. It requires creativity, finesse. Special ability to do it just right. Did you like your girlie in the bikini?"

Suddenly Diana was in his head again, dressed like a schoolgirl, hair in pigtails, wearing a school uniform that included a miniskirt. With no underwear.

"I like that schoolgirl look. I could put all sorts of images in your head. Like schoolgirl takes on the whole football team."

Tom tried to stand but barely moved in his seat. His muscles refused to respond.

"Gives new meaning to fucking with your head, don't it?" Sinclair grinned. "There's an art to this. You wanted to believe I could help you. Easy to get you to lower your guard. You didn't want me to bang your girlfriend but I planted the thought that I was into her with a few horny looks."

Lord tried to get up with every ounce of willpower he had. Nothing.

"Actually, she's not my type. Too small, too muscular. I like big portions of everything." He picked up his cell phone and dialed a number.

"Yes, they're ready for transport," he said, smiling. "No problems at all. C'mon up."

He returned his attention to Lord. "In case you haven't figured it out, working with Kroll I learned how to disguise my thoughts."

He stood over Lord and slapped his face.

"Can't damage the merchandise, Mr. Sensitive. Dr. Ed still thinks you're the prize. I'm going to be well rewarded. Ka-ching! I brought up thoughts of that towards the end. You probably saw it and thought I was thinking of your ridiculous lawsuit. Context is everything." He slapped Tom again and made a tut-tutting noise. "It was so much fun watching you get excited over that bullshit lawsuit idea. No jury would ever believe you. You're a loser with zero credibility.

"Kroll's got a bunch of PRI people who will swear it was great. Myself included. You talk about your ESP, they're going to see you as more psychotic than psychic."

Sinclair took another sip of wine. "If you're curious, the drug was in the *gouda*. I planted thoughts encouraging both of you to eat it. It's the cheapest cheese I have. I wouldn't want to ruin a good cheese. Or wine."

He pinched Tom's nose and laughed. "Dr. Ed finally realized how important my skills are, better than you stuck up reader assholes."

Tom struggled to speak but it was as useless as trying to stand. He wanted to tell Sinclair that Kroll thrived on playing people off against each other, that Tom didn't have "I'm better than you thoughts," that Sinclair was still being manipulated. But most of all Tom wanted to bash Sean's smug face into a bloody pulp and get Diana away.

"I was center court when the Bulls beat the Jazz for the second three-peat. I never thought there'd be anything better," he said, smirking. "I was wrong."

The doorbell rang.

Chapter Thirty-Eight

Hector Vasquez answered the phone on the first ring.

"Yes?"

"This is Chris Pruitt."

"Jeremy is in trouble?" Vasquez asked, halfway between a statement and a question.

"How did you know?"

"You were largely a clairvoyant if I recall correctly? Space not a significant factor for your thoughts. I was, I am, a precog. Time is equally fluid and flexible,' Vasquez said. "Kroll has captured him? Where?"

"In Chicago. But they are in transit to New York."

"He plans to ship him overseas. In my dreams last night, I saw snowballs made of money thrown at Kroll. Voices in a foreign language, not English or Spanish. Kroll handing money to a sharp-faced blond man. Blood all over. Jeremy and Diana in a cage like at the zoo."

"Whose blood?"

"I couldn't tell."

"Will you help us?"

"He saved my life," Vasquez said. "I'm still stitched up from the attack. But I have a debt. I will do whatever to help Jeremy and his lady friend."

Randy Pruitt had been listening in. Based on what Lord had said, he had backtracked on major news stories in the Los Angeles Area, telling Chris the names of people involved. Every fire, fatal car accident and homicide that was on a police blotter anywhere in Southern California. But when she heard the name Hector Vasquez, she had said, "That's the one!"

After she was done with the phone call she rested for a few minutes. Randy saw the toll it was taking but knew there was no stopping her. She gave him a peck on the lips and picked up the disposable phone he had bought early that morning. She punched in the numbers he had given her.

"Who is this?" Shorty snapped.

"Chris. You knew me as Chris Daniels. I'm married now, Chris Pruitt."

"Chris Daniels?"

"At the Psychological Research Institute."

"The only Chris I remember there was this wimpy little guy."

"That was me."

"But you're, oh shit, you're one of those transvestites."

"Actually it's transgender, but yes."

"Jesus H. Christ. It's unnatural."

"I'm not calling to debate sexual identity," she said firmly. "Jeremy needs you. He mentioned a few things that allowed my husband to track you down."

"Your husband. Yeesh."

She ignored his comment. "Jeremy has been in contact with you."

"Yeah, he came by. Tom Lord he calls himself now."

"He's in trouble."

"And I should care why? He's been in a pissing match with Dr. K for decades."

"They're going to ship him off to Russia. With Diana."

McGuire grumbled.

* * *

Lying in the darkness, Tom felt worse than he ever had. His abilities had failed him. Failed Diana. There had been many times in the past when he'd been unable to read someone's mind. But he had known it. He had never had the experience of reading someone's mind and being so very, very wrong. Ruining his life. And Diana's. He had fallen in love and brought another woman into the pit.

For the first time in his life, he had thoughts of suicide. Just end it. Kroll would never get his brain. Time passed with his soul in a darker place than his body.

He thought of Diana and leaving her on her own. She would have no value to their pursuers. He would be killing both of them. He had to be stronger than he felt. He had to keep fighting.

Breathe in, breathe out. Just this moment. No matter how bad it was.

He was in total darkness but felt no blindfold against his face. A dark room? He heard vague noises, heavy machinery, through walls that he couldn't tell how far away they were. Breathe in, breathe out.

His hands were cuffed behind his back. His legs tied together. He was lying on a very slightly cushioned floor. Rubberized mats? No gag, so their captors were confident that no one could hear a cry for help. Was he alone or was she nearby?

"Diana? Diana?"

"I'm here."

She was alive and near him. He felt a wave of relief. Then a surge of guilt and hopelessness. She was as trapped as he was.

"Are you okay?" he asked.

"No real pain, kind of groggy. That dipshit drugged us."

"Yeah. I'm sorry."

"For what?"

"For not realizing he was a dipshit who'd drug us. For all the trouble I've caused you."

"You do owe me a heck of a dinner."

"I mean it."

"I know you do. But if I hear any self-pity in your voice, I'm going to roll over there and make you feel sorrier than you ever were. You got a plan for getting out of here?"

"I'm trussed up tight."

"Think! What would Houdini do?"

"He would've fixed things beforehand. Had a shim for the cuffs, a false bottom on the case."

"A while back you told me with a bobby pin you could get out of most cuffs," she whispered. "Was that true?"

"Yes. But I can feel they took my wallet that had a couple of little picks in it. And I can't get to the handcuffs anyway."

"When you told me that, I listened."

"You..."

"I've got a couple in my hair."

With a few minutes of wiggling and wriggling, soon he was next to Diana. Who had been barely six feet away. Another five minutes and he plucked out the hair pin with his lips. For close to a half hour, he thrusted and maneuvered the bobby pin in her handcuffs. He dropped it a couple times and had to lick it up off the floor, in the dark, to reposition it in his mouth. Then the ecstatic clicks of the cuffs ratcheting open.

A few minutes after that, they were free. Standing and stretching stiff muscles. A quick hug and a kiss in the pitch blackness.

"You're amazing," he told her.

"I just kept the bobby pins. You always give the credit to your special mental abilities… I've also said your lips are magical."

They kissed again.

"I, I was ready to give up back there," he admitted.

"So?"

"I mean, I was so scared. Still am."

"So?"

"You don't mind that I'm a coward."

"You're not a coward," she said, grabbing his wrist hard enough to hurt. "Never say that. Never think that. My father taught me if you're not scared sometimes, you're nuts. Or a fool. The brave person is the one who pushes forward, pushes through it. Feel the fear and do it anyway."

He was glad she couldn't see his face. He was fighting back tears. Not of fear or sadness, but joy that he had her in his life. He knew then that he could die for her and not regret it.

"I wish I had met your father," Lord said.

"I do too." He heard a catch in her voice. "You get knocked down, but you get up again."

"Are you getting all Chumbawumba on me?"

They hugged in the total darkness. He began humming *Tubthumping*. They briefly joined in on the chorus, "I get knocked down, but I get up again, you're never gonna keep me down."

"We'll go out singing," he said.

"When you say going out, you better be referring to leaving this shithole. If you're talking anything more permanent than that…"

"I'm just referring to getting out of here. I'm more scared of your anger than anything these bastards can do."

"Good. You got your priorities right."

Then he extended his arms and paced out the space. About 30 feet long, seven and a half feet wide and high. There were metal bars on one end from a locking mechanism.

"I'm guessing we're in a cargo container," he said.

"Agreed. We're not moving."

"Yup. The floor feels a bit cushy, rubberized or something."

"Agreed," she said.

"No noticeable smells."

"Agree again," she said. "I have a vague recollection of riding in a van. For a long time. I don't think we're in Chicago."

"I've got to pee something fierce. Hungry but not starving. So I'm guessing it's somewhere between 12 and 24 hours since we were in Sinclair's place. Whatever drug they gave us probably slowed our systems down."

"Ditto to the bio functions. You want to choose a corner of this place and claim it?" They were standing near the end with the rods that probably worked the door.

After they had each done their business in the same far corner, she asked, "Can you pick up anything through the walls?"

He pressed his ear against the metal wall. Industrial noises. The grind of heavy machinery, metal on metal, mammoth motors making big efforts. A rhythmic thump every thirty seconds or so. A pile driver? Hydraulic whines. Cranes? An industrial area. A shipping yard or dock? He leaned against the wall and let his brain scan. So hard his head ached.

"It's real weak and it comes and goes, but I believe I'm hearing someone thinking in Russian. I can't understand it obviously. But a definite Slavic flavor."

There was no way to open the door from the inside. The temperature was dropping and they both were lightly dressed. They held each other for warmth. And comfort.

He detected the presumed sentry's presence about every 20 minutes. The timing was a guess since they had taken their watches, as well as phones, keys and wallets.

Diana asked for the bobby pin.

"You worried about your hair?" he joked.

"I'm going to make it into a t-shape I can tuck in my fist. Go for the eyes or throat."

"Remind me to never piss you off."

"It's too late for that, sonny boy."

He couldn't see her face, but he hoped she was smiling.

"When they open the door, I go through first," he said.

"No offense Sir Lancelot, but I've got more of a chance of kicking ass."

"None taken," he said. "No offense to you, but in their eyes, you're expendable. I'm the goose they want to lay golden eggs. Besides, you're smaller. Stay behind me until it's safe for you to go after someone."

"You want me to use you as a human shield?"

"It's not a great plan. But it's the best we've got at this point."

"Not a great plan is an understatement."

"Okay. What I think we should do until we get the door open is practice. Can I go into your mind?"

"Sure. Why?"

"I'd like you to run drills. Imagine the door opens. There's things we can visualize. You've got much more experience with hand-to-hand combat than I do. We can guess the guard is most likely a righty."

"Yes. Odds are with a shotgun or short-barreled automatic. The barrel will probably be pointing left."

"Run different scenarios in your head. Different heights, weapons, even left-handed. I'm going to eavesdrop inside that kind and gentle brain of yours and calculate how you're going to mangle them. I need to move to distract and then get out of the way."

"It's sort of a weird dance."

"Dancing with the Guards."

"Ugh, you're lucky I can't see you. You'd need to be worrying about a bobby pin in the throat."

"I love you too."

They found each other, kissed briefly, and began the mental rehearsal.

* * *

The Pruitts, Shorty and the Priest watched the car pull in from atop a three-cargo container high stack about 200 yards from the guardhouse. They were inside a warehouse the size of an airplane hangar. A vast space, six stories high with no interior floors, just a catwalk running across bare metal struts five stories up. The two-story high door they peered through would allow a couple of trucks to come and go simultaneously, with room to spare.

The warehouse was relatively quiet. Only a few workers tidying up.

Various docks had different levels of activity. On one of the nearby ones, forklifts scuttled about. Trucks dropped off loads. Other trucks picked up loads. But the giant cranes were moving less as the day shift checked out and the smaller evening shift checked in.

Randy had a scoped Marlin lever action 30-06 he'd brought from home. Shorty had his Raptor shotgun and a Beretta. Randy had brought a Dan Wesson .357 revolver which he'd given to Vasquez in a leg holster. All weapons had been dutifully transported in checked, hard-sided baggage that had been declared. Along with McGuire's Ka-Bar knife and a couple hundred rounds of ammunition. Christina had a pair of Bushnell 10x36 binoculars.

They had first met up just outside of JFK, in a parking lot near the airport. Shorty had been wary of Christina and Hector but bonded instantly with Randy when he found out the reporter was also "One of the best shots in South Dakota." Christina had said it and Randy was modestly quiet. "He's been that way ever since he was a 4H-er with a .22."

"How good?" Shorty challenged.

"He won first prize at the state fair two years in a row," Christina said proudly. "If he goes out hunting, you better not be a deer. Or an elk. Or a bear."

Randy looked like he was about to blush.

"You ever been in the military?" McGuire growled.

"Chief Petty Officer on the USS Saratoga," Chris answered.

"Swabbie," McGuire muttered. "Ever shoot a man?"

Randy shook his head.

"It's different. The trick is don't think of him as a man. Acquire the target and neutralize it." Shorty grilled him about his guns and Randy detailed his four rifles, two shotguns, and three handguns. Shorty talked about his arsenal and Randy asked the right questions. As well as being suitably impressed by Shorty's choices. In the rented car they had looked at each other's weapons. All guns were clean, well-oiled, and clearly much loved.

Chris and Hector exchanged an amused look as the two men became bros.

"How about you?" Shorty asked Hector. "You okay with shooting someone? Got any 10 commandment issues?"

"I am a man of god, but I was a child of the streets."

"You ever shot someone?" McGuire asked with a smirk.

"That's between me and the Lord," Vasquez said. "There are no statutes of limitations on some crimes. Only our Father's forgiveness."

McGuire smiled. More respectfully. "You might have to pray for more forgiveness today."

"It will be God's will."

"I like your attitude, padre. I used to have a jacket that said, 'Kill 'em all, let God sort 'em out.'"

Shorty turned to Christina. "So you know where Diana is?"

"Roughly," Chris said. "I had a clear image of a pier. Randy was able to use Google Earth and narrow it down. It's in Brooklyn."

They had managed to sneak in to the docks during shift change. As a reporter, Randy had bluffed his way inside many places where he shouldn't be. They had needed a limited disguise—bright yellow safety vests, hard hats and clipboards. Shorty and Randy had been in the front seat. Hector in the back seat. Chris in the trunk, with all the firepower.

They had waited until dusk turned to night before leaving the car and heading out. Without the vests, hardhats and clipboards, but with the arsenal.

* * *

"The sentry is passing," Tom said. "Ready?"

"Let's do it," Diana responded.

He began banging on the door.

Chapter Thirty-Nine

"There's two men in that small office trailer," Chris said from atop the cargo container lookout, pointing to the 20-foot trailer on the dock with the sign ABC Import-Export.

"You're sure?" McGuire asked.

She nodded. "They're sleeping. I also see something that looks like guns leaning against the wall."

"You're sure of that too?"

"No. I just see shapes, not that clear. It could be tools, brooms, cleaning equipment."

Shorty rubbed his chin.

"There are other men," Vasquez said. "I saw it in my dream last night."

"That's just great," Shorty said sarcastically. "You care to share anything else you saw in your dreams?"

"Things are going to get violent," Vasquez said.

"Jesus H. Christ. You don't have to be a psychic to figure that out."

"There will be blood."

Shorty sighed. "Thanks for the heads up. I thought we would just tell them the secret password from Miss Gender Bender here and then we'd all go out for cupcakes."

Randy shot Shorty a dirty look. He was about to say something but Christina squeezed his arm and shook her head.

Vasquez didn't say he had seen death on both sides. And not for Kroll.

Shorty gazed around the dock. "I got an idea. From one of the movies I was in. Maybe with Stallone. Though it might have been Statham. Anyone see any heavy rope or cable?"

Chris closed her eyes and made a slight humming noise. Randy took the binoculars from her and scanned adjacent piers. Vasquez just stared off into the distance.

Chris opened her eyes and pointed. "Behind that building two docks over I see a coil. I can't tell what it is."

"There's also one toward the end of this dock," Randy said, pointing.

Shorty took the binoculars and looked through them. "I'm gonna go with what I can see."

He and Vasquez drove down to the end of the dock. They found 100 feet of weathered white eight strand hawser line tied to a mammoth cleat. Shorty sawed at the heavy rope with his Ka-Bar knife until it was free. It took both men to lift the thick line into the trunk of the car.

They drove back and Shorty parked near the trailer. He explained to Vasquez what he wanted to do. The priest grinned.

They began quickly looping the rope around the trailer, grateful that a stack of containers blocked the view from the gatehouse.

The trailer was quickly wrapped, holding the outward-opening door shut and making exit through the four small windows impossible.

They had just finished their work when they saw the black Escalade pull up to the gate.

* * *

Ivan was on duty at the gatehouse. It was dark, nearing 6 p.m. Two of the other Russians, scheduled for guard duty starting at midnight, were sleeping in the trailer 100 yards further up the giant dock in Red Hook. The fourth Russian was on sentry duty, conscientiously walking the length of the dock, through the parking lot, and into the warehouse. Roughly every 20 minutes passing the container where Diana and Tom were imprisoned.

"Good evening," Ivan said when he recognized the driver.

"Same to you," Klimke said. "Dr. Kroll wants to see Lord before he gets shipped off."

"No one goes in is my order." Ivan said.

Kroll leaned forward from the back seat. Klimke hated the positioning, not liking anyone behind him, not liking feeling like a chauffeur. But Kroll always insisted. Just one more reason he would be glad when the job was done, he got his bonus, and moved on.

"Mr. Klimke has told me what a fine soldier you are," Kroll said respectfully. "I hope you understand that it was my plan which allowed this mission to be a success. Please allow me a few minutes to see Mr. Lord before he goes off to serve the *Rodina*."

Klimke thought Kroll was laying it on too thick, but Ivan seemed receptive.

Ivan looked at Klimke and said, "You good soldier too. Not always best to follow all the rules from desk jockstraps. For you I do it." He lifted the yellow and black striped wooden gate.

"*Bolshoi spasiba*," Kroll said, and the car pulled in.

* * *

The cargo container door mechanism creaked and squealed as the guard opened it.

Lord stepped forward, arms behind his back as if he was still handcuffed, clearly not threatening. The guard's attention was focused on him. The guard had a bushy black beard and thick head of hair. Lord thought of him as Rasputin.

Tom feinted like he was moving to the right, then juked to the left.

Diana exploded from behind Tom.

The Escalade pulled up as Diana caught the guard's face with the bobby pin spike. He was raising his weapon but managed to pivot. The point missed his eye but embedded in his cheek.

Diana grabbed the barrel of his AK-47. She surprised him by shoving it forward, rather than trying to pull it away. He was quick but she was quicker, catching his jaw with an elbow as she rolled into him.

But Klimke was out of the car, gun drawn. Lord stepped in front of them, blocking a clear shot at her. The mercenary slammed his gun into Lord's temple and he fell to the ground. Dizzy. Warm blood running down his face. Lord struggled to stand.

"Be careful!" Kroll snapped at Klimke.

Klimke aimed at Wynne.

Lord threw himself at the mercenary's wiry legs. Lord hit Klimke's thigh with his shoulder. Klimke didn't fall but his shot went wild, skimming off the concrete. The noise was masked by the sounds of industry.

"Freeze!" Klimke barked and Diana did.

Rasputin pulled the bobby pin out of his cheek. "*Pizda!*" he growled, swinging at Diana. She blocked and went into a defensive crouch.

"Enough!" Kroll commanded and everybody froze.

"Jeremy, I suggest you and Ms. Wynne stop this instant. Any further action and I'm afraid you'll be traveling alone. And comrade if either one of them is hurt unnecessarily, I'll make sure Moscow knows who is responsible."

Rasputin alternated glaring at Wynne and Kroll.

Klimke had a flat stare, a cat ready to pounce, every muscle controlled.

* * *

From the gatehouse, Ivan saw the skirmish. He grabbed his shotgun and started running toward the container.

From off to the side of the small trailer where the two Russians slept, Vasquez and McGuire trotted toward the fight.

From his position atop the cargo containers in the warehouse, Randy looked down the rifle. His hands trembled.

He had ear plugs in place, as did Chris. He had warned her that if he fired, the boom of the rifle would be deafening in the warehouse. "But at least the echoes should make it hard to pinpoint where we are."

Randy was unable to control his shaking hands. "I got buck fever," he said. "I can't do it."

"Just take out his leg. Now or never, sugar," Chris said, her voice a mix of comfort and command.

Randy timed his shot, waiting until the big hydraulic thump masked the noise. He fired and 9.8 grams of lead traveling at 3000 feet per second slammed into Ivan's knee, tearing cartilage and shattering bone. Ivan fell.

The sonic boom echoed around the warehouse, painful even with earplugs in place.

* * *

McGuire and Vasquez walked toward where Lord and Wynne stood with Kroll, Klimke and the sentry. Everyone but Kroll, Diana and Tom had a gun.

With weapons drawn, Shorty and Hector looked like gunslingers walking down a main street in Tombstone. Rasputin had his weapon trained on Shorty, who held the shotgun level at his hip.

"This is a time for reason, not bloodshed," Kroll said soothingly.

Klimke looked indifferent, almost bored. An eerie calm, scarier than agitation. He would kill Diana without hesitation.

"Please, everybody stop!" Lord said. He tried to probe Kroll's thoughts to find an area of vulnerability. He sensed only anxiety—if he didn't deliver Lord, his life would be ruined. Much of his mind was shut off. There was no angle Lord could exploit.

"We got a bunch of reinforcements here," Shorty said, moving closer. "Let Diana and Tom go, asshole, and we don't have to kill you."

"Not possible," Rasputin said.

* * *

From atop the container, Chris watched the scene through binoculars. "The guard with the gun, he's wearing a bulletproof vest."

"I see," Randy said, watching through his scope.

"You hit him in the vest, he won't die. Maybe some broken ribs. But you'll have his attention."

Randy looked away from his gun, over at his wife. "You're such an angel."

He sighted down his weapon and waited until the thump of the hydraulic press.

The bullet slammed into Rasputin's chest, knocking him to the ground.

Lord had shifted to Klimke's thoughts and found something to work with. He stepped in closer, hands still raised in a seeming gesture of surrender.

Klimke was momentarily distracted but his gun remained trained on Diana. She was too far away to attack him. And Klimke knew it.

Lord was a little more than arm's distance away but Klimke dismissed him as a threat.

"You're not fast enough," he told Lord.

"Not with my hands or feet."

He spit in Klimke's face, a glob that landed in the mercenary's eye.

The hypochondriac mercenary panicked. He pulled his hand up to wipe his face.

Diana was on him, her left arm keeping his gun aloft, the other slamming an elbow into his jaw. In close, she fired off knees at his groin that he managed to deflect, absorbing the force on his thighs. She stomped his foot.

They exchanged flurries of fast punches and kicks. Many of the blows would have been incapacitating if they landed. Diana was holding her own. Barely. The mercenary seemed to be getting stronger from the conflict.

Lord was wobbly but tried to get in to help. They looked like a speeded-up movie, a spinning blur of arms and legs. Lord got a punch in on Klimke but it didn't seem to register. They rolled and bumped into Lord. He got knocked down again.

Rasputin staggered to his feet and Lord charged him as he lifted his weapon. Lord jammed it back toward him, hitting the spot on his ribs where Lord sensed he hurt most. It wasn't hard to guess as there was a big divot where the bullet had hit.

Dazed with pain, Rasputin still managed to swing the weapon in Lord's direction.

Kroll shouted, "No!"

Vasquez put two rounds into the Russian's head and he fell to the floor.

Shorty was trying to intercede in the battle between Wynne and Klimke, to no avail.

The Russians in the trailer had been unable to force the door open. At one of the windows, they saw the heavy rope trapping them. They fired all eight rounds from the RMb-93 pump action shotgun, shredding the rope.

But the first one to climb out was hit in the chest by a round from Randy's gun. He fell back into the trailer.

"They'll try coming out the other side soon," Randy predicted. "I won't be able to hit them from here."

Klimke ducked a punch from Diana and landed a punch to her temple that rocked her back. He pulled the knife from his leg sheath.

He cocked his arm back to stab. Shorty jumped in, hooking the arm and twisting.

Klimke turned his attention to Shorty. The mercenary threw a punch but the stuntman was used to dodging blows. He hit Klimke with all his strength but the senior stuntman's blow had minimal effect on the battle-hardened mercenary. Then Klimke fired off a flurry of punches. A few got through. Shorty fell backwards. Klimke plunged the knife into his clavicle.

A battered Diana scuttled over to where Klimke's gun had fallen. As Klimke pulled back the knife to stab again, Diana fired. Three quick shots. Chest, chest, head.

Klimke fell.

The only sound was the industrial background noise. Day to day work continued despite the life and death.

"All this bloodshed," Kroll said to Tom. "All unnecessary if you had just cooperated." His tone was accusatory, as if Lord's misbehavior was responsible for the mayhem.

Vasquez had the revolver aimed at the psychologist.

"That's not really necessary," Kroll said calmly. "I'm not going to attack anyone. Nor run away."

Lord went into Kroll's mind, sensing fear for the first time in all the years he had known the psychologist. Not of Lord or Wynne but of the Russians, and the punishment for the psychologist if he didn't deliver Lord. His shields were down and Lord saw the ultimatum he had been given and the consequences.

Diana pushed herself up off the ground, still holding Klimke's weapon.

"You're the one behind all of this misery, all this suffering," she said to Kroll.

"Don't!" Lord said.

As she pulled the trigger Tom stepped forward, knocking the weapon aside. The bullet creased Kroll's shoulder. He looked indignant.

Then his face grew slack. He fell to the ground. He had a stunned expression, the right corner of his mouth drooping. He tried to speak but could only make a bit of noise that almost sounded like drunken slurring. He tried to push himself up with his left arm as his right arm lay limp, getting only a few inches off the ground before falling back.

Diana ignored him. She knelt over Shorty, pressing down on the arterial wound. Blood oozed around her hand.

"It's my time," Shorty said in a coarse whisper.

"You're not going to die," she insisted.

"Not a bad way to go, saving Gotta Wynne's daughter."

"No! We'll get you to the hospital."

There were sirens in the distance. Workers nearby had recognized that the gunfire was not the usual industrial noise.

"Maybe I'll see him in heaven," McGuire said. "Or hell. Wherever old soldiers go."

"Stop talking like that."

He tried to say something else but it was unintelligible. Then his eyes rolled.

Tom grabbed Diana's shoulder. "We've got to get out of here."

Holding the gun in her hand, she pointed to Kroll who lay on the ground, thrashing.

"Don't shoot him," Tom said.

"You want to help him," she spat venomously, shrugging Lord off and standing up. "Take him to the hospital and nurse him back to health?"

"Leave him. Let's go!"

The two Russians from the trailer ran toward them.

Before they could aim, Hector emptied the revolver and Diana fired her remaining rounds. That plus Randy's covering fire allowed them to sprint to the car. Randy started the engine as the others threw themselves in and slammed the door.

Randy drove, right at the speed limit. Police cars raced past with sirens and flashing lights.

Seeing Rasputin lying on the ground, one police car crashed through the gate. The officer jumped out. Gun drawn, on the radio, no doubt confirming that shots indeed had been fired.

One of the Russians from the trailer fired a shot at the cop. The officer, and the next two officers that arrived seconds later, focused their attention on the trigger-happy guard.

Ivan wisely lay still, pulling taut the tourniquet on his leg he had made from his belt.

Randy drove with Tom riding shotgun, Diana, Hector and Chris in the back. They simultaneously let out their breaths in a collective sigh when they were about 10 blocks from the dock.

More and more sirens.

"We should get rid of the guns," Vasquez said calmly. Clearly not his first time wrestling with that issue. To Lord and Wynne, he said, "I don't know about the rest of us, but I suspect your fingerprints are in that trailer. Start thinking about what you will tell the police when they come."

Tom looked over at Diana who was staring out the window. Breathing hard. She held the emptied gun in her hand, a blank expression on her face.

Epilogue

The media went wild with the story of a shootout at the docks involving apparent Russian mobsters, a once prominent psychologist, and a retired survivalist stunt man with a checkered past.

Kroll's connection with ESP research surfaced immediately but McGuire's name hadn't been in any declassified documents.

Chris told Lord that her remote viewing had begun to fade, images harder to pull up. "The only image I want right now is to be in my kitchen trying out a new recipe for apple pie," she said.

"Let's make that happen," Randy said, throwing a big arm around her and pulling her to him. They left for South Dakota the next day. But Randy tipped off his NY Times reporter contact about how Kroll and McGuire were connected.

Also a couple days after the incident, Vasquez headed back to Los Angeles. He told the couple, "I've got a lot of Hail Marys to say. It's been exciting, amigo, but I cannot wait to get back to worrying about what my sermon is going to be and if someone is going to get too drunk at the *quinceañera.*"

The police took a few days to find the fingerprints. Or at least that's how long it took before the detectives showed up at the couple's door. They were ordered to not leave town and checked into a nice Airbnb in Williamsburg.

Randy asked with his New York media contacts for a defense attorney with an impressive track record. Susan Brainard was pricey, with a $1000 an hour meter ticking. "There's sharks and there's fat tunas with a fake fin strapped on their back," an editor had said. "This one is universally agreed to be a great white."

Covered by the attorney-client privilege, Brainard assured Lord he could tell her everything in complete confidence. So he did. They sat in her office, with a view down Fifth Avenue. She took notes with a *Montblanc* pen, looking up occasionally to meet his eyes with an intense stare. Her advice, after he spoke for nearly an hour, was four words: "Keep your mouth shut."

The partial prints were not the greatest quality and their attorney cited Brandon Mayfield and other cases of false arrest based on bad fingerprints. At the end of the week, with multiple visits to the precinct and hours spent being questioned, one aggressive detective growled that they would be charged with felonies, "With up to seven years in the joint" for the fake IDs the couple were carrying.

Their wonderful pet shark snapped back that, "In New York State, unless authorities could prove an intent to defraud or use the ID in furtherance of another crime, it was not considered an offense. To allow you time to brush up on the law, detective, our session today is done." They marched out.

It had taken no small effort to track down the management of the parking lot where Diana had parked the car they had stolen. But Tom found the owner and called, telling him somewhat truthfully that they were stuck in New York due to the unexpected death of a friend. He was sympathetic and agreed to not have the car towed, particularly after Tom offered to pay $500 above whatever the daily rate was when they finally got back to Chicago. The fake ID in the car and Diana's bow were what made walking away from the vehicle not an option.

Esteban Rodriguez broke his first big story in the Times three days after the shootout. It had details about the

PRI institute research. The reporter called, pressing for information.

Rodriguez was persistent, as were a couple other reporters, but Brainard made it clear that if Lord talked to the press, he would need to get a new lawyer. He would have loved to have media attention in the past and now he was dodging their calls.

"You don't need them now," the lawyer stressed. "Kroll is out of commission. Keep your mouth shut and things will blow over. You start talking about this ESP crap and who knows which way it will go. It's hard to get off with an insanity defense." Brainard was not shy about letting Lord know she was not a believer.

The couple was called back several times to the precinct. Brainard was always present. The cops bluffed hard on "damning new evidence."

They didn't know they couldn't bluff Lord. Some knew about his telepathy but were as skeptical as Brainard. Maybe more so. A few times, Lord played around out of spite.

Like the late afternoon interrogation, where he picked up the detective was hungry and craving a meatball hero sandwich from his favorite Italian restaurant.

They sat in the small, windowless room, with three walls of grime-streaked cinderblock and one dominated by a big mirror. Lord said, "I know you're hungry to make an arrest. To bite into a suspect like they were a big meatball sandwich. With thick marinara sauce, melted provolone, parmesan cheese."

Tom could hear his stomach grumble.

"Putting together a case is like making a good dish. Just the right amount of garlic, onion, green peppers. Sautéed in olive oil." The cop ended the session early, glaring at Tom with a confused expression.

The toughest interrogator was a woman who seemed past the retirement age. She had close-cropped hair and a permanent scowl. She was super quick-witted, and her thoughts jumped quickly from one line of questioning to another. Lord couldn't sense any vulnerability. As soon as he answered one question, she brought in another from left field. She mainly poked and prodded at their alibi.

Diana and Tom claimed they were in their room making love at the time when the violence was happening at the docks. The detective questioned them closely but the couple both claimed blurry memories of exactly what they'd been doing.

"No one saw you," the detective persisted.

"Of course, we're not exhibitionists."

"There's no footage of you entering the hotel," she pressed.

"And there's no footage of them leaving," our attorney countered. "Or being at your crime scene. Listen, detective, my clients have stayed in the city even though your order to have them do so has all the legal weight of a bubblegum wrapper. You better take their cooperativeness into consideration. I'm going to instruct them to go back and resume their lives. Any further inquiries can be directed to my office."

Kroll hadn't been able to help the detectives. The shoulder wound was superficial but the stroke that followed was near fatal. Quick intervention at the hospital had saved his life but his voluntary motor skills on his left side and his speech were all but gone. He was strapped into a wheelchair and going to be transferred to a rehab facility in a few days. The once articulate psychologist babbled near words like a child learning to speak. His frustration was evident.

Some of the investigation made it into brief news items. But Tom got updates through Randy Pruitt, who had media sources and filled in details that didn't make the cut. TV journalists had already moved on to fresher stories.

Randy told them they had a lucky break—there were two homicides in that precinct in the days following the shootout at the docks. "Like the old New York. One seems to be a mugging, the other a drug deal gone bad. But it means resources have been diverted from your case," he explained. "I guess I should say our case. Also on the good news front, Kroll's finances have imploded. Banks, other creditors calling in loans. His financing is peculiar enough that the FBI and the IRS are stepping in. They suspect the Russians but there's layers and layers of cutouts and holding companies to dig through."

Tom thanked him for the info. And everything else he and his wife had done.

"My pleasure. I'm just glad Chris is back to her old self. It scared the shit out of me the way she was," he said. "If you and Diana are ever out this way, there's a lot of beautiful country we like to show off."

"I appreciate that."

They ended the call. Tom didn't tell him how precarious things were between Diana and him.

"It wasn't your right to stop me from killing him," she had told Tom.

"That wasn't self-defense, it was an execution."

"And what was it for Lisa?"

Neither one would change their mind. There was lots of silence and no romance.

No family members had claimed McGuire's body. Diana arranged for him to get a veteran's funeral and burial. On a chilly, dark gray morning, the couple were the only ones present graveside, aside from the three young soldiers in an honor guard. They blew taps and folded up the flag. Diana accepted it. She fought back tears but the sobs broke through. She leaned into Tom's arms. Then pulled away.

Lord and Wynne returned to favored routines. He did an hour of *tai chi, qi gong,* and mindfulness most mornings. Weather permitting, he did slow set at Grand Ferry Park, a small park with minimal development but gorgeous views of the East River and Manhattan. Diana would run for 30 to 60 minutes, sometimes on the track at McCarren Park, sometimes all over the neighborhood. Sometimes into Bed Stuy, Linden Hill, Ridgewood, Fort Greene, and Sunnyside. And beyond. Occasionally across the bridge into Manhattan.

On her return from her run, they exercised together. At least partially. He stopped after 100 pushups, 200 crunches, three minutes of planks and demanding yoga moves. She was just warming up.

Esteban Rodriguez called Tom many times, trying to get information.

Lord's attorney forcefully repeated her four-word advice. "Even if half of the shit you told me is true, Kroll is not really an issue anymore," she said. "Do you really want to poke that bear?"

Lord told Rodriquez, "No comment. For now."

Tom found out through Randy when Kroll was transferred to a nursing home in Queens.

"I'm going to go visit him," Tom told Diana. "Would you like to come?"

"What sort of sick relationship do you two have?" she asked.

"I want closure."

They took a Lyft out to Jackson Heights. Kroll was at a mildly rundown house in a neighborhood of mildly rundown houses. The Romanian woman who ran it was hesitant about letting the couple in. She had angry dark eyes. Tom claimed he was Kroll's nephew, visiting from out of state. He made it clear he only wanted to visit for a few minutes but would complain to the authorities if he couldn't see Kroll.

"No more than 10 minutes," she growled.

The place smelled of disinfectant trying to mask urine as the couple walked upstairs to his small room.

Kroll's wheelchair was parked facing the window. The view out of it was the garbage strewn backyard of a neighboring house. A dog on a chain yapped continuously.

"Uncle Eddie," Tom said, smiling broadly as the couple entered the room.

The house manager turned the wheelchair to face the couple.

Kroll's expression was frozen.

"It's been way too long," Tom said cheerily.

Diana stood in the doorway, staring. The house manager stood next to her, arms folded across her stout body.

"I have so many memories," Lord said to Kroll. "I just want you to know I haven't forgotten all you did." Lord stepped close and patted his shoulder.

"Don't worry, I'm sure you'll get the great care you deserve here. I might not be able to check in on you for a long time. And there's no one else in the family, or friends. But you'll do fine."

Tom patted him again. "Have a nice day."

Diana and Tom walked out. She didn't say anything until they were outside.

"Did you go into his mind?" she asked.

"Yes."

"What was he thinking?"

"He knew I was reading him. He was wallowing in his failure, his hopelessness, his being so alone. And he was begging."

"For what? Forgiveness?"

"No. For me to help him die."

She was quiet.

"Want me to get us a Lyft?" Tom asked.

"If you're up for it, I'd like to walk for a while."

"Sure."

They walked down Roosevelt Avenue, the subway screeching above them. Stores from a dozen different countries. Twice that many different languages spoken by passersby. The diverse opposite of South Dakota but the couple was equally out of place.

She looped her arm into his. "You wanted me to see that there are some things worse than death."

"Yeah. But I also did want closure. It was for me too."

They walked another dozen blocks.

"So what now?" she asked.

"I want to track down that valet in Portland where we swiped the car. Maybe help him out if he got jammed up because of what we did. Maybe go back to the Yakama reservation, hang out with Frank. But before that, I figure I have to stop in Chicago. Settle my account with Sean Sinclair."

"Really?"

"Yeah. They say revenge is a dish best served cold. I figure Chicago right now is pretty damn chilly."

"You have something in mind?"

"Not quite yet. I want it to be something that will hurt him forever."

"You've got a nasty streak under all that nice."

They walked another few blocks.

"I like that in a man," she said.

Acknowledgments

My gratitude to the late Dr. Charles Honorton who included me in the federally-funded ESP experiments that helped inspire this book. Dr. Honorton was absolutely nothing like the villainous Edward Kroll.

Thank you to Michael Aloisi and AM Ink Publishing for welcoming me into your family. It has been a collaborative and supportive experience right from the get-go.

And my appreciation to friends, family and advanced readers who gave me feedback as far as the gremlins that creep into any book length work. Thanks to Eli Pahl, LCSW, Brian Park, MD, and Michael Sekaquaptewa. Any mistakes or missteps that remain are mine alone.

Special thanks to Emily Schorr, M.D. and Ben Schorr, for all the feedback you gave, and all the joy you have given me over the years.

And to Kitty Church, for feedback and for her time as my special companion in recent years.

About the Author

Mark Schorr is the author of eleven previous published mysteries/thrillers. He was nominated for an Edgar award, had books published in France, Spain and Japan, and had three books optioned by Hollywood. He's also the author of hundreds of articles, with work published in *The New York Times*, *New York Magazine*, *Esquire*, and *The Oregonian*. He's been on staff for the *Los Angeles Herald Examiner*, *USA Today*, *CBS* and *NBC*.

Aside from his work as a writer, he's been a bookstore manager, a bouncer at Studio 54, a private investigator, an international courier, a crisis de-escalation trainer, and a decoy during training for TSA's bomb-sniffing dogs.

He is currently a mental health and addictions counselor in Portland, Oregon.